A Life's Secret

A Life's Secret

Mrs. Henry Wood

MINT EDITIONS

A Life's Secret was first published in 1862.

This edition published by Mint Editions 2021.

ISBN 9781513281094 | E-ISBN 9781513286112

Published by Mint Editions®

minteditionbooks.com

Publishing Director: Jennifer Newens
Design & Production: Rachel Lopez Metzger
Project Manager: Micaela Clark
Typesetting: Westchester Publishing Services

Contents

PART THE FIRST

I

Was the Lady Mad?

On the outskirts of Ketterford, a town of some note in the heart of England, stood, a few years ago, a white house, its green lawn, surrounded by shrubs and flowers, sloping down to the high road. It probably stands there still, looking as if not a day had passed over its head since, for houses can be renovated and made, so to say, new again, unlike men and women. A cheerful, bright, handsome house, of moderate size, the residence of Mr. Thornimett.

At the distance of a short stone's-throw, towards the open country, were sundry workshops and sheds—a large yard intervening between them and the house. They belonged to Mr. Thornimett; and the timber and other characteristic materials lying about the yard would have proclaimed their owner's trade without the aid of the lofty sign-board—"Richard Thornimett, Builder and Contractor." His business was extensive for a country town.

Entering the house by the pillared portico, and crossing the black-and-white floor-cloth of the hall to the left, you came to a room whose windows looked towards the timber-yard. It was fitted up as a sort of study, or counting-house, though the real business counting-house was at the works. Matting was on its floor; desks and stools stood about; maps and drawings, plain and coloured, were on its walls; not finished and beautiful landscapes, such as issue from the hands of modern artists, or have descended to us from the great masters, but skeleton designs of various buildings—churches, bridges, terraces—plans to be worked out in actuality, not to be admired on paper. This room was chiefly given over to Mr. Thornimett's pupil: and you may see him in it now.

A tall, gentlemanly young fellow, active and upright; his name, Austin Clay. It is Easter Monday in those long-past years—and yet not so very long past, either—and the works and yard are silent to-day. Strictly speaking, Austin Clay can no longer be called a pupil, for he is twenty-one, and his articles are out. The house is his home; Mr. and Mrs. Thornimett, who have no children of their own, are almost as his father and mother. They have said nothing to him about leaving, and he has said nothing to them. The town, in its busy interference, gratuitously opined that "Old Thornimett would be taking him into partnership." Old Thornimett had given no indication of what he might intend to do, one way or the other.

Austin Clay was of good parentage, of gentle birth. Left an orphan at the age of fourteen, with very small means, not sufficient to complete his education, Ketterford wondered what was to become of him, and whether he had not better get rid of himself by running away to sea. Mr. Thornimett stepped in and solved the difficulty. The late Mrs. Clay—Austin's mother—and Mrs. Thornimett were distantly related, and perhaps a certain sense of duty in the matter made itself heard; that, at least, combined with the great fact that the Thornimett household was childless. The first thing they did was to take the boy home for the Christmas holidays; the next, was to tell him he should stay there for good. Not to be adopted as their son, not to leave him a fortune hereafter, Mr. Thornimett took pains to explain to him, but to make him into a man, and teach him to earn his own living.

"Will you be apprenticed to me, Austin?" subsequently asked Mr. Thornimett.

"Can't I be articled, sir?" returned Austin, quickly.

"Articled?" repeated Mr. Thornimett, with a laugh. He saw what was running in the boy's mind. He was a plain man himself; had built up his own fortunes just as he had built the new house he lived in; had risen, in fact, as many a working man does rise: but Austin's father was a gentleman. "Well, yes, you can be articled, if you like it better," he said; "but I shall never call it anything but apprenticed; neither will the trade. You'll have to work, young sir."

"I don't care how hard I work, or what I do," cried Austin, earnestly. "There's no degradation in work."

Thus it was settled; and Austin Clay became bound pupil to Richard Thornimett.

"Old Thornimett and his wife have done it out of charity," quoth Ketterford.

No doubt they had. But as the time passed on they grew very fond of him. He was an open-hearted, sweet-tempered, generous boy, and one of them at least, Mr. Thornimett, detected in him the qualities that make a superior man. Privileges were accorded him from the first: the going on with certain of his school duties, for which masters came to him out of business hours—drawing, mathematics, and modern languages chiefly—and Austin went on himself with Latin and Greek.

With the two latter Mrs. Thornimett waged perpetual war. What would be the use of them to him, she was always asking, and Austin, in his pleasant, laughing way, would rejoin that they might help to make him a gentleman. He was that already: Austin Clay, though he might not know it, was a true gentleman born.

Had they repented their bargain? He was twenty-one now, and out of his articles, or his time, as it was commonly called. No, not for an instant. Never a better servant had Richard Thornimett; never, he would have told you, one so good. With all his propensity to be a "gentleman," Austin Clay did not shrink from his work; but did it thoroughly. His master in his wisdom had caused him to learn his business practically; but, that accomplished, he kept him to overlooking, and to other light duties, just as he might have done by a son of his own. It had told well.

Easter Monday, and a universal holiday Mr. Thornimett had gone out on horseback, and Austin was in the pupil's room. He sat at a desk, his stool on the tilt, one hand unconsciously balancing a ruler, the other supporting his head, which was bent over a book.

"Austin!"

The call, rather a gentle one, came from outside the door. Austin, buried in his book, did not hear it.

"Austin Clay!"

He heard that, and started up. The door opened in the same moment, and an old lady, dressed in delicate lavender print, came briskly in. Her cap of a round, old-fashioned shape, was white as snow, and a bunch of keys hung from her girdle. It was Mrs. Thornimett.

"So you are here!" she exclaimed, advancing to him with short, quick steps, a sort of trot. "Sarah said she was sure Mr. Austin had not gone out. And now, what do you mean by this?" she added, bending her spectacles, which she always wore, on his open book. "Confining yourself indoors this lovely day over that good-for-nothing Hebrew stuff!"

Austin turned his eyes upon her with a pleasant smile. Deep-set grey eyes they were, earnest and truthful, with a great amount of thought in them for a young man. His face was a pleasing, good-looking face, without being a handsome one, its complexion pale, clear, and healthy, and the hair rather dark. There was not much of beauty in the countenance, but there was plenty of firmness and good sense.

"It is not Hebrew, Mrs. Thornimett. Hebrew and I are strangers to each other. I am only indulging myself with a bit of old Homer."

"All useless, Austin. I don't care whether it is Greek or Hebrew, or Latin or French. To pore over those rubbishing dry books whenever you get the chance, does you no good. If you did not possess a constitution of iron, you would have been laid upon a sick-bed long ago."

Austin laughed outright. Mrs. Thornimett's prejudices against what she called "learning," had grown into a proverb. Never having been troubled with much herself, she, like the Dutch professor told of by George Primrose, "saw no good in it." She lifted her hand and closed the book.

"May I not spend my time as I like upon a holiday?" remonstrated Austin, half vexed, half in good humour.

"No," said she, authoritatively; "not when the day is warm and bright as this. We do not often get so fair an Easter. Don't you see that I have put off my winter clothing?"

"I saw that at breakfast."

"Oh, you did notice that, did you? I thought you and Mr. Thornimett were both buried in that newspaper. Well, Austin, I never make the change till I think warm weather is really coming in: and so it ought to be, for Easter is late this year. Come, put that book up."

Austin obeyed, a comical look of grievance on his face. "I declare you order me about just as you did when I came here first, a miserable little muff of fourteen. You'll never get another like me, Mrs. Thornimett. As if I had not enough outdoor work every day in the week! And I don't know where on earth to go to. It's like turning a fellow out of house and home!"

"You are going out for me, Austin. The master left a message for the Lowland farm, and you shall take it over, and stay the day with them. They will make as much of you as they would of a king. When Mrs. Milton was here the other day, she complained that you never went over now; she said she supposed you were growing above them."

"What nonsense!" said Austin, laughing. "Well, I'll go there for you at once, without grumbling. I like the Miltons."

"You can walk, or you can take the pony gig: whichever you like."

"I will walk," replied Austin, with alacrity, putting his book inside the large desk. "What is the message, Mrs. Thornimett?"

"The message—"

Mrs. Thornimett came to a sudden pause, very much as if she had fallen into a dream. Her eyes were gazing from the window into the far distance, and Austin looked in the same direction: but there was not anything to be seen.

"There's nothing there, lad. It is but my own thoughts. Something is troubling me, Austin. Don't you think the master has seemed very poorly of late?"

"N—o," replied Austin, slowly, and with some hesitation, for he was half doubting whether something of the sort had not struck him. Certainly the master—as Mr. Thornimett was styled indiscriminately on the premises both by servants and workpeople, so that Mrs. Thornimett often fell into the same habit—was not the brisk man he used to be. "I have not noticed it particularly."

"That is like the young; they never see anything," she murmured, as if speaking to herself. "Well, Austin, I have; and I can tell you that I do not like the master's looks, or the signs I detect in him. Especially did I not like them when he rode forth this morning."

"All that I have observed is that of late he seems to be disinclined for business. He seems heavy, sleepy, as though it were a trouble to him to rouse himself, and he complains sometimes of headache. But, of course—"

"Of course, what?" asked Mrs. Thornimett. "Why do you hesitate?"

"I was going to say that Mr. Thornimett is not as young as he was," continued Austin, with some deprecation.

"He is sixty-six, and I am sixty-three. But, you must be going. Talking of it, will not mend it. And the best part of the day is passing."

"You have not given me the message," he said, taking up his hat which lay beside him.

"The message is this," said Mrs. Thornimett, lowering her voice to a confidential tone, as she glanced round to see that the door was shut. "Tell Mr. Milton that Mr. Thornimett cannot answer for that timber merchant about whom he asked. The master fears he might prove a slippery customer; he is a man whom he himself would trust as far as he could see, but no farther. Just say it into Mr. Milton's private ear, you know."

"Certainly. I understand," replied the young man, turning to depart.

"You see now why it might not be convenient to despatch any one but yourself. And, Austin," added the old lady, following him across the hall, "take care not to make yourself ill with their Easter cheesecakes. The Lowland farm is famous for them."

"I will try not," returned Austin.

He looked back at her, nodding and laughing as he traversed the lawn, and from thence struck into the open road. His way led him past the workshops, closed then, even to the gates, for Easter Monday in that part of the country is a universal holiday. A few minutes, and he turned into the fields; a welcome change from the dusty road. The field way might be a little longer, but it was altogether pleasanter. Easter was late that year, as Mrs. Thornimett observed, and the season was early. The sky was blue and clear, the day warm and lovely; the hedges were budding into leaf, the grass was growing, the clover, the buttercups, the daisies were springing; and an early butterfly fluttered past Austin.

"You have taken wing betimes," he said, addressing the unconscious insect. "I think summer must be at hand."

Halting for a moment to watch the flight, he strode on the quicker afterwards. Supple, active, slender, his steps—the elastic, joyous, tread of youth—scarcely seemed to touch the earth. He always walked fast when busy with thought, and his mind was buried in the hint Mrs. Thornimett had spoken, touching her fears for her husband's health. "If he is breaking, it's through his close attention to business," decided Austin, as he struck into the common and was nearing the end of his journey. "I wish he would take a jolly good holiday this summer. It would set him up; and I know I could manage things without him."

A large common; a broad piece of waste land, owned by the lord of the manor, but appropriated by anybody and everybody; where gipsies encamped and donkeys grazed, and geese and children were turned out to roam. A wide path ran across it, worn by the passage of farmer's carts and other vehicles. To the left it was bordered in the distance by a row of cottages; to the right, its extent was limited, and terminated in some dangerous gravel pits—dangerous, because they were not protected.

Austin Clay had reached the middle of the path and of the common, when he overtook a lady whom he slightly knew. A lady of very strange manners, popularly supposed to be mad, and of whom he once stood in considerable awe, not to say terror, at which he laughed now. She was a Miss Gwinn, a tall bony woman of remarkable strength, the sister of Gwinn, a lawyer of Ketterford. Gwinn the lawyer did not bear the best of characters, and Ketterford reviled him when they could do it secretly. "A low, crafty, dishonest practitioner, whose hands couldn't have come clean had he spent his days and nights in washing them," was amidst the complimentary terms applied to him. Miss Gwinn, however, seemed honest enough, and but for her rancorous manners Ketterford might have grown to feel a sort of respect for her as a woman of sorrow. She had come suddenly to the place many years before and taken up her abode with her brother. She looked and moved and spoke as one half-crazed with grief: what its cause was, nobody knew; but it was accepted by all, and mysteriously alluded to by herself on occasion.

"You have taken a long walk this morning, Miss Gwinn," said Austin, courteously raising his hat as he came up with her.

She threw back her grey cloak with a quick, sharp movement, and turned upon him. "Oh, is it you, Austin Clay? You startled me. My thoughts were far away: deep upon another. *He* could wear a fair outside, and accost me in a pleasant voice, like you."

"That is rather a doubtful compliment, Miss Gwinn," he returned, in his good-humoured way. "I hope I am no darker inside than out. At any rate, I don't try to appear different from what I am."

"Did I accuse you of it? Boy! you had better go and throw yourself into one of those gravel pits and die, than grow up to be deceitful," she vehemently cried. "Deceit has been the curse of my days. It has made me what I am; one whom the boys hoot after, and call—"

"No, no; not so bad as that," interrupted Austin, soothingly. "You have been cross with them sometimes, and they are insolent, mischievous little ragamuffins. I am sure every thoughtful person respects you, feeling for your sorrow."

"Sorrow!" she wailed. "Ay. Sorrow, beyond what falls to the ordinary lot of man. The blow fell upon *me*, though I was not an actor in it. When those connected with us do wrong, we suffer; we, more than they. I may be revenged yet," she added, her expression changing to anger. "If I can only come across *him*."

"Across whom?" naturally asked Austin.

"Who are you, that you should seek to pry into my secrets?" she passionately resumed. "I am five-and-fifty to-day—old enough to be your mother, and you presume to put the question to *me*! Boys are coming to something."

"I beg your pardon; I but spoke heedlessly, Miss Gwinn, in answer to your remark. Indeed I have no wish to pry into anybody's business. And as to 'secrets,' I have eschewed them, since, a little chap in petticoats, I crept to my mother's room door to listen to one, and got soundly whipped for my pains."

"It is a secret that you will never know, or anybody else; so put its thoughts from you. Austin Clay," she added, laying her hand upon his arm, and bending forward to speak in a whisper, "it is fifteen years, this very day, since its horrors came out to me! And I have had to carry it about since, as I best could, in silence and in pain."

She turned round abruptly as she spoke, and continued her way along the broad path; while Austin Clay struck short off towards the gravel pits, which was his nearest road to the Lowland farm. Silent and abandoned were the pits that day; everybody connected with them was enjoying holiday with the rest of the world. "What a strange woman she is!" he thought.

It has been said that the gravel pits were not far from the path. Austin was close upon them, when the sound of a horse's footsteps caused him to turn. A gentleman was riding fast down the common path, from the opposite side to the one he and Miss Gwinn had come, and Austin shaded his eyes with his hand to see if it was any one he knew. No; it was a stranger. A slender man, of some seven-and-thirty years, tall, so far as could be judged, with thin, prominent aquiline features, and dark eyes. A fine face; one of those that impress the beholder at first sight, as it did Austin, and, once seen, remain permanently on the memory.

"I wonder who he is?" cried Austin Clay to himself. "He rides well."

Possibly Miss Gwinn might be wondering the same. At any rate, she had fixed her eyes on the stranger, and they seemed to be starting from her head with the gaze. It would appear that she recognised him, and with no pleasurable emotion. She grew strangely excited. Her face turned of a ghastly whiteness, her hands closed involuntarily, and, after standing for a moment in perfect stillness, as if petrified, she darted forward in his pathway, and seized the bridle of his horse.

"So! you have turned up at last! I knew—I knew you were not dead!" she shrieked, in a voice of wild raving. "I knew you would some time be brought face to face with me, to answer for your wickedness."

Utterly surprised and perplexed, or seeming to be, at this summary attack, the gentleman could only stare at his assailant, and endeavour to get his bridle from her hand. But she held it with a firm grasp.

"Let go my horse," he said. "Are you mad?"

"*You* were mad," she retorted, passionately. "Mad in those old days; and you turned another to madness. Not three minutes ago, I said to myself that the time would come when I should find you. Man! do you remember that it is fifteen years ago this very day that the—the—crisis of the sickness came on? Do you know that never afterwards—"

"Do not betray your private affairs to me," interrupted the gentleman.

"They are no concern of mine. I never saw you in my life. Take care! the horse will do you an injury."

"No! you never saw me, and you never saw somebody else!" she panted, in a tone that would have been mockingly sarcastic, but for its wild passion. "You did not change the current of my whole life! you did not turn another to madness! These equivocations are worthy of *you*."

"If you are not insane, you must be mistaking me for some other person," he replied, his tone none of the mildest, though perfectly calm. "I repeat that, to my knowledge, I never set eyes upon you in my life. Woman! have you no regard for your own safety? The horse will kill you! Don't you see that I cannot control him?"

"So much the better if he kills us both," she shrieked, swaying up and down, to and fro, with the fierce motions of the angry horse. "You will only meet your deserts: and, for myself, I am tired of life."

"Let go!" cried the rider.

"Not until you have told me where you live, and where you may be found. I have searched for you in vain. I will have my revenge; I will force you to do justice. You—"

In her sad temper, her dogged obstinacy, she still held the bridle. The horse, a spirited animal, was passionate as she was, and far stronger. He reared bolt upright, he kicked, he plunged; and, finally, he shook off the obnoxious control, to dash furiously in the direction of the gravel pits. Miss Gwinn fell to the ground.

To fall into the pit would be certain destruction to both man and horse. Austin Clay had watched the encounter in amazement, though he could not hear the words of the quarrel. In the humane impulse of the moment, disregarding the danger to himself, he darted in front of the horse, arrested him on the very brink of the pit, and threw him back on his haunches.

Snorting, panting, the white foam breaking from him, the animal, as if conscious of the doom he had escaped, now stood in trembling quiet, obedient to the control of his master. That master threw himself from his back, and turned to Austin.

"Young gentleman, you have saved my life."

There was little doubt of that. Austin accepted the fact without any fuss, feeling as thankful as the speaker, and quite unconscious at the moment of the wrench he had given his own shoulder.

"It would have been an awkward fall, sir. I am glad I happened to be here."

"It would have been a *killing* fall," replied the stranger, stepping to the brink, and looking down. "And your being here must be owing to God's wonderful Providence."

He lifted his hat as he spoke, and remained a minute or two silent and uncovered, his eyes closed. Austin, in the same impulse of reverence, lifted his.

"Did you see the strange manner in which that woman attacked me?" questioned the stranger.

"Yes."

"She must be insane."

"She is very strange at times," said Austin. "She flies into desperate passions."

"Passions! It is madness, not passion. A woman like that ought to be shut up in Bedlam. Where would be the satisfaction to my wife and family, if, through her, I had been lying at this moment at the bottom there, dead? I never saw her in my life before; never."

"Is she hurt? She has fallen down, I perceive."

"Hurt! not she. She could call after me pretty fiercely when my horse shook her off. She possesses the rage and strength of a tiger. Good fellow! good Salem! did a mad woman frighten and anger you?" added the stranger, soothing his horse. "And now, young sir," turning to Austin, "how shall I reward you?"

Austin broke into a smile at the notion.

"Not at all, thank you," he said. "One does not merit reward for such a thing as this. I should have deserved sending over after you, had I not interposed. To do my best was a simple matter of duty—of obligation; but nothing to be rewarded for."

"Had he been a common man, I might have done it," thought the stranger; "but he is evidently a gentleman. Well, I may be able to repay it in some manner as you and I pass through life," he said, aloud, mounting the now subdued horse. "Some neglect the opportunities, thrown in their way, of helping their fellow-creatures; some embrace them, as you have just done. I believe that whichever we may give—neglect or help—will be returned to us in kind: like unto a corn of wheat, that must spring up what it is sown; or a thistle, that must come up a thistle."

"As to embracing the opportunity—I should think there's no man living but would have done his best to save you, had he been standing here."

"Ah, well; let it go," returned the horseman. "Will you tell me your name? and something about yourself?"

"My name is Austin Clay. I have few relatives living, and they are distant ones, and I shall, I expect, have to make my own way in the world."

"Are you in any profession? or business?"

"I am with Mr. Thornimett, of Ketterford: the builder and contractor."

"Why, I am a builder myself!" cried the stranger, a pleasing accent of surprise in his tone. "Shall you ever be visiting London?"

"I daresay I shall, sir. I should like to do so."

"Then, when you do, mind you call upon me the first thing," he rejoined, taking a card from a case in his pocket and handing it to Austin. "Come to me should you ever be in want of a berth: I might help you to one. Will you promise?"

"Yes, sir; and thank you."

"I fancy the thanks are due from the other side, Mr. Clay. Oblige me by not letting that Bess o' Bedlam obtain sight of my card. I might have her following me."

"No fear," said Austin, alluding to the caution.

"She must be lying there to regain the strength exhausted by passion," carelessly remarked the stranger. "Poor thing! it is sad to be mad, though! She is getting up now, I see: I had better be away. That town beyond, in the distance, is Ketterford, is it not?"

"It is."

"Fare you well, then. I must hasten to catch the twelve o'clock train. They have horse-boxes, I presume, at the station?"

"Oh, yes."

"All right," he nodded. "I have received a summons to town, and cannot afford the time to ride Salem home. So we must both get conveyed by train, old fellow"—patting his horse, as he spoke to it. "By the way, though—what is the lady's name?" he halted to ask.

"Gwinn. Miss Gwinn."

"Gwinn? Gwinn? Never heard the name in my life. Fare you well, in all gratitude."

He rode away. Austin Clay looked at the card. It was a private visiting card—"Mr. Henry Hunter" with an address in the corner.

"He must be one of the great London building firm, 'Hunter and Hunter,'" thought Austin, depositing the card in his pocket. "First class people. And now for Miss Gwinn."

For his humanity would not allow him to leave her unlooked-after, as the molested and angry man had done. She had risen to her feet, though slowly, as he stepped back across the short worn grass of the common. The fall had shaken her, without doing material damage.

"I hope you are not hurt?" said Austin, kindly.

"A ban light upon the horse!" she fiercely cried. "At my age, it does not do to be thrown on the ground violently. I thought my bones were broken; I could not rise. And he has escaped! Boy! what did he say to you of me—of my affairs?"

"Not anything. I do not believe he knows you in the least. He says he does not."

The crimson passion had faded from Miss Gwinn's face, leaving it wan and white. "How dare you say you believe it?"

"Because I do believe it," replied Austin. "He declared that he never saw you in his life; and I think he spoke the truth. I can judge when a man tells truth, and when he tells a lie. Mr. Thornimett often says he wishes he could read faces—and people—as I can read them."

Miss Gwinn gazed at him; contempt and pity blended in her countenance. "Have you yet to learn that a bad man can assume the semblance of goodness?"

"Yes, I know that; and assume it so as to take in a saint," hastily spoke Austin. "You may be deceived in a bad man; but I do not think you can in a good one. Where a man possesses innate truth and honour, it shines out in his countenance, his voice, his manner; and there can be no mistake. When you are puzzled over a bad man, you say to yourself, 'He *may* be telling the truth, he *may* be genuine;' but with a good man you know it to be so: that is, if you possess the gift of reading countenances. Miss Gwinn, I am sure there was truth in that stranger."

"Listen, Austin Clay. That man, truthful as you deem him, is the very incarnation of deceit. I know as much of him as one human being can well know of another. It was he who wrought the terrible wrong upon my house; it was he who broke up my happy home. I'll find him now. Others said he must be dead; but I said, 'No, he lives yet.' And, you see he does live. I'll find him."

Without another word she turned away, and went striding back in the direction of Ketterford—the same road which the stranger's horse had taken. Austin stood and looked after her, pondering over the strange events of the hour. Then he proceeded to the Lowland farm.

A pleasant day amidst pleasant friends spent he; rich Easter cheesecakes being the least of the seductions he did *not* withstand; and Ketterford clocks were striking half-past ten as he approached Mrs. Thornimett's. The moonlight walk was delightful; there was no foreboding of ill upon his spirit, and he turned in at the gate utterly unconscious of the news that was in store for him.

Conscious of the late hour—for they were early people—he was passing across the lawn with a hasty step, when the door was drawn silently open, as if some one stood there watching, and he saw Sarah, one of the two old maid-servants, come forth to meet him. Both had lived in the family for years; had scolded and ordered Austin about when a boy, to their heart's content, and for his own good.

"Why, Sarah, is it you?" was his gay greeting. "Going to take a moonlight ramble?"

"Where *have* you stayed?" whispered the woman in evident excitement. "To think you should be away this night of all others, Mr. Austin! Have you heard what has happened to the master?"

"No. What?" exclaimed Austin, his fears taking alarm.

"He fell down in a fit, over at the village where he went; and they brought him home, a-frightening us two and the missis almost into fits ourselves. Oh, Master Austin!" she concluded, bursting into tears, "the doctors don't think he'll live till morning. Poor dear old master!"

Austin, half paralysed at the news, stood for a moment against the wall inside the hall. "Can I go and see him?" he presently asked.

"Oh, you may go," was the answer; "the mistress has been asking for you, and nothing rouses *him*. It's a heavy blow; but it has its side of brightness. God never sends a blow but he sends mercy with it."

"What is the mercy—the brightness?" Austin waited to ask, thinking she must allude to some symptom of hope. Sarah put her shrivelled old arm on his in solemnity, as she answered it.

"He was fit to be taken. He had lived for the next world while he was living in this. And those that do, Master Austin, never need shrink from sudden death."

II

Changes

To reflect upon the change death makes, even in the petty every-day affairs of life, must always impart a certain awe to the thoughtful mind. On the Easter Monday, spoken of in the last chapter, Richard Thornimett, his men, his contracts, and his business in progress, were all part of the life, the work, the bustle of the town of Ketterford. In a few weeks from that time, Richard Thornimett—who had not lived to see the morning light after his attack—was mouldering in the churchyard; and the business, the workshops, the artisans, all save the dwelling-house, which Mrs. Thornimett retained for herself, had passed into other hands. The name, Richard Thornimett, as one of the citizens of Ketterford, had ceased to be: all things were changed.

Mrs. Thornimett's friends and acquaintances had assembled to tender counsel, after the fashion of busybodies of the world. Some recommended her to continue the business; some, to give it up; some, to take in a gentleman as partner; some, to pay a handsome salary to an efficient manager. Mrs. Thornimett listened politely to all, without the least intention of acting upon anybody's opinion but her own. Her mind had been made up from the first. Mr. Thornimett had died fairly well off, and everything was left to her—half of the money to be hers for life, and then to go to different relatives; the other half was bequeathed to her absolutely, and was at her own disposal. Rumours were rife in the town, that, when things came to be realized, she would have about twelve thousand pounds in money, besides other property.

But before making known her decision abroad, she spoke to Austin Clay. They were sitting together one evening when she entered upon the subject, breaking the silence that reigned with some abruptness.

"Austin, I shall dispose of the business; everything as it stands. And the goodwill."

"Shall you?" he exclaimed, taken by surprise, and his voice betraying a curious disappointment.

Mrs. Thornimett nodded in answer.

"I would have done my best to carry it on for you, Mrs. Thornimett. The foreman is a man of experience; one we may trust."

"I do not doubt you, Austin; and I do not doubt him. You have got your head on your shoulders the right way, and you would be faithful and true. So well do I think of your abilities, that, were you in a position to pay down only half the purchase-money, I would give you the refusal of the business, and I am certain success would attend you. But you are not; so that is out of the question."

"Quite out of the question," assented Austin. "If ever I get a business of my own, it must be by working for it. Have you quite resolved upon giving it up?"

"So far resolved, that the negotiations are already half concluded," replied Mrs. Thornimett. "What should I, a lone woman, do with an extensive business? When poor widows are left badly off, they are obliged to work; but I possess more money than I shall know how to spend. Why should I worry out my hours and days trying to amass more? It would not be seemly. Rolt and Ransom wish to purchase it."

Austin lifted his head with a quick movement. He did not like Rolt and Ransom.

"The only difference we have in the matter, is this: that I wish them to take you on, Austin, and they think they shall find no room for you. Were you a common workman, it would be another thing, they say."

"Do not allow that to be a difference any longer, Mrs. Thornimett," he cried, somewhat eagerly. "I should not care to be under Rolt and Ransom. If they offered me a place to-morrow, and *carte blanche* as to pay, I do not think I could bring myself to take it."

"Why?" asked Mrs. Thornimett, in surprise.

"Well, they are no favourites of mine. I know nothing against them, except that they are hard men—grinders; but somehow I have always felt a prejudice against that firm. We do have our likes and dislikes, you are well aware. Young Rolt is prominent in the business, too, and I am sure there's no love lost between him and me; we should be at daggers drawn. No, I should not serve Rolt and Ransom. If they succeed to your business, I think I shall go to London and try my fortune there."

Mrs. Thornimett pushed back her widow's cap, to which her head had never yet been able to get reconciled—something like Austin with regard to Rolt and Ransom. "London would not be a good place for you, Austin. It is full of pitfalls for young men."

"So are other places," said Austin, laughingly, "if young men choose to step into them. I shall make my way, Mrs. Thornimett, never fear. I am thorough master of my business in all its branches, higher and lower as you know, and I am not afraid of putting my own shoulder to the wheel, if there's necessity for it. As to pitfalls—if I do stumble in the dark into any, I'll manage to scramble out again; but I will try and take care not to step into them wilfully. Had you continued the business, of course I would have remained with you; otherwise, I should like to go to London."

"You can be better trusted, both as to capabilities and steadiness, than some could at your age," deliberated Mrs. Thornimett. "But they are wrong notions that you young men pick up with regard to London. I believe there's not one of you but thinks its streets are sprinkled with diamonds."

"*I* don't," said Austin. "And while God gives me hands and brains to work with, I would rather earn my diamonds, than stoop to pick them up in idleness."

Mrs. Thornimett paused. She settled her spectacles more firmly on her eyes, turned them full on Austin, and spoke sharply.

"Were you disappointed when you heard the poor master's will read?"

Austin, in return, turned his eyes upon her, and opened them to their utmost width in his surprise. "Disappointed! No. Why should I be?"

"Did it never occur to you to think, or to expect, that he might leave you something?"

"Never," earnestly replied Austin. "The thought never so much as crossed my mind. Mr. Thornimett had near relatives of his own—and so have you. Who am I, that I should think to step in before them?"

"I wish people would mind their own business!" exclaimed the old lady, in a vexed tone. "I was gravely assured, Austin, that young Clay felt grievously ill-used at not being mentioned in the will."

"Did you believe it?" he rejoined.

"No, I did not."

"It is utterly untrue, Mrs. Thornimett, whoever said it. I never expected Mr. Thornimett to leave me anything; therefore, I could not have been disappointed at the will."

"The poor master knew I should not forget you, Austin; that is if you continue to be deserving. Some time or other, when my old bones are laid beside him, you may be the better for a trifle from me. Only a trifle, mind; we must be just before we are generous."

"Indeed, you are very kind," was Austin Clay's reply; "but I should not wish you to enrich me at the expense of others who have greater claims." And he fully meant what he said. "I have not the least fear of making my own way up the world's ladder. Do you happen to know anything of the London firm, Hunter and Hunter?"

"Only by reputation," said Mrs. Thornimett.

"I shall apply to them, if I go to London. They would interest themselves for me, perhaps."

"You'd be sure to do well if you could get in there. But why should they help you more than any other firm would?"

"There's nothing like trying," replied Austin, too conscious of the evasive character of his reply. He was candour itself; but he feared to speak of the circumstances under which he had met Mr. Henry Hunter, lest Miss Gwinn should find out it was to him he had gone, and so track Mr. Henry Hunter home. Austin deemed that it was no business of his to help her to find Mr. Hunter, whether he was or not the *bête noire* of whom she had spoken. He might have told of the encounter at the time, but for the home calamity that supervened upon it; that drove away other topics. Neither had he mentioned it at the Lowland farm. For all Miss Gwinn's violence, he felt pity for her, and could not expose the woman.

"A first-rate firm, that of Hunter and Hunter," remarked Mrs. Thornimett. "Your credentials will be good also, Austin."

"Yes; I hope so."

It was nearly all that passed upon the subject. Rolt and Ransom took possession of the business, and Austin Clay prepared to depart for London. Mrs. Thornimett felt sure he would get on well—always provided that he kept out of "pit-falls." She charged him not to be above his business, but to *work* his way upwards: as Austin meant to do.

A day or two before quitting Ketterford, it chanced that he and Mrs. Thornimett, who were out together, encountered Miss Gwinn. There was a speaking acquaintance between the two ladies, and Miss Gwinn stopped to say a kind word or two of sympathy for the widow and her recent loss. She could be a lady on occasion, and a gentle one. As the conversation went on, Mrs. Thornimett incidentally mentioned that Mr. Clay was going to leave and try his fortune in London.

"Oh, indeed," said Miss Gwinn, turning to him, as he stood quietly by Mrs. Thornimett's side. "What does he think of doing there?"

"To get a situation, of course. He means first of all to try at Hunter and Hunter's."

The words had left Mrs. Thornimett's lips before Austin could interpose—which he would have given the world to do. But there was no answering emotion on Miss Gwinn's face.

"Hunter and Hunter?" she carelessly repeated. "Who are they?"

"'Hunter Brothers,' they are sometimes called," observed Mrs. Thornimett. "It is a building firm of eminence."

"Oh," apathetically returned Miss Gwinn. "I wish you well," she added, to Austin.

He thanked her as they parted. The subject, the name, evidently bore for her no interest whatever. Therefore Austin judged, that although she might have knowledge of Mr. Henry Hunter's person, she could not of his name.

III

Away to London

A heavy train, drawn by two engines, was dashing towards London. Whitsuntide had come, and the public took advantage of the holiday, and the trains were crammed. Austin Clay took advantage of it also; it was a saving to his pocket, the fares having been lowered; and he rather liked a cram. What he did not like, though, was the being stuffed into a first-class carriage with its warm mats and cushions. The crowd was so great that people sat indiscriminately in any carriage that came first. The day was intensely hot, and he would have preferred one open on all sides. They were filled, however, before he came. He had left Ketterford, and was on his road to London to seek his fortune—as old stories used to say.

Seated in the same compartment as himself was a lady with a little girl. The former appeared to be in very delicate health; she remarked more than once, that she would not have travelled on so crowded a day, had she given it proper thought. The little girl was chiefly remarkable for making herself troublesome to Austin; at least, her mamma perpetually reproached her with doing so. She was a lovely child, with delicately carved features, slightly aquiline, but inexpressibly sweet and charming. A bright colour illumined her cheeks, her eyes were large and dark and soft, and her brown curls were flowing. He judged her to be perhaps eleven years old; but she was one of those natural, unsophisticated children, who appear much younger than they are. The race has pretty nearly gone out of the world now: I hope it will come back again.

"Florence, how *can* you be so tiresome? Pushing yourself before the gentleman against that dangerous door! it may fly open at any moment. I am sure he must be tired of holding you."

Florence turned her bright eye—sensible, honest eyes, bright though they were—and her pretty hot cheeks upon the gentleman.

"Are you tired, sir?"

Austin smiled. "It would take rather more than this to tire me," he said. "Pray allow her to look out," he added, to the lady, opposite to whom he sat; "I will take every care of her."

"Have you any little girls of your own?" questioned the young damsel.

Austin laughed outright. "No."

"Nor any sisters?"

"Nor any sisters. I have scarcely any relatives in the world. I am not so fortunate as you."

"I have a great many relatives, but no brothers or sisters. I had a little sister once, and she died when she was three years old. Was it not three, mamma?"

"And how old are you?" inquired Austin.

"Oh, pray do not ask," interposed the lady. "She is so thoroughly childish, I am ashamed that anybody should know her age. And yet she does not want sense."

"I was twelve last birthday," cried the young lady, in defiance of all conventionalism. "My cousin Mary is only eleven, but she is a great deal bigger than I."

"Yes," observed the lady, in a tone of positive resentment. "Mary is quite a woman already in ideas and manners: you are a child, and a very backward one."

"Let her be a child, ma'am, while she may," impulsively spoke Austin; "childhood does not last too long, and it never comes again. Little girls are women nowadays: I think it is perfectly delightful to meet with one like this."

Before they reached London other passengers had disappeared from the carriage, and they were alone. As they neared the terminus, the young lady was peremptorily ordered to "keep her head in," or perhaps she might lose it.

"Oh dear! if I must, I must," returned the child. "But I wanted to look out for papa; he is sure to be waiting for us."

The train glided into its destination. And the bright quick eyes were roving amidst the crowd standing on the platform. They rested upon a gentleman.

"There's Uncle Henry! there's Uncle Henry! But I don't see papa. Where's papa?" she called out, as the gentleman saw them and approached.

"Papa's not come; he has sent me instead, Miss Florence." And to Austin Clay's inexpressible surprise, he recognised Mr. Henry Hunter.

"There is nothing the matter? James is not ill?" exclaimed the lady, bending forward.

"No, no; nothing of that. Being a leisure day with us, we thought we would quietly go over some estimates together. James had not finished the calculations, and did not care to be disturbed at them. Your carriage is here."

Mr. Henry Hunter was assisting her to alight as he spoke, having already lifted down Florence. A maid with a couple of carpet-bags appeared presently, amidst the bustle, and Austin saw them approach a private carriage. He had not pushed himself forward. He did not intend to do so then, deeming it not the most fitting moment to challenge the notice of Mr. Henry Hunter; but that gentleman's eye happened to fall upon him.

Not at first for recognition. Mr. Hunter felt sure it was a face he had seen recently; was one he ought to know; but his memory was puzzled. Florence followed his gaze.

"That gentleman came up in the same carriage with us, Uncle Henry. He got in at a place they called Ketterford. I like him so much."

Austin came forward as he saw the intent look; and recollection flashed over the mind of Mr. Henry Hunter. He took both the young man's hands in his and grasped them.

"You like him, do you, Miss Florence?" cried he, in a half-joking, half-fervent tone. "I can tell you what, young lady; but for this gentleman, you would no longer have possessed an Uncle Henry to plague; he would have been dead and forgotten."

A word or two of explanation from Austin, touching what brought him to London, and his intention to ask advice of Mr. Henry Hunter. That gentleman replied that he would give it willingly, and at once, for he had leisure on his hands that day, and he could not answer for it that he would have on another. He gave Austin the address of his office.

"When shall I come, sir?" asked Austin.

"Now, if you can. A cab will bring you. I shall not be there later in the day."

So Austin, leaving his portmanteau, all the luggage he had at present brought with him, in charge at the station, proceeded in a cab to the address named, Mr. Henry Hunter having driven off in the carriage.

The offices, yards, buildings, sheds, and other places pertaining to the business of Hunter and Hunter, were situated in what may be considered a desirable part of the metropolis. They encroached neither upon the excessive bustle of the City, nor upon the aristocratic exclusiveness of the gay West end, but occupied a situation midway between the two. Sufficiently open was the district in their immediate neighbourhood, healthy, handsome, and near some fine squares; but a very, very little way removed, you came upon swarming courts, and close dwellings, and squalor, and misery, and all the bad features of what we are pleased to call Arab life. There are many such districts in London, where wealth and ease contrast with starvation and improvidence, *all but* within view of each other; the one gratifying the eye, the other causing it pain.

The yard and premises were of great extent. Austin had thought Mr. Thornimett's pretty fair for size; but he could laugh at them, now that he saw the Messrs. Hunters'. They were enclosed by a wall, and by light iron gates. Within the gates on the left-hand side were the offices, where the in-door business was transacted. A wealthy, important, and highly considered firm was that of the Messrs. Hunter. Their father had made the business what it was, and had bequeathed it to them jointly at his death. James, whose wife and only child you have seen arriving by the train, after a week's visit to the country, was the elder brother, and was usually styled Mr. Hunter; the younger was known as Mr. Henry Hunter, and he had a large family. Each occupied a handsome house in a contiguous square.

Mr. Henry Hunter came up almost as Austin did, and they entered the offices. In a private room, warmly carpeted, stood two gentlemen. The one, had he not been so stout, would have borne a great likeness to Mr. Henry Hunter. It was Mr. Hunter. In early life the likeness between the brothers had been remarkable; the same dark hair and eyes; the well-formed acquiline features, the same active, tall, light figure; but, of late years, James had grown fat, and the resemblance was in part lost. The other gentleman was Dr. Bevary, a spare man of middle height, the brother of Mrs. James Hunter. Mr. Henry Hunter introduced Austin Clay, speaking of the service rendered him, and broadly saying as he had done to Florence, that but for him he should not now have been alive.

"There you go, Henry," cried Dr. Bevary. "That's one of your exaggerations, that is: you were always given to the marvellous, you know. Not alive!"

Mr. Henry Hunter turned to Austin. "Tell the truth, Mr. Clay. Should I, or not?" And Austin smiled, and said he believed *not*.

"I cannot understand it," exclaimed Dr. Bevary, after some explanation had been given by Mr. Henry Hunter. "It is incredible to suppose a strange woman would attack you in that manner, unless she was mad."

"Mad, or not mad, she did it," returned Mr. Henry Hunter. "I was riding Salem—you know I took him with me, in that week's excursion

I made at Easter—and the woman set upon me like a tigress, clutching hold of Salem, who won't stand such jokes. In his fury, he got loose from her, dashing he neither knew nor cared whither, and this fine fellow saved us on the very brink of the yawning pit—risking the chance of getting killed himself. Had the horse not been arrested, I don't see how he could have helped being knocked over with us."

Mr. Hunter turned a warm grateful look on Austin. "How was it you never spoke of this, Henry?" he inquired of his brother.

"There's another curious phase of the affair," laughed Mr. Henry Hunter. "I have had a dislike to speak of it, even to think of it. I cannot tell you why; certainly not on account of the escaped danger. And it was over: so, what signified talking of it?"

"Why did she attack you?" pursued Dr. Bevary.

"She evidently, if there was reason in her at all, mistook me for somebody else. All sorts of diabolical things she was beginning to accuse me of; that of having evaded her for some great number of years, amongst the rest. I stopped her; telling her I had no mind to be the depository of other people's secrets."

"She solemnly protested to me, after you rode away, sir, that you *were* the man who had done her family some wrong," interposed Austin. "I told her I felt certain she was mistaken; and so drew down her anger upon me."

"Of what nature was the wrong?" asked Dr. Bevary.

"I cannot tell," said Austin. "I seemed to gather from her words that the wrong was upon her family, or upon some portion of her family, rather than upon her. I remember she made use of the expression, that it had broken up her happy home."

"And you did not know her?" exclaimed the doctor, looking at Mr. Henry Hunter.

"Know her?" he returned, "I never set eyes on her in all my life until that day. I never was in the place before, or in its neighbourhood. If I ever did work her wrong, or ill, I must have done it in my sleep; and with miles of distance intervening. Who is she? What is her name? You told it me, Mr. Clay, but I forget what it was."

"Her name is Gwinn," replied Austin. "The brother is a lawyer and has scraped together a business. One morning, many years ago, a lady arrived at his house, without warning, and took up her abode with him. She turned out to be his sister, and the people at Ketterford think she is mad. It is said they come from Wales. The little boys call after her, "the mad Welsh woman." Sometimes Miss Gwinn."

"What did you say the name was?" interrupted Dr. Bevary, with startling emphasis. "Gwinn?—and from Wales?"
"Yes."
Dr. Bevary paused, as if in deep thought. "What is her Christian name?" he presently inquired.
"It is a somewhat uncommon one," replied Austin. "Agatha."
The doctor nodded his head, as if expecting the answer. "A tall, spare, angular woman, of great strength," he remarked.
"Why, what do you know of her?" exclaimed Mr. Henry Hunter to the doctor, in a surprised tone.
"Not a great deal. We medical men come across all sorts of persons occasionally," was the physician's reply. And it was given in a concise, laconic manner, as if he did not care to be questioned further. Mr. Henry Hunter pursued the subject.
"If you know her, Bevary, perhaps you can tell whether she is mad or sane."
"She is sane, I believe: I have no reason to think her otherwise. But she is one who can allow angry passion to master her at moments: I have seen it do so. Do you say her brother is a lawyer?" he continued, to Austin Clay.
"Yes, he is. And not one of the first water, as to reputation; a grasping, pettifogging practitioner, who will take up any dirty case that may be brought to him. And in that, I fancy, he is a contrast to his sister; for, with all her strange ways, I should not judge her to be dishonourable. It is said he speculates, and that he is not over particular whose money he gets to do it with."
"I wonder that she never told me about this brother," dreamily exclaimed the doctor, in an inward tone, as if forgetting that he spoke aloud.
"Where did you meet with her? When did you know her?" interposed Mr. Henry Hunter.
"Are you sure that *you* know nothing about her?" was the doctor's rejoinder, turning a searching glance upon Mr. Henry Hunter.
"Come, Bevary, what have you got in your head? I do *not* know her. I never met with her until she saw and accosted me. Are you acquainted with her history?"
"With a dark page in it."
"What is the page?"
Dr. Bevary shook his head. "In the course of a physician's practice

he becomes cognisant of many odds and ends of romance, dark or fair; things that he must hold sacred, and may not give utterance to."

Mr. Henry Hunter looked vexed. "Perhaps you can understand the reason of her attacking me?"

"I could understand it, but for your assertion of being a stranger to her. If it is so, I can only believe that she mistook you for another."

"*If* it is so," repeated Mr. Henry Hunter. "I am not in the habit of asserting an untruth, Bevary."

"Nor, on the other hand, is Miss Gwinn one to be deceived. She is keen as a razor."

"Bevary, what are you driving at?"

"At nothing. Don't be alarmed, Henry. I have no cause to suppose you know the woman, or she you. I only thought—and think—she is one whom it is almost impossible to deceive. It must, however, have been a mistake."

"It was a mistake—so far as her suspicion that she knew me went," decisively returned Mr. Henry Hunter.

"Ay," acquiesced Dr. Bevary. "But here am I gossiping my morning away, when a host of patients are waiting for me. We poor doctors never get a holiday, as you more favoured mortals do."

He laughed as he went out, nodding a friendly farewell to Austin. Mr. Henry Hunter stepped out after him. Then Mr. Hunter, who had not taken part in the discussion, but had stood looking from the window while they carried it on, wheeled round to Austin and spoke in a low, earnest tone.

"What *is* this tale—this mystery—that my brother and the doctor seem to be picking up?"

"Sir, I know no more than you have heard me say. I witnessed her attack on Mr. Henry Hunter."

"I should like to know further about it: about her. Will you—Hush! here comes my brother back again. Hush!"

His voice died away in the faintest whisper, for Mr. Henry Hunter was already within the room. Was Mr. Hunter suspecting that his brother had more cognisance of the affair than he seemed willing to avow? The thought, that it must be so, crossed Austin Clay; or why that warning "hush" twice repeated?

It happened that business was remarkably brisk that season at Hunter and Hunter's. They could scarcely get hands enough, or the work done. And when Austin explained the cause which had brought him to town, and frankly proffered the question of whether they could recommend him to employment, they were glad to offer it themselves. He produced his credentials of capacity and character, and waited. Mr. Henry Hunter turned to him with a smile.

"I suppose you are not above your work, Mr. Clay?"

"I am not above anything in the world that is right, sir. I have come to seek work."

He was engaged forthwith. His duties at present were to lie partly in the counting-house, partly in overlooking the men; and the salary offered was twenty-five pounds per quarter.

"I can rise above that in time, I suppose," remarked Austin, "if I give satisfaction?"

Mr. Hunter smiled. "Ay, you can rise above that, if you choose. But when you get on, you'll be doing, I expect, as some of the rest do."

"What is that, sir?"

"Leaving us, to set up for yourself. Numbers have done so as soon as they have become valuable. I do not speak of the men, you understand, but of those who have been with us in a higher capacity. A few of the men, though, have done the same; some have risen into influence."

"How can they do that without capital?" inquired Austin. "It must take money, and a good deal of it, to set up for themselves."

"Not so much as you may think. They begin in a small way—take piece-work, and work early and late, often fourteen and fifteen hours a day, husbanding their earnings, and getting a capital together by slow but sure degrees. Many of our most important firms have so risen, and owe their present positions to sheer hard work, patience, and energy."

"It was the way in which Mr. Thornimett first rose," observed Austin. "He was once a journeyman at fourteen shillings a week. *He* got together money by working over hours."

"Ay, there's nothing like it for the industrious man," said Mr. Hunter.

Preliminaries were settled, advice given to him where he might find lodgings, and Austin departed, having accepted an invitation to dine at six at Mr. Henry Hunter's.

And all through having performed an unpremeditated but almost necessary act of bravery.

IV

Daffodil's Delight

Turning to the right after quitting the business premises of the Messrs. Hunter, you came to an open, handsome part, where the square in which those gentlemen dwelt was situated, with other desirable squares, crescents, and houses. But, if you turned to the left instead of to the right, you very speedily found yourself in the midst of a dense locality, not so agreeable to the eye or to the senses.

And yet some parts of this were not much to be complained of, unless you instituted a comparison between them and those open places; but in this world all things are estimated by comparison. Take Daffodil's Delight, for example. "Daffodil's Delight! what's that?" cries the puzzled reader, uncertain whether it may be a fine picture or something to eat. Daffodil's Delight was nothing more than a tolerably long street, or lane, or double row of houses—wide enough for a street, dirty enough for a lane, the buildings irregular, not always contiguous, small gardens before some, and a few trees scattered here and there. When the locality was mostly fields, and the buildings on them were scanty, a person of the name of Daffodil ran up a few tenements. He found that they let well, and he ran up more, and more, and more, until there was a long, long line of them, and he growing rich. He called the place Daffodil's Delight—which we may suppose expressed his own complacent satisfaction at his success—and Daffodil's Delight it had continued, down to the present day. The houses were of various sizes, and of fancy appearance; some large, some small; some rising up like a narrow tower, some but a storey high; some were all windows, some seemed to have none; some you could only gain by ascending steps; to others you pitched down as into a cellar; some lay back, with gardens before their doors, while others projected pretty nearly on to the street gutter. Nothing in the way of houses could be more irregular, and what Mr. Daffodil's motive could have been in erecting such cannot be conjectured—unless he formed an idea that he would make a venture to suit various tastes and diverse pockets.

Nearly at the beginning of this locality, in its best part, before the road became narrow, there stood a detached white house; one of only six rooms, but superior in appearance, and well kept; indeed, it looked more like a gentleman's cottage residence than a working man's. Verandah blinds were outside the windows, and green wire fancy stands held geraniums and other plants on the stone copings, against their lower panes, obviating the necessity for inside blinds. In this house lived Peter Quale. He had begun life carrying hods of mortar for masons, and covering up bricks with straw—a half-starved urchin, his feet as naked as his head, and his body pretty nearly the same. But he was steady, industrious, and persevering—just one of those men that *work on* for decent position, and acquire it. From two shillings per week to four, from four to six, from six to twelve—such had been Peter Quale's beginnings. At twelve shillings he remained for some time stationary, and then his advance was rapid. Now, he was one of the superior artisans of the Messrs. Hunters' yard; was, in fact, in a post of trust, and his wages had grown in proportion. Daffodil's Delight said that Quale's earnings could not be less than 150*l.* per annum. A steady, sensible, honest, but somewhat obstinate man, well-read, and intelligent; for Peter, while he advanced his circumstances, had not neglected his mind. He had cultivated that far more than he had his speech or his manner; a homely tone and grammar, better known to Daffodil's Delight than to polite ears, Peter favoured still.

In the afternoon of Whit Monday, the day spoken of already, Peter sat in the parlour of his house, a pipe in his mouth, and a book in his hand. He looked about midway between forty and fifty, had a round bald head, surmounted just now by a paper cap, a fair complexion, grey whiskers, and a well-marked forehead, especially where lie the perceptive faculties. His eyes were deeply sunk in his head, and he was by nature a silent man. In the kitchen behind, "washing up" after dinner, was his helpmate, Mrs. Quale. Although so well to do, and having generally a lodger, she kept no servant—"wouldn't be bothered with 'em," she said—but did her own work; a person coming in once a week to clean.

A rattling commotion in the street caused Peter Quale to look up from his book. A large pleasure-van was rumbling down it, drawing up at the next door to his.

"Nancy!" called out he to his wife.

"Well?" came forth the answer, in a brisk, bustling voice, from the depths of the kitchen.

"The Shucks, and that lot, be actually going off now?"

The news appeared to excite the curiosity of Mrs. Quale, and she came hastily in; a dark-eyed, rosy-cheeked little woman, with black curls. She wore a neat white cap, a fresh-looking plum-coloured striped gown of some thin woollen material, and a black apron; a coarse apron being pinned round her. Mrs. Quale was an inveterate busybody, knew every incident that took place in Daffodil's Delight, and possessed a free-and-easy tongue; but she was a kindly woman withal, and very popular. She put her head outside the window above the geraniums, to reconnoitre.

"Oh, they be going, sure enough! Well, they are fools! That's just like Slippery Sam! By to-morrow they won't have a threepenny piece to bless themselves with. But, if they must have went, they might have started earlier in the day. There's the Whites! And—why!—there's the Dunns! The van won't hold 'em all. As for the Dunns, they'll have to pinch for a month after it. She has got on a dandy new bonnet with pink ribbons. Aren't some folks idiots, Peter?"

Peter rejoined, with a sort of a grunt, that it wasn't no business of his, and applied himself again to his pipe and book. Mrs. Quale made everybody's business hers, especially their failings and shortcomings; and she unpinned the coarse apron, flung it aside, and flew off to the next house.

It was inhabited by two families, the Shucks and the Baxendales. Samuel Shuck, usually called Slippery Sam, was an idle, oily-tongued chap, always slipping from work—hence the nickname—and spending at the "Bricklayers' Arms" what ought to have been spent upon his wife and children. John Baxendale was a quiet, reserved man, living respectably with his wife and daughter, but not saving. It was singular how improvident most of them were. Daffodil's Delight was chiefly inhabited by the workmen of the Messrs. Hunter; they seemed to love to congregate there as in a nest. Some of the houses were crowded with them, a family on a floor—even in a room; others rented a house to themselves, and lived in comfort.

Assembled inside Sam Shuck's front room, which was a kitchen and not a parlour, and to which the house door opened, were as many people as it could well hold, all in their holiday attire. Abel White, his wife and family; Jim Dunn, and his; Patrick Ryan and the childer (Pat's wife was dead); and John Baxendale and his daughter, besides others; the whole host of little Shucks, and half-a-dozen outside stragglers. Mrs. Quale might well wonder how all the lot could be stuffed into the pleasure-van. She darted into their midst.

"You never mean to say you be a-going off, like simpletons, at this time o' day?" quoth she.

"Yes, we be," answered Sam Shuck, a lanky, serpent sort of man in frame, with a prominent black eye, a turned-up nose, and, as has been said, an oily tongue. "What have you got to say again it, Mrs. Quale? Come!"

"Say!" said that lady, undauntedly, but in a tone of reason rather than rebuke, "I say you may just as well fling your money in the gutter as to go off to Epping at three o'clock in the afternoon. Why didn't you start in the morning? If I hired a pleasure-van I'd have my money's worth out of it."

"It's just this here," said Sam. "It was ordered to be here as St. Paul's great bell was a striking break o' day, but the wheels wasn't greased; and they have been all this time a greasing 'em with the best fresh butter at eighteen-pence a pound, had up from Devonshire on purpose."

"You hold your tongue, Sam," reprimanded Mrs. Quale. "You have been a greasing your throat pretty strong, I see, with an extra pot or two; you'll be in for it as usual before the day's out. How is it you are going now?" she added, turning to the women.

"It's just the worst managed thing as I ever had to do with," volubly spoke up Jim Dunn's wife, Hannah. "And it's all the fault o' the men: as everything as goes wrong always is. There was a quarrel yesterday over it, and nothing was settled, and this morning when we met they began a jawing again. Some would go, and some wouldn't; some 'ud have a van to the Forest, and some 'ud take a omnibus ride to the Zoological Gardens, and see the beasts, and finish up at the play; some 'ud sit at home, and smoke, and drink, and wouldn't go nowhere; and most of the men got off to the 'Bricklayers' Arms' and stuck there; and afore the difference was settled in favour of the van and the Forest, twelve o'clock struck, and then there was dinner to be had, and us to put ourselves to rights and the van to be seen after. And there it is, now three o'clock's gone."

"It'll be just a ride out, and a ride in," cried Mrs. Quale; "you won't have much time to stop. Money must be plentiful with you, a fooling it away like that. I thought some of you had better sense."

"We spoke against it, father and I," said quiet Mary Baxendale, in Mrs. Quale's ear; "but as we had given our word to join in it and share in the expense, we didn't like to go from it again. Mother doesn't feel strong to-day, so she's stopping at home."

"It does seem stupid to start at this late hour," spoke up a comely woman, mild in speech, Robert Darby's wife. "Better to have put it off till to-morrow, and taken another day's holiday, as I told my master. But when it was decided to go, we didn't say nay, for I couldn't bear to disappoint the children."

The children were already being lifted into the van. Sundry baskets and bundles, containing provisions for tea, and stone bottles of porter for the men, were being lifted in also. Then the general company got in; Daffodil's Delight, those not bound on the expedition, assembling to witness the ceremony, and Peter casting an eye at it from his parlour. After much packing, and stowing, and laughing, and jesting, and the gentlemen declaring the ladies must sit upon their laps three deep, the van and its four horses moved off, and went lumbering down Daffodil's Delight.

Mrs. Quale, after watching the last of it, was turning into her own gate, when she heard a tapping at the window of the tenement on the *other* side of her house. Upon looking round, it was thrown open, and a portly matron, dressed almost well enough for a lady, put out her head. She was the wife of George Stevens, a very well-to-do workman, and most respectable man.

"Are they going off to the Forest at this hour, that lot?"

"Ay," returned Mrs. Quale; "was ever such nonsense known? I'd have made a day of it, if I had went. They'll get home at midnight, I expect, fit to stand on their heads. Some of the men have had a'most as much as is good for them now."

"I say," continued Mrs. Stevens, "George says, will you and your master come in for an hour or two this evening, and eat a bit of supper with us? We shall have a nice dish o' beefsteaks and onions, or some relishing thing of that sort, and the Cheeks are coming."

"Thank ye," said Mrs. Quale. "I'll ask Peter. But don't go and get anything hot."

"I must," was the answer. "We had a shoulder of lamb yesterday, and we finished it up to-day for dinner, with a salad; so there's nothing cold in the house, and I'm forced to cook a bit of something. I say, don't make it late; come at six. George—he's off somewhere, but he'll be in."

Mrs. Quale nodded acquiescence, and went indoors. Her husband was reading and smoking still.

"I'd have put it off till ten at night, and went then!" ironically cried she, in allusion to the departed pleasure-party. "A bickering and contending they have been over it, Hannah Dunn says; couldn't come to an agreement what they'd do, or what they wouldn't do! Did you ever see such a load! Them poor horses 'll have enough of it, if the others don't. I say, the Stevenses want us to go in there to supper to-night. Beefsteaks and onions."

Peter's head was bent attentively over a map in his book, and it continued so bent for a minute or two. Then he raised it. "Who's to be there?"

"The Cheeks," she said. "I'll make haste and put the kettle on, and we'll have our tea as soon as it boils. She says don't go in later than six."

Pinning on the coarse apron, Mrs. Quale passed into the kitchen to her work. From the above slight sketch, it may be gathered that Daffodil's Delight was, take it for all in all, in tolerably comfortable circumstances. But for the wasteful mode of living generally pervading it; the improvidence both of husbands and wives; the spending where they need not have spent, and in things they would have been better without—it would have been in *very* comfortable circumstances: for, as is well known, no class of operatives earn better wages than those connected with the building trade.

"Is this Peter Quale's?"

The question proceeded from a stranger, who had entered the house passage, and thence the parlour, after knocking at its door. Peter raised his eyes, and beheld a tall, young, very gentleman-like man, in grey travelling clothes and a crape band on his black hat. Of courteous manners also, for he lifted his hat as he spoke, though Peter was only a workman and had a paper cap on his head.

"I am Peter Quale," said Peter, without moving.

Perhaps you may have already guessed that it was Austin Clay. He stepped forward with a frank smile. "I am sent here," he said, "by the Messrs. Hunter. They desired me to inquire for Peter Quale."

Peter was not wont to put himself out of the way for strangers: had a Duke Royal vouchsafed him a visit, I question if Peter would have been more than barely civil; but he knew his place with respect to his employers, and what was due to them—none better; and he rose up at their name, and took off his paper cap, and laid his pipe inside the fender, and spoke a word of apology to the gentleman before him.

"Pray do not mention it; do not disturb yourself," said Austin, kindly. "My name is Clay. I have just entered into an engagement with the Messrs. Hunter, and am now in search of lodgings as conveniently near their yard as may be. Mr. Henry Hunter said he thought you had rooms which might suit me: hence my intrusion."

"Well, sir, I don't know," returned Peter, rather dubiously. He was one of those who are apt to grow bewildered with any sudden proposition; requiring time, as may be said, to take it in, before he could digest it.

"You are from the country, sir, maybe?"

"I am from the country. I arrived in London but an hour ago, and my portmanteau is yet at the station. I wish to settle where I shall lodge, before I go to get it. Have you rooms to let?"

"Here, Nancy, come in!" cried Peter to his wife. "The rooms are in readiness to be shown, aren't they?"

Mrs. Quale required no second call. Hearing a strange voice, and gifted in a remarkable degree with what we are taught to look upon as her sex's failing—curiosity—she had already discarded again the apron, and made her appearance in time to receive the question.

"Ready and waiting," answered she. "And two better rooms for their size you won't find, sir, search London through," she said, volubly, turning to Austin. "They are on the first floor—a nice sitting-room, and a bedchamber behind it. The furniture is good, and clean, and handsome; for, when we were buying of it, we didn't spare a few pounds, knowing such would keep good to the end. Would you please step up, sir, and take a look at them?"

Austin acquiesced, motioning to her to lead the way. She dropped a curtsey as she passed him, as if in apology for taking it. He followed, and Peter brought up the rear, a dim notion penetrating Peter's brain that the attention was due from him to one sent by the Messrs. Hunter.

Two good rooms, as she had said; small, but well fitted up. "You'd be sure to be comfortable, sir," cried Mrs. Quale to Austin. "If *I* can't make lodgers comfortable, I don't know who can. Our last gentleman came to us three years ago, and left but a month since. He was a barrister's clerk, but he didn't get well paid, and he lodged in this part for cheapness."

"The rooms would suit me, so far as I can judge," said Austin, looking round; "suit me very well indeed, if we can agree upon terms. My pocket is but a shallow one at present," he laughed.

"I would make *them* easy enough for any gentleman sent by the masters," struck in Peter. "Did you say your name was Clay, sir?"

"Clay," assented Austin.

Mrs. Quale wheeled round at this, and took a free, full view of the gentleman from head to foot. "Clay? Clay?" she repeated to herself. "And there *is* a likeness, if ever I saw one! Sir," she hastily inquired, "do you come from the neighbourhood of Ketterford?"

"I come from Ketterford itself," replied he.

"Ah, but you were not born right in the town. I think you must be Austin Clay, sir; the orphan son of Mr. Clay and his wife—Miss Austin that used to be. They lived at the Nash farm. Sir, I have had you upon my lap scores of times when you were a little one."

"Why—who are you?" exclaimed Austin.

"You can't have forgot old Mr. Austin, the great-uncle, sir? though you were only seven years old when he died. I was Ann Best, cook to the old gentleman, and I heard all the ins and outs of the marriage of your father and mother. The match pleased neither family, and so they just took the Nash farm for themselves, to be independent and get along without being beholden for help to anybody. Many a fruit puff have I made for you, Master Austin; many a currant cake: how things come round in this world! Do take our rooms, sir—it will seem like serving my old master over again."

"I will take them willingly, and be glad to fall into such good hands. You will not require references now?"

Mrs. Quale laughed. Peter grunted resentfully. References from anybody sent by the Messrs. Hunter! "I would say eight shillings a week, sir," said Peter, looking at his wife. "Pay as you like; monthly, or quarterly, or any way."

"That's less than I expected," said Austin, in his candour. "Mr. Henry Hunter thought they would be about ten shillings."

Peter was candid also. "There's the neighbourhood to be took into consideration, sir, which is not a good one, and we can only let according to it. In some parts—and not far off, neither—you'd pay eighteen or twenty shillings for such rooms as these; in Daffodil's Delight it is different, though this is the best quarter of it. The last gentleman paid us nine. If eight will suit you, sir, it will suit us."

So the bargain was struck; and Austin Clay went back to the station for his luggage. Mrs. Quale, busy as a bee, ran in to tell her next-door neighbour that she could not be one of the beef-steak-and-onion eaters that night, though Peter might, for she should have her hands full with their new lodger. "The nicest, handsomest young fellow," she wound up with; "one it will be a pleasure to wait on."

"Take care what you be at, if he's a stranger," cried cautious Mrs. Stevens. "There's no trusting those country folks: they run away sometimes. It looks odd, don't it, to come after lodgings one minute, and enter upon 'em the next?"

"Very odd," assented Mrs. Quale, with a laugh. "Why, it was Mr. Henry Hunter sent him round here; and he has got a post in their house."

"What sort of one?" asked Mrs. Stevens, sceptical still.

"Who knows? Something superior to the best of us workpeople, you may be sure. He belongs to gentlefolks," concluded Mrs. Quale. "I knew him as a baby. It was in his mother's family I lived before I married. He's as like his mother as two peas, and a handsome woman was Mrs. Clay. Good-bye: I'm going to get the sheets on to his bed now."

Mrs. Quale, however, found that she was, after all, able to assist at the supper; for, when Austin came back, it was only to dress himself and go out, in pursuance of the invitation he had accepted to dine at Mr. Henry Hunter's. With all his haste it had struck six some minutes when he got there.

Mrs. Henry Hunter, a very pretty and very talkative woman, welcomed him with both hands, and told her children to do the same, for it was "the gentleman who saved papa." There was no ceremony; he was received quite *en famille*; no other guest was present, and three or four of the children dined at table. He appeared to find favour with them all. He talked on business matters with Mr. Henry Hunter; on lighter topics with his wife; he pointed out some errors in Mary Hunter's drawings, which she somewhat ostentatiously exhibited to him, and showed her how to rectify them. He entered into the school life of the two young boys, from their classics to their scrapes; and nursed a pretty little lady of five, who insisted on appropriating his knee—bearing himself throughout all with the modest reticence—the refinement of the innate gentleman. Mrs. Henry Hunter was charmed with him.

"How do you think you shall like your quarters?" she asked. "Mr. Hunter told me he recommended you to Peter Quale's."

"Very well. At least they will do. Mrs. Quale, it appears, is an old friend of mine."

"An old friend! Of yours!"

"She claims me as one, and says she has nursed me many a time when I was a child. I had quite forgotten her, and all about her, though I now remember her name. She was formerly a servant in my mother's family, near Ketterford."

Thus Austin Clay had succeeded without delay or difficulty in obtaining employment, and was, moreover, received on a footing of equality in the house of Mr. Henry Hunter. We shall see how he gets on.

V

Miss Gwinn's Visit

Were there space, it might be well to trace Austin Clay's progress step by step—his advancements and his drawbacks—his smooth-sailing and his difficulties; for, that his course was not free from difficulties and drawbacks you may be very sure. I do not know whose is. If any had thought he was to be represented as perfection, they were mistaken. Yet he managed to hold on his way without moral damage, for he was high-principled in every sense of the word. But there is neither time nor space to give to these particulars that regard himself alone.

Austin Clay sat one day in a small room of the office, making corrections in a certain plan, which had been roughly sketched. It was a hot day for the beginning of autumn, some three or four months having elapsed since his installation at Hunter and Hunter's. The office boy came in to interrupt him.

"Please, sir, here's a lady outside, asking if she can see young Mr. Clay."

"A lady!" repeated Austin, in some wonder. "Who is it?"

"I think she's from the country, sir," said the sharp boy. "She have got a big nosegay in her hand and a brown reticule."

"Does she wear widow's weeds?" questioned Austin hastily, an idea flashing over him that Mrs. Thornimett might have come up to town.

"Weeds?" replied the boy, staring, as if at a loss to know what "weeds" might mean. "She have got a white veil on, sir."

"Oh," said Austin. "Well, ask her to come in. But I don't know any lady that can want me. Or who has any business to come here if she does," he added to himself.

The lady came in: a very tall one. She wore a dark silk dress, a shepherd's plaid shawl, a straw bonnet, and a white veil. The reticule spoken of by the boy was in her hand; but the nosegay she laid down on a bench just outside the door. Austin rose to receive her.

"You are doubtless surprised to see me, Austin Clay. But, as I was coming to London on business—I always do at this season of the year—I got your address from Mrs. Thornimett, having a question to put to you."

Without ceremony, without invitation, she sat herself down on a chair. More by her voice than her features—for she kept her veil before her face—did Austin recognise her. It was Miss Gwinn. He recognised her with dismay. Mr. Henry Hunter was about the premises, liable to come in at any moment, and then might occur a repetition of that violent scene to which he had been a witness. Often and often had his mind recurred to the affair; it perplexed him beyond measure. Was Mr. Henry Hunter the stranger to her he asserted himself to be, or was he not? "What shall I do with her?" thought Austin.

"Will you shut the door?" she said, in a peremptory, short tone, for the boy had left it open.

"I beg your pardon, Miss Gwinn," interrupted Austin, necessity giving him courage. "Though glad to see you myself, I am at the present hour so busy that it is next to impossible for me to give you my attention. If you will name any place where I can wait upon you after business hours, this, or any other evening, I shall be happy to meet you."

Miss Gwinn ranged her eyes round the room, looking possibly, for confirmation of his words. "You are not so busy as to be unable to spare a minute to me. You were but looking over a plan."

"It is a plan that is being waited for." Which was true. "And you must forgive me for reminding you—I do it in all courtesy—that my time and this room do not belong to me, but to my employers."

"Boy! what is your motive for seeking to get rid of me?" she asked, abruptly. "That you have one, I can see."

Austin was upon thorns. He had not taken a seat. He stood near the door, pencil in hand, hoping it would induce her to move. At that moment footsteps were heard, and the office-door was pushed wide open.

It was Mr. Hunter. He stopped on the threshold, seeing a lady, an unusual sight there, and came to the conclusion that it must be some stranger for Mr. Clay. Her features, shaded by the thick white veil, were indistinct, and Mr. Hunter but glanced at her. Miss Gwinn on the contrary looked full at him, as she did at most people, and bent her head as a slight mark of courtesy. He responded by lifting his hat, and went out again.

"One of the principals, I suppose?" she remarked.

"Yes," he replied, feeling thankful that it was not Mr. Henry. "I believe he wants me, Miss Gwinn."

"I am not going to keep you from him. The question I wish to put to you will be answered in a sentence. Austin Clay, have you, since—"

"Allow me one single instant first, then," interrupted Austin, resigning himself to his fate, "just to speak a word of explanation to Mr. Hunter."

He stepped out of the room and closed the door behind him. Standing at the outer door, close by, open to the yard, was Mr. Hunter. Austin, in his haste and earnestness, grasped his arm.

"Find Mr. Henry, sir," he whispered. "Wherever he may be, let him keep there—out of sight—until she—this person—has gone. It is Miss Gwinn."

"Who? What do you say?" cried Mr. Hunter, staring at Austin.

"It is that Miss Gwinn. The woman who set upon Mr. Henry in that strange manner. She—"

Miss Gwinn opened the door at this juncture, and looked out upon them. Mr. Hunter walked briskly away in search of his brother. Austin turned back again.

She closed the door when he was inside the room, keeping her hand upon it. She did not sit down, but stood facing Austin, whom she held before her with the other hand.

"Have you, since you came to London, seen aught of my enemy?—that man whom you saved from his death in the gravel pits? Boy! answer me truthfully."

He remained silent, scarcely seeing what his course ought to be; or whether in such a case a lie of denial might not be justifiable. But the hesitation spoiled that, for she read it arightly.

"No need of your affirmative," she said. "I see you have met him. Where is he to be found?"

There was only one course for him now; and he took it, in all straightforward openness.

"It is true I have seen that gentleman, Miss Gwinn, but I can tell you nothing about him."

She looked fixedly at him. "That you cannot, or that you will not? Which?"

"That I will not. Forgive the seeming incivility of the avowal, but I consider that I ought not to comply with your request—that I should be doing wrong?"

"Explain. What do you mean by 'wrong?'"

"In the first place, I believe you were mistaken with regard to the gentleman: I do not think he was the one for whom you took him. In the second place, even if he be the one, I cannot make it my business to bring you into contact with him, and so give rise—as it probably would—to further violence."

There was a pause. She threw up her veil and looked fixedly at him, struggling for composure, her lips compressed, her face working.

"You know who he is, and where he lives," she jerked forth.

"I acknowledge that."

"How dare you take part against me?" she cried, in agitation.

"I do not take part against you, Miss Gwinn," he replied, wishing some friendly balloon would come and whirl her away; for Mr. Hunter might not find his brother to give the warning. "I do not take his part more than I take yours, only in so far as that I decline to tell you who and where he is. Had he the same ill-feeling towards you, and wished to know where you might be found, I would not tell him."

"Austin Clay, you *shall* tell me."

He drew himself up to his full height, speaking in all the quiet consciousness of resolution. "Never of my own free will. And I think, Miss Gwinn, there are no means by which you can compel me."

"Perhaps the law might?" She spoke dreamily, not in answer to him, but in commune with herself, as if debating the question. "Fare you well for the present, young man; but I have not done with you."

To his intense satisfaction she turned out of the office, catching up the flowers as she went. Austin attended her to the outer gate. She strode straight on, not deigning to cast a glance to the busy yard, with its sheds, its timber, its implements of work, and its artisans, all scattered about it.

"Believe me," he said, holding out his hand as a peace-offering, "I am not willingly discourteous. I wish I could see my way clear to help you."

She did not take the hand; she walked away without another word or look, and Austin went back again. Mr. Hunter advanced to meet him from the upper end of the yard, and went with him into the small room.

"What was all that, Clay? I scarcely understood."

"I daresay not, sir, for I had no time to be explanatory. It seems she—Miss Gwinn—has come to town on business. She procured my address from Mrs. Thornimett, and came here to ask of me if I had seen anything of her enemy—meaning Mr. Henry Hunter. I feared lest he should be coming in; I could only beg of you to find Mr. Henry, and warn him not. That is all, sir."

Mr. Hunter stood with his back to Austin, softly whistling—his habit when in deep thought. "What can be her motive for wanting to find him?" he presently said.

"She speaks of revenge. Of course I do not know for what: I cannot give a guess. There's no doubt she is mistaken in the person, when she accuses Mr. Henry Hunter."

"Well," returned Mr. Hunter, "I said nothing to my brother, for I did not understand what there was to say. It will be better not to tell him now; the woman is gone, and the subject does not appear to be a pleasant one. Do you hear?"

"Very well, sir."

"I think I understood, when the affair was spoken of some time ago, that she does not know him as Mr. Hunter?"

"Of course she does not," said Austin. "She would have been here after him before now if she did. She came this morning to see me, not suspecting she might meet him."

"Ah! Better keep the visit close," cried Mr. Hunter, as he walked away.

Now, it had occurred to Austin that it would be better to do just the opposite thing. *He* should have told Mr. Henry Hunter, and left that gentleman to seek out Miss Gwinn, or not, as he might choose. A sudden meeting between them in the office, in the hearing of the yard, and with the lady in excitement, was not desirable; but that Mr. Henry Hunter should clear himself, now that she was following him up, and convince her it was not he who was the suspected party, was, Austin thought, needful—that is, if he could do it. However, he could only obey Mr. Hunter's suggestions.

Austin resumed his occupation. His brain and fingers were busy over the plan, when he saw a gig drive into the yard. It contained the great engineer, Sir Michael Wilson. Mr. Henry Hunter came down the yard to meet him; they shook hands, and entered the private room together. In a few minutes Mr. Henry came to Austin.

"Are you particularly engaged, Clay?"

"Only with this plan, sir. It is wanted as soon as I can get it done."

"You can leave it for a quarter of an hour. I wish you to go round to Dr. Bevary. I was to have been at his house now—half-past eleven—to accompany him on a visit to a sick friend. Tell him that Sir Michael has come, and I have to go out with him, therefore it is impossible for me to keep my engagement. I am very sorry, tell Bevary: these things always happen crossly. Go right into his consulting-room, Clay; never mind patients; or else he will be chafing at my delay, and grumble the ceiling off."

Austin departed. Dr. Bevary occupied a good house in the main street, to the left of the yard, to gain which he had to pass the turning to Daffodil's Delight. Had Dr. Bevary lived to the right of the yard, his practice might have been more exclusive; but doctors cannot always choose their localities, circumstances more frequently doing that for them. He had a large connexion, and was often pressed for time.

Down went Austin, and gained the house. Just inside the open door, before which a close carriage was standing, was the doctor's servant.

"Dr. Bevary is engaged, sir, with a lady patient," said the man. "He is very particularly engaged for the moment, but I don't think he'll be long."

"I'll wait," said Austin, not deeming it well strictly to follow Mr. Henry Hunter's directions; and he turned, without ceremony, to the little box of a study on the left of the hall.

"Not there, sir," interposed the man hastily, and he showed him into the drawing-room on the right; Dr. Bevary and his patient being in the consulting-room.

Ten minutes of impatience to Austin. What could any lady mean by keeping him so long, in his own house? Then they came forth. The lady, a very red and portly one, rather old, was pushed into her carriage by the help of her footman, Austin watching the process from the window. The carriage then drove off.

The doctor did not come in. Austin concluded the servant must have forgotten to tell him he was there. He crossed the hall to the little study, the doctor's private room, knocked and entered.

"I am not to care for patients," called out he gaily, believing the doctor was alone; "Mr. Henry Hunter says so." But to his surprise, a patient was sitting there—at least, a lady; sitting, nose and knees together, with Dr. Bevary, and talking hurriedly and earnestly, as if they had the whole weight of the nation's affairs on their shoulders.

It was Miss Gwinn. The flowers had apparently found their home, for they were in a vase on the table. Austin took it all in at a glance.

"So it is you, is it, Austin Clay?" she exclaimed. "I was acquainting Dr. Bevary with your refusal to give me that man's address, and asking his opinion whether the law could compel you. Have you come after me to say you have thought better of it?"

Austin was decidedly taken aback. It might have been his fancy, but he thought he saw a look of caution go out to him from Dr. Bevary's eyes.

"Was your visit to this lady, Mr. Clay?"

"No, sir, it was to you. Sir Michael Wilson has come down on business, and Mr. Henry Hunter will not be able to keep his appointment with you. He desired me to say that he was sorry, but that it was no fault of his."

Dr. Bevary nodded. "Tell him I was about to send round to say that I could not keep mine with him so it's all right. Another day will—"

A sharp cry. A cry of passion, of rage, almost of terror. It came from Miss Gwinn; and the doctor, breaking off his sentence, turned to her in amazement.

It was well he did so; it was well he caught her hands. Another moment, and she would have dashed them through the window, and perhaps herself also. Driving by, in the gig, were Sir Michael Wilson and Mr. Henry Hunter. It was at the latter she gazed, at him she pointed.

"Do you see him? Do you see him?" she panted to the doctor. "That's the man; not the one driving; the other—the one sitting this way. Oh, Dr. Bevary, will you believe me now? I told you I met him at Ketterford; and there he is again! Let me go!"

She was strong almost as a wild animal, wrestling with the doctor to get from him. He made a motion to Austin to keep the door, and there ensued a sharp struggle. Dr. Bevary got her into an arm-chair at last, and stood before her, holding her hands, at first in silence. Then he spoke calmly, soothingly, as he would to a child.

"My dear lady, what will become of you if you give way to these fits of violence? But for me, I really believe you would have been through the window. A pretty affair of spikes that would be! I should have had you laid up in my house for a month, covered over with sticking-plaster."

"If you had not stopped me I might have caught that gig," was her passionate rejoinder.

"Caught that gig! A gig going at the rate of ten miles an hour, if it was going one! By the time you had got down the steps of my door it would have been out of sight. How people can drive at that random rate in London streets, *I* can't think."

"*How* can I find him? How can I find him?"

Her tone was quite a wail of anguish. However they might deprecate her mistaken violence, it was impossible but that both her hearers should feel compassion for her. She laid her hand on the doctor's arm.

"Will you not help me to find him, Dr. Bevary? Did you note him?"

"So far as to see that there were two persons in the gig, and that they were men, not women. Do you feel sure it was the man you speak of? It is so easy to be mistaken in a person who is being whirled along swiftly."

"Mistaken!" she returned, in a strangely significant tone. "Dr. Bevary, I am sure it was he. I have not kept him in my mind for years, to mistake him now. Austin Clay," she fiercely added, turning round upon Austin, "*you* speak; speak the truth; I saw you look after them. Was it, or was it not, the man whom I met at Ketterford?"

"I believe it was," was Austin's answer. "Nevertheless, Miss Gwinn, I do not believe him to be the enemy you spoke of—the one who worked you ill. He denies it just as solemnly as you assert it; and I am sure he is a truthful man."

"And that I am a liar?"

"No. That you believe what you assert is only too apparent. I think it a case, on your side, of mistaken identity."

Happening to raise his eyes, Austin caught those of Dr. Bevary fixed upon him with a keen, troubled, earnest gaze. It asked, as plainly as a gaze could ask, "*Do* you believe so? or is the falsehood on *his* side?"

"Will you disclose to Dr. Bevary the name of that man, if you will not to me?"

Again the gentlemen's eyes met, and this time an unmistakeable warning of caution gleamed forth from Dr. Bevary's. Austin could only obey it.

"I must decline to speak of him in any way, Miss Gwinn," said he; "you had my reasons before. Dr. Bevary, I have given you the message I was charged with. I must wish you both good day."

Austin walked back, full of thought, his belief somewhat wavering. "It is very strange," he reflected. "Could a woman, could any one be so positive as she is, unless thoroughly sure? What *is* the mystery, I wonder? That it was no sentimental affair between them, or rubbish of that sort, is patent by the difference of their ages; she looks pretty nearly old enough to be his mother. Mr. Henry Hunter's is a remarkable face—one that would alter little in a score of years."

The bell was ringing twelve as he approached the yard, and the workmen were pouring out of it, on their way home to dinner. Plentiful tables awaited them; little care was on their minds; flourishing was every branch of the building trade then. Peter Quale came up to Austin.

"Sam Shuck have just been up here, sir, a-eating humble pie, and praying to be took on again. But the masters be both absent; and Mr. Mills, he said he didn't choose, in a thing like this, to act on his own responsibility, for he heard Mr. Hunter say Shuck shouldn't again be employed."

"I would not take him on," replied Austin, "if it rested with me; an idle, skulking, deceitful vagabond, drunk and incapable at one time, striving to spread discontent among the men at another. He has been on the loose for a fortnight now. But it is not my affair, Quale; Mr. Mills is manager."

The yard, between twelve and one, was pretty nearly deserted. The gentleman, spoken of as Mr. Mills, and Austin, usually remained; the principals would sometimes be there, and an odd man or two. The timekeeper lived in the yard. Austin rather liked that hour; it was quiet. He was applying to his plan with a zest, when another interruption came, in the shape of Dr. Bevary. Austin began to think he might as well put the drawing away altogether.

"Anybody in the offices, Mr. Clay, except you?" asked the doctor.

"Not indoors. Mills is about somewhere."

Down sat the doctor, and fixed his keen eyes upon Austin. "What took place here this morning with Miss Gwinn?"

"No harm, sir," replied Austin, briefly explaining. "As it happened, Mr. Henry kept away. Mr. Hunter came in and saw her; but that was all."

"What is your opinion?" abruptly asked the doctor. "Come, give it freely. You have your share of judgment, and of discretion too, or I should not ask it. Is she mistaken, or is Henry Hunter false?"

Austin did not immediately reply. Dr. Bevary mistook the cause of his silence.

"Don't hesitate, Clay. You know I am trustworthy; and it is not I who would stir to harm a Hunter. If I seek to come to the bottom of this affair, it is that I may do what I can to repair damage; to avert some of the fruits of wrong-doing."

"If I hesitated, Dr. Bevary, it was that I am really at a loss what answer to give. When Mr. Henry Hunter denies that he knows the woman, or that he ever has known her, he appears to me to speak open truth. On the other hand, these recognitions of Miss Gwinn's, and her persistency, are, to say the least of them, suspicious and singular. Until within an hour I had full trust in Mr. Henry Hunter; now I do not know what to think. She seemed to recognise him in the gig so surely."

"He does not appear"—Dr. Bevary appeared to be speaking to himself, and his head was bent—"like one who carries about with him some dark secret."

"Mr. Henry Hunter? None less. Never a man whose outside gave indications of a clearer conscience. But, Dr. Bevary, if her enemy be Mr. Henry Hunter, how is it she does not know him by name?"

"Ay, there's another point. She evidently attaches no importance to the name of Hunter."

"What was the name of—of the enemy she talks of?" asked Austin. "We must call him 'enemy' for want of a better name. Do you know it, doctor?"

"No. Can't get it out of her. Never could get it out of her. I asked her again to-day, but she evaded the question."

"Mr. Hunter thought it would be better to keep her visit this morning a secret from his brother, as they had not met. I, on the contrary, should have told him of it."

"No," hastily interposed Dr. Bevary, putting up his hand with an alarmed, warning gesture. "The only way is, to keep her and Henry Hunter apart."

"I wonder," mused Austin, "what brings her to town?"

The doctor threw his penetrating gaze into Austin's eyes. "Have you no idea what it is?"

"None, sir. She seemed to intimate that she came every year."

"Good. Don't try to form any, my young friend. It would not be a pleasant secret, even for you to hold!"

He rose as he spoke, nodded, and went out, leaving Austin Clay in a state of puzzled bewilderment. It was not lessened when, an hour later, Austin encountered Dr. Bevary's close carriage, driving rapidly along the street, the doctor seated inside it, and Miss Gwinn beside him.

VI

Tracked Home

I think it has been mentioned that the house next door to the Quales', detached from it however, was inhabited by two families: the lower part by Mr. Samuel Shuck, his wife, and children; the upper and best part by the Baxendales. No two sets of people could be more dissimilar; the one being as respectable as the other was disreputable. John Baxendale's wife was an invalid; she had been so, on and off, for a long while. There was an only daughter, and she and her mother held themselves very much aloof from the general society of Daffodil's Delight.

On the morning following the day spoken of in the last chapter as distinguished by the advent of Miss Gwinn in London, Mrs. Baxendale found herself considerably worse than usual. Mr. Rice, the apothecary, who was the general attendant in Daffodil's Delight, and lived at its corner, had given her medicine, and told her to "eat well and get up her strength." But, somehow, the strength and the appetite did not come; on the contrary, she got weaker and weaker. She was in very bad spirits this morning, was quite unable to get up, and cried for some time in silence.

"Mother, dear," said Mary Baxendale, going into her room, "you'll have the doctor gone out, I fear."

"Oh, Mary! I cannot get up—I cannot go," was the answer, delivered with a burst of sobbing sorrow. "I shall never rise from my bed again."

The words fell on the daughter with a terrible shock. Her fears in regard to her mother's health had long been excited, but this seemed like a confirmation of a result she had never dared openly to face. She was not a very capable sort of girl—the reverse of what is called strong-minded; but the instinct imparted by all true affection warned her to make light of her mother's words.

"Nay, mother, it's not so bad as that," she said, checking her tears. "You'll get up again fast enough. You are feeling low, maybe, this morning."

"Child, I am too weak to get up—too ill. I don't think I shall ever be about again."

Mary sat down in a sort of helpless perplexity.

"What is to be done?" she cried.

Mrs. Baxendale asked herself the same question as she lay. Finding herself no better under Mr. Rice's treatment, she had at length determined to do what she ought to have done at first—consult Dr. Bevary.

From half-past eight to ten, three mornings in the week, Dr. Bevary gave advice gratis; and Mrs. Baxendale was on this one to have gone to him—rather a formidable visit, as it seemed to her, and perhaps the very thought of it had helped to make her worse.

"What is to be done?" repeated Mary.

"Could you not wait upon him, child, and describe my symptoms?" suggested the sick woman, after weighing the dilemma in her mind. "It might do as well. Perhaps he can write for me."

"Oh, mother, I don't like to go!" exclaimed Mary, in the impulse of the moment.

"But, my dear, what else is to be done?" urged Mrs. Baxendale. "We can't ask a great gentleman like that to come to me."

"To be sure—true. Oh, yes, I'll go, mother."

Mary got herself ready without another word. Mrs. Baxendale, a superior woman for her station in life, had brought up her daughter to be thoroughly dutiful. It had seemed a formidable task to the mother, the going to this physician, this "great gentleman;" it seemed a far worse to the daughter, and especially the having to explain symptoms and ailments at second-hand. But the great physician was a very pleasant man, and would nod good-humouredly to Mary, when by chance he met her in the street.

"Tell him, with my duty, that I am not equal to coming myself," said Mrs. Baxendale, when Mary stood ready in her neat straw bonnet and light shawl. "I ought to have gone weeks ago, and that's the truth. Don't forget to describe the pain in my right side, and the flushings of heat."

So Mary went on her way, and was admitted to the presence of Dr. Bevary, where she told her tale with awkward timidity.

"Ah! a return of the old weakness that she had years ago," remarked the doctor. "I told her she must be careful. Too ill to get up? Why did she not come to me before?"

"I suppose, sir, she did not much like to trouble you," responded Mary. "She has been hoping from week to week that Mr. Rice would do her good."

"*I* can't do her good, unless I see her," cried the doctor. "I might prescribe just the wrong thing, you know."

Mary repressed her tears.

"I am afraid, then, she must die, sir. She said this morning she thought she should never get up from her bed again."

"I'll step round some time to-day and see her," said Dr. Bevary. "But now, don't you go chattering that to the whole parish. I should have every sick person in it expecting me, as a right, to call and visit them."

He laughed pleasantly at Mary as he spoke, and she departed with a glad heart. The visit had been so much less formidable in reality than in anticipation.

As she reached Daffodil's Delight, she did not turn into it, but continued her way to the house of Mrs. Hunter. Mary Baxendale took in plain sewing, and had some in hand at present from that lady. She inquired for Dobson. Dobson was Mrs. Hunter's own maid, and a very consequential one.

"Not able to get Miss Hunter's night-dresses home on Saturday!" grumbled Dobson, when she appeared and heard what Mary had to say. "But you must, Mary Baxendale. You promised them, you know."

"I should not have promised had I known that my mother would have grown worse," said Mary. "A sick person requires a deal of waiting on, and there's only me. I'll do what I can to get them home next week, if that will do."

"I don't know that it will do," snapped Dobson. "Miss Florence may be wanting them. A promise is a promise, Mary Baxendale."

"Yes, it will do, Mary," cried Florence Hunter, darting forward from some forbidden nook, whence she had heard the colloquy, and following Mary down the steps into the street. A fair sight was that child to look upon, with her white muslin dress, her blue ribbons, her flowing hair, and her sweet countenance, radiant as a summer's morning. "Mamma is not downstairs yet, or I would ask her—she is ill, too—but I know I do not want them. Never you mind them, and never mind Dobson either, but nurse your mother."

Dobson drew the young lady back, asking her if such behaviour was not enough to "scandalize the square;" and Mary Baxendale returned home.

Dr. Bevary paid his visit to Mrs. Baxendale about mid-day. His practised eye saw with certainty what others were only beginning to suspect—that Death had marked her. He wrote a prescription, gave some general directions, said he would call again, and told Mrs. Baxendale she would be better out of bed than in it.

Accordingly, after his departure, she got up and went into the front room, which they made their sitting-room. But the exertion caused her to faint; she was certainly on this day much worse than usual. John Baxendale was terribly concerned, and did not go back to his work after dinner. When the bustle was over, and she seemed pretty comfortable again, somebody burst into the room, without knocking or other ceremony. It was one of the Shucks, a young man of eight, in tattered clothes, and a shock head of hair. He came to announce that Mrs. Hunter's maid was asking for Mary, and little Miss Hunter was there, too, and said, might she come up and see Mrs. Baxendale.

Both were requested to walk up. Dobson had brought a gracious message from her mistress (not graciously delivered, though), that the sewing might wait till it was quite convenient to do it; and Florence produced a jar, which she had insisted upon carrying herself, and had thereby split her grey kid gloves, it being too large for her hands.

"It is black-currant jelly, Mrs. Baxendale," she said, with the prettiest, kindest air, as she freely sat down by the sick woman's side. "I asked mamma to let me bring some, for I remember when I was ill I only liked black-currant jelly. Mamma is so sorry to hear you are worse, and she will come to see you soon."

"Bless your little heart, Miss Florence!" exclaimed the invalid. "The same dear child as ever—thinking of other people and not of yourself."

"I have no need to think for myself," said Florence. "Everything I want is got ready for me. I wish you did not look so ill. I wish you would have my uncle Bevary to see you. He cures everybody."

"He has been kind enough to come round to-day, Miss," spoke up John Baxendale, "and he'll come again, he says. I hope he will be able to do the missis good. As you be a bit better," he added to his wife, "I think I'll go back to my work."

"Ay, do, John. There's no cause for you to stay at home. It was some sort of weakness, I suppose, that came over me."

John Baxendale touched his hair to Florence, nodded to Dobson, and went downstairs and out. Florence turned to the open window to watch his departure, ever restless, as a healthy child is apt to be.

"There's Uncle Henry!" she suddenly called out.

Mr. Henry Hunter was walking rapidly down Daffodil's Delight. He encountered John Baxendale as the man went out of his gate.

"Not back at work yet, Baxendale?"

"The missis has been taken worse, sir," was the man's reply. "She fainted dead off just now, and I declare I didn't know what to think about her. She's all right again, and I am going round."

At that moment there was heard a tapping at the window panes, and a pretty little head was pushed out beneath them, nodding and laughing, "Uncle Henry! How do you do, Uncle Henry?"

Mr. Henry Hunter nodded in reply, and pursued his way, unconscious that the lynx eye of Miss Gwinn was following him, like a hawk watching its prey.

It happened that she had penetrated Daffodil's Delight, hoping to catch Austin Clay at his dinner, which she supposed he might be taking about that hour. She held his address at Peter Quale's from Mrs. Thornimett. Her object was to make a further effort to get from him what he knew of the man she sought to find. Scarcely had she turned into Daffodil's Delight, when she saw Mr. Henry Hunter at a distance. Away she tore after him, and gained upon him considerably. She reached the house of John Baxendale just as he, Baxendale, was re-entering it; for he had forgotten something he must take with him to the yard. Turning her head upon Baxendale for a minute as she passed, Miss Gwinn lost sight of Mr. Henry Hunter.

How had he disappeared? Into the ground? or into a house? or down any obscure passage that might be a short cut between Daffodil's Delight, and some other Delight? or into that cab that was now whirling onwards at such a rate? That he was no longer visible, was certain: and Miss Gwinn was exceeding wroth. She came to the conclusion that he had seen her, and hid himself in the cab, though she had not heard it stop.

But she had seen him spoken to from the window of that house, where the workman had just gone in, and she determined to make inquiries there, and so strode up the path. In the Shucks' kitchen there were only three or four children, too young to give an answer. Miss Gwinn picked her way through them, over the dirt and grease of the floor, and ascended to the sitting-room above. She stood a minute to take in its view.

John Baxendale was on his knees, hunting among some tools at the bottom of a closet; Mary was meekly exhibiting the progress of the nightgowns to Dobson, who sat in state, sour enough to turn milk into curd; the invalid was lying, pale, in her chair; while the young lady appeared to be assisting at the tool-hunting, on her knees also, and chattering as fast as her tongue could go. All looked up at the apparition of the stranger, who stood there gazing in upon them.

"Can you tell me where a gentleman of the name of Lewis lives?" she began, in an indirect, diplomatic, pleasant sort of way, for she no doubt deemed it well to discard violence for tact. In the humour she was in yesterday, she would have said, sharply and imperiously, "Tell me the name of that man I saw now pass your gate."

John Baxendale rose. "Lewis, ma'am? I don't know anybody of the name."

A pause. "It is very unfortunate," she mildly resumed. "I am in search of the gentleman, and have not got his address. I believe he belongs to this neighbourhood. Indeed, I am almost sure I saw him talking to you just now at the gate—though my sight is none of the clearest from a distance. The same gentleman to whom that young lady nodded."

"That was my uncle Henry," called out the child.

"Who?" cried she, sharply.

"It was Mr. Henry Hunter, ma'am, that was," spoke up Baxendale.

"Mr. Henry Hunter!" she repeated, as she knit her brow on John Baxendale. "That gentleman is Mr. Lewis."

"No, that he is not," said John Baxendale. "I ought to know, ma'am; I have worked for him for some years."

Here the mischief might have ended; there's no telling; but that busy little tongue of all tongues—ah! what work they make!—began clapping again.

"Perhaps you mean my papa? Papa's name is Lewis—James Lewis Hunter. But he is never called Mr. Lewis. He is brother to my uncle Henry."

A wild flush of crimson flashed over Miss Gwinn's sallow face. Something within her seemed to whisper that her search was over. "It is possible I mistook the one for the other in the distance," she observed, all her new diplomacy in full play. "Are they alike in person?" she continued to John Baxendale.

"Not so much alike now, ma'am. In years gone by they were the very model of one another; but Mr. Hunter has grown stout, and it has greatly altered him. Mr. Henry looks just like what Mr. Hunter used to look."

"And who are you, did you say?" she asked of Florence with an emphasis that would have been quite wild, but that it was in a degree suppressed. "You are not Mr. Lewis Hunter's daughter?"

"I am," said Miss Florence.

"And—you have a mother?"

"Of course I have," repeated the child.

A pause: the lady looked at John Baxendale. "Then Mr. Lewis Hunter is a married man?"

"To be sure he is," said John, "ever so many years ago. Miss Florence is twelve."

"Thank you," said Miss Gwinn abruptly turning away. "Good morning."

She went down the stairs at a great rate, and did not stay to pick her steps over the grease of the Shucks' floor.

"What a mistake to make!" was her inward comment, and she laughed as she said it. "I did not sufficiently allow for the lapse of years. If that younger one had lost his life in the gravel pits, he would have died an innocent man."

Away to the yard now, as fast as her legs would carry her. In turning in, she ran against Austin Clay.

"I want to speak with Mr. Hunter," she imperiously said. "Mr. Lewis Hunter—not the one I saw in the gig."

"Mr. Hunter is out of town, Miss Gwinn," was Austin's reply. "We do not expect him at the yard to-day; he will not be home in time to come to it."

"Boy! you are deceiving me!"

"Indeed I am not," he returned. "Why should I? Mr. Hunter is not in the habit of being denied to applicants. You might have spoken to him yesterday when you saw him, had it pleased you so to do."

"I never saw him yesterday."

"Yes, you did, Miss Gwinn. That gentleman who came into the office and bowed to you was Mr. Hunter."

She stared Austin full in the face, as if unable to believe what he said. "*That* Mr. Hunter?—Lewis Hunter?"

"It was."

"If so, *how* he is altered!" And, throwing up her arms with a strange, wild gesture, she turned and strode out of the yard. The next moment Austin saw her come into it again.

"I want Mr. Lewis Hunter's private address, Austin Clay."

But Austin was on his guard now. He did not relish the idea of giving anybody's private address to such a person as Miss Gwinn, who might or might not be mad.

She detected his reluctance.

"Keep it from me if you choose, boy," she said, with a laugh that had a ring of scorn. "Better for you perhaps to be on the safe side. The first workman I meet will give it me, or a court guide."

And thus saying, she finally turned away. At any rate for the time being.

Austin Clay resumed his work, and the day passed on to evening. When business was over, he went home to make some alteration in his dress, for he had to go by appointment to Mr. Hunter's, and on these occasions he generally remained with them. It was beginning to grow dusk, and a chillness seemed to be in the air.

The house occupied by Mr. Hunter was one of the best in the west-central square. Ascending to it by a flight of steps, and passing through a pillared portico, you found yourself in a handsome hall, paved in imitation of mosaic. Two spacious sitting-rooms were on the left: the front one was used as a dining-room, the other opened to a conservatory. On the right of the hall, a broad flight of stairs led to the apartments above, one of which was a fine drawing-room, fitted up with costly elegance.

Mr. and Mrs. Hunter were seated in the dining-room. Florence was there likewise, but not seated; it may be questioned if she ever did sit, except when compelled. Dinner was over, but they frequently made this their evening sitting-room. The drawing-room upstairs was grand, the room behind was dull; this was cheerful, and looked out on the square. Especially cheerful it looked on this evening, for a fire had been lighted in the grate, and it cast a warm glow around in the fading twilight.

Austin Clay was shown in, and invited to a seat by the fire, near Mrs. Hunter. He had come in obedience to orders from Mr. Hunter, issued to him when he, Mr. Hunter, had been going out that morning. His journey had been connected with certain buildings then in process, and he thought he might have directions to give with respect to the following morning's early work.

A few minutes given by Austin and his master to business matters, and then the latter left the room, and Austin turned to Mrs. Hunter. Unusually delicate she looked, as she half sat, half lay back in her chair, the firelight playing on her features. Florence had dragged forth a stool, and was sitting on it in a queer sort of fashion, one leg under her, at Austin's feet. He was a great favourite of hers, and she made no secret of the liking.

"You are not looking well this evening," he observed, in a gentle tone, to Mrs. Hunter.

"I am not feeling well. I scarcely ever do feel well; never strong. I sometimes think, Mr. Clay, what a mercy it is that we are not permitted to foresee the future. If we could, some of us might be tempted to—to—" she hesitated, and then went on in a lower tone—"to pray that God might take us in youth."

"The longer we live, the more we become impressed with the wonderful wisdom that exists in the ordering of all things," replied Austin. "My years have not been many, comparatively speaking; but I see it always, and I know that I shall see it more and more."

"The confirmed invalid, the man of care and sorrow, the incessant battle for existence with those reduced to extreme poverty—had they seen their future, as in a mirror, how could they have borne to enter upon it?" dreamily observed Mrs. Hunter. "And yet, I have heard people exclaim, 'How I wish I could foresee my destiny, and what is to happen to me!'"

"But the cares and ills of the world do not come near you, Mrs. Hunter," spoke Austin, after a pause of thought.

Mrs. Hunter smiled. "From the cares and crosses of the world, as we generally estimate cares and crosses, I am free. God has spared them to me. He does not overwhelm us with ills; if one ill is particularly our portion, we are generally spared from others. Mine lie in my want of health, and in the thought that—that—I am rarely free from pain and suffering," she concluded. But Austin felt that it was not what she had been about to say.

"What should we do if *all* the ills came to us, mamma?" cried Florence, who had been still, and was listening.

"My dear, if all the ills came to us, God would show us a way to bear them. You know that He has promised so much; and His promises cannot fail."

"Clay," cried Mr. Hunter, returning to the room and resuming his seat, "did any one in particular call and want me to-day?"

"No, sir. Several came, but Mr. Henry saw them."

"Did Arkwright come?" resumed Mr. Hunter.

"I think not; I did not see him. That—lady—who was there yesterday, came again. She asked for you."

A pause. Then Mr. Hunter spoke up sharply. "For my brother, you mean. She must have wanted him."

"She certainly asked for you, sir. For Mr. Lewis Hunter."

Those little ears pricked themselves up, and their owner unceremoniously wheeled herself round on her stool, holding on by Austin's knee, as she faced her father.

"There was a lady came to John Baxendale's rooms to-day, when I and Dobson were there, and she asked for Mr. Lewis Hunter. At least—it was the funniest thing, papa—she saw Uncle Henry talking to John Baxendale, and she came up and said he was Mr. Lewis, and asked where he lived. John Baxendale said it was Mr. Henry Hunter, and she said no, it was not Mr. Henry Hunter, it was Mr. Lewis. So then we found out that she had mistaken him for you, and that it was you she wanted. Who was she, papa?"

"She—she—her business was with Henry," spoke Mr. Hunter, in so confused, so startled a sort of tone, not as if answering the child, more as if defending himself to any who might be around, that Austin looked up involuntarily. His face had grown lowering and angry, and he moved his position, so that his wife's gaze should not fall upon it. Austin's did, though.

At that moment there was heard a knock and ring at the house door, the presumable announcement of a visitor. Florence, much addicted to acting upon natural impulse, and thereby getting into constant hot water with her governess, who assured her nothing could be more unbefitting a young lady, quitted her stool and flew to the window. By dint of flattening her nose and crushing her curls against a corner of one of its panes, she contrived to obtain a partial view of the visitor.

"Oh dear! I hoped it was Uncle Bevary. Mamma's always better when he comes; he tells her she is not so ill as she fancies. Papa!"

"What?" cried Mr. Hunter, quickly.

"I do believe it is that same lady who came to John Baxendale's. She is as tall as a house."

What possessed Mr. Hunter? He started up; he sprung half way across the room, hesitated there, and glided back again. Glided stealthily as it were; and stealthily touching Austin Clay, motioned him to follow him. His hands were trembling; and the dark frown, full of embarrassment, was still upon his features. Mrs. Hunter noticed nothing unusual; the apartment was shaded in twilight, and she sat with her head turned to the fire.

"Go to that woman, Clay!" came forth in a whisper from Mr. Hunter's compressed lips, as he drew Austin outside the room. "I cannot see her. *You* go."

"What am I to say?" questioned Austin, feeling surprised and bewildered.

"Anything; anything. Only keep her from me."

He turned back into the room as he spoke, and closed the door softly, for Miss Gwinn was already in the hall. The servant had said his master was at home, and was conducting her to the room where his master and mistress sat, supposing it was some friend come to pay an hour's visit. Austin thought he heard Mr. Hunter slip the bolt of the dining-room, as he walked forward to receive Miss Gwinn.

Austin's words were quick and sharp, arresting the servant's footsteps. "Not there, Mark! Miss Gwinn," he courteously added, presenting himself before her, "Mr. Hunter is unable to see you this evening."

"Who gave *you* authority to interfere, Austin Clay?" was the response, not spoken in a raving, angry tone, but in one of cold, concentrated determination. "I demand an interview with Lewis Hunter. That he is at home, I know, for I saw him through the window, in the reflection of the firelight, as I stood on the steps; and here I will remain until I obtain speech of him, be it until to-morrow morning, be it until days to come. Do you note my words, meddling boy? I *demand* the interview; I do not crave it: he best knows by what right."

She sat deliberately down on one of the hall chairs. Austin, desperately at a loss what to do, and seeing no means of getting rid of her save by forcible expulsion, knocked gently at the room door again. Mr. Hunter drew it cautiously open to admit him; then slipped the bolt, entwined his arm within Austin's, and drew him to the window. Mrs. Hunter's attention was absorbed by Florence, who was chattering to her.

"She has taken a seat in the hall, sir," he whispered. "She says she will remain there until she sees you, though she should have to wait until the morning. I am sure she means it: stop there, she will. She says she demands the interview as a right."

"No," said Mr. Hunter, "she possesses no *right*. But—perhaps I had better see her, and get it over: otherwise she may make a disturbance. Tell Mark to show her into the drawing-room, Clay; and you stay here and talk to Mrs. Hunter."

"What is the matter, that you are whispering? Does any one want you?" interrupted Mrs. Hunter, whose attention was at length attracted.

"I am telling Clay that people have no right to come to my private house on business matters," was the reply given by Mr. Hunter. "However, as the person is here, I must see her, I suppose. Do not let us be interrupted, Louisa."

"But what does she want?—it was a lady, Florence said. Who is she?" reiterated Mrs. Hunter.

"It is a matter of business of Henry's. She ought to have gone to him." Mr. Hunter looked at his wife and at Austin as he spoke. The latter was leaving the room to do his bidding, and Miss Gwinn suffered herself to be conducted quietly to the drawing-room.

A full hour did the interview last. The voices seemed occasionally to be raised in anger, so that the sound penetrated to their ears downstairs, from the room overhead. Mrs. Hunter grew impatient; the tea waited on the table, and she wanted it. At length they were heard to descend, and to cross the hall.

"James is showing her out himself," said Mrs. Hunter. "Will you tell him we are waiting tea, Mr. Clay?"

Austin stepped into the hall, and started when he caught sight of the face of Mr. Hunter. He was turning back from closing the door on Miss Gwinn, and the bright rays of the hall-lamp fell full upon his countenance. It was of ghastly whiteness; its expression one living aspect of terror, of dread. He staggered, rather than walked, to a chair, and sank into it. Austin hastened to him.

"Oh, sir, what is it? You are ill?"

The strong man, the proud master, calm hitherto in his native self-respect, was for the moment overcome. He leaned his forehead upon Austin's arm, hiding its pallor, and put up his finger for silence.

"I have had a stab, Clay," he whispered. "Bear with me, lad, for a minute. I have had a cruel stab."

Austin really did not know whether to take the words literally. "A stab?" he hesitatingly repeated.

"Ay; here," touching his heart. "I wish I was dead, Clay. I wish I had died years ago; or that *she* had. Why was she permitted to live?—to live to work me this awful wrong?" he dreamily wailed. "An awful wrong to me and mine!"

"What is it?" spoke Austin, upon impulse. "A wrong? Who has done it?"

"She has. The woman now gone out. She has done it all."

He rose, and appeared to be looking for his hat. "Mrs. Hunter is waiting tea, sir," said the amazed Austin.

"Tea!" repeated Mr. Hunter, as if his brain were bewildered; "I cannot go in again to-night; I cannot see them. Make some excuse for me, Clay—anything. *Why* did that woman work me this crying wrong?"

He took his hat, opened the hall door, and shut it after him with a bang, leaving Austin in wondering consternation.

He returned to the dining-room, and said Mr. Hunter had been obliged to go out on business; he did not know what else to say. Florence was sent to bed after tea, but Austin sat a short while longer with Mrs. Hunter. Something led back to the previous conversation, when Mrs. Hunter had been alluding to her state of health, and to some sorrow that was her daily portion.

"What is it?" said Austin, in his impulsive manner.

"The thought that I shall have to leave Florence without a mother."

"Dear Mrs. Hunter, surely it is not so serious as that! You may get better."

"Yes; I know I may. Dr. Bevary tells me that I shall. But, you see, the very fear of it is hard to bear. Sometimes I think God is reconciling me to it by slow degrees."

Later in the evening, as Austin was going home, he passed a piece of clear ground, to be let for building purposes, at the end of the square. There, in its darkest corner, far back from the road, paced a man as if in some mental agony, his hat carried in his hands, and his head bared to the winds. Austin peered through the night with his quick sight, and recognised Mr. Hunter.

VII

Mr. Shuck at Home

Daffodil's Delight was in a state of commotion. It has often been remarked that there exists more real sympathy between the working classes, one for another, than amongst those of a higher grade; and experience generally seems to bear it out. From one end of Daffodil's Delight to the other, there ran just now a deep feeling of sorrow, of pity, of commiseration. Men made inquiries of each other as they passed in the street; women congregated at their doors to talk, concern on their faces, a question on their lips—"How is she? What does the doctor say?"

Yes; the excitement had its rise in one cause alone—the increased illness of Mrs. Baxendale. The physician had pronounced his opinion (little need to speak it, though, for the fact was only too apparent to all who used their eyes), and the news had gone forth to Daffodil's Delight—Mrs. Baxendale was past recovery; was, in fact, dying!

The concern, universal as it was, showed itself in various ways. Visits and neighbourly calls were so incessant, that the Shucks openly rebelled at the "trampling up and down through their living-room," by which route the Baxendale apartments could alone be gained. The neighbours came to help; to nurse; to shake up the bed and pillows; to prepare condiments over the fire; to condole; and, above all, to gossip: with tears in their eyes and lamentation in their tones, and ominous shakes of the head, and uplifted hands; but still, to gossip: *that* lies in human female nature. They brought offerings of savoury delicacies; or things that, in their ideas, stood for delicacies—dainties likely to tempt the sick. Mrs. Cheek made a pint jug of what she called "buttered beer," a miscellaneous compound of scalding-hot porter, gin, eggs, sugar, and spice. Mrs. Baxendale sipped a little; but it did not agree with her fevered palate, and she declined it for the future, with "thanks, all the same," and Mrs. Cheek and a crony or two disposed of it themselves with great satisfaction. All this served to prove two things—that good feeling ran high in Daffodil's Delight, and that means did not run low.

Of all the visitors, the most effectual assistant was Mrs. Quale. She gossiped, it is true, or it had not been Mrs. Quale; but she gave efficient help; and the invalid was always glad to see her come in, which could not be said with regard to all. Daffodil's Delight was not wrong in the judgment it passed upon Mary Baxendale—that she was a "poor creature." True; poor as to being clever in a domestic point of view, and in attending upon the sick. In mind, in cultivation, in refinement, in gentleness, Mary Baxendale beat Daffodil's Delight hollow; she was also a beautiful seamstress; but in energy and capability Mary was sadly wanting. She was timid always—painfully timid in the sick-room; anxious to do for her mother all that was requisite, but never knowing how to set about it. Mrs. Quale remedied this; she did the really efficient part; Mary gave love and gentleness; and, between the two, Mrs. Baxendale was thankful and happy.

John Baxendale, not a demonstrative man, was full of concern and grief. His had been a very happy home, free from domestic storms and clouds; and, to lose his wife, was anything but a cheering prospect. His wages were good, and they had wanted for nothing, not even for peace. To such, when trouble comes, it seems hard to bear—it almost seems as if it came as a *wrong*.

"Just hold your tongue, John Baxendale," cried Mrs. Quale one day, upon hearing him express something to this effect. "Because you have never had no crosses, is it any reason that you never shall? No. Crosses come to us all sometime in our lives, in one shape or other."

"But it's a hard thing for it to come in this shape," retorted Baxendale, pointing to the bed. "I'm not repining or rebelling against what it pleases God to do; but I can't *see* the reason of it. Look at some of the other wives in Daffodil's Delight; shrieking, raving trollops, turning their homes into a bear-garden with their tempers, and driving their husbands almost mad. If some of them were taken they'd never be missed: just the contrary."

"John," interposed Mrs. Baxendale, in her quiet voice, "when I am gone up there"—pointing with her finger to the blue October sky—"it may make you think more of the time when you must come; may help you to be preparing for it, better than you have done."

Mary lifted her wan face, glowing now with the excitement of the thought. "Father, *that* may be the end—the reason. I think that troubles are sent to us in mercy, not in anger."

"Think!" exclaimed Mrs. Quale, tossing back her head with a manner less reverent than her words. "Before you shall have come to my age, girl, it's to be hoped you'll *know* they are. Isn't it time for the medicine?" she continued, seeing no other opening for a reprimand just then.

It was time for the medicine, and Mrs. Quale poured it out, raised the invalid from her pillow, and administered it. John Baxendale looked on. Like his daughter Mary, he was in these matters an incapable man.

"How long is it since Dr. Bevary was here?" he asked.

"Let's see?" responded Mrs. Quale, who liked to have most of the talking to herself, wherever she might be. "This is Friday. Tuesday, wasn't it, Mary? Yes, he was here on Tuesday."

"But why does he not come oftener?" cried John, in a tone of resentment. "That's what I was wanting to ask about. When one is as ill as she is—in danger of dying—is it right that a doctor should never come a near for three or four days?"

"Oh, John! a great physician like Dr. Bevary!" remonstrated his wife. "It is so very good of him to come at all. And for nothing, too! He as good as said to Mary he didn't mean to charge."

"I can pay him; I'm capable of paying him, I hope," spoke John Baxendale. "Who said I wanted my wife to be attended out of charity?"

"It's not just that, father, I think," said Mary. "He comes more in a friendly way."

"Friendly or not, it isn't come to the pass yet, that I can't pay a doctor," said John Baxendale. "Who has let it go abroad that I couldn't?"

Taking up his hat, he went out on the spur of the moment, and bent his steps to Dr. Bevary's. There he was civil and humble enough, for John Baxendale was courteous by nature. The doctor was at home, and saw him at once.

"Listen, my good man," said Dr. Bevary, when he had caught somewhat of his errand. "If, by going round often, I could do any good to your wife, I should go. Twice a day; three times a day—by night, too, if necessary. But I cannot do her good: had she a doctor over her bed constantly, he could render no service. I step round now and then, because I see that it is a satisfaction to her, and to those about her; not for any use I can be. I told you a week ago the end was not very far off, and that she would meet it calmly. She will be in no further pain—no worse than she is now."

"I am able to pay you, sir."

"That is not the question. If you paid me a guinea every time I came round, I should visit her no more frequently than I do."

"And, if you please, sir, I'd rather pay you," continued the man. "I'm sure I don't grudge it; and it goes against the grain to have it said that John Baxendale's wife is attended out of charity. We English workmen, sir, are independent, and proud of being so."

"Very good," said Dr. Bevary. "I should be sorry to see the day come when English workmen lost their independence. As to 'charity,' we will talk a bit about that. Look here, Baxendale," the doctor added, laying his hand upon his shoulder, in his kind and familiar way, "you and I can speak reasonably together, as man to man. We both have to work for our living—you with the hands, I chiefly with the head—so, in that, we are equal. I go twice a week to see your wife; I have told you why it is useless to go oftener. When patients come to me, they pay me a guinea, and I see them twice for it, which is equivalent to half a guinea a visit; but, when I go to patients at their own houses, my fee is a guinea each time. Now, would it seem to you a neighbourly act that I should take two guineas weekly from your wages?—quite as much, or more, than you gain. What does my going round cost me? A few minutes' time; a gossip with Mrs. Quale, touching the doings of Daffodil's Delight, and a groan at those thriftless Shucks, in their pigsty of a room. That is the plain statement of facts; and I should like to know what there is in it that need put your English spirit up. Charity! We might call it by that name, John Baxendale, if I were the guinea each time out of pocket, through medicines or other things furnished to you."

John Baxendale smiled; but he looked only three parts convinced.

"Tush, man!" said the doctor; "I may be asking you to do me some friendly service, one of these days, and then, you know, we should be quits. Eh, John?"

John Baxendale half put out his hand, and the doctor shook it.

"I think I understand now, sir; and I thank you heartily for what you have said. I only wish you could do some good to the wife."

"I wish I could, Baxendale," he replied, throwing a kindly glance after the man as he was moving away. "I shan't bring an action against you in the county court for these unpaid fees, Baxendale, for it wouldn't stand," called out the doctor. "I never was called in to see your wife—I went of my own accord, and have so continued to go, and shall so continue. Good day."

As John Baxendale was descending the steps of the house door, he encountered Mrs. Hunter. She stopped him to inquire after his wife.

"Getting weaker daily, ma'am, thank you. The doctor has just told me again that there's no hope."

"I am truly sorry to hear it," said Mrs. Hunter. "I will call in and see her. I did intend to call before, but something or other has caused me to put it off."

John Baxendale touched his hat, and departed. Mrs. Hunter went in to her brother.

"Oh, is it you, Louisa?" he exclaimed. "A visit from you is somewhat a rarity. Are you feeling worse?"

"Rather better, I think, than usual. I have just met John Baxendale," continued Mrs. Hunter, sitting down, and untying her bonnet strings. "He says there is no hope for his wife. Poor woman! I wish it had been different. Many a worse woman could have been better spared."

"Ah," said the doctor, "if folks were taken according to our notions of whom might be best spared, what a world this would be! Where's Miss Florence?"

"I did not bring her out with me, Robert. I came round to say a word to you about James," resumed Mrs. Hunter, her voice insensibly lowering itself to a tone of confidence. "Something is the matter with him, and I cannot imagine what."

"Been eating too many cucumbers again, no doubt," cried the doctor. "He *will* go in at that cross-grained vegetable, let it be in season, or out."

"Eating!" returned Mrs. Hunter, "I wish he did eat. For at least a fortnight—more, I think—he has not eaten enough to support a bird. That he is ill is evident to all—must be evident; but when I ask him what is the matter, he persists in it that he is quite well; that I am fanciful: seems annoyed, in short, that I should allude to it. Has he been here to consult you?"

"No," replied Dr. Bevary; "this is the first I have heard of it. How does he seem? What are his symptoms?"

"It appears to me," said Mrs. Hunter, almost in a whisper, "that the malady is more on the mind. There is no palpable disorder. He is restless, nervous, agitated; so restless at night, that he has now taken to sleep in a room apart from mine—not to disturb me, he says. I fear—I fear he may have been attacked with some dangerous inward malady, that he is concealing. His father, you know, died of—"

"Pooh! Nonsense! You are indeed becoming fanciful, Louisa," interrupted the doctor. "Old Mr. Hunter died of an unusual disorder, I admit; but, if the symptoms of such appeared in either James or Henry, they would come galloping to me in hot haste, asking if my skill could suggest a preventive. It is no 'inward malady,' depend upon it. He has been smoking too much: or going in at the cucumbers."

"Robert, it is something far more serious than that," quietly rejoined Mrs. Hunter.

"When did you first notice him to be ill?"

"It is, I say, about a fortnight since. One evening there came a stranger to our house, a lady, and she *would* see him. He did not want to see her: he sent young Clay to her, who happened to be with us; but she insisted upon seeing James. They were closeted together a long while before she left; and then James went out—on business, Mr. Clay said."

"Well?" cried Dr. Bevary. "What has the lady to do with it?"

"I am not sure that she has anything to do with it. Florence told an incomprehensible story about the lady's having gone into Baxendale's that afternoon, after seeing her uncle Henry in the street and mistaking him for James. A Miss—what was the name?—Gwinn, I think."

Dr. Bevary, who happened to have a small glass phial in his hand, let it fall to the ground: whether by inadvertence, or that the words startled him, he best knew. "Well?" was all he repeated, after he had gathered the pieces in his hand.

"I waited up till twelve o'clock, and James never came in. I heard him let himself in afterwards with his latch-key, and came up into the dressing-room. I called out to know where he had been, it is so unusual for him to stay out, and he said he was much occupied, and that I was to go to sleep, for he had some writing to do. But, Robert, instead of writing, he was pacing the house all night, out of one room into another; and in the morning—oh, I wish you could have seen him!—he looked wild, wan, haggard, as one does who has got up out of a long illness; and I am positive he had been weeping. From that time I have noticed the change I tell you of. He seems like one going into his grave. But, whether the illness is upon the body or the mind, I know not."

Dr. Bevary appeared intent upon putting together the pieces of his phial, making them fit into each other.

"It will all come right, Louisa; don't fret yourself: something must have gone cross in his business. I'll call in at the office and see him."

"Do not say that I have spoken to you. He seems to have quite a nervous dread of its being observed that anything is wrong with him; has spoken sharply, not in anger, but in anguish, when I have pressed the question."

"As if the lady could have anything to do with it!" exclaimed Dr. Bevary, in a tone of satire.

"I do not suppose she had. I only mentioned the circumstances because it is since that evening he has changed. You can see what you think of him, and tell me afterwards."

The answer was only a nod; and Mrs. Hunter went out. Dr. Bevary remained in a brown study. His servant came in with an account that patient after patient was waiting for him, but the doctor replied by a repelling gesture, and the man did not again dare to intrude. Perplexity and pain sat upon his brow; and, when at last he did rouse himself, he raised aloft his hands, and gave utterance to words that sounded very like a prayer:

"I pray heaven it may not be so! It would kill Louisa."

The pale, delicate face of Mrs. Hunter was at that moment bending over the invalid in her bed. In her soft grey silk dress and light shawl, her simple straw bonnet with its white ribbons, she looked just the right sort of visitor for a sick-chamber; and her voice was sweet, and her manner gentle.

"No, ma'am, don't speak of hope to me," murmured Mrs. Baxendale. "I know that there is none left, and I am quite reconciled to die. I have been an ailing woman for years, dear lady; and it is wonderful how those that are so get to look upon death, if they can but presume to hope their soul is safe, with satisfaction, rather than with dread. Though I dare not say as much yet to my poor husband."

"I have long been ailing, too," softly replied Mrs. Hunter. "I am rarely free from pain, and I know that I shall never be healthy and strong again. But still—I do fear it would give me pain to die, were the fiat to come forth."

"Never fear, dear lady," cried the invalid, her eyes brightening. "Before the fiat does come, be assured that God will have reconciled you to it. Ah, ma'am, what matters it, after all? It is a journey we must take; and, when once we are prepared, it seems but the setting off a little sooner or a little later. I got Mary to read me the burial service on Sunday: I was always fond of it; but I am past reading now. In one part thanks are given to God for that he has been pleased to deliver the dead out of the miseries of this sinful world. Ma'am, if He did not remove us to a better and a happier home, would the living be directed to give thanks for our departure from this?"

"A spirit ripe for heaven," thought Mrs. Hunter, when she took her leave.

It was Mrs. Quale who piloted her through the room of the Shucks. Of all scenes of disorder and discomfort, about the worst reigned there. Sam had been—you must excuse the inelegance of the phrase, but it was much in vogue in Daffodil's Delight—"on the loose" again for a couple of days. He sat sprawling across the hearth, a pipe in his mouth, and a pot of porter at his feet. The wife was crying with her hair down; the children were quarrelling in tatters; the dirt in the place, as Mrs. Quale expressed it, stood on end; and Mrs. Hunter wondered how people could bear to live so.

"Now, Sam Shuck, don't you see who is a standing in your presence?" sharply cried Mrs. Quale.

Sam, his back to the staircase door, really had not seen. He threw his pipe into the grate, started up, and pulled his hair to Mrs. Hunter in a very humble fashion. In his hurry he turned over a small child, and the contents of the pewter pot upon it. The child roared; the wife took it up and shook its clothes in Sam's face, restraining her tongue till the lady should be gone; and Mrs. Hunter stepped into the garden out of the *mêlée*—glad to get there: Sam following her in a spirit of politeness.

"How is it you are not at work to-day, Shuck?" she asked.

"I am going to-morrow—I shall go for certain, ma'am."

"You know, Shuck, I never do interfere with Mr. Hunter's men," said Mrs. Hunter. "I consider that intelligent workmen, as you are, ought to be above any advice that I could offer. But I cannot help saying how sad it is that you should waste your time. Were you not discharged a little while ago, and taken on again under a specific promise, made by you to Mr. Henry Hunter, that you would be diligent in future?"

"I am diligent," grumbled Sam. "But why, ma'am—a chap must take holiday now and then. 'Tain't in human nature to be always having the shoulder at the wheel."

"Well, pray be cautious," said Mrs. Hunter. "If you offend again, and get discharged, I know they will not be so ready to take you back. Remember your little children, and be steady for their sakes."

Sam went indoors to his pipe, to his wife's tongue, and to despatch a child to get the pewter pot replenished.

VIII

Five Thousand Pounds!

Mrs. Hunter, turning out of Mr. Shuck's gate, stepped inside Mrs. Quale's, who was astonishing her with the shortcomings of the Shucks, and prophesying that their destiny would be the workhouse, when Austin Clay came forth. He had been home to dinner, and was now going back to the yard. Mrs. Hunter said good morning to her talkative friend, and walked away by Austin's side—Mrs. Baxendale, Sam Shuck, and Daffodil's Delight generally, forming themes of converse. Austin raised his hat to her when they came to the gates of the yard.

"No, I am not about to part; I am going in with you," said Mrs. Hunter. "I want to speak just a word to my husband, if he is at liberty. Will you find him for me?"

"He has been in his private room all the morning, and is probably there still," said Austin. "Do you know where Mr. Hunter is?" he inquired of a man whom they met.

"In his room, sir," was the reply, as the man touched his cap to Mrs. Hunter.

Austin led the way down the passage, and knocked at the door, Mrs. Hunter following him. There was no answer; and believing, in consequence, that it was empty, he opened it.

Two gentlemen stood within it, near a table, paper and pens and ink before them, and what looked like a cheque-book. They must have been deeply absorbed not to have heard the knock. One was Mr. Hunter: the other—Austin recognised him—Gwinn, the lawyer of Ketterford. "I will not sign it!" Mr. Hunter was exclaiming, with passionate vehemence. "Five thousand pounds! it would cripple me for life."

"Then you know the alternative. I go this moment and—"

"Mrs. Hunter wishes to speak to you, sir," interposed Austin, drowning the words and speaking loudly. The gentlemen turned sharply round: and when Mr. Hunter caught sight of his wife, the red passion of his face turned to a livid pallor. Lawyer Gwinn nodded familiarly to Austin.

"How are you, Clay? Getting on, I hope. *Who* is this person, may I ask?"

"This lady is Mrs. Hunter," haughtily replied Austin, after a pause, surprised that Mr. Hunter did not take up the words—the offensive manner in which they were spoken—the insulting look that accompanied them. But Mr. Hunter did not appear in a state to take anything up just then.

Gwinn bent his body to the ground.

"I beg the lady's pardon. I had no idea she was Mrs. Hunter."

But so ultra-courteous were the tones, so low the bow, that Austin Clay's cheeks burnt at the covert irony.

"James, you are ill," said Mrs. Hunter, advancing in her quiet, composed manner, but taking no notice whatever of the stranger. "Can I get anything for you? Shall we send for Dr. Bevary?"

"No, don't do that; it is going off. You will oblige me by leaving us," he whispered to her. "I am very busy."

"You seem too ill for business," she rejoined. "Can you not put it off for an hour? Rest might be of service to you."

"No, madam, the business cannot be put off," spoke up Lawyer Gwinn.

And down he sat in a chair, with a determined air of conscious power—just as his sister had sat *her*self down, a fortnight before, in Mr. Hunter's hall.

Mrs. Hunter quitted the room at once, leaving her husband and the stranger in it. Austin followed her. Her face wore a puzzled, vexed look, as she turned it upon Austin. "Who is that person?" she asked. "His manner to me appeared to be strangely insolent."

An instinct, for which Austin perhaps could not have accounted had he tried, caused him to suppress the fact that it was the brother of the Miss Gwinn who had raised a commotion at Mr. Hunter's house. He answered that he had not seen the person at the office previously, his tone being as careless a one as he could assume. And Mrs. Hunter, who was of the least suspicious nature possible, let it pass. Her mind, too, was filled with the thought of her husband's suffering state.

"Does Mr. Hunter appear to you to be ill?" she asked of Austin, somewhat abruptly.

"He looked so, I think."

"Not now; I am not alluding to the present moment," she rejoined. "Have you noticed before that he does not seem well?"

"Yes," replied Austin; "this week or two past."

There was a brief pause.

"Mr. Clay," she resumed, in a quiet, kind voice, "my health, as you are aware, is not good, and any sort of uneasiness tries me much. I am going to ask you a confidential question. I would not put it to many, and the asking it of you proves that my esteem for you is great. That Mr. Hunter is ill, there is no doubt; but whether mentally or bodily I am unable to discover. To me he observes a most unusual reticence, his object probably being to spare me pain; but I can battle better with a known evil than with an unknown one. Tell me, if you can, whether any vexation has arisen in business matters?"

"Not that I am aware of," promptly replied Austin. "I feel sure that nothing is amiss in that quarter."

"Then it is as I suspected, and he must be suffering from some illness that he is concealing."

She wished Austin good morning. He saw her out of the gate, and then proceeded to the room he usually occupied when engaged indoors. Presently he heard Mr. Hunter and his visitor come forth, and saw the latter pass the window. Mr. Hunter came into the room.

"Is Mrs. Hunter gone?"

"Yes, sir."

"Do you know what she wanted?"

"I do not think it was anything particular. She said she should like to say a word to you, if you were disengaged."

Mr. Hunter did not speak immediately. Austin was making out certain estimates, and his master looked over his shoulder. Not *to look*; his mind was evidently all pre-occupied.

"Did Mrs. Hunter inquire who it was that was with me?" he presently said.

"She inquired, sir. I did not say. I told her I had not seen the person here before."

"*You* knew?" in a quick, sharp accent.

"Oh, yes."

"Then why did you not tell her? What was your motive for concealing it?"

The inquiry was uttered in a tone that could not be construed as proceeding from any emotion but that of fear. A flush came into Austin's ingenuous face.

"I beg your pardon, sir. I never wish to be otherwise than open. But, as you had previously desired me not to speak of the lady who came to your house that night, I did not know but the same wish might apply to the visit of to-day."

"True, true," murmured Mr. Hunter; "I do *not* wish this visit of the man's spoken of. Never mention his name, especially to Mrs. Hunter. I suppose he did not impose upon me," added he, with a poor attempt at a forced smile: "it *was* Gwinn, of Ketterford, was it not?"

"Certainly," said Austin, feeling surprised. "Did you not know him previously, sir?"

"Never. And I wish I had not known him now."

"If—if—will you forgive my saying, sir, that, should you have any transaction with him, touching money matters, it is necessary to be wary. Many a one has had cause to rue the getting into the clutches of Lawyer Gwinn."

A deep, heavy sigh, burst from Mr. Hunter. He had turned from Austin. The latter spoke again in his ardent sympathy.

"Sir, is there any way in which I can serve you?—*any* way? You have only to command me."

"No, no, Clay. I fell into that man's clutches—as you have aptly termed it—years ago, and the penalty must be paid. There is no help for it."

"Not knowing him, sir?"

"Not knowing him. And not knowing that I owed it, as I certainly did not know, until a week or two back. I no more suspected that—that I was indebted there, than I was indebted to you."

Mr. Hunter had grown strangely confused and agitated, and the dew was rising on his livid face. He made a hollow attempt to laugh it off, and seemed to shun the gaze of his clerk.

"This comes of the freaks of young men," he observed, facing Austin after a pause, and speaking volubly. "Austin Clay, I will give you a piece of advice. Never put your hand to a bill. You may think it an innocent bit of paper, which can cost you at most but the sum that is marked upon it: but it may come back to you in after years, and you must purchase it with thousands. Have nothing to do with bills, in any way; they will be a thorn in your side."

"So, it is a money affair!" thought Austin. "I might have known it was nothing else, where Gwinn was concerned. Here's Dr. Bevary coming in, sir," he added aloud.

The physician was inside the room ere the words had left Austin's lips. Mr. Hunter had seized upon a stray plan, and seemed bent upon its examination.

"Rather a keen-looking customer, that, whom I met at your gate," began the doctor. "Who was it?"

"Keen-looking customer?" repeated Mr. Hunter.

"A fellow dressed in black, with a squint and a white neckerchief; an ill-favoured fellow, whoever he is."

"How should I know about him?" replied Mr. Hunter, carelessly. "Somebody after the men, I suppose."

But Austin Clay felt that Mr. Hunter *did* know; that the description could only apply to Gwinn of Ketterford. Dr. Bevary entwined his arm within his brother-in-law's, and led him from the room.

"James, do you want doctoring?" he inquired, as they entered the one just vacated by Lawyer Gwinn.

"No, I don't. What do you mean?"

"If you don't, you belie your looks; that's all. Can you honestly affirm to me that you are in robust health?"

"I am in good health. There is nothing the matter with me."

"Then there's something else in the wind. What's the trouble?"

A flush rose to the face of Mr. Hunter.

"I am in no trouble that you can relieve; I am quite well. I repeat that I do not understand your meaning."

The doctor gazed at him keenly, and his tone changed to one of solemn earnestness.

"James, I suspect that you *are* in trouble. Now, I do not wish to pry into it unnecessarily; but I would remind you of the sound wisdom that lies in the good old proverb: 'In the multitude of counsellors there is safety.'"

"And if there is?" returned Mr. Hunter.

"If you will confide the trouble to me, I will do what I can to help you out of it—*whatever it may be*—to advise with you as to what is best to be done. I am your wife's brother; could you have a truer friend?"

"You are very kind, Bevary. I am in no danger. When I am, I will let you know."

The tone—one of playful mockery—grated on the ear of Dr. Bevary. "Is it assumed to hide what he dare not betray?" thought he.

Mr. Hunter cut the matter short by crossing the yard to the time-keeper's office; and Dr. Bevary went out talking to himself: "A wilful man must have his own way."

Austin Clay sat up late that night, reading one of the quarterly reviews; he let the time slip by till the clock struck twelve. Mr. and Mrs. Quale had been in bed some time; when nothing was wanted for Mr. Clay, Mrs. Quale was rigid in retiring at ten. Early to bed, and early to rise, was a maxim she was fond of, both in precept and practice. The striking of the church clock aroused him; he closed the book, left it on the table, pulled aside the crimson curtain, and opened the window to look out at the night before going into his chamber.

A still, balmy night. The stars shone in the heavens, and Daffodil's Delight, for aught that could be heard or seen just then, seemed almost as peaceful as they. Austin leaned from the window; his thoughts ran not upon the stars or upon the peaceful scene around, but upon the curious trouble which seemed to be overshadowing Mr. Hunter. "Five thousand pounds!" His ears had caught distinctly the ominous sum. "Could he have fallen into Lawyer Gwinn's 'clutches' to *that* extent?"

There was much in it that Austin could not fathom. Mr. Hunter had hinted at "bills;" Miss Gwinn had spoken of the "breaking up of her happy home;" two calamities apparently distinct and apart. And how was it that they were in ignorance of his name, his existence, his—

A startling interruption came to Austin's thoughts. Mrs. Shuck's door was pulled hastily open, and some one panting with excitement, uttering faint, sobbing cries, came running down their garden into Peter Quale's. It was Mary Baxendale. She knocked sharply at the door with nervous quickness.

"What is it, Mary?" asked Austin.

She had not seen him; but, of course, the words caused her to look up. "Oh! sir," the tears streaming from her eyes as she spoke, "would you please call Mrs. Quale, and ask her to step in? Mother's on the wing."

"I'll call her. Mary!"—for she was speeding back again—"can I get any other help for you? If I can be of use, step back and tell me."

Sam Shuck came out of his house as Austin spoke, and went flying up Daffodil's Delight. He had gone for Dr. Bevary. The doctor had desired to be called, should there be any sudden change. Of course, he did not mean the change of *death*. He could be of no use in that; but how could they discriminate?

Mrs. Quale was dressed and in the sick chamber with all speed. Dr. Bevary was not long before he followed her. Neighbours on either side put their heads out.

Ten minutes at the most, and Dr. Bevary was out again. Austin was then leaning over Peter Quale's gate. He had been in no urgent mood for bed before, and this little excitement, though it did not immediately concern him, afforded an excuse for not going to it.

"How is she, sir?"

"Is it you?" responded Dr. Bevary. "She is gone. I thought it would be sudden at the last."

"Poor thing!" exclaimed Austin.

"Poor thing? Ay, that's what we are all apt to say when our friends die. But there is little cause when the change has been prepared for, the spirit made ripe for heaven. She's gone to a world where there's neither sickness nor pain."

Austin made no reply. The doctor spoke again after a pause.

"Clay—to go from a solemn subject to one that—that may, however, prove not less solemn in the end—you heard me mention a stranger I met at the gates of the yard to-day, and Mr. Hunter would not take my question. Was it Gwinn of Ketterford?"

The doctor had spoken in a changed, low tone, laying his hand, in his earnestness, on Austin's shoulder. Austin paused. He did not know whether he ought to answer.

"You need not hesitate," said the doctor, divining his scruples. "I can understand that Mr. Hunter may have forbidden you to mention it, and that you would be faithful to him. Don't speak; your very hesitation has proved it to me. Good night, my young friend; we would both serve him if we only knew how."

Austin watched him away, and then went indoors, for Daffodil's Delight began to be astir, and to collect itself around him, Sam Shuck having assisted in spreading the news touching Mrs. Baxendale. Daffodil's Delight thought nothing of leaving its bed, and issuing forth in shawls and pantaloons upon any rising emergency, regarding such interludes of disturbed rest as socially agreeable.

IX

The Separation of Hunter and Hunter

Austin Clay sat at his desk at Hunter and Hunter's, sorting the morning letters, which little matter of employment formed part of his duties. It was the morning subsequent to the commotion in Daffodil's Delight. His thoughts were running more on that than on the letters, when the postmark "Ketterford" on two of them caught his eye.

The one was addressed to himself, the other to "Mr. Lewis Hunter," and the handwriting of both was the same. Disposing of the rest of the letters as usual, placing those for the Messrs. Hunter in their room, against they should arrive, and dealing out any others there might be for the hands employed in the firm, according to their address, he proceeded to open his own.

To the very end of it Austin read; and then, and not till then, he began to suspect that it could not be meant for him. No name whatever was mentioned in the letter; it began abruptly, and it ended abruptly; not so much as "Sir," or "Dear Sir," was it complimented with, and it was simply signed "A. G." He read it a second time, and then its awful meaning flashed upon him, and a red flush rose to his brow and settled there, as if burnt into it with a branding iron. He had become possessed of a dangerous secret.

There was no doubt that the letter was written by Miss Gwinn to Mr. Hunter. By some extraordinary mischance, she had misdirected it. Possibly the letter now lying on Mr. Hunter's desk, might be for Austin. Though, what could she be writing about to him?

He sat down. He was quite overcome with the revelation; it was, indeed, of a terrible nature, and he would have given much not to have become cognizant of it. "Bills!" "Money!" So that had been Mr. Hunter's excuse for the mystery! No wonder he sought to turn suspicion into any channel but the real one.

Austin was poring over the letter like one in a nightmare, when Mr. Hunter interrupted him. He crushed it into his pocket with all the aspect of a guilty man; any one might have taken him in his confusion so to be. Not for himself was he confused, but he feared lest Mr. Hunter should discover the letter. Although certainly written for him, Austin did not dare hand it to him, for it would never do to let Mr. Hunter know that he possessed the secret. Mr. Hunter had come in, holding out the other letter from Ketterford.

"This letter is for you, Mr. Clay. It has been addressed to me by mistake, I conclude."

Austin took it, and glanced his eyes over it. It contained a few abrupt lines, and a smaller note, sealed, was inside it.

> "My brother is in London, Austin Clay. I have reason to think he will be calling upon the Messrs. Hunter. Will you watch for him, and give him the inclosed note? Had he told me where he should put up in town, I should have had no occasion to trouble you.
>
> A. Gwinn

Austin did not lift his eyes to Mr. Hunter's in his usual candid open manner. He could not bear to look him in the face; he feared lest his master might read in his the dreadful truth.

"What am I to do, sir?" he asked. "Watch for Gwinn, and give him the note?"

"Do this with them," said Mr. Hunter.

Striking a wax match, he held both Austin's note and the sealed one over the flame until they were consumed.

"You could not fulfil the request if you wished, for the man went back to Ketterford last night."

He said no more. He went away again, and Austin lighted another match, and burnt the crushed letter in his pocket, thankful, so far, that it had escaped Mr. Hunter.

Trouble came. Ere many days had elapsed, there was dissension in the house of Hunter and Hunter. Thoroughly united and cordial the brothers had always been; but now a cause of dispute arose, and it seemed that it could not be arranged. Mr. Hunter had drawn out five thousand pounds from the bank, and refused to state for what, except that it was for a "private purpose." The business had been a gradually increasing one, and nearly all the money possessed by both was invested in it; so much as was not actually out, lay in the bank in their joint names, "Hunter and Hunter." Each possessed a small private account, but nothing like sufficient to meet a cheque for five thousand pounds.

Words ran high between them, and the sound penetrated to ears outside their private room.

His face pale, his lips compressed, his tone kept mostly subdued, James Hunter sat at his desk, his eyes falling on a ledger he was not occupied with, and his hand partially shading his face. Mr. Henry, more excited, giving way more freely to his anger, paced the carpet, occasionally stopping before the desk and before his brother.

"It is the most unaccountable thing in the world," he reiterated, "that you should refuse to say what it has been applied to. Draw out, surreptitiously, a formidable sum like that, and not account for it! It is monstrous."

"Henry, I have told you all I can tell you," replied Mr. Hunter, concealing his countenance more than ever. "An old debt was brought up against me, and I was forced to satisfy it."

Mr. Henry Hunter curled his lip.

"A debt to that amount! Were you mad?"

"I did not—know—I—had—contracted it," stammered Mr. Hunter, very nearly losing his self possession. "At least, I thought it had been paid. Youth's errors do come home to us sometimes in later life."

"Not to the tune of five thousand pounds," retorted Mr. Henry Hunter. "It will cripple the business; you know it will. It is next door to ruin."

"Nonsense, Henry! The loss of five thousand pounds will neither cripple the business nor bring ruin. It will be my own loss: not yours."

"How on earth could you think of giving it away? Five thousand pounds!"

"I could not help myself. Had I refused to pay it—"

"Well?" for Mr. Hunter had stopped in embarrassment.

"I should have been compelled to do so. There. Talking of it will not mend it."

Mr. Henry Hunter took a few turns, and then wheeled round sharply. "Perhaps there are other claims for 'youth's follies' to come behind it?"

The words seemed to arouse Mr. Hunter. Not to anger; but to what looked very like fear—almost to an admission that it might be so.

"Were any such further claim to come, I would not satisfy it," he cried, wiping his face. "No, I would not; I would go into exile first."

"We must part," said Mr. Henry Hunter the expression of his brother's face quite startling him. "There is no alternative. I cannot risk the beggaring of my wife and children."

"If it must be so, it must," was all the reply given.

"Tell me the truth, James," urged Mr. Henry in a more conciliatory tone. "I don't want to part. Tell me all, and let me be the judge. Surely, man! it can't be anything so very dreadful. You didn't set fire to your neighbour's house, I suppose?"

"I never thought the claim could come upon me. That is all I can tell you."

"Then we part," decisively returned Mr. Henry Hunter.

"Yes, it may be better. If I am to go to ruin, it is of no use to drag you down into it."

"If you are to go to ruin!" echoed Mr. Henry, regarding his brother attentively. "James! is that an admission that other mysterious claims may really follow this one?"

"No, I think they will not. But we had better part. Only—let the cause of our separation be kept from the world."

"I should be clever to betray the cause, seeing that you leave me in ignorance of what it may be," answered Mr. Henry Hunter, who was feeling vexed, puzzled, and very angry.

"I mean—let no shadow of the truth get abroad. The business is large enough for two firms, and we have agreed to carry it on apart. Let that be the plea."

"You take it coolly, James."

A strange expression—a *wrung* expression—passed over the face of James Hunter. "I cannot help myself, Henry. The five thousand pounds are gone, and of course it is right that I should bear the loss alone—or any other loss it may bring in its train."

"But why not impart to me the facts?"

"No. It could not possibly do good; and it might make matters infinitely worse. One advantage our separation will have; there is a great deal of money owing to us from different quarters, and this will call it in."

"Or I don't see how you would carry anything on for your part, minus your five thousand pounds," retorted Mr. Henry, in a spirit of satire.

"Will you grant me a favour, Henry?"

"That depends upon what it may be."

"Let the real grounds of our separation—this miserable affair that has led to it—be equally a secret from your wife, as from the world. I should not ask it without an urgent reason."

"Don't you mean to tell Louisa?"

"No. The matter is one entirely my own; I do not wish to talk of it even to my wife. Will you give me the promise?"

"Very well. If it be of the consequence you seem to intimate. I cannot fathom you, James."

"Let us apply ourselves now to the ways and means of the dissolution. That, at any rate, may be amicable."

It was quite evident that he fully declined further allusion to the subject. And Mr. Henry Hunter obtained no better elucidation, then or later.

It fell upon the world like a thunderbolt—that is, the world connected with Hunter and Hunter. *They* separate? so flourishing a firm as that? The world at first refused to believe it; but the world soon found it was true.

Mr. Hunter retained the yard where the business was at present carried on. Mr. Henry Hunter found other premises to suit him; not far off; a little more to the west. Considerably surprised were Mrs. Hunter and Mrs. Henry Hunter; but the same plausible excuse was given to them; and they were left in ignorance of the true cause.

"Will you remain with me?" pointedly asked Mr. Hunter of Austin Clay. "I particularly wish it."

"As you and Mr. Henry may decide, sir," was the reply given. "It is not for me to choose."

"We could both do with you, I believe. I had better talk it over with him."

"That will be the best plan," sir.

"What do you part for?" abruptly inquired Dr. Bevary one day of the two brothers, coming into the counting-house and catching them together.

Mr. Henry raised his eyebrows. Mr. Hunter spoke volubly.

"The business is getting too large. It will be better divided."

"Moonshine!" cried the doctor, quietly. "That's what you have been cramming your wives with; it won't do for me. When a concern gets unwieldy, a man takes a partner to help him on with it; *you* are separating. There's many a firm larger than yours. Do you remember the proverb of the bundle of sticks?"

But neither Dr. Bevary nor anybody else got at a better reason than that for the measure. The dissolution of partnership took place; it was duly gazetted, and the old firm became two. Austin remained with Mr. Hunter, and he was the only living being who gave a guess, or who could give a guess, at the real cause of separation—the drawing out of that five thousand pounds.

And yet—it was not the drawing out of that first five thousand pounds, that finally decided Mr. Henry Hunter to enforce the step, so much as the thought that other thousands might perhaps be following it. He could not divest his mind of the fear.

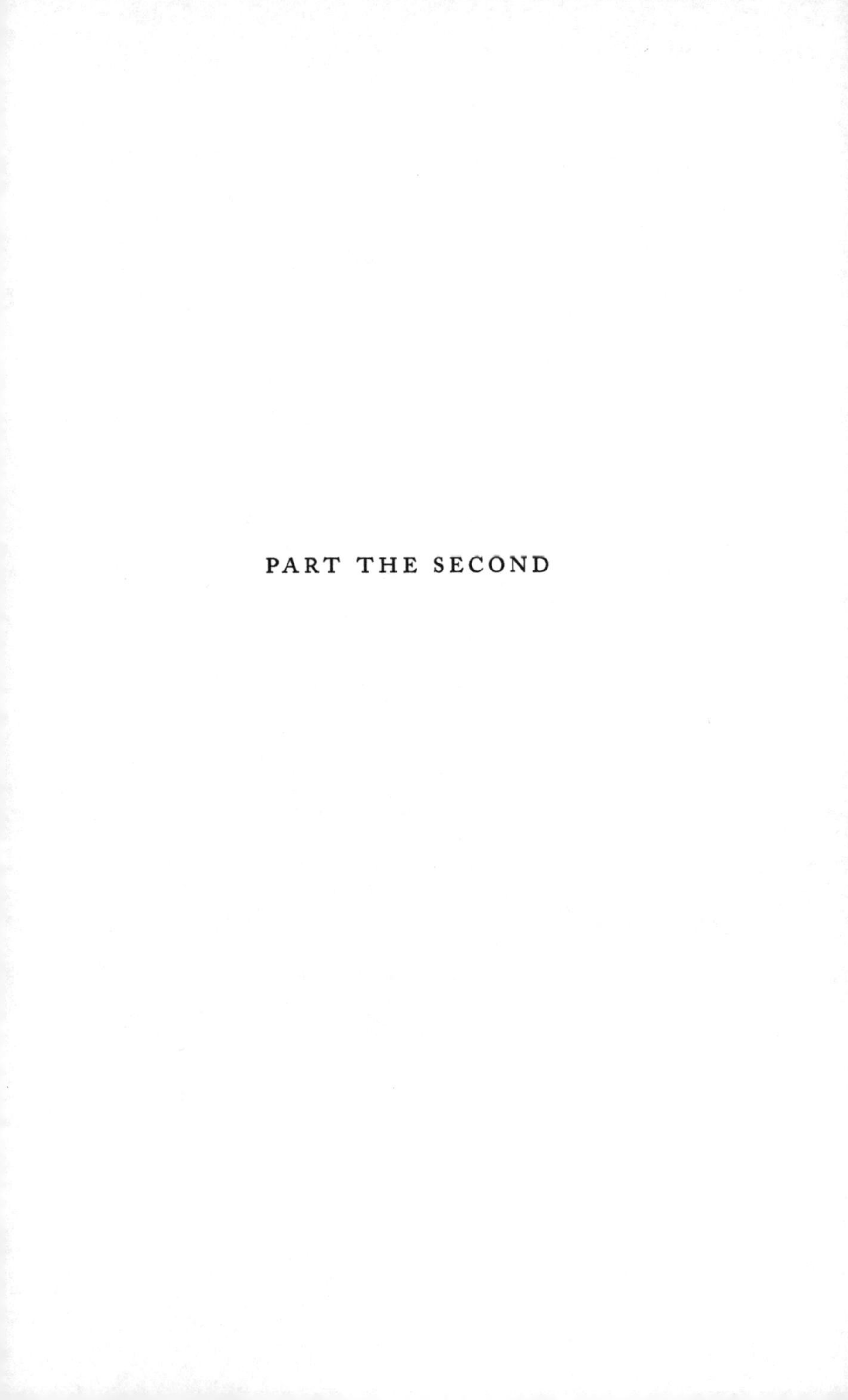

PART THE SECOND

I

A Meeting of the Workmen

For several years after the separation of Hunter and Hunter, things went on smoothly; at least there was no event sufficiently marked that we need linger to trace it. Each had a flourishing business, though Mr. Hunter had some difficulty in staving off embarrassment in the financial department: a fact which was well known to Austin Clay, who was now confidential manager—head of all, under Mr. Hunter.

He, Austin Clay, was getting towards thirty years of age. He enjoyed a handsome salary, and was putting by money yearly. He still remained at Peter Quale's, though his position would have warranted a style of living far superior. Not that it could have brought him more respect: of that he enjoyed a full share, both from master and men. Clever, energetic, firm, and friendly, he was thoroughly fitted for his post—was liked and esteemed. But for him, Mr. Hunter's business might not have been what it was, and Mr. Hunter knew it. *He* was a broken-spirited man, little capable now of devoting energy to anything. The years, in their progress, had terribly altered James Hunter.

A hot evening in Daffodil's Delight; and Daffodil's Delight was making it a busy one. Uninterrupted prosperity is sometimes nearly allied to danger; or, rather, danger may grow out of it. Prosperity begets independence, and independence often begets assumption—very often, a selfish, wrong view of surrounding things. If any workmen had enjoyed of late years (it may be said) unlimited prosperity, they were those connected with the building trade. Therefore, being so flourishing, it struck some of their body, who in a degree gave laws to the rest, that the best thing they could do was to make themselves more flourishing still. As a preliminary, they began to agitate for an increase of wages: this was to be accomplished by reducing the hours of labour, the proposition being to work nine hours per day instead of ten. They said nothing about relinquishing the wages of the extra hour: they would be paid for ten hours and work nine. The proposition was first put by the men of a leading metropolitan firm to their principals, and, failing to obtain it, they threatened to strike. This it was that was just now agitating Daffodil's Delight.

In the front room of one of the houses that abutted nearly on the gutter, and to which you must ascend by steps, there might be read in the window, inscribed on a piece of paper, the following notice: "The Misses Dunn's, Milliner and Dressmakers. Ladies own materiels made up." The composition of the *affiche* was that of the two Miss Dunns jointly, who prided themselves upon being elegant scholars. A twelvemonth's apprenticeship had initiated them into the mysteries of dressmaking; millinery had come to them, as Mark Tapley would say, spontaneous, or by dint of practice. They had set up for themselves in their father's house, and could boast of a fair share of the patronage of Daffodil's Delight. Showy damsels were they, with good-humoured, turned-up noses, and light hair; much given to gadding and gossiping, and fonder of dressing themselves than of getting home the dresses of their customers.

On the above evening, they sat in their room, an upper one, stitching away. A gown was in progress for Mrs. Quale, who often boasted that she could do any work in the world, save make her own gowns. It had been in progress for two weeks, and that lady had at length come up in a temper, as Miss Jemima Dunn expressed it, and had demanded it to be returned, done or undone. They, with much deprecation, protested it should be home the first thing in the morning, and went to work. Four or five visitors, girls of their own age, were performing the part of lookers-on, and much laughter prevailed.

"I say," cried out Martha White—a pleasant-looking girl, who had perched herself aloft on the edge of a piece of furniture, which appeared to be a low chest of drawers by day, and turn itself into a bed at night—"Mary Baxendale was crying yesterday, because of the strike; saying, it would be bad for all of us, if it came. Ain't she a soft?"

"Baxendale's again it, too," exclaimed Miss Ryan, Pat Ryan's eldest trouble. "Father says he don't think Baxendale 'll go in for it all."

"Mary Baxendale's just one of them timid things as is afraid of their own shadders," cried Mary Ann Dunn. "If she saw a cow a-coming at the other end of the street, she'd turn tail and run. Jemimer, whatever are you at? The sleeves is to be in plaits, not gathers."

"She do look ill, though, does Mary Baxendale," said Jemima, after some attention to the sleeve in hand. "It's my belief she'll never live to see Christmas; she's going the way her mother went. Won't it be prime when the men get ten hours' pay for nine hours' work? I shall think about getting married then."

"You must find somebody to have you first," quoth Grace Darby. "You have not got a sweetheart yet."

Miss Jemima tossed her head. "I needn't to wait long for that. The chaps be as plentiful as sprats in winter. All you have got to do is to pick and choose."

"What's that?" interrupted Mrs. Dunn, darting into the room, with her sharp tongue and her dirty fine cap. "What's that as you're talking about, miss?"

"We are a-talking of the strike," responded Jemima, with a covert glance to the rest. "Martha White and Judy Ryan says the Baxendales won't go in for it."

"Not go in for it? What idiots they must be!" returned Mrs. Dunn, the attractive subject completely diverting her attention from Miss Jemima and her words. "Ain't nine hours a-day enough for the men to be at work? I can tell the Baxendales what—when we have got the nine hours all straight and sure, we shall next demand eight. 'Taint free-born Englishers as is going to be put upon. It'll be glorious times, girls, won't it? We shall get a taste o' fowls and salmon, may be, for dinner then!"

"My father says he does not think the masters will come-to, if the men do strike," observed Grace Darby.

"Of course they won't—till they are forced," retorted Mrs. Dunn, in a spirit of satire. "But that's just what they are a-going to be. Don't you be a fool, Grace Darby!"

Lotty Cheek rushed in, a girl with a tongue almost as voluble as Mrs. Dunn's, and rough hair, the colour of a tow-rope. "What d'ye think?" cried she, breathlessly. "There's a-going to be a meeting of the men to-night in the big room of the Bricklayers' Arms. They are a-filing in now. I think it must be about the strike."

"D'ye suppose it would be about anything else?" retorted Mrs. Dunn. "I'd like to be one of 'em! I'd hold out for the day's work of eight hours, instead of nine, I would. So 'ud they, if they was men."

Mrs. Dunn's speech was concluded to an empty room. All the girls had flown down into the street, leaving the parts of Mrs. Quale's gown in closer contact with the dusty floor than was altogether to their benefit.

The agitation in the trade had hitherto been chiefly smouldering in an under-current: now, it was rising to the surface. Lotty Cheek's inference was right; the meeting of this evening had reference to the strike. It had been hastily arranged in the day; was quite an informal sort of affair, and confined to the operatives of Mr. Hunter.

Not in a workman's jacket, but in a brown coat dangling to his heels, with a slit down the back and ventilating holes for the elbows, first entered he who had been chiefly instrumental in calling the meeting. It was Mr. Samuel Shuck; better known, you may remember, as Slippery Sam. Somehow, Sam and prosperity could not contrive to pull together in the same boat. He was one of those who like to live on the fat of the land, but are too lazy to work for their share of it. And how Sam had contrived to exist until now, and keep himself and his large family out of the workhouse, was a marvel to all. In his fits of repentance, he would manage to get in again at one or other of the yards of the Messrs. Hunter; but they were growing tired of him.

The room at the Bricklayers' Arms was tolerably commodious, and Sam took up a conspicuous position in it.

"Well," began Sam, when the company had assembled, and were furnished with pipes and pewter pots, "you have heard that that firm won't accept the reduction in the hours of labour, so the men have determined on a strike. Now, I have got a question to put to you. Is there most power in one man, or in a few dozens of men?"

Some laughed, and said, "In the dozens."

"Very good," glibly went on Sam, whose tongue was smoother than oil, and who was gifted with a sort of oratory and some learning when he chose to put it out. "Then, the measure I wish to urge upon you is, make common cause with those men; we are not all obliged to strike at the same time; it will be better not; but by degrees. Let every firm in London strike, each at its appointed time," he continued, raising his voice to vehemence. "We must stand up for ourselves; for our rights; for our wives and children. By making common cause together, we shall bowl out the masters, and bring them to terms."

"Hooroar!" put in Pat Ryan.

"Hooroar!" echoed a few more.

An aged man, Abel White's father, usually called old White, who was past work, and had a seat at his son's chimney corner, leaned forward and spoke, his voice tremulous, but distinct. "Samuel Shuck, did you ever know strikes do any good, either to the men or the masters? Friends," he added, turning his venerable head around, "I am in my eightieth year: and I picked up some experience while them eighty years was passing. Strikes have ruined some masters, in means; but they have ruined men wholesale, in means, in body, and in soul."

"Hold there," cried Sam Shuck, who had not brooked the interruption patiently. "Just tell us, old White, before you go on, whether coercion answers for British workmen?"

"It does not," replied the old man, lifting his quiet voice to firmness. "But perhaps you will tell me in your turn, Sam Shuck, whether it's likely to answer for masters?"

"It *has* answered for them," returned Sam, in a tone of irony. "I *have* heard of back strikes, where the masters were coerced and coerced, till the men got all they stood out for."

"And so brought down ruin on their own heads," returned the old man, shaking his. "Did you ever hear of a lock-out, Shuck?"

"Ay, ay," interposed quiet, respectable Robert Darby. "Did you ever hear of that, Slippery Sam?"

Slippery Sam growled. "Let the masters lock-out if they dare! Let 'em. The men would hold out to the death."

"And death it will be, with some of us, if the strike comes, and lasts. I came down here to-night, on my son's arm, just for your good, my friends, not for mine. At your age, I thought as some of you do; but I have learnt experience now. I can't last long, any way; and it's little matter to me whether famine from a strike be my end, or—"

"Famine" derisively retorted Slippery Sam.

"Yes, famine," was the quiet answer. "Strikes never yet brought nothing but misery in the end. Let me urge upon you all not to be led away. My voice is but a feeble one; but I think the Lord is sometimes pleased to show out things clearly to the aged, almost as with a gift of prophecy; and I could only come and beseech you to keep upon the straight-forrard path. Don't have anything to do with a strike; keep it away from you at arm's length, as you would keep away the evil one."

"What's the good of listening to him?" cried Slippery Sam, in anger. "He is in his dotage."

"Will you listen to me then?" spoke up Peter Quale; "I am not in mine. I didn't intend to come here, as may be guessed; but when I found so many of you bending your steps this way to listen to Slippery Sam, I thought it time to change my mind, and come and tell you what *I* thought of strikes."

"*You!*" rudely replied Slippery Sam. "A fellow like you, always in full work, earning the biggest wages, is sure not to favour strikes. You can't be much better off than you are."

"That admission of yours is worth something, Slippery Sam, if there's any here have got the sense to see it," nodded Peter Quale. "Good workmen, on full wages, *don't* favour strikes. I have rose up to what I am by sticking to my work patiently, and getting on step by step. It's open to every living man to get on as I have done, if he have got skill and pluck to work. But if I had done as you do, Sam, gone in for labour one day and for play two, and for drinking, and strikes, and rebellion, because money, which I was too lazy to work for didn't drop from the skies into my hands, then I should just have been where you be."

"Is it right to keep a man grinding and sweating his life out for ten hours a-day?" retorted Sam. "The masters would be as well off if we worked nine, and the surplus men would find employment."

"It isn't much of your life that you sweat out, Sam Shuck," rejoined Peter Quale, with a cough that especially provoked his antagonist. "And, as to the masters being as well off, you had better ask them about that. Perhaps they'd tell you that to pay ten hours' wages for nine hours' work would be the hour's wage dead loss to their pockets."

"Are you rascal enough to go in for the masters?" demanded Sam, in a fiery heat. "Who'd do that, but a traitor?"

"I go in for myself, Sam," equably responded Peter Quale. "I know on which side my bread's buttered. No skilful workman, possessed of prudent thought and judgment, ever yet went blindfold into a strike. At least, not many such."

Up rose Robert Darby. "I'd just say a word, if I can get my meaning out, but I'm not cute with the tongue. It seems to me, mates, that it would be a great boon if we could obtain the granting of the nine hours' movement; and perhaps in the end it would not affect the masters, for they'd get it out of the public. I'd agitate for this in a peaceful way, in the shape of reason and argument, and do my best in that way to get it. But I'd not like, as Peter Quale says, to plunge blindfold into a strike."

"I look at it in this light, Darby," said Peter Quale, "and it seems to me it's the only light as 'll answer to look at it in. Things in this world are estimated by comparison. There ain't nothing large nor small *in itself*. I may say, this chair's big: well, so it is, if you match it by that there bit of a stool in the chimbley corner; but it's very small if you put it by the side of a omnibus, or of one of the sheds in our yard. Now, if you compare our wages with those of workmen in most other trades, they are large. Look at a farm labourer, poor fellow, with his ten shillings (more or less) a-week, hardly keeping body and soul together. Look at what a man earns in the malting districts in the country; fifteen shillings and his beer, is reckoned good wages. Look at a policeman, with his pound a-week. Look at a postman. Look at—"

"Look at ourselves," intemperately interrupted Jim Dunn. "What's other folks to us? We work hard, and we ought to be paid according."

"So I think we are," said Peter Quale. "Thirty-three shillings is *not* bad wages, and it is only a delusion to say it is. Neither is ten hours a-day an unfair or oppressive time to work. I'd be as glad as anybody to have the hour took off, if it could be done pleasantly; but I am not going to put myself out of work and into trouble to stand out for it. It's a thing that I am convinced the masters never will give; and if Pollock's men strike for it, they'll do it against their own interests—"

Hisses, and murmurs of disapprobation from various parts of the room, interrupted Peter Quale.

"You'd better wait and understand, afore you begin to hiss," phlegmatically recommended Peter Quale, when the noise had subsided. "I say it will be against their interests to strike, because, I think, if they stop on strike for twelve months, they'll be no nearer getting their end. I may be wrong, but that's my opinion. There's always two sides to a question—our own, and the opposite one; and the great fault in most folks is, that they look only at their own side, and it causes them to see things in a partial view. I have looked as fair as I can at our own side, trying to put away my bias *for it*; and I have put myself in thought on the master's side, asking myself, what would *I* do, were I one of them. Thus I have tried to judge between them and us, and the conclusion I have drawed is, that they won't give in."

"The masters have been brought to grant demands more unreasonable than this," rejoined Sam Shuck. "If you know anything about back strikes, you must know that, Quale."

"And that's one of the reasons why I argue they won't grant this," said Peter. "If they go on granting and granting, they may get asking themselves where the demands 'll stop."

"Let us go back to 1833," spoke up old White again, and the man's age and venerable aspect caused him to be listened to with respect. "I was then working in Manchester, and belonged to the Trades' Union; a powerful Union as ever was formed. In our strength, we thought we should like a thing or two altered, and we made a formal demand upon the master builders, requiring them to discontinue the erection of buildings on sub-contracts. The masters fell in with it. You'll understand, friends," he broke off to say, "that, looking at things now, and looking at 'em then, is just as if I saw 'em in two opposite aspects. Next, we gave out a set of various rules for the masters, and required them to abide by such—about the making of the wages equal; the number of apprentices they should take; the machinery they should or should not use, and other things. Well, the masters gave us that also, and it put us all cock-a-hoop, and we went on to dictate to 'em more and more. If they—the masters—broke any of our rules, we levied fines on 'em, and made 'em pay up; we ordered them before us at our meetings, found fault with 'em, commanded 'em to obey us, to take on such men as we pointed out, and to turn off others; in short, forced 'em to do as we chose. People might have thought that we was the masters and they the operatives. Pretty well, that, wasn't it?"

The room nodded acquiescence. Slippery Sam snapped his fingers in delight.

"The worst was, it did not last," resumed the old man. "Like too many other folks emboldened with success, we wasn't content to let well alone, but went on a bit too far. The masters took up their own defence at last; and the wonder to me now, looking back, is, that they didn't do it before. They formed themselves into a Union, and passed a resolve to employ no man unless he signed a pledge not to belong to a Trades' Union. Then we all turned out. Six months the strike was on, and the buildings was at a standstill, and us out of work."

"Were wages bad at that time?" inquired Robert Darby.

"No. The good workmen among us had been earning in the summer thirty-five shillings a-week; and the bricklayers had just had a rise of three shillings. We was just fools: that's my opinion of it now. Awful misery we were reduced to. Every stick we had went to the pawn-shop; our wives was skin and bone, our children was in rags; and some of us just laid our heads down on the stones, clammed to death."

"What was the trade in other places about, that it didn't help you?" indignantly demanded Sam Shuck.

"They did help us. Money to the tune of eighteen thousand pounds came to us; but we was a large body—many mouths to feed, and the strike was prolonged. We had to come-to at last, for the masters wouldn't; and we voted our combination a nuisance, and went humbly to 'em, like dogs with their tails between their legs, and craved to be took on again upon their own terms. But we couldn't get took back; not all of us: the masters had learnt a lesson. They had got machinery to work, and had collected workmen from other parts, so that we was not wanted. And that's all the good the strike brought to us! I came away on the tramp with my family, and got work in London after a deal of struggle and privation: and I made a vow never to belong willingly to a strike again."

"Do you see where the fault lay in that case?—the blame?—the whole gist of the evil?"

The question came from a gentleman who had entered the room as old White was speaking. The men would have risen to salute him, but he signed to them to be still and cause no interruption—a tall, noble man, with calm, self-reliant countenance.

"It lay with the masters," he resumed, nobody replying to him. "Had those Manchester masters resisted the first demand of their men—a demand made in the insolence of power, not in need—and allowed them fully to understand that they were, and would be, masters, we should, I believe, have heard less of strikes since, than we have done. I never think of those Manchester masters but my blood boils. When a principal suffers himself to be dictated to by his men, he is no longer a master, or worthy of the name."

"Had you been one of them, and not complied, you might have come to ruin, sir," cried Robert Darby. "There's a deal to be said on both sides."

"Ruin!" was the answer. "I never would have conceded an inch, though I had known that I must end my days in the workhouse through not doing it."

"Of course, sir, you'd stand up for the masters, being hand in glove with 'em, and likely to be a master yourself," grumbled Sam Shuck, a touch of irony in his tone.

"I should stand up for whichever side I deemed in the right, whether it was the masters' or the men's," was the emphatic answer. "Is it well—is it in accordance with the fitness of things, that a master should be under the control of his men? Come! I ask it of your common sense."

"No." It was readily acknowledged.

"Those Manchester masters and those Manchester operatives were upon a par as regards shame and blame."

"Sir! Shame and blame?"

"They were upon a par as regards shame and blame," was the decisive repetition; "and I make no doubt that both equally deemed themselves to have been so, when they found their senses. The masters came to them: the men were brought to theirs."

"You speak strongly, sir."

"Because I feel strongly. When I become a master, I shall, if I know anything of myself, have my men's interest at heart; but none of them shall ever presume to dictate to me. If a master cannot exercise his own authority in firm self-reliance, let him give up business."

"Have masters a right to oppress us, sir?—to grind us down?—to work us into our coffins?" cried Sam Shuck.

The gentleman raised his eyebrows, and a half smile crossed his lips. "Since when have you been oppressed, and ground down into your coffins?"

Some of the men laughed—at Sam's oily tongue.

"If you *are*—if you have any complaint of that sort to make, let me hear it now, and I will convey it to Mr. Hunter. He is ever ready, you know, to—What do you say, Shuck? The nine hours' concession is all you want? If you can get the masters to give you ten hours' pay for nine hours' work, so much the better for you. *I* would not: but it is no affair of mine. To be paid what you honestly earn, be it five pounds per week or be it one, is only justice; but to be paid for what you don't earn, is the opposite thing. I think, too, that the equalization of wages is a mistaken system, quite wrong in principle: one which can bring only discontent in the long run. Let me repeat that with emphasis—the equalization of wages, should it ever take place, can bring only discontent in the long run."

There was a pause. No one spoke, and the speaker resumed—

"I conclude you have met here to discuss this agitation at the Messrs. Pollocks?"

Pollocks' men are a-going to strike," said Slippery Sam.

"Oh, they are, are they?" returned the gentleman, some mockery in his tone. "I hope they may find it to their benefit. I don't know what the Messrs. Pollocks may do in the matter; but I know what I should."

"You'd hold out to the last against the men?"

"I should; to the last and the last: were it for ten years to come. Force a measure upon *me*! coerce *me*!" he reiterated, drawing his fine form to its full height, while the red flush mantled in his cheeks. "No, my men, I am not made of that yielding stuff. Only let me be persuaded that my judgment is right, and no body of men on earth should force me to act against it."

The speaker was Austin Clay, as I daresay you have already guessed. He had not gone to the meeting to interrupt it, or to take part in it, but in search of Peter Quale. Hearing from Mrs. Quale that her husband was at the Bricklayers' Arms—a rare occurrence, for Peter was not one who favoured public-houses—Austin went thither in search of him, and so found himself in the midst of the meeting. His business with Peter related to certain orders he required to give for the early morning. Once there, however, the temptation to have his say was too great to be resisted. That over, he went out, making a sign to the man to follow him.

"What are those men about to rush into, Quale?" he demanded, when his own matter was over.

"Ah, what indeed?" returned the man. "If they do get led into a strike, they'll repent it, some of them."

"You are not one of the malcontents, then?"

"I?" retorted Peter, utter scorn in his tone. "No, sir. There's a proverb which I learnt years ago from an old book as was lent me, and I've not forgotten it, sir—'Let well alone.' But you must not think all the men you saw sitting there be discontented agitators, Mr. Clay. It's only Shuck and a few of that stamp. The rest be as steady and cautious as I am."

"If they don't get led away," replied Austin Clay, and his voice betrayed a dubious tone. "Slippery Sam, in spite of his loose qualifications, is a ringleader more persuasive than prudent. Hark! he is at it again, hammer and tongs. Are you going back to them?"

"No, sir. I shall go home now."

"We will walk together, then," observed Austin. "Afterwards I am going on to Mr. Hunter's."[1]

---

1. "It need scarcely be remarked, that Sam Shuck and his followers represent only the ignorant and unprincipled section of those who engage in strikes. Working men are perfectly right in combining to seek the best terms they can get, both as to wages and time; provided there be no interference with the liberty either of masters or fellow-workmen.—*Ed.* L. H., February, 1862."

II

Called to Ketterford

Austin Clay was not mistaken. Rid of Peter Quale, who was a worse enemy of Sam's schemes than even old White, Sam had it nearly his own way, and went at it "hammer and tongs." He poured his eloquent words into the men's ears—and Sam, as you have heard, really did possess the gift of eloquence: of a rough and rude sort: but that tells well with the class now gathered round him. He brought forth argument upon argument, fallacious as they were plausible; he told the men it depended upon *them*, whether the boon they were standing out for should be accorded, not upon the masters. Not that Sam called it a boon; he spoke of it as a *right*. Let them only be firm and true to themselves, he said, and the masters must give in: there was no help for it, they would have no other resource. Sam finally concluded by demanding, with fierce looks all round, whether they were men, or whether they were slaves, and the men answered, with a cheer and a shout, that Britons never should be slaves: and the meeting broke up in excitement and glorious spirits, and went home elated, some with the anticipation of the fine time that was dawning for them, others with having consumed a little too much half-and-half.

Slippery Sam reeled away to his home. A dozen or so attended him, listening to his oratory, which was continued still: though not exactly to the gratification of Daffodil's Delight, who were hushing their unruly babies to sleep, or striving to get to sleep themselves. Much Sam cared whom he disturbed! He went along, flinging his arms and his words at random—inflammatory words, carrying poisoned shafts that told. If somebody came down upon you and upon me, telling us that, with a little exertion on our part, we should inevitably drop into a thousand a year, and showing plausible cause for the same, should we turn a deaf ear? The men shook hands individually with Slippery Sam, and left him propped against his own door; for Sam, with all deference be it spoken, was a little overcome himself—with the talking, of course.

Sam's better half greeted him with a shrill tongue: she and Mrs. Dunn might be paired in that respect! and Sam's children, some in the bed in the corner, some sitting up, greeted him with a shrill cry also, clamouring for a very common-place article, indeed—"some *bread*!" Sam's family seemed inconveniently to increase; for the less there appeared to be to welcome them with, the surer and faster they arrived. Thirteen Sam could number now; but several of the elder ones were out in the world "doing for themselves"—getting on, or starving, as it might happen to be.

"You old sot! you have been at that drinking-can again," were Mrs. Sam's words of salutation; and I wish I could soften them down to refinement for polite ears; but if you are to have the truth, you must take them as they were spoken.

"Drinking-can!" echoed Sam, who was in too high glee to lose his temper, "never mind the drinking-can, missis: my fortian's made. I drawed together that meeting, as I telled ye I should," he added, discarding his scholarly eloquence for the familiar home phraseology, "and they come to it, every man jack on 'em, save thin-skinned Baxendale upstairs. Never was such a full meeting knowed in Daffodil's Delight."

"Who cares for the meeting!" irascibly responded Mrs. Sam. "What we wants is, some'at to fill our insides with. Don't come bothering home here about a meeting, when the children be a starving. If you'd work more and talk less, it 'ud become ye better."

"I got the ear of the meeting," said Sam, braving the reproof with a provoking wink. "A despicable set our men is, at Hunter's, a humdrumming on like slaves for ever, taking their paltry wages and making no stir. But I've put the brand among 'em at last, and sent 'em home all on fire, to dream of short work and good pay. Quale, he come, and put in his spoke again' it; and that wretched old skeleton of a White, what's been cheating the grave this ten year, he come, and put in his; and Mr. Austin Clay, he must thrust his nose among us, and talk treason to the men: but I think my tongue have circumvented the lot. If it haven't, my name's not Sam Shuck."

"If you and your circumventions and your tongue was all at the bottom of the Thames, 'twouldn't be no loss, for all the good they does above it," sobbed Mrs. Shuck, whose anger generally ended in tears. "Here's me and the children a clemming for want o' bread, and you can waste your time over a idle good-for-nothing meeting. Ain't you ashamed, not to work as other men do?"

"Bread!" loftily returned Sam, with the air of a king, "'tisn't bread I shall soon be furnishing for you and the children: it's mutton chops. My fortian's made, I say."

"Yah!" retorted Mrs. Sam. "It have been made forty times in the last ten year, to listen to you. What good has ever come of the boast? I'd shut up my mouth if I couldn't talk sense."

Sam nodded his head oracularly, and entered upon an explanation. But for the fact of his being a little "overcome"—whatever may have been its cause—he would have been more guarded. "I've had overtures," he said, bending forward his head and lowering his voice, "and them overtures, which I accepted, will be the making of you and of me. Work!" he exclaimed, throwing his arms gracefully from him with a repelling gesture, "I've done with work now; I'm superior to it; I'm exalted far above that lowering sort of toil. The leaders among the London Trade Union have recognised eloquence, ma'am, let me tell you; and they've made me one of their picked body—appointed me agitator to the firms of Hunter. 'You get the meeting together, and prime 'em with the best of your eloquence, and excite 'em to recognise and agitate for their own rights, and you shall have your appointment, and a good round weekly salary.' Well, Mrs. S., I did it. I got the men together, and I *have* primed 'em, and some of 'em's a busting to go off; and all I've got to do from henceforth is to keep 'em up to the mark, by means of that tongue which you are so fond of disparaging, and to live like a gentleman. There's a trifling instalment of the first week's money."

Sam threw a sovereign on the table. Mrs. Shuck, with a grunt of disparagement still, darted forward to seize upon it through her tears. The children, uttering a wild shriek of wonder, delight, and disbelief, born of incipient famine, darted forward to seize it too. Sam burst into a fit of laughter, threw himself back to indulge it, and not being just then over steady on his legs, lost his equilibrium, and toppled over the fender into the ashes.

Leaving Mrs. Shuck to pick him up, or to leave him there—which latter negative course was the one she would probably take—let us return to Austin Clay.

At Peter Quale's gate he was standing a moment to speak to the man before proceeding onwards, when Mrs. Quale came running down the garden path.

"I was coming in search of you, sir," she said to Austin Clay. "This has just been brought, and the man made me sign my name to a paper."

Austin took what she held out to him—a telegraphic despatch. He opened it; read it; then in the prompt, decisive manner usual with him, requested Mrs. Quale to put him up a change of things in his portmanteau, which he would return for; and walked away with a rapid step.

"Whatever news is it that he has had?" cried Mrs. Quale, as she stood with her husband, looking after him. "Where can he have been summoned to?"

"'Tain't no business of ours," retorted Peter; "if it had been, he'd have enlightened us. Did you ever hear of that offer that's always pending?—Five hundred a year to anybody as 'll undertake to mind his own business, and leave other folks's alone."

Austin was on his way to Mr. Hunter's. A very frequent evening visitor there now, was he. But this evening he had an ostensible motive for going; a boon to crave. That alone may have made his footsteps fleet.

In the soft twilight of the summer evening, in the room of their own house that opened to the conservatory, sat Florence Hunter—no longer the impulsive, charming, and somewhat troublesome child, but the young and lovely woman. Of middle height and graceful form, her face was one of great sweetness; the earnest, truthful spirit, the pure innocence, which had made its charm in youth, made it now: to look on Florence Hunter, was to love her.

She appeared to be in deep thought, her cheek resting on her hand, and her eyes fixed on vacancy. Some movement in the house aroused her, and she arose, shook her head, as if she would shake care away, and bent over a rare plant in the room's large opening, lightly touching the leaves.

"I fear that mamma is right, and I am wrong, pretty plant!" she murmured. "I fear that you will die. Is it that this London, with its heavy atmosphere—"

The knock of a visitor at the hall door resounded through the house. Did Florence *know* the knock, that her voice should falter, and the soft pink in her cheeks should deepen to a glowing crimson? The room door opened, and a servant announced Mr. Clay.

In that early railway journey when they first met, Florence had taken a predilection for Austin Clay. "I like him so much!" had been her gratuitous announcement to her uncle Harry. The liking had ripened into an attachment, firm and lasting—a child's attachment: but Florence grew into a woman, and it could not remain such. Thrown much together, the feeling had changed, and love mutually arose: they fell into it unconsciously. Was it quite prudent of Mr. Hunter to sanction, nay, to court the frequent presence at his house of Austin Clay? Did he overlook the obvious fact, that he was one who possessed attractions, both of mind and person, and that Florence was now a woman grown? Or did Mr. Hunter deem that the social barrier, which he might assume existed between his daughter and his dependent, would effectually prevent all approach of danger? Mr. Hunter must himself account for the negligence: no one else can do it. It was certain that he did have Austin very much at his house, but it was equally certain that he never cast a thought to the possibility that his daughter might be learning to love him.

The strange secret, whatever it may have been, attaching to Mr. Hunter, had shattered his health to that extent that for days together he would be unequal to go abroad or to attend to business. Then Austin, who acted as principal in the absence of Mr. Hunter, would arrive at the house when the day was over, to report progress, and take orders for the next day. Or, rather, consult with him what the orders should be; for in energy, in capability, Austin was now the master spirit, and Mr. Hunter bent to it. That over, he passed the rest of the evening in the society of Florence, conversing with her freely, confidentially; on literature, art, the news of the day; on topics of home interest; listening to her music, listening to her low voice, as she sang her songs; guiding her pencil. There they would be. He with his ready eloquence, his fund of information, his attractive manners, and his fine form, handsome in its height and strength; she with her sweet fascinations, her gentle loveliness. What could be the result? But, as is almost invariably the case, the last person to give a suspicion to it was he who positively looked on, and might have seen all—Mr. Hunter. Life, in the presence of the other, had become sweet to each as a summer's dream—a dream that had stolen over them ere they knew what it meant. But consciousness came with time.

Very conscious of it were they both as he entered this evening. Austin took her hand in greeting; a hand always tremulous now in his. She bent again over the plant she was tending, her eyelids and her damask cheeks drooping.

"You are alone, Florence!"

"Just now. Mamma is very poorly this evening, and keeps her room. Papa was here a few minutes ago."

He released her hand, and stood looking at her, as she played with the petals of the flower. Not a word had Austin spoken of his love;

not a word was he sure that he might speak. If he partially divined that it might be acceptable to her, he did not believe it would be to Mr. Hunter.

"The plant looks sickly," he observed.

"Yes. It is one that thrives in cold and wind. It came from Scotland. Mamma feared this close London atmosphere would not suit it; but I said it looked so hardy, it would be sure to do well. Rather than it should die, I would send it back to its bleak home."

"In tears, Florence? for the sake of a plant?"

"Not for that," she answered, twinkling the moisture from her eyelashes, as she raised them to his with a brave smile. "I was thinking of mamma; she appears to be fading rapidly, like the plant."

"She may grow stronger when the heat of summer shall have passed."

Florence slightly shook her head, as if she could not share in the suggested hope. "Mamma herself does not seem to think she shall, Austin. She has dropped ominous words more than once latterly. This afternoon I showed her the plant, that it was drooping. 'Ay, my dear,' she remarked, "it is like me—on the wane." And I think my uncle Bevary's opinion has become unfavourable."

It was a matter on which Austin could not urge hope, though, for the sake of tranquillizing Florence, he might suggest it, for he believed that Mrs. Hunter was fading rapidly. All these years she seemed to have been getting thinner and weaker; it was some malady connected with the spine, causing her at times great pain. Austin changed the subject.

"I hope Mr. Hunter will soon be in, Florence. I am come to ask for leave of absence."

"Papa is not out; he is sitting with mamma. That is another reason why I fear danger for her. I think papa sees it; he is so solicitous for her comfort, so anxious to be with her, as if he would guard her from surprise or agitating topics. He will not suffer a visitor to enter at hazard; he will not let a note be given her until he has first seen it."

"But he has long been thus anxious," replied Austin, who was aware that what she spoke of had lasted for years.

"I know. But still, latterly—however, I must hope against hope," broke off Florence. "I think I do: hope is certainly a very strong ingredient in my nature, for I cannot realize the parting with my dear mother. Did you say you have come for leave of absence? Where is it that you wish to go?"

"I have had a telegraphic despatch from Ketterford," he replied, taking it from his pocket. "My good old friend, Mrs. Thornimett, is dying, and I must hasten thither with all speed."

"Oh!" uttered Florence, almost reproachfully. "And you are wasting the time with me!"

"Not so. The first train that goes there does not start for an hour yet, and I can get to Paddington in half of one. The news has grieved me much. The last time I was at Ketterford—you may remember it—Mrs. Thornimett was so very well, exhibiting no symptoms whatever of decay."

"I remember it," answered Florence. "It is two years ago. You stayed a whole fortnight with her."

"And had a battle with her to get away then," said Austin, smiling with the reminiscence, or with Florence's word "whole"—a suggestive word, spoken in that sense. "She wished me to remain longer. I wonder what illness can have stricken her? It must have been sudden."

"What is the relationship between you?"

"A distant one. She and my mother were second cousins. If I—"

Austin was stopped by the entrance of Mr. Hunter. *So* changed, *so* bent and bowed, since you, reader, last saw him! The stout, upright figure had grown thin and stooping, the fine dark hair was grey, the once calm, self-reliant face was worn and haggard. Nor was that all; there was a constant *restlessness* in his manner and in the turn of his eye, giving a spectator the idea that he lived in a state of ever-present, perpetual fear.

Austin put the telegraphic message in his hand. "It is an inconvenient time, I know, sir, for me to be away, busy as we are, and with this agitation rising amongst the men; but I cannot help myself. I will return as soon as it is possible."

Mr. Hunter did not hear the words. His eyes had fallen on the word "Ketterford," in the despatch, and that seemed to scare away his senses. His hands shook as he held the paper, and for a few moments he appeared incapable of collected thought, of understanding anything. Austin exclaimed again.

"Oh, yes, yes, it is only—it is Mrs. Thornimett who is ill, and wants you—I comprehend now." He spoke in an incoherent manner, and with a sigh of the most intense relief. "I—I—saw the word 'dying,' and it startled me," he proceeded, as if anxious to account for his agitation. "You can go, Austin; you must go. Remain a few days there—a week, if you find it necessary."

"Thank you, sir. I will say farewell now, then."

He shook hands with Mr. Hunter, turned to Florence, and took hers. "Remember me to Mrs. Hunter," he said in a low tone, which, in spite of himself, betrayed its own tenderness, "and tell her I hope to find her better on my return."

A few paces from the house, as he went out, Austin encountered Dr. Bevary. "Is she much worse?" he exclaimed to Austin, in a hasty tone.

"Is who much worse, doctor?"

"Mrs. Hunter. I have just had a message from her."

"Not very much, I fancy. Florence said her mamma was poorly this evening. I am off to Ketterford, doctor, for a few days."

"To Ketterford!" replied Dr. Bevary, with an emphasis that showed the news had startled him. "What are you going there for? For—for Mr. Hunter?"

"For myself," said Austin. "A good old friend is ill—dying, the message says—and has telegraphed for me."

The physician looked at him searchingly. "Do you speak of Miss Gwinn?"

"I should not call her a friend," replied Austin. "I allude to Mrs. Thornimett."

"A pleasant journey to you, then. And, Clay, steer clear of those Gwinns; they would bring you no good."

It was in the dawn of the early morning that Austin entered Ketterford. He did not let the grass grow under his feet between the railway terminus and Mrs. Thornimett's, though he was somewhat dubious about disturbing the house. If she was really "dying," it might be well that he should do so; if only suffering from a severe illness, it might not be expected of him; and the wording of the message had been ambiguous, leaving it an open question. As he drew within view of the house, however, it exhibited signs of bustle; lights not yet put out in the dawn, might be discerned through some of the curtained windows, and a woman, having much the appearance of a nurse, was coming out at the door, halting on the threshold a moment to hold converse with one within.

"Can you tell me how Mrs. Thornimett is?" inquired Austin, addressing himself to her.

The woman shook her head. "She is gone, sir. Not more than an hour ago."

Sarah, the old servant whom we have seen before at Mrs. Thornimett's, came forward, weeping. "Oh, Mr. Austin! oh, sir: why could not you get here sooner?"

"How could I, Sarah?" was his reply. "I received the message only last evening, and came off by the first train that started."

"I'd have took a engine to myself, and rode upon its chimbley, but what I'd have got here in time," retorted Sarah. 'Twice in the very last half hour of her life she asked after you. "Isn't Austin come?" "Isn't he yet come? My dear old mistress!"

"Why was I not sent for before?" he asked, in return.

"Because we never thought it was turning serious," sobbed Sarah. "She caught cold some days ago, and it flew to her throat, or her chest, I hardly know which. The doctor was called in; and it's my belief *he* didn't know: the doctors nowadays bain't worth half what they used to be, and they call things by fine names that nobody can understand. However it may have been, nobody saw any danger, neither him nor us. But at midday yesterday there was a change, and the doctor said he'd like further advice to be brought in. And it was had; but they could not do her any good; and she, poor dear mistress, was the first to say that she was dying. 'Send for Austin,' she said to me; and one of the gentlemen, he went to the wire telegraph place, and wrote the message."

Austin made no rejoinder: he seemed to be swallowing down a lump in his throat. Sarah resumed. "Will you see her, sir? She is just laid out."

He nodded acquiescence, and the servant led the way to the death chamber. It had been put straight, so to remain until all that was left of its many years' occupant should be removed. She lay on the bed in placid stillness; her eyes closed, her pale face calm, a smile upon it; the calm of a spirit at peace with heaven. Austin leaned over her, losing himself in solemn thoughts. Whither had the spirit flown? to what bright unknown world? Had it found the company of sister spirits? had it seen, face to face, its loving Saviour? Oh! what mattered now the few fleeting trials of this life that had passed over her! how worse than unimportant did they seem by the side of death! A little, more or less, of care; a lot, where shade or sunshine shall have predominated; a few friends gained or lost; struggle, toil, hope—all must merge in the last rest. It was over; earth, with its troubles and its petty cares, with its joys and sorrows, and its "goods stored up for many years;" as completely over for Mary Thornimett, as though it had never, been. In the higher realms whither her spirit had hastened—

"I told Mrs. Dubbs to knock up the undertaker, and desire him to come here at once and take the measure for the coffin."

Sarah's interruption recalled Austin to the world. It is impossible, even in a death-chamber, to run away from the ordinary duties of daily life.

III

Two Thousand Pounds

"You will stay for the funeral, Mr. Clay?"

"It is my intention to do so."

"Good. Being interested in the will, it may be agreeable to you to hear it read."

"Am I interested?" inquired Austin, in some surprise.

"Why, of course you are," replied Mr. Knapley, the legal gentleman with whom Austin was speaking, and who had the conduct of Mrs. Thornimett's affairs. "Did you never know that you were a considerable legatee?"

"I did not," said Austin. "Some years ago—it was at the death of Mr. Thornimett—Mrs. Thornimett hinted to me that I might be the better some time for a trifle from her. But she has never alluded to it since: and I have not reckoned upon it."

"Then I can tell you—though it is revealing secrets beforehand—that you are the better to the tune of two thousand pounds."

"Two thousand pounds!" uttered Austin, in sheer amazement. "How came she to leave me so much as that?"

"Do you quarrel with it, young sir?"

"No, indeed: I feel all possible gratitude. But I am surprised, nevertheless."

"She was a clever, clear-sighted woman, was Mrs. Thornimett," observed the lawyer. "I'll tell you about it—how it is you come to have so much. When I was taking directions for Mr. Thornimett's will—more than ten years back now—a discussion arose between him and his wife as to the propriety of leaving a sum of money to Austin Clay. A thousand pounds was the amount named. Mr. Thornimett was for leaving you in his wife's hands, to let her bequeath it to you at her death; Mrs. Thornimett wished it should be left to you then, in the will I was about to make, that you might inherit it on the demise of Mr. Thornimett. He took his own course, and did *not* leave it, as you are aware."

"I did not expect him to leave me anything," interrupted Austin.

"My young friend, if you break in with these remarks, I shall not get to the end of my story. After her husband's burial, Mrs. Thornimett spoke to me. 'I particularly wished the thousand pounds left now to Austin Clay,' she said, 'and I shall appropriate it to him at once.' 'Appropriate it in what manner?' I asked her. 'I should like to put it out to interest, that it may be accumulating for him,' she replied, 'so that at my death he may receive both principal and interest.' 'Then, if you live as long as it is to be hoped you will, madam, you may be bequeathing him two thousand pounds instead of one,' I observed to her. 'Mr. Knapley,' was her answer, 'if I choose to bequeath him three, it is my own money that I do it with; and I am responsible to no one.' She had taken my remark to be one of remonstrance, you see, in which spirit it was not made: had Mrs. Thornimett chosen to leave you the whole of her money she had been welcome to do it for me. 'Can you help me to a safe investment for him?' she resumed; and I promised to look about for it. The long and the short of it is, Mr. Clay, that I found both a safe and a profitable investment, and the one thousand pounds *has* swollen itself into two—as you will hear when the will is read."

"I am truly obliged for her kindness, and for the trouble you have taken," exclaimed Austin, with a glowing colour. "I never thought to get rich all at once."

"You only be prudent and take care of it," said Mr. Knapley. "Be as wise in its use as I and Mrs. Thornimett have been. It is the best advice I can give you."

"It is good advice, I know, and I thank you for it," warmly responded Austin.

"Ay. I can tell you that less than two thousand pounds has laid the foundation of many a great fortune."

To a young man whose salary is only two hundred a year, the unexpected accession to two thousand pounds, hard cash, seems like a great fortune. Not that Austin Clay cared so very much for a "great fortune" in itself; but he certainly did hope to achieve a competency, and to this end he made the best use of the talents bestowed upon him. He was not ambitious to die "worth a million;" he had the rare good sense to know that excess of means cannot bring excess of happiness. The richest man on earth cannot eat two dinners a day, or wear two coats at a time, or sit two thoroughbred horses at once, or sleep on two beds. To some, riches are a source of continual trouble. Unless rightly used, they cannot draw a man to heaven, or help him on his road thither. Austin Clay's ambition lay in becoming a powerful man of business; such as were the Messrs. Hunter. He would like to have men under him, of whom he should be the master; not to control them with an iron hand, to grind them to the dust, to hold them at a haughty distance, as if they were of one species of humanity and he of another. No; he would hold intact their relative positions of master and servant—none more strictly than he; but he would be their considerate friend, their firm advocate, regardful ever of their interests as he was of his own. He would like to have capital sufficient for all necessary business operations, that he might fulfil every obligation justly and honourably: so far, money would be welcome to Austin. Very welcome did the two thousand pounds sound in his ears, for they might be the stepping-stone to this. Not to the "great fortune" talked of by Mr. Knapley, who avowed freely his respect for millionaires: he did not care for that. They might also be a stepping-stone to something else—the very thought of which caused his face to glow and his veins to tingle—the winning of Florence Hunter. That he would win her, Austin fully believed now.

On the day previous to the funeral, in walking through the streets of Ketterford, Austin found himself suddenly seized by the shoulder. A window had been thrown open, and a fair arm (to speak with the gallantry due to the sex in general, rather than to that one arm in particular) was pushed out and laid upon him. His captor was Miss Gwinn.

"Come in," she briefly said.

Austin would have been better pleased to avoid her, but as she had thus summarily caught him, there was no help for it: to enter into a battle of contention with *her* might be productive of neither honour nor profit. He entered her sitting-room, and she motioned him to a chair.

"So you did not intend to call upon me during your stay in Ketterford, Austin Clay?"

"The melancholy occasion on which I am here precludes much visiting," was his guarded reply. "And my sojourn will be a short one."

"Don't be a hypocrite, young man, and use those unmeaning words. 'Melancholy occasion!' What did you care for Mrs. Thornimett, that her death should make you 'melancholy?'"

"Mrs. Thornimett was my dear and valued friend," he returned, with an emotion born of anger. "There are few, living, whom I would not rather have spared. I shall never cease to regret the not having arrived in time to see her before she died."

Miss Gwinn peered at him from her keen eyes, as if seeking to know whether this was false or true. Possibly she decided in favour of the latter, for her face somewhat relaxed its sternness. "What has Dr. Bevary told you of me and of my affairs?" she rejoined, passing abruptly to another subject.

"Not anything," replied Austin. He did not lift his eyes, and a scarlet flush dyed his brow as he spoke; nevertheless it was the strict truth. Miss Gwinn noted the signs of consciousness.

"You can equivocate, I see."

"Pardon me. I have not equivocated to you. Dr. Bevary has disclosed nothing; he has never spoken to me of your affairs. Why should he, Miss Gwinn?"

"Your face told a different tale."

"It did not tell an untruth, at any rate," he said, with some hauteur.

"Do you never see Dr. Bevary?"

"I see him sometimes."

"At the house of Mr. Hunter, I presume. How is *she*?"

Again the flush, whatever may have called it up, crimsoned Austin Clay's brow. "I do not know of whom you speak," he coldly said.

"Of Mrs. Hunter."

"She is in ill-health."

"Ill to be in danger of her life? I hear so."

"It may be. I cannot say."

"Do you know, Austin Clay, that I have a long, long account to settle with you?" she resumed, after a pause: "years and years have elapsed since, and I have never called upon you for it. Why should I?" she added, relapsing into a dreamy mood, and speaking to herself rather than to Austin; "the mischief was done, and could not be recalled. I once addressed a brief note to you at the office of the Messrs. Hunter, requesting you to give a letter, enclosed in it, to my brother. Why did you not?"

Austin was silent. He retained only too vivid a remembrance of the fact.

"Why did you not give it him, I ask?"

"I could not give it him, Miss Gwinn. When your letter reached me, your brother had already been at the office of the Messrs. Hunter, and was then on his road back to Ketterford. The enclosure was burnt unopened."

"Ay!" she passionately uttered, throwing her arms upwards in mental pain, as Austin had seen her do in the days gone by, and holding commune with herself, regardless of his presence, "such has been my fate through life. Thwarted, thwarted on all sides. For years and years I had lived but in the hope of finding him; the hope of it kept life in me: and when the time came, and I did find him, and was entering upon my revenge, then this brother of mine, who has been the second bane of my existence, stepped in and reaped the benefit. It was my fault. Why, in my exultation, did I tell him the man was found? Did I not know enough of his avarice, his needs, to have made sure that he would turn it to his own account? Why," she continued, battling with her hands as at some invisible adversary, "was I born with this strong principle of justice within me? Why, because he stepped in with his false claims and drew gold—a fortune—of the man, did I deem it a reason for dropping *my* revenge?—for letting it rest in abeyance? In abeyance it is still; and its unsatisfied claims are wearing out my heart and my life—"

"Miss Gwinn," interrupted Austin, at length, "I fancy you forget that I am present. Your family affairs have nothing to do with me, and I would prefer not to hear anything about them. I will wish you good day."

"True. They have nothing to do with you. I know not why I spoke before you, save that your sight angers me."

"Why so?" Austin could not forbear asking.

"Because you live on terms of friendship with that man. You are as his right hand in business; you are a welcome guest at his house; you regard and respect the house's mistress. Boy! but that she has not wilfully injured me; but that she is the sister of Dr. Bevary, I should—"

"I cannot listen to any discussion involving the name of Hunter," spoke Austin, in a repellant, resolute tone, the colour again flaming in his cheeks. "Allow me to bid you good day."

"Stay," she resumed, in a softer tone, "it is not with you personally that I am angry—"

An interruption came in the person of Lawyer Gwinn. He entered the room without his coat, a pen behind each ear, and a dirty straw hat on his head. It was probably his office attire in warm weather.

"I thought I heard a strange voice. How do you do, Mr. Clay?" he exclaimed, with much suavity.

Austin bowed. He said something to the effect that he was on the point of departing, and retreated to the door, bowing his final farewell to Miss Gwinn. Mr. Gwinn followed.

"Ketterford will have to congratulate you, Mr. Clay," he said. "I understand you inherit a very handsome sum from Mrs. Thornimett."

"Indeed!" frigidly replied Austin. "Mrs. Thornimett's will is not yet read. But Ketterford always knows everybody's business better than its own."

"Look you, my dear Mr. Clay," said the lawyer, holding him by the button-hole. "Should you require a most advantageous investment for your money—one that will turn you in cent. per cent. and no risk—I can help you to one. Should your inheritance be of the value of a thousand pounds, and you would like to double it—as all men, of course, do like—just trust it to me; I have the very thing now open."

Austin shook himself free—rather too much in the manner that he might have shaken himself from a serpent. "Whether my inheritance may be of the value of one thousand pounds or of ten thousand, Mr. Gwinn, I shall not require your services in the disposal of it. Good morning."

The lawyer looked after him as he strode away. "So, you carry it with a high hand to me, do you, my brave gentleman! with your vain person, and your fine clothes, and your imperious manner! Take you care! I hold your master under my thumb; I may next hold you!"

"The vile hypocrite!" exclaimed Austin to himself, walking all the faster to leave the lawyer's house behind him. "She is bad enough, with her hankering after revenge, and her fits of passion; but she is an angel of light compared to him. Heaven help Mr. Hunter! It would have been sufficient to have had *her* to fight, but to have *him*! Ay, Heaven help him!"

"How d'ye do, Mr. Clay?"

Austin returned the nod of the passing acquaintance, and continued his way, his thoughts reverting to Miss Gwinn.

"Poor thing! there are times when I pity her! Incomprehensible as the story is to me, I can feel compassion; for it was a heavy wrong done her, looking at it in the best light. She is not all bad; but for the wrong, and for her evil temper, she might have been different. There is something good in the hint I gathered now from her lips, if it be true—that she suffered her own revenge to drop into abeyance, because her brother had pursued Mr. Hunter to drain money from him: she would not go upon him in both ways. Yes, there was something in it both noble and generous, if those terms can ever be applied to—"

"Austin Clay, I am sure! How are you?"

Austin resigned his hand to the new comer, who claimed it. His thoughts could not be his own to-day.

The funeral of Mrs. Thornimett took place. Her mortal remains were laid beside her husband, there to repose peacefully until the last trump shall sound. On the return of the mourners to the house, the will was read, and Austin found himself the undoubted possessor of two thousand pounds. Several little treasures, in the shape of books, drawings, and home knicknacks, were also left to him. He saw after the packing of these, and the day following the funeral he returned to London.

It was evening when he arrived; and he proceeded without delay to the house of Mr. Hunter—ostensibly to report himself, really to obtain a sight of Florence, for which his tired heart was yearning. The drawing-room was lighted up, by which he judged that they had friends with them. Mr. Hunter met him in the hall: never did a visitor's knock sound at his door but Mr. Hunter, in his nervous restlessness, strove to watch who it might be that entered. Seeing Austin, his face acquired a shade of brightness, and he came forward with an outstretched hand.

"But you have visitors," Austin said, when greetings were over, and Mr. Hunter was drawing him towards the stairs. He wore deep mourning, but was not in evening dress.

"As if anybody will care for the cut of your coat!" cried Mr. Hunter. "There's Mrs. Hunter wrapped up in a woollen shawl."

The room was gay with light and dress, with many voices, and with music. Florence was seated at the piano, playing, and singing in a glee with others. Austin, silently greeting those whom he knew as he passed, made his way to Mrs. Hunter. She was wrapped in a warm shawl, as her husband had said; but she appeared better than usual.

"I am so glad to see you looking well," Austin whispered, his earnest tone betraying deep feeling.

"And I am glad to see you here again," she replied, smiling, as she held his hand. "We have missed you, Austin. Yes, I feel better! but it is only a temporary improvement. So you have lost poor Mrs. Thornimett. She died before you could reach her."

"She did," replied Austin, with a grave face. "I wish we could get transported to places, in case of necessity as quickly as the telegraph brings us news that we are wanted. A senseless and idle wish, you will say; but it would have served me in this case. She asked after me twice in her last half hour."

"Austin," breathed Mrs. Hunter, "was it a happy death-bed? Was she ready to go?"

"Quite, quite," he answered, a look of enthusiasm illumining his face. "She had been ready long."

"Then we need not mourn for her; rather praise God that she is taken. Oh, Austin, what a happy thing it must be for such to die! But you are young and hopeful; you cannot understand that, yet."

So, Mrs. Hunter had learnt that great truth! Some years before, she had not so spoken to the wife of John Baxendale, when *she* was waiting in daily expectation of being called on her journey. It had come to her ere her time of trial—as the dying woman had told her it would.

The singing ceased, and in the movement which it occasioned in the room, Austin left Mrs. Hunter's side, and stood within the embrasure of the window, half hidden by the curtains. The air was pleasant on that warm summer night, and Florence, resigning her place at the instrument to some other lady, stole to the window to inhale its freshness. There she saw Austin. She had not heard him enter the room—did not know, in fact, that he was back from Ketterford.

"Oh!" she uttered, in the sudden revulsion of feeling that the sight brought to her, "is it you?"

He quietly took her hands in his, and looked down at her. Had it been to save her life, she could not have helped betraying emotion.

"Are you glad to see me, Florence?" he softly whispered.

She coloured even to tears. Glad! The time might come when she should be able to tell him so; but that time was not yet.

"Mrs. Hunter is glad of my return," he continued, in the same low tone, sweeter to her ear than all music. "She says I have been missed. Is it so, Florence?"

"And what have you been doing?" asked Florence, not knowing in the least what she said in her confusion, as she left his question unanswered, and drew her hands away from him.

"I have not been doing much, save the seeing a dear old friend laid in the earth. You know that Mrs. Thornimett is dead. She died before I got there."

"Papa told us that. He heard from you two or three times, I think. How you must regret it! But why did they not send for you in time?"

"It was only the last day that danger was apprehended," replied Austin. "She grew worse suddenly. You cannot think, Florence, how strangely this gaiety"—he half turned to the room—"contrasts with the scenes I have left: the holy calm of her death-chamber, the laying of her in the grave."

"An unwelcome contrast, I am sure it must be."

"It jars on the mind. All events, essentially of the world, let them be ever so necessary or useful, must do so, when contrasted with the solemn scenes of life's close. But how soon we forget those solemn scenes, and live in the world again!"

"Austin," she gently whispered, "I do not like to talk of death. It reminds me of the dread that is ever oppressing me."

"She looks so much better as to surprise me," was his answer, unconscious that it betrayed his undoubted cognisance of the "dread" she spoke of.

"If it would but last!" sighed Florence. "To prolong mamma's life, I think I would sacrifice mine."

"No, you would not, Florence—in mercy to her. If called upon to lose her you would grow reconciled to it; to do so, is in the order of nature. *She* could not spare *you*."

Florence believed that she never could grow reconciled to it: she often wondered *how* she should bear it when the time came. But there rose up before her now, as she spoke with Austin, one cheering promise, "As thy day is, so shall thy strength be."

"What should you say, if I tell you I have come into a fortune!" resumed Austin, in a lighter tone.

"I should say—But, is it true?" broke off Florence.

"Not true, as you and Mr. Hunter would count fortunes," smiled Austin; "but true, as poor I, born without silver spoons in my mouth, and expecting to work hard for all I shall ever possess, have looked upon them. Mrs. Thornimett has behaved to me most kindly, most generously; she has bequeathed to me two thousand pounds."

"I am delighted to hear it," said Florence, her glad eyes sparkling. "Never call yourself poor again."

"I cannot call myself rich, as Mr. and Mrs. Hunter compute riches. But, Florence, it may be a stepping-stone to become so."

"A stepping-stone to become what?" demanded Dr. Bevary, breaking in upon the conference.

"Rich," said Austin, turning to the doctor. "I am telling Florence that I have come into some money since I went away."

Mr. Hunter and others were gathering around them, and the conversation became general. "What is that, Clay?" asked Mr. Hunter. "You have come into a fortune, do you say?"

"I said, *not* into a fortune, sir, as those accustomed to fortune would estimate it. That great physician, standing there and listening to me, he would laugh at the sum: I daresay he makes more in six months. But it may prove a stepping-stone to fortune, and to—to other desirable things."

"Do not speak so vaguely," cried the doctor, in his quaint fashion. "Define the 'desirable things.' Come! it's my turn now."

"I am not sure that they have taken a sufficiently tangible shape as yet, to be defined," returned Austin, in the same tone. "You might laugh at them for day-dreams."

Unwittingly his eye rested for a moment upon Florence. Did she deem the day-dreams might refer to her, that her eye-lids should droop, and her cheeks turn scarlet? Dr. Bevary noticed both the look and the signs; Mr. Hunter saw neither.

"Day-dreams would be enchanting as an eastern fairy-tale, only that they never get realized," interposed one of the fair guests, with a pretty simper, directed to Austin Clay and his attractions.

"I will realize mine," he returned, rather too confidently, "Heaven helping me!"

"A better stepping-stone, that help, to rely upon, than the money you have come into," said Dr. Bevary, with one of his peculiar nods.

"True, doctor," replied Austin. "But may not the money have come from the same helping source? Heaven, you know, vouchsafes to work with humble instruments."

The last few sentences had been interchanged in a low tone. They now passed into the general circle, and the evening went on to its close.

Austin and Dr. Bevary were the last to leave the house. They quitted it together, and the doctor passed his arm within Austin's as they walked on.

"Well," said he, "and what have you been doing at Ketterford?"

"I have told you, doctor. Leaving my dear old friend and relative in her grave; and, realizing the fact that she has bequeathed to me this money."

"Ah, yes; I heard that," returned the doctor. "You've been seeing friends too, I suppose. Did you happen to meet the Gwinns?"

"Once. I was passing the house, and Miss Gwinn laid hands upon me from the window, and commanded me in. I got out again as soon as I could. Her brother made his appearance as I was leaving."

"And what did he say to you?" asked the doctor, in a tone meant to be especially light and careless.

"Nothing; except that he told me if I wanted a safe and profitable investment for the money I had inherited under Mrs. Thornimett's will, he could help me to one. I cut him very short, sir."

"What did *she* say?" resumed Dr. Bevary. "Did she begin upon her family affairs—as she is rather fond of doing?"

"Well," said Austin, his tone quite as careless as the doctor's, "I did not give her the opportunity. Once, when she seemed inclined to do so, I stopped her; telling her that her private affairs were no concern of mine, neither should I listen to them."

"Quite right, my young friend," emphatically spoke the doctor.

Not another word was said until they came to Daffodil's Delight. Here they wished each other good night The doctor continued his way to his home, and Austin turned down towards Peter Quale's.

But what could be the matter? Had Daffodil's Delight miscalculated the time, believing it to be day, instead of night? Women leaned out of their windows in night-caps; children had crept from their beds and come forth to tumble into the gutter naked, as some of them literally were; men crowded the doorway of the Bricklayers' Arms, and stood about with pipes and pint pots; all were in a state of rampant excitement. Austin laid hold of the first person who appeared sober enough to listen to him. It happened to be a woman, Mrs. Dunn.

"What is this?" he exclaimed. "Have you all come into a fortune?" the recent conversation at Mr. Hunter's probably helping him to the remark.

"Better nor that," shrieked Mrs. Dunn. "Better nor *that*, a thousand times! We have circumvented the masters, and got our ends, and now we shall just have all we want—roast goose and apple pudding for dinner, and plenty of beer to wash it down with."

"But what is it that you have got?" pursued Austin, who was completely at sea.

"Got! why, we have got the Strike," she replied, in joyful excitement. "Pollocks' men struck to-day. Where have you been, sir, not to have heered on it?"

At that moment a fresh crowd came jostling down Daffodil's Delight, and Austin was parted from the lady. Indeed, she rushed up to the mob to follow in their wake. Many other ladies followed in their wake—half Daffodil's Delight, if one might judge by numbers. Shouting, singing, exulting, dancing; it seemed as if they had, for the nonce, gone mad. Sam Shuck, in his long-tailed coat, ornamented with its holes and its slits, was leading the van, his voice hoarse, his face red, his legs and arms executing a war-dance of exaltation. He it was who had got up the excitement and was keeping it up, shouting fiercely: "Hurrah for the work of this day! Rule Britanniar! Britons never shall be slaves! The Strike has begun, friends! H—o—o—o—o—o—r—rah! Three cheers for the Strike!"

Yes. The Strike had begun.

IV

Agitation

The men of an influential metropolitan building firm had struck, because their employers declined to accede to certain demands, and Daffodil's Delight was, as you have seen, in a high state of excitement, particularly the female part of it. The men said they struck for a diminution in the hours of labour; the masters told them they struck for an increase of wages. Seeing that the non-contents wanted the hours reduced and *not* the pay, it appears to me that you may call it which you like.

The Messrs. Hunters' men—with whom we have to do, for it was they who chiefly filled Daffodil's Delight—though continuing their work as usual, were in a most unsettled state; as was the case in the trade generally. The smouldering discontent might have died away peacefully enough, and probably would, but that certain spirits made it their business to fan it into a flame.

A few days went on. One evening Sam Shuck posted himself in an angle formed by the wall at the top of Daffodil's Delight. It was the hour for the men to quit work; and, as they severally passed him on their road home, Sam's arm was thrust forward, and a folded bit of paper put into their hands. A mysterious sort of missive apparently; for, on opening the paper, it was found to contain only these words, in the long, sprawling hand of Sam himself: "Barn at the back of Jim Dunn's. Seven o'clock."

Behind the house tenanted by the Dunns were premises occupied until recently by a cowkeeper. They comprised, amidst other accommodation, a large barn, or shed. Being at present empty, and to let, Sam thought he could do no better than take French leave to make use of it.

The men hurried over their tea, or supper (some took one on leaving work for the night, some the other, some a mixture of both, and some neither), that they might attend to the invitation of Sam. Peter Quale was seated over a substantial dish of batter pudding, a bit of neck of mutton baked in the midst of it, when he was interrupted by the entrance of John Baxendale, who had stepped in from his own rooms next door.

"Be you a going to this meeting, Quale?" Baxendale asked, as he took a seat.

"I don't know nothing about it," returned Peter. "I saw Slippery Sam a giving out papers, so I guessed there was something in the wind. He took care to pass me over. I expect I'm the greatest eyesore Sam has got just now. Have a bit?" added Peter, unceremoniously, pointing to the dish before him with his knife.

"No, thank ye; I have just had tea at home. That's the paper"—laying it open on the table-cloth. "Sam Shuck is just now cock-a-hoop with this strike."

"He is no more cock-a-hoop than the rest of Daffodil's Delight is," struck in Mrs. Quale, who had finished her own meal, and was at leisure to talk. "The men and women is all a going mad together, I think, and Slippery Sam's leading 'em on. Suppose you all do strike—which is what they are hankering after—what good 'll it bring?"

"That's just it," replied Baxendale. "One can't see one's way clear. The agitation might do us some good, but it might do us a deal of harm; so that one doesn't know what to be at. Quale, I'll go to the meeting, if you will?"

"If I go, it will be to give 'em a piece of my mind," retorted Peter.

"Well, it's only right that different sides should be heard. Sam 'll have it all his own way else."

"He'll manage to get that, by the appearance things wears," said Mrs. Quale, wrathfully. "How you men can submit to be led by such a fellow as him, just because his tongue is capable of persuading you that black's white, is a marvel to me. Talk of women being soft! let the men talk of theirselves. Hold up a finger to 'em, and they'll go after it: like the Swiss cows Peter read of the other day, a flocking in a line after their leader, behind each other's tails."

"I wish I knew what was right," said Baxendale, "or which course would turn out best for us."

"I'd be off and listen to what's going on, at any rate," urged Mrs. Quale.

The barn was filling. Sam Shuck, perched upon Mrs. Dunn's washing-tub turned upside down, which had been rolled in for the occasion, greeted each group as it arrived with a gracious nod. Sam appeared to be progressing in the benefits he had boasted to his wife he should derive, inasmuch as that the dilapidated clothes had been discarded for better ones: and he stood on the tub's end in all the glory of a black frock coat, a crimson neck-tie with lace ends, and peg-top pantaloons: the only attire (as a ready-made outfitting shop had assured him) that a gentleman could wear. Sam's eye grew less complacent when it rested on Peter Quale, who was coming in with John Baxendale.

"This is a pleasure we didn't expect," said he.

"Maybe not," returned Peter Quale, drily. "The barn's open to all."

"Of course it is," glibly said Sam, putting a good face upon the matter. "All fair and above board, is our mottor: which is more than them native enemies of ours, the masters, can say: they hold their meetings in secret, with closed doors."

"Not in secret—do they?" asked Robert Darby. "I have not heard of that."

"They meet in their own homes, and they shut out strangers," replied Sam. "I'd like to know what you call that, but meeting in secret?"

"I should not call it secret; I should call it private," decided Darby, after a minute's pause, given to realize the question. "We might do the same. Our homes are ours, and we can shut out whom we please."

"Of course we *might*," contended Sam. "But we like better to be open; and if a few of us assemble together to consult on the present aspect of affairs, we do it so that the masters, if they choose, might come and hear us. Things are not equalized in this world. Let us attempt secret meetings, and see how soon we should be looked up by the law, and accused of hatching treason and sedition, and all the rest of it. That sharp-eyed *Times* newspaper would be the first to set on us. There's one law for the masters, and another for the men."

"Is that Slippery Sam?" exclaimed a new comer, at this juncture. "Where did you get that fine new toggery, Shuck?"

The disrespectful interruption was spoken in simple surprise: no insidious meaning prompting it. Sam Shuck had appeared in ragged attire so long, that the change could not fail to be remarkable. Sam loftily turned a deaf ear to the remark, and continued his address.

"I am sure that most of you can't fail to see that things have come to a crisis in our trade. The moment that brought it, was when that great building firm refused the reasonable demands of their men; and the natural consequence of which was a strike. Friends, I have been just *riled* ever since. I have watched you go to work day after day like tame cats, the same as if nothing had happened; and I have said to myself: 'Have those men of Hunter's got souls within them, or have they got none?'"

"I don't suppose we have parted from our souls," struck in a voice.

"You have parted with the feelings of them, at any rate," rejoined Sam, beginning to dance in the excitement of contention, but remembering in time that his *terra firma* was only a creaky tub. "What's that you ask me? How have you parted with them? Why, by not following up the strike. If you possessed a grain of the independence of free men, you'd have hoisted your colours before now; what would have been the result? Why, the men of other firms in the trade would have followed suit, and all struck in a body. It's the only way that will bring the masters to reason: the only way by which we can hope to obtain our rights."

"You see there's no knowing what would be the end of a strike, Shuck," argued John Baxendale.

"There's no knowing what may be the inside of a pie until you cut him open," said Jim Dunn, whose politics were the same as Mr. Shuck's, red-hot for a strike. "But 'tain't many as 'ud shrink from putting in the knife to see."

The men laughed, and greeted Jim Dunn with applause.

"I put it to you all," resumed Sam, who took his share of laughing with the rest, "whether there's sense or not in what I say. Are we likely to get our grievances redressed by the masters, unless we force it? Never: not if we prayed our hearts out."

"Never," and "never," murmured sundry voices.

"What *are* our grievances?" demanded Peter Quale, putting the question in a matter-of-fact tone, as if he really asked for information.

"Listen!" ironically exclaimed Sam. "He asks what our grievances are! I'll answer you, Quale. They are many and great. Are we not kept to work like beasts of burden, ten hours a day? Does that leave us time for the recreation of our wearied bodies, for the improvement of our minds, for the education of our children, for the social home intercourse in the bosoms of our families? By docking the day's labour to nine hours—or to eight, which we shall get, may be, after awhile," added Sam, with a wink—"it would leave us the extra hour, and be a blessing."

Sam carried the admiring room with him. That hard, disbelieving Peter Quale, interrupted the cheering.

"A blessing, or the conterairy, as it might turn out," cried he. "It's easy to talk of education, and self-improvement; but how many is there that would use the accorded hour that way?"

"Another grievance is our wages," resumed Sam, drowning the words, not caring to court discussion on what might be a weak point. "We call ourselves men, and Englishmen, and yet we lie down contented with five-and-sixpence a day. Do you know what our trade gets in Australia? Oh, you do, some of you? then I'll tell those that don't. From twelve to fifteen shillings per day: and even more than that. *Twelve shillings!* and that's the minimum rate of pay," slowly repeated Sam, lifting up his arm and one peg-top to give emphasis to the words.

A murmur of envy at the coveted rate of pay in Australia shook the room to the centre.

"But the price of provisions and other necessaries is enormous in that quarter," debated Abel White. "So it may come to the same in the end—be about as broad as long. Old father and me was talking about it last night."

"If everybody went in for your old father's sentiments, we should soon be like him—in our dotage," loftily observed Sam.

"But things are dear there," persisted Sam's antagonist. "I have heard what is sometimes given for shoes there; but I'm afraid to say, it was so much. The wages in Australia can't be any guide for us."

"No, they can't," said Peter Quale. "Australia is one place, and this is another. Where's the use of bringing up that?"

"Oh, of course not," sarcastically uttered Sam. "Anything that tends to show how we are put upon, and how we might be made more comfortable, it's of no use bringing up. The long and the short of it is this: we want to be regarded as MEN: to have our voices considered, and our plaints attended to; to be put altogether upon a better footing. Little enough is it we ask at present: only for a modicum of ease in our day's hard labour, just the thin end of the wedge inserted to give it. That's all we are agitating for. It depends upon ourselves whether we get it or not. Let us display manly courage and join the strike, and it is ours to-morrow."

The response did not come so quickly as Sam deemed it ought. He went on in a persuasive, ringing tone.

"Consider the wives of your bosoms; consider your little children; consider yourselves. Were you born into the world to be slaves—blackymoors; to be ground into the dust with toil? Never."

"Never," uproariously echoed three parts of the room.

"The motto of a true man is, or ought to be, 'Do as little as you can, and get as much for it;'" said Sam, dancing in his enthusiasm, and thereby nearly losing his perch on the tub. "With an hour's work less a day, and the afternoon holiday on the Saturday, we shall—"

"What's the good of a afternoon Saturday holiday? We don't want that, Sam Shuck."

This ignominious interruption to the proceedings came from a lady. Buzzing round the entrance door and thrusting in their heads at a square hole, which might originally have been intended for a window were a dozen or two of the gentler sex. This irregularity had not been unobserved by the chairman, who faced them: the chairman's audience, densely packed, had their backs that way. It was not an orthodox adjunct to a trade meeting, that was certain, and the chairman would probably have ordered the ladies away, had he deemed there was a chance of his getting obeyed; but too many of them had the reputation of being the grey mares. So he winked at the irregularity, and had added one or two flourishes of oratory for their especial ears. The interruption came from Mrs. Cheek, Timothy Cheek's wife.

"What's the good of a afternoon Saturday holiday? We don't want that, Sam Shuck. Just when we be up to our eyes in muck and cleaning, our places routed out till you can't see the colour of the boards, for brooms, and pails, and soap and water, and the chairs and things is all topsy-turvy, one upon another, so as the children have to be sent out to grub in the gutter, for there ain't no place for 'em indoors, do you think we want the men poking their noses in? No; and they'd better not try it on. Women have got tempers given to 'em as well as you."

"And tongues too," rejoined Sam, unmindful of the dignity of his office.

"It is to be hoped they have," retorted Mrs. Cheek, not inclined to be put down; and her sentiments appeared to be warmly joined in by the ladies generally. "Don't you men go a agitating for the Saturday's half-holiday! What 'ud you do with it, do you suppose? Why, just sot it away at the publics."

Some confusion ensued; and the women were peremptorily ordered to mind their own business, and "make theirselves scarce," which not one of them attempted to obey. When the commotion had subsided, a very respectable man took up the discourse—George Stevens.

"The gist of the whole question is this," he said: "Will agitation do us good, or will it do us harm? We look upon ourselves as representing one interest; the masters consider they represent another. If it comes to open warfare between the two, the strongest would win."

"In other words, whichever side's funds held out the longest," said Robert Darby. "That is as I look upon it."

"Just so," returned Stevens. "I cannot say, seeing no farther than we can see at present, that a strike would be advisable."

"Stevens, do you want to better yourself, or not?" asked Sam Shuck.

"I'd be glad enough to better myself, if I saw my way clear to do it," was the reply. "But I don't."

"We don't want no strikes," struck in a shock-headed hard-working man. "What is it we want to strike for? We have got plenty of work, and full wages. A strike won't fill our pockets. Them may vote for strikes that like 'em; I'll keep to my work."

Partial applause.

"It is as I said," cried Sam. "There's poor, mean-spirited creatures among you, as won't risk the loss of a day's pay for the common good, or put out a hand to help the less fortunate. I'd rather be buried alive, five feet under the earth, than I'd show cat so selfish."

"What is the interest of one of us is the interest of all," observed Stevens. "And a strike, if we went into it, would either benefit us all in the end, or make us all suffer. It is sheer nonsense to attempt to make out that one man's interest is different from another's; our interests are the same. I'd vote for striking to-morrow, if I were sure we should come out of it with whole skins, and get what we struck for: but I must see that a bit clearer first."

"How can we get it, unless we try for it?" demanded Sam. "If the masters find we're all determined, they'll give in to us. I appeal to you all"—raising his hands over the room—"whether the masters can do without us?"

"That has got to be seen," said Peter Quale, significantly. "One thing is plain: we could not do without them."

"Nor they without us—nor they without us," struck in voices from various parts of the barn.

"Then why shilly-shally about the question of a strike?" asked Sam of the barn, in a glib tone of reason. "If a universal strike were on, the masters would pretty soon make terms that would end it. Why, a six months' strike would drive half of them into the *Gazette*—"

"But it might drive us into the workhouse at the same time," interrupted John Baxendale.

"Let me finish," went on Sam; "it's not perlite to take up a man in the middle of a sentence. I say that a six months' strike would send many of the masters to the bankruptcy court. Well now, there has been a question debated among us"—Sam lowered his voice—"whether it would not be policy to let things go on quietly, as they are, till next spring—"

"A question among who?" interposed Peter Quale, regardless of the reproof just administered to John Baxendale.

"Never you mind who," returned Sam, with a wink: "among those that are hard at work for your interest. With their contracts for the season signed, and their works in full progress, say about next May, then would be the time for a strike to tell upon the masters. However, it has been thought better not to delay it. The future's but an uncertainty: the present is ours, and so must the strike be. *Have* you wives?" he pathetically continued; "*have* you children? *have* you spirits of your own? Then you will all, with one accord, go in for the strike."

"But what are our wives and children to do while the strike is on?" asked Robert Darby. "You say yourself it might last six months, Shuck. Who would support them?"

"Who!" rejoined Sam, with an indignant air, as if the question were a superfluous one. "Why the Trades' Unions, of course. *That's* all settled. The Unions are prepared to take care of all who are out on strike, standing up, like brave Britons, for their privileges, and keep 'em like fighting-cocks. Hooroar for that blessed boon, the Trades' Unions!"

"Hooroar for the Trades' Unions!" was shouted in chorus. "Keep us like fighting-cocks, will they! Hooroar!"

"Much good you'll get from the Trades' Unions!" burst forth a dissentient voice. "They are the greatest pests as ever was allowed in a free country."

The opposition caused no little commotion. Standing by the door, having pushed his way through the surrounding women, who had *not* made themselves "scarce," was a man in a flannel jacket, a cap in his hand, and his head white with mortar. He was looking excited as he spoke.

"This is not regular," said Sam Shuck, displaying authority. "You have no business here: you don't belong to us."

"Regular or irregular, I'll speak my mind," was the answer. "I have been at work for Jones the builder, down yonder. I have done my work steady and proper, and I have had my pay. A man comes up to me yesterday and says, 'You must join the Trades' Union.' 'No,' says I, 'I shan't; I don't want nothing of the Trades' Union, and the Union don't want nothing of me.' So they goes to my master. 'If you keep on employing this man, your other men will strike,' they says to him; and he, being in a small way, got intimidated, and sent me off to-day. And here I am, throwed out of work, and I have got a sick wife and nine young children to keep. Is that justice? or is it tyranny? Talk about emancipating the slaves! let us emancipate ourselves at home."

"Why don't you join the Union?" cried Sam. "All do, who are good men and true."

"All good men and true *don't*," dissented the man. "Many of the best workmen among us won't have anything to do with Unions; and you know it, Sam Shuck."

"Just clear out of this," said Sam.

"When I've had my say," returned the man, "not before. If I would join the Union, I can't. To join it, I must pay five shillings, and I have not got them to pay. With such a family as mine, you may guess every shilling is forestalled afore it comes in. I kept myself to myself, doing my work in quiet, and interfering with nobody. Why should they interfere with me?"

"If you have been in full work, five shillings is not much to pay to the Union," sneered Sam.

"If I had my pockets filled with five-shilling pieces, I would not pay one to it," fearlessly retorted the man. "Is it right that a free-born Englishman should give in to such a system of intimidation? No: I never will. You talk of the masters being tyrants: it's you who are the tyrants, one to another. What is one workman better than his fellow, that he should lay down laws and say, You shall do this, and you shall do that, or you shan't be allowed to work at all? That rule you want to get passed—that a skilled, thorough workman shouldn't do a full day's work because some of his fellows can't—who's agitating for it? Why, naturally those that can't or won't do the full work. Would an honest, capable man go in for it? Of course he'd not. I tell you what"—turning his eyes on the room—"the Trades' Unions have been called a protection to the working man; but, if you don't take care, they'll grow into a curse. When Sam Shuck, and other good-for-naughts like him, what never did a full week's work for their families yet, are paid in gold and silver to spread incendiarism among you, it's time you looked to yourselves."

He turned away as he spoke; and Sam, in a dance of furious passion, danced off his tub. The interlude had not tended to increase the feeling of the men in Sam's favour—that is, in the cause he advocated. Not a man present but wanted to better himself could he do so with safety, but they were afraid to enter on aggressive measures. Indiscriminate talking ensued; diverse opinions were disputed, and the meeting was prolonged to a late hour. Finally the men dispersed as they came, nothing having been resolved upon. A few set their faces resolutely against the proposed strike; a few were red-hot for it; but the majority were undecided, and liable to be swayed either way.

"It will come," nodded Sam Shuck, as he went home to a supper of pork chops and gin-and-water.

But Sam was destined to be—as he would have expressed it—circumvented. It cannot be supposed that this unsatisfactory state of things was unnoticed by the masters: and they took their measures accordingly. Forming themselves into an association, they discussed the measures best to be adopted, and determined upon a lock-out; that is, to close their yards until the firm, whose workmen had struck, should resume work. They also resolved to employ only those men who would sign an agreement, or memorandum, affirming that they were not connected with any society which interfered with the arrangements of the master whose service they entered, or with the hours of labour, and acknowledging the rights both of masters and men to enter into any trade arrangements on which they might mutually agree. This paper of agreement was not relished by the men at all; they styled it "the odious document." Neither was the lock-out relished: it was of course equivalent, in one sense, to a strike; only that the initiative had come from the masters' side, and not from theirs. It commenced early in August. Some of the masters closed their works without a word of explanation to their men: in one sense it was not needed, for the men knew of the measure beforehand. Mr. Hunter chose to assemble them together, and state what he was about to do. Somewhat of his old energy appeared to have been restored to him for the moment, as he stood before them and spoke—Austin Clay by his side.

"You have brought it upon yourselves," he said, in answer to a remark from one who boldly, but respectfully, asked whether it was fair to resort to a lock-out, and so punish all alike, contents and non-contents. "I will meet the question upon your own grounds. When the Messrs. Pollocks' men struck because their demands, to work nine hours a day, were not acceded to, was it not in contemplation that you should join them—that the strike should be universal? Come, answer me candidly."

The men, true and honest, did not deny it.

"And possibly by this time you would have struck," said Mr. Hunter. "How much more 'fair' would that have been towards us, than this locking-out is towards you? Do you suppose that you alone are to meet and pass your laws, saying you will coerce the masters, and that the masters will not pass laws in return? Nonsense, my men!"

A pause.

"When have the masters attempted to interfere with your privileges, either by saying that your day's toil shall consist of longer hours, or by diminishing your wages, and threatening to turn you off if you do not fall in with the alteration? Never. Masters have rights as well as men; but some of you, of late, have appeared to ignore the fact. Let me ask you another question: Were you well treated under me, or were you not? Have I shown myself solicitous for your interests, for your welfare? Have I ever oppressed you, ever put upon you?"

No, Mr. Hunter had never sought to oppress them: they acknowledged it freely. He had ever been a good master.

"My men, let me give you my opinion. While condemning your conduct, your semblance of discontent—it has been semblance rather than reality—I have been sorry for you, for it is not with you that the chief blame lies. You have suffered evil persuaders to get access to your ears, and have been led away by their pernicious counsels. The root of the evil lies there. I wish you could bring your own good sense to bear upon these points, and to see with your own eyes. If so, there will be nothing to prevent our resuming together amicable relations; and, for my own part, I care not how soon the time shall come. The works are for the present closed.

PART THE THIRD

I

A Premature Avowal

Daffodil's Delight was in all the glory of the lock-out. The men, having nothing to do, improved their time by enjoying themselves; they stood about the street, or lounged at their doors, smoking their short pipes and quaffing draughts of beer. Let money run ever so short, you will generally see that the beer and the pipes can be found. As yet, the evils of being out of work were not felt; for weekly pay, sufficient for support, was supplied them by the Union Committee. The men were in high spirits—in that sort of mood implied by the words "Never say die," which phrase was often in their mouths. They expressed themselves determined to hold out; and this determination was continually fostered by the agents of the Union, of whom Sam Shuck was the chief: chief as regarded Daffodil's Delight—inferior as regarded other agents elsewhere. Many of the more temperate of the men, who had not particularly urged the strike, were warm supporters now of the general opinion, for they regarded the lock-out as an unwarrantable piece of tyranny on the part of the masters. As to the ladies, they were over-warm partisans, generally speaking, making the excitement, the unsettled state of Daffodil's Delight, an excuse for their own idleness (they are only too ready to do so when occasion offers), and collected in groups round the men, or squatted themselves on door steps, proclaiming their opinion of existing things, and boasting that they'd hold out for their rights till death.

It was almost like a summer's day. Seated in a chair at the bottom of her garden, just within the gate, was Mary Baxendale. Not that she was there to join in the gossip of the women, little knots of whom were dotting the street, or had any intention of joining in it: she was simply sitting there for air.

Mary Baxendale was fading. Never very strong, she had, for the last year or two, been gradually declining, and, with the excessive heat of the past summer, her remaining strength appeared to have gone out. Her occupation, that of a seamstress, had not tended to keep her in health; she had a great deal of work offered her, her skill being superior, and she had sat at it early and late. Mary was thoughtful and conscientious, and she was anxious to contribute a full share to the home support. Her father had married again, had now two young children, and it almost appeared to Mary as if she were an interloper in the paternal home. Not that the new Mrs. Baxendale made her feel this: she was a bustling, hearty woman, fond of show and spending, and of setting off her babies; but she was kind to Mary.

The capability of exertion appeared to be past, and Mary's days were chiefly spent in a quiescent state of rest, and in frequently sitting out of doors. This day—it was now the beginning of September—was an unusually bright one, and she drew her invalid shawl round her, and leaned back in her seat, looking out on the lively scene, at the men and women congregating in the road, and inhaling the fresh air. At least, as fresh as it could be got in Daffodil's Delight.

"How do you feel to-day, Mary?"

The questioner was Mrs. Quale. She had come out of her house in her bonnet and shawl, bent on some errand and stopped to accost Mary.

"I am pretty well to-day. That is, I should be, if it were not for the weakness."

"Weakness, ay!" cried Mrs. Quale, in a snapping sort of tone, for she was living in a state of chronic tartness, not approving of matters in general just now. "And what have you had this morning to fortify you against the weakness?"

A faint blush rose to Mary's thin face. The subject was a sore one to the mind of Mrs. Quale, and that lady was not one to spare her tongue. The fact was, that at the present moment, and for some little time past, Mary's condition and appetite had required unusual nourishment; but, since the lock-out, this had not been procurable by John Baxendale. Sufficient food the household had as yet, but it was of a plain coarse sort, not suitable for Mary; and Mrs. Quale, bitter enough against the existing condition of things before, touching the men and their masters, was not by this rendered less so. Poor Mary, in her patient meekness, would have subsided into her grave with famine, rather than complain of what she saw no help for.

"Did you have an egg at eleven o'clock?"

"Not this morning. I did not feel greatly to care for it."

"Rubbish!" responded Mrs. Quale. "I may say I don't care for the moon, because I know I can't get it."

"But I really did not feel to have any appetite just then," repeated Mary.

"And if you had an appetite, I suppose you couldn't have been any the nearer satisfying it!" returned Mrs. Quale, in a raised voice. "You let your stomach get empty, and, after a bit, the craving goes off and sickness comes on, and then you say you have no appetite. But, there! it is not your fault; where's the use of my—"

"Why, Mary, girl, what's the matter?"

The interruption to Mrs. Quale proceeded from Dr. Bevary. He was passing the gate with Miss Hunter. They stopped, partly at sight of Mary, who was looking strikingly ill, partly at the commotion Mrs. Quale was making. Neither of them had known that Mary was in this state. Mrs. Quale was the first to take up the discourse.

"She don't look over flourishing, do she, sir?—do she Miss Florence? She have been as bad as this—oh, for a fortnight, now."

"Why did you not send my uncle word, Mary?" spoke Florence, impulsive in the cause of kindness, as she had been when a child. "I am sure he would have come to see you."

"You are very kind, Miss, and Dr. Bevary, also," said Mary. "I could not think of troubling him with my poor ailments, especially as I feel it would be useless. I don't think anybody can do me good on this side the grave, sir."

"Tush, tush!" interposed Dr. Bevary. "That's what many sick people say; but they get well in spite of it. Let us see you a bit closer," he added, going inside the gate. "And now tell me how you feel."

"I am just sinking, sir, as it seems to me; sinking out of life, without much ailment to tell of. I have a great deal of fever at night, and a dry cough. It is not so much consumption as—"

"Who told you it was consumption?" interrupted Dr. Bevary.

"Some of the women about here call it so, sir. My step-mother does: but I should say it was more of a waste."

"Your step-mother is fond of talking of what she knows nothing about, and so are the women," remarked Dr. Bevary. "Have you much appetite?"

"Yes, and that's the evil of it," struck in Mrs. Quale, determined to lose no opportunity of propounding her view of the case. "A pretty time this is for folks to have appetites, when there's not a copper being earned. I wish all strikes and lock-outs was put down by law, I do. Nothing comes of 'em but empty cubbarts."

"Your cupboard need not be any the emptier for a lock-out," said Dr. Bevary, who sometimes, when conversing with the women of Daffodil's Delight, would fall familiarly into their mode of speech.

"No, I know that; we have been providenter than that, sir," returned Mrs. Quale. "A pity but what others could say the same. You might take a walk through Daffodil's Delight, sir, from one end of it to the other, and not find half a dozen cubbarts with plenty in 'em just now. Serve 'em right! they should have put by for a rainy day."

"Ah!" returned Dr. Bevary, "rainy days come to most of us as we go through life, in one shape or other. It is well to provide for them when we can."

"And it's well to keep out of 'em where it's practicable," wrathfully remarked Mrs. Quale. "There no more need have been this disturbance between masters and men, than there need be one between you and me, sir, this moment, afore you walk away. They be just idiots, are the men; the women be worse, and I'm tired of telling 'em so. Look at 'em," added Mrs. Quale, directing the doctor's attention to the female ornaments of Daffodil's Delight. "Look at their gowns in jags, and their dirty caps! they make the men's being out of work an excuse for their idleness, and they just stick theirselves out there all day, a crowing and a gossiping."

"Crowing?" exclaimed the doctor.

"Crowing; every female one of 'em, like a cock upon its dunghill," responded Mrs. Quale, who was not given to pick her words when wrath was moving her. "There isn't one as can see an inch beyond her own nose. If the lock-out lasts, and starvation comes, let 'em see how they'll crow then. It'll be on t'other side their mouths, I fancy!"

"Money is dealt out to them by the Trades' Union, sufficient to live," observed Dr. Bevary.

"Sufficient not to starve," independently corrected Mrs. Quale. "What is it, sir, the bit of money they get, to them that have enjoyed their thirty-five shillings a-week, and could hardly make that do, some of 'em? Look at the Baxendales. There's Mary, wanting more food than she did in health; ay, and craving for it. A good bit of meat once or twice in the day, an egg now and then, a cup of cocoa and milk, or good tea—not your wishy-washy stuff, bought in by the ounce—how is she to get it all? The allowance dealt out to John Baxendale keeps 'em in bread and cheese; I don't think it does in much else." They were interrupted by John Baxendale himself. He came out of his house, touching his hat to the doctor and to Florence. The latter had been leaning over Mary, inquiring softly into her ailments, and the complaint of Mrs. Quale, touching the short-comings of Mary's comforts, had not reached her ears; that lady, out of regard to the invalid, having deemed it well to lower her tone.

"I am sorry, sir, you should see her so poorly," said Baxendale, alluding to his daughter. "She'll get better, I hope."

"I must try what a little of my skill will do towards it," replied the doctor. "If she had sent me word she was ill, I would have come before."

"Thank ye, sir. I don't know as I should have been backward in asking you to come round and take a look at her; but a man don't like to ask favours when he has got no money in his pocket; it makes him feel little, and look little. Things are not in a satisfactory state with us all just now."

"They are not indeed."

"I never thought the masters would go to the extreme of a lock-out," resumed Baxendale. "It was a harsh measure."

"On the face of it it does seem so," responded Dr. Bevary. "But what else could they have done? Have kept open their works, that those on strike might have been supported from the wages they paid their men, and probably have found those men also striking at last? If you and others had wanted to escape a lock-out, Baxendale, you should have been cautious not to lend yourselves to the agitation that was smouldering."

"Sir, I know there's a great deal to be said on both sides," was the reply. "I never was for the agitation; I did not urge the strike; I set my face nearly dead against it. The worst is, we all have to suffer for it alike."

"Ay, that is the worst of things in this world," responded the doctor. "When people do wrong, the consequences are rarely confined to themselves, they extend to the innocent. Come, Florence. I will see you again later, Mary."

The doctor and his niece walked away. Mrs. Quale had already departed on her errand.

"He was always a kind man," observed John Baxendale, looking after Dr. Bevary. "I hope he will be able to cure you, Mary."

"I don't feel that he will, father," was the low answer. But Baxendale did not hear it; he was going out at the gate, to join a knot of neighbours, who were gathered together at a distance.

"Will Mary Baxendale soon get well, do you think, uncle?" demanded Florence, as they went along.

"No, my dear, I do not think she will."

There was something in the doctor's tone that startled Florence. "Uncle Bevary! you do not fear she will die?"

"I do fear it, Florence; and that she will not be long first."

"Oh!" Then, after she had gone a few paces further, Florence withdrew her arm from his. "I must go back and stay with her a little while. I had no idea of this."

"Mind you don't repeat it to her in your chatter," called out the doctor; and Florence shook her head by way of answer.

"I am in no hurry to go home, Mary; I thought I would return and stay a little longer with you," was her greeting, when she reached the invalid. "You must feel it dull, sitting here alone."

"Dull! oh no, Miss Florence. I like sitting by myself and thinking."

Florence smiled. "What do you think about?"

"Oh, miss, I quite lose myself in thinking. I think of my Saviour, of how kind he was to everybody; and I think of the beautiful life we are taught to expect after this life. I can hardly believe that I shall soon be there."

Florence paused, feeling as if she did not know what to say. "You do not seem to fear death, Mary. You speak rather as if you wished it."

"I do not fear it, Miss Florence; I have been learning not to fear it ever since my poor mother died. Ah, miss! it is a great thing to learn; a great boon, when once it's learnt."

"But surely you do not want to die!" exclaimed Florence, in surprise.

"Miss Florence, as to that, I feel quite satisfied to let it be as God pleases. I know I am in His good hands. The world now seems to me to be full of care and trouble."

"It is very strange," murmured Florence. "Mamma, too, believes she is near death, and she expresses no reluctance, no fear. I do not think she feels any."

"Miss Florence, it is only another proof of God's mercies," returned the sick girl. "My mother used to say that you could not be quite ripe for death until you felt it; that it came of God's goodness and Christ's love. To such, death seems a blessing instead of a terror, so that when their time is drawing near, they are glad to die. There's a gentleman waiting to speak to you, miss."

Florence lifted her head hastily, and encountered the smile and the outstretched hand of Austin Clay. But that Mary Baxendale was unsuspicious, she might have gathered something from the vivid blush that overspread her cheeks.

"I thought it was you, Florence," he said. "I caught sight of a young lady from my sitting-room window; but you kept your head down before Mary."

"I am sorry to see Mary looking so ill. My uncle was here just now, but he has gone. I suppose you were deep in your books?" she said, with a smile, her face regaining its less radiant hue. "This lock-out must be a fine time for you."

"So fine, that I wish it were over," he answered. "I am sick of it already, Florence. A fortnight's idleness will tire out a man worse than a month's work."

"Is there any more chance of its coming to an end, sir?" anxiously inquired Mary Baxendale.

"I do not see it," gravely replied Austin. "The men appear to be too blind to come to any reasonable terms."

"Oh, sir, don't cast more blame on them than you can help!" she rejoined, in a tone of intense pain. "They are all led away by the Trades' Unions; they are, indeed. If once they enrol under them, they must only obey."

"Well, Mary, it comes to what I say—that they are blinded. They should have better sense than to be led away."

"You speak as a master, sir."

"Probably I do; but I have brought my common sense to bear upon the question, both on the side of the masters and of the men; and I believe that this time the men are wrong. If they had laboured under any real grievance, it would have been different; but they did not labour under any. Their wages were good, work was plentiful—"

"I say, Mary, I wish you'd just come in and sit by the little ones a bit, while I go down to the back kitchen and rinse out the clothes."

The interruption came from Mrs. Baxendale, who had thrown up her window to speak. Mary rose at once, took her pillow from the chair, wished Florence good day, and went indoors.

Austin held the gate open for Florence to pass out: he was not intending to accompany her. She stood a moment, speaking to him, when some one, who had come up rapidly and stealthily, laid his great hand on Austin's arm. Absorbed in Florence, Austin had not observed him, and he looked up with a start. It was Lawyer Gwinn, of Ketterford, and he appeared to be in some anger or excitement.

"Young Clay, where is your master to-day?"

Neither the salutation nor the manner of the man pleased Austin; his appearance, there and then, especially displeased him. His answer was spoken in haughty defiance. Not in policy: and in a cooler moment he would have remembered the latter to have been the only safe diplomacy.

A strangely bitter smile of conscious power parted the man's lips. "So you take part with him, do you, sir! It may be better for both you and him, that you bring me face to face with him. They have denied me to him at his house; their master is out of town, they say; but I know it to be a lie: I know that the message was sent out to me by Hunter himself. I had a great mind to force—"

Florence, who was looking deadly white, interrupted, her voice haughty as Austin's had been.

"You labour under a mistake, sir. My father is out of town. He went this morning."

Mr. Gwinn wheeled round to her. Neither her tone nor Austin's was calculated to abate his anger.

"You are his daughter, then!" he uttered, with the same insolent stare, the same displayed irony he had once used to her mother. "The young lady whom people envy as that spoiled and only child, Miss Hunter! What if I tell you a secret?—that you—"

"Be still!" shouted Austin, in uncontrollable emotion. "Are you a man, or a demon? Miss Hunter, allow me," he cried, grasping the hand of Florence, and drawing her peremptorily towards Peter Quale's door, which he threw open. "Go upstairs, Florence, to my sitting-room: wait there until I come to you. I must be alone with this man."

Florence looked at him in amazement, as he pushed her into the passage. He was evidently in the deepest agitation: every vestige of colour had forsaken his face, and his manner was authoritative as any father's could have been. She bowed to its power unconsciously, not a thought of resistance crossing her mind, and went straight upstairs to his sitting room—although it might not be precisely correct for a young lady so to do. Not a soul, save herself, appeared to be in the house.

A short colloquy and an angry one, and then Mr. Gwinn was seen returning the way he had come. Austin came springing up the stairs three at a time.

"Will you forgive me, Florence? I could not do otherwise."

What with the suddenness of the proceedings, their strangeness, and her own doubts and emotion, Florence burst into tears. Austin lost his head: at least, all of prudence that was in it. In the agitation of the moment he suffered his long-controlled feelings to get the better of him, and spoke words that he had hitherto successfully repressed.

"My darling!" he whispered, taking her hand, "I wish I could have shielded you from it! Florence, you know—you must long have known—

that my dearest object in life is you—your happiness, your welfare. I had not intended to say this so soon; it has been forced from me: you must pardon me for saying it here and now."

She gently disengaged the hand, and he did not attempt to retain it. Her wet eyelashes fell on her blushing cheeks; they were like a damask rose glistening in the morning dew. "But this mystery?—it certainly seems one," she exclaimed, striving to speak with matter-of-fact calmness. "Is not that man Gwinn, of Ketterford?"

"Yes."

"Brother to the lady who seemed to cause so much emotion to papa. Ah! I was but a child at the time, but I noticed it. Austin, I think there must be some dreadful secret. What is it? He comes to our house at periods and is closeted with papa, and papa is more miserable than ever after it."

"Whether there is or not, it is not for us to inquire into it. Men engaged in business often have troublesome people to deal with. I hastened you in," he quickly went on, not caring to be more explanatory, and compelled to speak with reserve. "I know the man of old, and his language is sometimes coarse, not fitted for a young lady's ears: so I sent you away. Florence," he whispered, his tone changing to one of deepest tenderness, "this is neither the time nor the place to speak, but I must say one word. I shall win you if I can."

Florence made no answer. She only ran downstairs as quickly as she could, she and her scarlet cheeks. Austin laughed at her haste, as he followed her. Mrs. Quale was coming in then, and met them at the door.

"See what it is to go gadding out!" cried Austin, to her. "When young ladies pay you the honour of a morning visit, they might find an empty house, but for my stay-at-home propensities."

Mrs. Quale turned her eyes from one to the other of them in puzzled doubt.

"The truth is," said Austin, vouchsafing an explanation, "there was a rude man in the road, talking nonsense, so I sent Miss Hunter indoors, and stopped to deal with him."

"I am sure I am sorry, Miss Florence," cried unsuspicious Mrs. Quale. "We often have rude men in this quarter: they get hold of a drop too much, the simpletons. And when the wine's in, the wit's out, you know, Miss."

Austin piloted her through Daffodil's Delight, possibly lest any more "rude men" should molest her, leaving her at her own door.

But when he came to reflect on what he had done, he was full of contrition and self-blame. The time had *not* come for him to aspire to the hand of Florence Hunter, at least in the estimation of the world, and he ought not to have spoken to her. There was only one course open to him now in honour; and that was, to tell the whole truth to her mother.

That same evening at dusk he was sitting alone with Mrs. Hunter. Mr. Hunter had not returned: that he had gone out of town for the day was perfect truth: and Florence escaped from the room when she heard Austin's knock.

After taking all the blame on himself for having been premature, he proceeded to urge his cause and his love, possibly emboldened to do so by the gentle kindness with which he was listened to.

"It has been my hope for years," he avowed, as he held Mrs. Hunter's hands in his, and spoke of the chance of Mr. Hunter's favour. "Dear Mrs. Hunter, do you think he will some time give her to me!"

"But, Austin—"

"Not yet; I do not ask for her yet; not until I have made a fitting home for her," he impulsively continued, anticipating what might have been the possible objection of Mrs. Hunter. "With the two thousand pounds left to me by Mrs. Thornimett, and a little more added to it, which I have myself saved, I believe I shall be able to make my way."

"Austin, you will make your way," she replied, in a tone of the utmost confidence and kindness. "I have heard Mr. Hunter himself anticipate a successful career for you. Even when you were, comparatively speaking, penniless, Mr. Hunter would say that talent and energy, such as yours, could not fail to find its proper outlet. Now that you have inherited the money, your success is certain. But—I fear you cannot win Florence."

The words fell on his heart like an icebolt. He had reckoned on Mrs. Hunter's countenance, though he had not been sure of her husband's. "What do you object to in me?" he inquired, in a tone of pain. "I am of gentle birth."

"Austin, *I* do not object. I have long seen that your coming here so much—and it was Mr. Hunter's pleasure to have you—was likely to lead to an attachment between you and Florence. Had I objected to you, I should have pointed out to Mr. Hunter the impolicy of your coming. I like *you*: there is no one in the world to whom I would so readily intrust the happiness of Florence. Other mothers might look to a higher alliance for her: but, Austin, when we get near the grave, we judge with a judgment not of this world. Worldly distinctions lose their charm."

"Then where lies the doubt—the objection?" he asked.

"I once—it is not long ago—hinted at this to Mr. Hunter," she replied. "He would not hear me out; he would not suffer me to conclude. It was an utter impossibility that you could ever marry Florence," he said: "neither was it likely that either of you would wish it."

"But we do wish it; the love has already arisen," he exclaimed, in agitation. "Dear Mrs. Hunter—"

"Hush, Austin! calm yourself. Mr. Hunter must have some private objection. I am sure he has; I could see so far; and one that, as was evident, he did not choose to disclose to me. I never inquire into his reasons when I perceive this. You must try and forget her."

A commotion was heard in the hall. Austin went out to ascertain its cause. There stood Gwinn of Ketterford, insisting upon an interview with Mr. Hunter.

Austin contrived to get rid of the man by convincing him Mr. Hunter was really not at home. Gwinn went out grumbling, promising to be there the first thing in the morning.

The interlude had broken up the confidence between Austin and Mrs. Hunter; and he went home in despondency: but vowing to win her, all the same, sooner or later.

II

Mr. Cox

Time had gone on. It was a gloomy winter's evening. Not that, reckoning by the seasons, it could be called winter yet; but it was getting near it, and the night was dark and sloppy, and blowing and rainy. The wind went booming down Daffodil's Delight, sending the fierce rain before it in showers, and the pools gleamed in the reflected light of the gas-lamps, as wayfarers splashed through them and stirred up their muddy waters.

The luxurious and comfortable in position—those at ease in the world, who could issue their orders to attentive tradespeople at their morning's leisure—had no necessity to be abroad on that inclement Saturday night. Not so Daffodil's Delight; there was not much chance (taking it collectively) of a dinner for the morrow, at the best; but, unless they went abroad, there was none. The men had not gone to work yet, and times were bad.

Down the street, to one particular corner shop, which had three gilt-coloured balls hanging outside it, flocked the stream—chiefly females. Not together. They mostly walked in units, and, some of them at least, in a covert sort of manner, keeping in the shade of dead walls, and of dark houses, as if not caring to be seen. Amongst the latter, stole one who appeared more especially fearful of being recognised. She was a young woman, comely once, but pale and hollow-eyed now, her bones too sharp for her skin. Well wrapped up, was she, against the weather; her cloth cloak warm, a fur round her neck, and india-rubber shoes. Choosing her time to approach the shop when the coast should be tolerably clear, she glanced cautiously in at the window and door, and entered.

Laying upon the counter a small parcel, which she carried folded in a handkerchief, she displayed a cardboard box to the sight of the shop's master, who came forward to attend to her. It contained a really handsome set of corals, fashioned like those worn in the days when our mothers were young; a necklace of six rows of small beads, with a gold snap made to imitate a rose, a long coral bead set in it. A pair of gold earrings, with large pendant coral drops, lay beside it, and a large and handsome gold brooch, set likewise with corals.

"What, is it *you*, Miss Baxendale?" he exclaimed, his tone expressive of some surprise.

"It is, indeed, Mr. Cox," replied Mary. "We all have to bend to these hard times. It's share and share alike in them. Will you please to look at these jewels?"

She tenderly drew aside the cotton which was over the trinkets—tenderly and reverently, almost as if a miniature live baby were lying there. Very precious were they to Mary. They were dear to her from association; and she also believed them to be of great value.

The pawnbroker glanced at them slightly, carelessly lifting one of the earrings in his hand, to feel its weight. The brooch he honoured with a closer inspection.

"What do you want upon them?" he asked.

"Nay," said Mary, "it is not for me to name a sum. What will you lend?"

"You are not accustomed to our business, or you would know that we like borrowers to mention their own ideas as to sum; and we give it if we can," he rejoined with ready words. "What do you ask?"

"If you would let me have four pounds upon them, began Mary, hesitatingly. But he snapped up the words.

"Four pounds! Why, Miss Baxendale, you can't know what you are saying. The fashion of these coral things is over and done with. They are worth next to nothing."

Mary's heart beat quicker in its sickness of disappointment.

"They are genuine, sir, if you'll please to look. The gold is real gold, and the coral is the best coral; my poor mother has told me so many a time. Her godmother was a lady, well-to-do in the world, and the things were a present from her."

"If they were not genuine, I'd not lend as many pence upon them," said the man. "With a little alteration the brooch might be made tolerably modern; otherwise their value would be no more than old gold. In selling them, I—"

"It will not come to that, Mr. Cox," interrupted Mary. "Please God spares me a little while—and, since the hot weather went out, I feel a bit stronger—I shall soon redeem them."

Mr. Cox looked at her thin face; he listened to her short breath; and he drew his own conclusions. There was a line of pity in his hard face, for he had long respected Mary Baxendale.

"By the way the strike seems to be lasting on, there doesn't seem much promise of a speedy end to it," quoth he, in answer. "I never was so over-done with pledges."

"My work does not depend upon that," said Mary. "Let me get up a little strength, and I shall have as much work as I can do. And I am well paid, Mr. Cox: I have a private connection. I am not like the poor seamstresses who make skirts for fourpence a-piece."

Mr. Cox made no immediate reply to this, and there was a pause. The open box lay before him. He took up the necklace and examined its clasp.

"I will lend you a sovereign upon them."

She lifted her face pitiably, and the tears glistened in her eyes.

"It would be of no use to me," she whispered. "I want the money for a particular purpose, otherwise I should never have brought here these gifts of my mother's. She gave them to me the day I was eighteen, and I have tenderly kept them from desecration."

Poor Mary! From desecration!

"I have heard her say what they cost; but I forget now. I know it was over ten pounds."

"But the day for this fashion has gone by. To ask four pounds upon them was preposterous; and you would know it to be so, were you acquainted with the trade."

"Will you lend me two pounds, then?"

The tone was tremblingly eager, the face beseeching—a wan face, telling of the coming grave. Possibly the thought struck the pawnbroker, and awoke some humanity within him.

"I shall lose by it, I know, if it comes to a sale. I'd not do it for anybody else, Miss Baxendale."

He proceeded to write out the ticket, his thoughts running upon whether—if it did come to a sale—he could not make three pounds by the brooch alone. As he was handing her the money, somebody rushed in, close to the spot occupied by Mary, and dashed down a large-sized paper parcel on the counter. She wore a black lace bonnet, which had once been white, frayed, and altogether the worse for wear, independent of its dirt. It was tilted on the back of her head, displaying a mass of hair in front, half grey, half black, and exceedingly in disorder; together with a red face. It was Mrs. Dunn.

"Well, to be sure! if it's not Mary Baxendale! I thought you was too much of the lady to put your nose inside a pop-shop. Don't it go again the grain?" she ironically added, for she did not appear to be in the sweetest of tempers.

"It does indeed, Mrs. Dunn," was the girl's meek answer, as she took her money and departed.

"Now then, old Cox, just attend to me," began Mrs. Dunn. "I have brought something as you don't get offered every day."

Mr. Cox, accustomed to the scant ceremony bestowed upon him by some of the ladies of Daffodil's Delight, took the speech with indifference, and gave his attention to the parcel, from which Mrs. Dunn was rapidly taking off the twine.

"What's this—silk?" cried he, as a roll of dress-silk, brown, cross-barred with gold, came forth to view.

"Yes, it is silk; and there's fourteen yards of it; and I want thirty shillings upon it," volubly replied Mrs. Dunn.

He took the silk between his fingers, feeling its substance, in his professionally indifferent and disparaging manner.

"Where did you get it from?" he asked.

"Where did I get it from?" retorted Mrs. Dunn. "What's that to you!" "D'ye think I stole it?"

"How do I know?" returned he.

"You insolent fellow! Is it only to-day as you have knowed me, Tom Cox? My name's Hannah Dunn; and I don't want you to testify to my honesty; I can hold up my head in Daffodil's Delight just as well as you can—perhaps a little better. Concern yourself with your own business. I want thirty shillings upon that."

"It isn't worth thirty shillings in the shop, new," was the rejoinder.

"What?" shrieked Mrs. Dunn. "It cost three-and-fourpence halfpenny a yard, every yard of it, and there's fourteen of'em, I tell you."

"I don't care if it cost six-and-fourpence halfpenny, it's not worth more than I say. I'll lend you ten shillings upon it, and I should lose then."

"Where do you expect to go to when you die?" demanded Mrs. Dunn, in a tone that might be heard half over the length and breadth of Daffodil's Delight. "I wouldn't tell such lies for the paltry sake of grinding folks down; no, not if you made me a duchess to-morrow for it."

"Here, take the silk off. I have not got time to bother: it's Saturday night."

He swept the parcel, silk, paper, and string, towards her, and was turning away. She leaned over the counter and seized upon him.

"You want a opposition in the place, that's what you want, Master Cox! You have been cock o' the walk over Daffodil's Delight so long, that you think you can treat folks as if they was dirt. You be over-done with business, that's what you be; you're a making gold as fast as they makes it in Aurstraliar; we shall have you a setting up your tandem next. What'll you give me upon that silk?"

"I'll give you ten shillings; I have said so. You may take it or not; it's at your own option."

More contending; but the pawnbroker was firm; and Mrs. Dunn was forced to accept the offer, or else take away her silk.

"How long is this strike going to last?" he asked, as he made out the duplicate.

The words excited the irascibility of Mrs. Dunn.

"Strike!" she uttered, in a flaming passion. "Who dares to call it a strike? It's not a strike; it's a lock-out."

"Lock-out, then. The two things come to the same, don't they? Is there a chance of its coming to an end?"

"No, they don't come to the same," shrieked Mrs. Dunn. "A strike's what it is—a strike; a act of noble independence which the British workman may be proud on. A lock-out is a nasty, mean, overbearing tyranny on the part of the masters. Now, old Cox! call it a strike again."

"But I hear the masters' shops are open again—for anybody to go to work that likes," replied Mr. Cox, quite imperturbable.

"They be open for slaves to go to work, not for free-born men," retorted Mrs. Dunn, her shrieking voice at a still higher pitch. "I hope the men'll hold out for ever, I do! I hope the masters 'll be drove, everyone of'em, into the dust and dregs of the bankruptcy court! I hope their sticks and stones 'll be sold up, down to their children's cradles—"

"There, that's enough," interposed the pawnbroker, as he handed her what he had to give. "You'll be collecting a crowd round the door, if you go on like that. Here's somebody else waiting for your place."

It was Mrs. Cheek, an especial friend of the lady's now being dismissed. Mrs. Cheek was carefully carrying a basket which contained various chimney ornaments—pretty enough in their places, but not of much value. The pawnbroker, after some haggling, not so intemperately carried on as the bargain just concluded, advanced six shillings on them.

"I had wanted twelve," she said; "and I can't do with less."

"I am willing to lend it," returned he, "if you bring goods accordingly."

"I have stripped the place of a'most all the light things as can be spared," said Mrs. Cheek. "One doesn't care to begin upon the heavy furniture and the necessaries."

"Is there no chance of the present state of affairs coming to an end?" inquired Mr. Cox, putting the same question to which he had not got a direct answer from Mrs. Dunn. "The men can go back to work if they like; the masters' yards are open again."

"Open!" returned Mrs. Cheek, in a guttural tone, as she threw back her head in disdain; "they have been open some time, if you call *that* opening 'em. If a man likes to go as a sneaking coward, and work upon the terms offered now, knuckling down to the masters, and putting his hand to their mean old odious document, severing himself from the Union, he can do it. It ain't many of our men as you'll find do that dirty work. If my husband was to attempt it, I'd be ready to skin him alive."

"But the men have gone back in some parts of the metropolis."

"*Men*, do you call 'em. A few may; one black sheep out of a flock. They ain't men, they are half-castes. Let them look to theirselves," concluded Mrs. Cheek significantly, as she quitted the pawnbroker's shop with a fling.

At the butcher's stall, a few paces further, she came up to Mrs. Dunn, who was standing in the glare of the blazing gaslight, in the incessant noise of the "Buy, buy, buy! what'll you buy?" Not less than a dozen women were congregated there, elbowing each other, as they turned over the scraps of meat set out for sale in small heaps—sixpence the lot, a shilling the lot, according to quality and quantity. In the prosperous time when their husbands were in full work, these ladies had scornfully disdained such heaps on a Saturday night. They had been wont then to buy a good joint for the Sunday's dinner. One of the women nudged another in her vicinity, directing her attention to the inside of the shop. "Just twig Mother Shuck; she's a being served, I hope!"

"Mother Shuck," Slippery Sam's better half, was making her purchases in the agreeable confidence of possessing money to pay for them—liver and bacon for the present evening's supper, and a breast of veal, to be served with savoury herbs, for the morrow's dinner. In the old times, while the throng of women now outside had been able to make the same or similar purchases, *she* had hovered without like a hungry hyena, hanging over the cheap portions with covetous eyes and fingers, as many another poor wife had done, whose husband could not or would not work. Times were changed.

"I can't afford nothing, hardly, I can't," grumbled Mrs. Cheek. "What's the good of six shillings for a Saturday night, when everything's wanted, from the rent down to a potater? The young 'uns have got their bare feet upon the boards, as may be said, for their shoes be without toes and heels; and who is to get 'em others? I wish that Cox was a bit juster. He's a getting rich upon our spoils. Six shillings for that lot as I took him in!"

"I wish he was smothered!" struck in Mrs. Dunn. "He took and asked me if I'd stole the silk. It was that lovely silk, you know, as I was fool enough to go and choose the week of the strike, on the strength of the good times a coming. We have had something else to do since, instead of making up silk gownds."

"The good times ain't come yet," said Mrs. Cheek, shortly. "I wish the old 'uns was back again, if we could get 'em without stooping to the masters."

"It was at the shop where Mary Ann and Jemimar deals, when they has to get in things for their customers' work," resumed Mrs. Dunn, continuing the subject of the silk. "I shouldn't have had credit at any other place. Fourteen yards I bought of it, and three-and-fourpence halfpenny I gave for every yard of it; I did, I protest to you, Elizar Cheek; and that swindling old screw had the conscience to offer me ten shillings for the whole!"

"Is the silk paid for?"—"Paid for!" wrathfully repeated Mrs. Dunn; "has it been a time to pay for silk gownds when our husbands be under a lock-out? Of course it's not paid for, and the shop's a beginning to bother for it; but they'll be none the nearer getting it. I say, master, what'll you weigh in these fag ends of mutton and beef at—the two together?" It will be readily understood, from the above conversation and signs, that in the several weeks that had elapsed since the commencement of the lock-out, things, socially speaking, had been going backwards. The roast goose and other expected luxuries had not come yet. The masters' works were open—open to any who would go to work in them, provided they renounced all connection with the Trades' Unions. Daffodil's Delight, taking it collectively, would not have this at any price, and held out. The worst aspect in the affair—I mean for the interests of the men—was, that strange workmen were assembling from different parts of the country, accepting the work which they refused. Of course this feature in the dispute was most bitter to the men; they lavished their abuse upon the masters for employing strange hands; and they would have been glad to lavish something worse than abuse up on the hands themselves. One of the masters compared them to the fable of the dog in the manger—they would not take the work, and they would not let (by their good will) anybody else take it. Incessant agitation was maintained. The workmen were in a sufficiently excited state, as it was; and, to help on that which need not have been helped, the agents of the Trades' Union kept the ball rolling—an incendiary ball, urging obstinacy and spreading discontent. But this little history has not so much to do with the political phases of the unhappy dispute, as with its social effects.

As Mary Baxendale was returning home from the pawnbroker's, she passed Mrs. Darby, who was standing at her own door looking at the weather. "Mary, girl," was the salutation, "this is not a night for you to be abroad."

"I was obliged to go," was the reply. "How are the children?"

"Come in and see them," said Mrs. Darby. She led the way into a back room, which, at the first glance, seemed to be covered with mattresses and children. A large family had Robert Darby—indeed, it was a complaint prevalent in Daffodil's Delight. They were of various ages; these, lying on the mattresses, six of them, were from four to twelve years. The elder ones were not at home. The room had a close, unhealthy smell, which struck especially on the senses of Mary, rendered sensitive from illness.

"What have you got them all in this room for?" she exclaimed, in the impulse of the moment.

"I have given up the rooms above," was Mrs. Darby's reply.

"But—when the children were ill—was it a time to give up rooms?" debated Mary.

"No," replied Mrs. Darby, who spoke as if she were heart-broken, in a sad, subdued tone, the very reverse of Mesdames Dunn and Cheek. "But how could we keep on the top rooms when we were unable to get together the rent, to pay for them? I spoke to the landlord, and he is letting the back rent stand a bit, not to sell us up; and I gave up to him the two top rooms; and we all sleep in here together."

"I wish the men would go back to work!" said Mary, with a sigh.

"Mary my heart's just failing within me," said Mrs. Darby, her tone a sort of wail. "Here's winter coming on, and all of them out of work. If it were not for my daughter, who is in service, and brings us her wages as she gets them, I believe we should just have starved. I *must* get medicine, for the children, though we go without bread."

"It is not medicine they want: it is nourishment," said Mary.

"It is both. Nourishment would have done when they were first ailing, but now that it has turned to low fever, they must have medicine, or it will grow into typhus. It's bark they have to take, and it costs—"

"Mother! mother!" struck up a plaintive voice, that of the eldest of the children lying there, "I want more of that nice drink!"

"I have not got it, Willy. You know that you had it all. Mrs. Quale brought me round a pot of black currant jelly," she explained to Mary, "and I poured boiling water on it to make drink. Their little parched throats did so relish it, poor things."

Mary knelt on the floor and put her hand on the child's moist brow. He was a pretty boy; fair and delicate, with light curls falling round his face. A gentle, thoughtful, intelligent boy he had ever been, but less healthy than some. "You are thirsty, Willy?"

He opened his heavy eyelids, and the large round blue eyes glistened with fever, as they were lifted to see who spoke.

"How do you do, Mary?" he meekly said. "Yes, I am so thirsty. Mother said perhaps she should have a sixpence to-night to buy a pot of jelly like Mrs. Quale's." Mrs. Darby coloured slightly; she thought Mary must reflect on the extravagance implied. Sixpence for jelly, when they were wanting money for a loaf!

"I did say it to him," she whispered, as she was quitting the room with Mary. "I thought I might spare a sixpence out of what Darby got from the society. But I can't; I can't. There's so many things we cannot do without, unless we just give up, and lie down and don't even try at keeping body and soul together. Rent, and coals, and candles, and soap; and we must eat something. Darby, too, of course he wants a trifle for beer and tobacco. Mary, I say I am just heart-faint. If the poor boy should die, it'll be upon my mind for ever, that the drink he craved for in his last illness couldn't be got for him."

"Does he crave for it?"

"Nothing was ever like it. All day long it has been his sad, pitiful cry. 'Have you got the jelly yet, mother? Oh, mother, if I could but have the drink!'"

As Mary went through the front room, Robert Darby was in it then. His chin rested on his hands, his elbows were on the table; altogether he looked very down-hearted.

"I have been to see Willy," she cried.

"Ah, poor little chap!" It was all he said; but the tone implied more.

"Things seem to be getting pretty low with us all. I wish there could be a change," continued Mary.

"How can there be, while the masters and the Unions are at loggerheads?" he asked. "Us men be between the two, and between the two we come to the ground. It's like sitting on two stools at once."

Mary proceeded to the shop where jelly was sold, an oilman's, bought a sixpenny pot, and took it back to Mrs. Darby's, handing it in at the door. "Why did you do it, Mary? You cannot afford it."

"Yes, I can. Give it to Willy, with my love."

"He will only be out of a world of care, if God does take him," sighed Mary to herself, as she bent her steps homeward. "Oh, father!" she continued aloud, encountering John Baxendale at their own gate, "I wish this sad state of things could be ended. There's the poor little Darbys worse instead of better. They are all lying in one room, down with fever."

"God help us if fever should come!" was the reply of John Baxendale.

"It is not catching fever yet. They have given up their top chambers, and are all sleeping in that back room. Poor Willie craved for a bit of jelly, and Mrs. Darby could not get it him."

"Better crave for that than for worse things," returned John Baxendale. "I am just a walking about here, because I can't bear to stop indoors. I *can't* pay the rent, and the things must go."

"No, father, they need not. He said if you would get up two pounds towards it, he would give time for the rest. If—"

"Two pounds!" exclaimed John Baxendale, "where am I to get two pounds from? Borrow of them that have been provident, and so are better off, in this distress, than me? No, that I never will."

Mary opened her hand, and displayed two sovereigns held in its palm. They sparkled in the gaslight. "The money is my own, father. Take it." A sudden revulsion of feeling came over Baxendale—he seemed to have passed from despair to hope.—"Child," he gently said, "did an angel send it?" And Mary, worn with weakness, with long-continued insufficient food, sad with the distress around her, burst into tears, and, bending her head upon his arm, sobbed aloud.

III

"I Think I Have Been a Fool"

The Shucks had got a supper party. On this same Saturday night, when the wind was blowing outside, and the rain was making the streets into pools, two or three friends had dropped into Sam Shuck's—idlers like Sam himself—and were hospitably invited to remain. Mrs. Shuck was beginning to fry the liver and bacon she had just brought in, with the accompaniment of a good peck of onions, and Sam and his friends were staying their appetites with pipes and porter. When Mary Baxendale and her father entered—Mary having lingered a minute outside, until her emotion had passed, and her eyes were dry—they could scarcely find their way across the kitchen, what with the clouds from the pipes, and the smoke from the frying-pan. There was a great deal of laughter going on. Prosperity had not yet caused the Shucks to change their residence for a better one. Perhaps that was to come: but Sam's natural improvidence stood in the way of much change.

"You are merry to-night," observed Mary, by way of being sociable.

"It's merrier inside nor out, a-wading through the puddles and the sharp rain," replied Mrs. Shuck, without turning round from her employment. "It's some'at new to see you out such a night as this, Mary Baxendale! Don't you talk about folks wanting sense again."

"I don't know that I ever do talk of it," was the inoffensive reply of Mary, as she followed her father up the stairs.

Mrs. Baxendale was hushing a baby when they entered their room. She looked very cross. The best-tempered will do so, under the long-continued embarrassment of empty purses and empty stomachs. "Who has been spreading it up and down the place that *we* are in trouble about the rent?" she abruptly demanded, in no pleasant voice. "That girl of Ryan's was here just now—Judy. She knew it, it seems, and she didn't forget to speak of it. Mary, what a simpleton you are, to be out in this rain!"

"Never mind who speaks of the rent, Mrs. Baxendale, so long as it can be paid," said Mary, sitting down in the first chair to get her breath up, after mounting the stairs. "Father is going to manage it, so that we shan't have any trouble at present. It's all right."

"However have you contrived it?" demanded Mrs. Baxendale of her husband, in a changed tone.

"Mary has contrived it—not I. She has just put two pounds into my hand. Where did you get it, child?"—"It does not signify your knowing that, father."

"If I don't know it, I shan't use the money," he answered, shortly.—"Why, surely, father, you can trust me!" she rejoined.

"That is not it, Mary," said John Baxendale. "I don't like to use borrowed money, unless I know who it has been borrowed from."

"It was not borrowed, in your sense of the word, father. I have only done what you and Mrs. Baxendale have been doing lately. I pledged that set of coral ornaments of my mother's. Had you forgotten them?"

"Why, yes, I had forgot 'em," cried he. "Coral ornaments! I declare they had as much slipped my memory, as if she had never possessed them."

"Cox would only lend me two pounds upon them. Father, I hope I shall some time get them redeemed." John Baxendale made no reply. He turned to pace the small room, evidently in deep thought. Mary, her poor short breath gathered again, took off her wet cloak and bonnet. Presently, Mrs. Baxendale put the loaf upon the table, and some cold potatoes.

"Couldn't you have brought in a sausage or two for yourself, Mary, or a red herring?" she said. "You had got a shilling in your pocket."

"I can eat a potato," said Mary; "it don't much matter about me."

"It matters about us all, I think," cried Mrs. Baxendale. "What a delicious smell of onions!" she added in a parenthesis. "Them Shucks have got the luck of it just now. Us, and the children, and you, are three parts starved—I know that, Mary. *We* may weather it—it's to be hoped we shall; but it will just kill you."

"No, it shan't," said John Baxendale, turning to them with a strangely stern decision marked upon his countenance. "This night has decided me, and I'll go and do it."

"Go and do what?" exclaimed his wife, a sort of fear in her tone.

"I'll go to Work, please God, Monday morning comes," he said, with emphasis. "The thought has been hovering in my mind this week past."

"It's just the thing you ought to have done weeks ago," observed Mrs. Baxendale.

"You never said it."—"Not I. It's best to let men come to their senses of their own accord. You mostly act by the rules of contrary, you men;

if I had advised your going to work next Monday morning, you'd just have stopped away."

Passing over this conjugal compliment in silence, John Baxendale descended the stairs. He possessed a large share of the open honesty of the genuine English workman. He disdained to do things in a corner. It would not suit him to return to work the coming Monday morning on what might be called "the sly;" he preferred to act openly, and to declare it to the Trades' Union previously, in the person of their paid agent, Sam Shuck. This he would do at once, and for that purpose entered the kitchen. The first instalment of the supper was just served: which was accomplished by means of a tin dish placed on the table, and the contents of the frying-pan being turned unceremoniously into it. Sam and the company deemed the liver and bacon were best served hot and hot, so they set themselves to eat, while Mrs. Shuck continued to fry.

"I have got just a word to say, Shuck; I shan't disturb you," began John Baxendale. But Shuck interrupted him.

"It's of no use, Baxendale, your remonstrating about the short allowance. Think of the many mouths there is to feed. It's hard times, we all know, thanks to the masters; but our duty, ay, and our pride too, must lie in putting up with them, like men."

"It's not very hard times with you, at any rate," said John Baxendale, sniffing involuntarily the savoury odour, and watching the tempting morsels consumed. "My business here is not to remonstrate at anything, but to inform you that I shall resume work on Monday."

The announcement took Sam by surprise. He dropped the knife with which he was cutting the liver, held upon his bread—for the repast was not served fashionably, with a full complement of plates and dishes—and stared at Baxendale—"What!" he uttered.

"I have had enough of it. I shall go back on Monday morning."

"Are you a fool, Baxendale? Or a knave?"

"Sometimes I think I must be a fool," was the reply, given without irritation. "Leastways, I have wondered lately whether I am or not: when there has been full work and full wages to be had for the asking, and I have not asked, but have let my wife and children and Mary go down to starvation point."

"You have been holding out for principle," remonstrated Sam.

"I know; and principle is a very good thing when you are sure it's the right principle. But flesh and blood can't stand out for ever."

"After standing out as long as this, I'd try and stand out a bit longer," cried Sam. "You *must*, Baxendale; you can't turn traitor now."

"You say 'a bit,' longer, Sam Shuck. It has been 'a bit longer,' and 'a bit longer,' for some time past; but the bit doesn't come to any ending. There's no more chance of the masters' coming to, than there was at first, but a great deal less. The getting of these men from the country will render them independent of us. What is to become of us then?"

"Rubbish!" said Sam Shuck. "The masters must come to: they can't stand against the Unions. Because a sprinkling of poor country workmen have thrust in their noses, and the masters are keeping open their works on the show of it, is that a reason why we should knuckle down? They are doing it to frighten us."

"Look here," said Baxendale. "I have two women and two children on my hands, and one of the women is next door to the grave; I am threatened—*you* know it, Sam Shuck—with a lodging for them in the street next week, because I have not been able to pay the rent; I have parted by selling and pledging, with nearly all there is to part with, of my household goods. There was what they call a Bible reader round last week, and he says, pleasantly, 'Why don't you kneel down and ask God to consider your condition, Mr. Baxendale?' Very good. But how can I do that? Isn't it just a mockery for me to pray for help to provide for me and mine? If God was pleased to answer us in words, would not the answer be, 'There is work, and to spare; you have only got to do it?'"

"Well, that's grand," put in one of Sam's guests, most of whom had been staring with open mouths. "As if folks asked God about such things as this!"

"Since my late wife died, I have thought about it more than I used to," said Baxendale, simply, "and I have got to see that there's no good to be done in anything without it. But how can I in reason ask for help now, when I don't help myself? The work is ready to my hand, and I don't take it. So, Sam, my mind's made up at last. You'll tell the Union."

"No, I shan't. You won't go to work."

"You'll see. I shall be glad to go. I haven't had a proper meal this—"

"You'll think better of it between now and Monday morning," interrupted Sam, drowning the words. "I'll have a talk with you to-morrow. Have a bit of supper, Baxendale?"

"No, thank ye. I didn't come in to eat your victuals," he added, moving to the door.

"We have got plenty," said Mrs. Shuck, turning round from the frying-pan. "Here, eat it up-stairs, if you won't stop, Baxendale." She took out a slice of liver and of bacon, and handed them to him on a saucer. What a temptation it was to the man, sick with hunger! However, he was about to refuse, when he thought of Mary.

"Thank ye, Mrs. Shuck. I'll take it, then, if you can spare it. It will be a treat to Mary." Like unto the appearance of water in the arid desert to the parched and exhausted traveller, was the sight of that saucer of meat to Mary. Terribly did she often crave for it. John Baxendale positively refused to touch any; so Mary divided it into two portions, giving one to Mrs. Baxendale. The woman's good-nature—her sense of Mary's condition—would have led her to refuse it; but she was not quite made up of self-denial, and she felt faint and sinking. John Baxendale cut a thick slice of bread, rubbed it over the remains of gravy in the saucer, and ate that. "Please God, this shall have an end," he mentally repeated. "I think I *have* been a fool!"

Mr. Hunter's yard—as it was familiarly called in the trade—was open just as were other yards, though as yet he had but few men at work in it; in fact, so little was doing that it was almost equivalent to a stand-still. Mr. Henry Hunter was better off. A man of energy, determined to stand no nonsense, as he himself expressed it, he had gone down to country places, and engaged many hands.

On the Monday following the above Saturday night, John Baxendale presented himself to Austin Clay and requested to be taken on again. Austin complied at once, glad to do so, and told the man he was wise to come to his senses. Mr. Hunter was not at business that day; "too unwell to leave home" was the message carried to Austin Clay. In the evening Austin went to the house: as was usual when Mr. Hunter did not make his appearance at the works in the day. Florence was alone when he entered. Evidently in distress; though she strove to hide it from him, to turn it off with gay looks and light words. But he noted the signs. "What is your grief, Florence?" he asked, speaking in an earnest tone of sympathy.

It caused the tears to come forth again. Austin took her hands and drew her to him, as either a lover or a brother might have done, leaving her to take it as she pleased.

"Let me share it, Florence, whatever it may be."

"It is nothing more than usual," she answered; "but somehow my spirits are low this evening. I try to bear up bravely; and I do bear up:

but, indeed, this is an unhappy home. Mamma is sinking fast; I see it daily. While papa—" But for making the abrupt pause, she would have broken down. Austin turned away: he did not choose that she should enter upon any subject connected with Mr. Hunter. This time Florence would not be checked: as she had been hitherto. "Austin, I cannot bear it any longer. What is it that is overshadowing papa?" she continued, her voice, her whole manner full of dread. "I am sure that some misfortune hangs over the house."

"I wish I could take you out of it," was the impulsive and not very relevant answer. "I can tell you nothing, Florence," he concluded more soberly. "Mr. Hunter has many cares in business; but the cares are his own."

"Austin, is it kind of you to try to put me off so? I can bear reality, whatever it may be, better than suspense. It is for papa I grieve. See how ill he is! And yet he has no ailment of body, only of mind. Night after night he paces his room, never sleeping."

"How do you know that?" Austin inquired.

"Because I listen to it."—"You should not do so."

"I cannot *help* listening to him. How is it possible? His room is near mine, and when his footsteps are sounding in it, in the midnight silence, hour after hour, my ears grow sensitively quick. I say that loving him, I cannot help it. Sometimes I think that if I only knew the cause, the nature of his sorrow, I might soothe it—perhaps help to remove it."

"As if young ladies could ever help or remove the cares of business!" he cried, speaking lightly.

"I am not a child, Austin," she resumed: "it is not kind of you to make pretence that I am, and try to put me off as one. Papa's trouble is *not* connected with business, and I am sure you know that as well as I do. Will you not tell me what it is?"

"Florence, you can have no grounds for assuming that I am cognisant of it."

"I feel very sure that you are. Can you suppose that I should otherwise speak of it to you?"

"I say that you can have no grounds for the supposition. By what do you so judge?"

"By signs," she answered. "I can read it in your countenance, your actions. I was pretty sure of it before that day when you sent me hastily into your rooms, lest I should hear what the man Gwinn was about to say; but I have been fully sure since. What he would have said related to it; and, in some way, the man is connected with the ill. Besides, you have been on confidential terms with papa for years."

"On business matters only: not on private ones. My dear Florence, I must request you to let this subject cease, now and always. I know nothing of its nature from your father; and if my own thoughts have in any way strayed towards it, it is not fitting that I should give utterance to them."

"Tell me one thing: could I be of any service, in any way?"

"Hush, Florence," he uttered, as if the words had struck upon some painful cord. "The only service you can render is, by taking no notice of it. Do not think of it if you can help; do not allude to it to your mother."

"I never do," she interrupted.—"That is well."

"You have sometimes said you cared for me."

"Well?" he rejoined, determined to be as contrary as he could.

"If you did, you would not leave me in this suspense. Only tell me the nature of papa's trouble, I will not ask further."

Austin gathered his wits together, thinking what plea he should invent. "It is a debt, Florence. Your papa contracted a debt many years ago; he thought it was paid; but by some devilry—pardon the word; I forgot I was talking to you—a lawyer, Gwinn of Ketterford, has proved that it was not paid, and he comes to press for instalments of it. That is all I know. And now you must give me your promise not to speak of this. I'll never tell you anything more if you do."

Florence had listened attentively, and was satisfied.

"I will never speak of it," she said. "I think I understand it now. Papa fears he shall have no fortune left for me. Oh, if he only knew—"

"Hush, Florence!" came the warning whisper, for Mrs. Hunter was standing at the door.

"Is it you, Austin? I heard voices here, and wondered who had come in."

"How are you, dear Mrs. Hunter?" he said to her as she entered. "Better this evening?"

"Not better," was Mrs. Hunter's answer, as she retained Austin's hand, and drew him on the sofa beside her. "There will be no 'better' for me in this world. Austin, I wish I could have gone from it under happier circumstances. Florence, I hear your papa calling."

"If *you* are not happy in the prospect of the future, who can be?" murmured Austin, as Florence left the room.

"I spoke not of myself. My concern is for Mr. Hunter. Austin, I would give every minute of my remaining days to know what terrible grief it is that has been so long upon him." Austin was silent. Had Mrs. Hunter and Florence entered into a compact to annoy him? "It has been like a dark shade upon our house for years. Florence and I have kept silence upon it to him, and to each other; to him we dare not speak, to each other we would not. Latterly it has seemed so much worse, that I was forced to whisper of it to her: I could not keep it in; the silence was killing me. We both agree that you are in his confidence; if so, perhaps you will satisfy me?"

Austin Clay felt himself in a dilemma. He could not speak of it in the light manner he had to Florence, or put off so carelessly Mrs. Hunter. "I am not in his confidence, indeed, Mrs. Hunter," he broke forth, glad to be able to say so much. "That I have observed the signs you speak of in Mr. Hunter, his embarrassment, his grief—"

"Say his fear, Austin."

"His fear. That I have noticed this it would be vain to deny. But, Mrs. Hunter, I assure you he has never given me his confidence upon the subject. Quite the contrary; he has particularly shunned it with me. Of course I can give a very shrewd guess at the cause—he is pressed for money. Times are bad; and when a man of Mr. Hunter's thoughtful temperament begins to be really anxious on the score of money matters, it shows itself in various ways."

Mrs. Hunter quitted the subject, perhaps partially reassured; at any rate convinced that no end would be answered by continuing it. "I was mistaken, I suppose," she said, with a sigh. "At least you can tell me, Austin, how business is going on. How will it go on?"

Very grave turned Austin's face now. This was an open evil—one to be openly met and grappled with; and what his countenance gained in seriousness it lost in annoyance. "I really do not see how it will go on," was his reply, "unless we can get to work soon. I want to speak to Mr. Hunter. Can I see him?"

"He will be in directly. He has not been down to-day yet. But I suppose you will wish to see him in private; I know he and you like to be alone when you talk upon business matters."

At present it was expedient that Mrs. Hunter, at any rate, should not be present, if she was to be spared annoyance; for Mr. Hunter's affairs were growing ominous. This was chiefly owing to the stoppage of works in process, and partly to the effect of a diminished capital. Austin as yet did not know all the apprehension, for Mr. Hunter contrived to keep some of it from him. That the diminishing of the capital was owing to

Gwinn of Ketterford, Austin did know; at least, his surmises amounted to certainty. When a hundred pounds, or perhaps two hundred pounds, mysteriously went out, and Austin was not made acquainted with the money's destination, he drew his own conclusions.

"Are the men not learning the error of their course yet?" Mrs. Hunter resumed.

"They seem further off learning it than ever. One of them, indeed, came back to-day: Baxendale."

"I felt sure he would be amongst the first to do so. He is a sensible man: how he came to hold out at all, is to me a matter of surprise."

"He told me this morning, when he came and asked to be taken on again, that he wished he never had held out," said Austin. "Mary is none the better for it."

"Mary was here to-day," remarked Mrs. Hunter. "She came to say that she was better, and could do some work if I had any. I fear it is a deceitful improvement. She is terribly thin and wan. No; this state of things must have been bad for her. She looks as if she were half famished."

"She only looks what she is," said Austin.

"Oh, Austin! I should have been so thankful to help her to strengthening food during this scarcity," Mrs. Hunter exclaimed, the tears rising in her eyes. "But I have not dared. You know what Mr. Hunter's opinion is—that the men have brought it upon themselves, and that, to help their families, only in the least degree, would be encouraging them to hold out, and would tend to prolong the contest. He positively forbade me helping any of them: and I could only obey. I have kept indoors as much as possible; that I might avoid the sight of the distress which I must not relieve. But I ordered Mary a good meal here this morning: Mr. Hunter did not object to that. Here he is." Mr. Hunter entered, leaning upon Florence. He looked like an old man, rather than one of middle age.

"Baxendale is back, sir," Austin observed, after a few words on business matters had passed in an under tone.

"Come to his senses at last, has he?" cried Mr. Hunter.

"That is just what I told him he had done, sir."

"Has he signed the declaration?"

"Of course he has. The men have to do that, you know, sir, before they get any work. He says he wishes he had come back at first."

"So do a good many others, in their hearts," answered Mr. Hunter, significantly. "But they can't pluck up the courage to acknowledge it."

"The men are most bitter against him—urged on, no doubt, by the Union. They—"

"Against Baxendale?"

"Against Baxendale. He came to speak to me before breakfast. I gave him the declaration to read and sign, and sent him to work at once. In the course of the morning it had got wind; though Baxendale told me he had given Sam Shuck notice of his intention on Saturday night. At dinner time, when Baxendale was quitting the yard, there were, I should say, a couple of hundred men assembled there—"

"The Daffodil Delight people?" interrupted Mr. Hunter.

"Yes. Our late men chiefly, and a sprinkling of Mr. Henry's. They were waiting there for Baxendale, and the moment he appeared, the yells, the hisses, the groans, were dreadful. I suspected what it was, and ran out. But for my doing so, I believe they would have set upon him."

"Mark you, Clay! I will protect my workmen to the very limit of the law. Let the malcontents lay but a finger upon any one of them, and they shall assuredly be punished to the uttermost," reiterated Mr. Hunter, bringing down his hand forcibly. "What did you do?"

"I spoke to them just as you have now spoken," said Austin. "Their threatenings to the man were terrible. I dared them to lay a finger upon him; I assured them that the language they were using was punishable. Had the police been in the way—but the more you want them, the less they are to be seen—I should have handed a few into custody."

"Who were the ringleaders?"—"I can scarcely tell. Ryan, the Irishman, was busy, and so was Jim Dunn; Cheek, also, backed by his wife."

"Oh, you had women also!"

"In plenty," said Austin. "One of them—I think it was Cooper's wife—roared out a challenge to fight *Mrs.* Baxendale, if her man, Cooper, as she expressed it, was too much of a woman to fight *him*. There will be bloodshed, I fear, sir, before the thing is over."

"If there is, let they who cause it look to themselves," said Mr. Hunter, speaking as sternly as he felt. "How did it end?"

"I cleared a passage for Baxendale, and they yelled and hooted him home," replied Austin. "I suppose they'd like to take my life, sir," he said to me; "but I think I am only doing right in returning to work. I could not let my family and Mary quite starve. This afternoon all was quiet; Quale told me the men were holding a meeting."

Florence was sitting with her hands clasped, her colour gradually rising. "If they should—set upon Baxendale, and—and injure him!" she breathed.

"Then the law would see what it could do towards getting some of them punished," sternly spoke Mr. Hunter.

"Oh, James!" interposed his wife, her pale cheeks flushing, as the words grated on her ears. "Can nothing be done to prevent it? Prevention is better than cure. Austin, will you not give notice to the police, and tell them to be on the alert?"

"I have done it," answered Austin.

"Papa," said Florence, "have you heard that Robert Darby's children are ill?—likely to die? They are suffering dreadfully from want. Mary Baxendale said so when she was here this morning."

"I know nothing about Robert Darby or his children," was the uncompromising reply of Mr. Hunter. "If a man sees his children starving before him, and will not work to feed them, he deserves to find them ill. Florence, I see what you mean—you would like to ask me to permit you to send them relief. *I will not.*"

Do not judge of Mr. Hunter's humanity by the words, or deem him an unfeeling man. He was far from that. Had the men been out of work through misfortune, he would have been the first to forward them succour; many and many a time had he done it in cases of sickness. He considered, as did most of the other London masters, that to help the men or their families in any way, would but tend to prolong the dispute. And there was certainly reason in their argument—if the men wished to feed their children, why did they not work for them?

"Sir," whispered Austin, when he was going, and Mr. Hunter went with him into the hall, "that bill of Lamb's came back to us to-day, noted."

"No!"—"It did, indeed. I had to take it up."

Mr. Hunter lifted his hands. "This wretched state of things! It will bring on ruin, it will bring on ruin. I heard one of the masters curse the men the other day in his perplexity and anger; there are times when I am tempted to follow his example. Ruin! for my wife and for Florence!"

"Mr. Hunter," exclaimed Austin, greatly agitated, and speaking in the moment's impulse, "why will you not give me the hope of winning her? I will make her a happy home—"

"Be silent!" sternly interrupted Mr. Hunter. "I have told you that Florence can never be yours. If you cannot put away this unthankful subject, at once and for ever, I must forbid you the house."

"Good night, sir," returned Austin. And he went away, sighing heavily.

IV

Somebody "Pitched into"

How do the poor manage to pull through illness? Through distress, through hunger, through cold, through nakedness; above all, through the close, unwholesome atmosphere in which too many of them are obliged to live, they struggle on from sickness back to health. Look at the children of Robert Darby. The low fever which attacked them had in some inexplicable way been subdued, without its going on to the dreaded typhus. If typhus had appeared at that untoward time in Daffodil's Delight, why, then, no earthly power could have kept many from the grave. Little pale, pinched forms, but with the disease gone, there sat Darby's children. Colder weather had come, and they had gathered round the bit of fire in their close room: fire it could scarcely be called, for it was only a few decaying embers. All sat on the floor, save Willy; he was in a chair, leaning his head back on a pillow. The boy had probably never been fitted by constitution for a prolonged life, though he might have lasted some years more under favourable surroundings; as it was, fever and privation had done their work with him, and the little spirit was nearly worn out. Mrs. Darby had taken him round to Mr. Rice. "He does not want me, he wants good nourishment, and plenty of it," was the apothecary's announcement! And Mrs. Darby took him home again. "Mother, the fire's nearly out."

"I can't help it, Willy. There's no coal, and nothing to buy it with."—"Take something, mother."

You may or may not, as you are acquainted or not with the habits of the poor, be aware that this sentence referred to the pawnbroker: spoken out fully it would have been, "Take something and pledge it, mother." In cases of long-continued general distress, the children of a family know just as much about its ways and means as the heads do. Mrs. Darby cast her eyes round the kitchen. There was nothing to take, nothing that would raise them help, to speak of. As she stood over Willy, parting the hair with her gentle finger upon his little pale brow, her tears dropped upon his face. The pillow on which his head leaned? Ay; she had thought of that with longing; but how would his poor aching head do without it? The last things put in pledge had been

Darby's tools. The latch of the door opened, and Grace entered. She appeared to be in some deep distress. Flinging herself on a chair, she clasped hold of her mother, sobbing wildly, clinging to her as if for protection. "Oh, mother, they have accused me of theft; the police have been had to me!" were the confused words that broke from her lips. Grace had taken a service in a baker's family, where there was an excessively cross mistress. She was a well-conducted, honest girl, and, since the distress had commenced at home, had brought her wages straight to her mother, whenever they were paid her. For the last week or two, the girl had brought something more. On the days when she believed she could get a minute to run home in the evening, she had put by her allowance of meat at dinner—they lived well at the baker's—and made it upon bread and potatoes. Had Grace for a moment suspected there was anything wrong or dishonest in this, she would not have done it: she deemed the meat was hers, and she took it to Willy. On this day, two good slices of mutton were cut for her; she put them by, ate her potatoes and bread, and after dinner, upon being sent on an errand past Daffodil's Delight, was taking them out with her. The mistress pounced upon her. She abused her, she reproached her with theft, she called her husband to join in the accusation; and finally, a policeman was brought in from the street, probably more to frighten the girl than to give her in charge. It did frighten her in no measured degree. She protested, as well as she could do it for her sobs, that she had no dishonest thought; that she had believed the meat to be hers to eat it or not as she pleased, and that she was going to take it to her little brother, who was dying. The policeman decided that it was not a case for charge at the police-court, and the baker's wife ended the matter by turning her out. All this, with sobs and moans, she by degrees explained now.

Robert Darby, who had entered during the scene, placed his hand, more in sorrow than in anger, upon Grace's shoulder, in his stern honesty. "Daughter, I'd far rather we all dropped down here upon the floor and died out with starvation, than that you should have brought home what was not yours to bring."

"There's no need for *you* to scold her, Robert," spoke Mrs. Darby, with more temper than she, meek woman that she was, often betrayed: and her conscience told her that she had purposely kept these little episodes from her husband. "It is the bits of meat she has fed him with twice or thrice a week that has just kept life in him; that's my firm belief."

"She shouldn't have done it; it was not hers to bring," returned Robert Darby.

"What else has he had to feed him?" proceeded the wife, determined to defend the girl. "What do any of us have? *You* are getting nothing." The tone was a reproachful one. With her starving children before her, and one of them dying, the poor mother's wrung heart could but speak out.

"I know I am getting nothing. Is it my fault? I wish I could get something. I'd work my fingers to the bone to keep my children."

"Robert, let me speak to you," she said in an imploring tone, the tears gushing from her eyes. "I have sat here this week and asked myself, every hour of it, what we shall do. All our things, that money can be made on, are gone; the pittance we get allowed by the society does not keep body and soul together; and this state of affairs gets worse, and will get worse. What is to become of us? What are we to do?" Robert Darby leaned in his old jacket—one considerably the worse for wear—against the kitchen wall, his countenance gloomy, his attitude bespeaking misery. He knew not what they were to do, therefore he did not attempt to say. Grace had laid down her inflamed face upon the edge of Willy's pillow and was sobbing silently. The others sat on the floor: very quiet; as semi-starved little ones are apt to be. "You have just said you would work your fingers to the bone to keep your children," resumed Mrs. Darby to her husband.

"I'd work for them till the flesh dropped off me. I'd ask no better than to do it," he vehemently said. "But where am I to get work to do now?"

"Baxendale has got it," she rejoined in a low tone.

Grace started from her leaning posture.

"Oh, father, do as Baxendale has done! don't let the children quite starve. If you had been in work, this dreadful thing would not have happened. It will be a slur upon me for life."

"So I would work, girl, but for the Trades' Unions."

"Father, the Trades' Unions seem to bring you no good; nothing but harm. Don't trust them any longer; trust the masters now."

Never was there a better meaning man than Robert Darby; but he was too easily swayed by others. Latterly it had appeared to him that the Trades' Unions did bring him harm, and his trust in them was shaken. He stood for a few moments, revolving the question in his own mind. "They'd cast me off, you see, the Trades' Unions would," he observed to his wife, in an irresolute tone.

"What if they did? The masters would take you on. Stand right with the masters—"

Mrs. Darby was interrupted by a shriek from Grace. Little Willy, whom nobody had been giving attention to, was lying back with a white face, senseless. Whether from the weakness of his condition, or from the unusual excitement of the scene going on around him, certain it was that the child had fainted. There was some little bustle in bringing him to, and Mrs. Darby sat down, the boy upon her lap.

"What ailed you, deary?" said Robert Darby, bending down to him.

"I don't know, father," returned the child. And his voice was fainter than ever.

Mrs. Darby pulled her husband's ear close to her lips. "When the boy's dead, you'll wish you had cared for him more than for the Trades' Unions; and worked for him."

The words told upon the man. Perhaps for the first time he had fully realized to his imagination the moment when he should see his boy lying dead before him. "I will work," he exclaimed. "Willy, boy, father will go and get work; and he'll soon bring you home something good to eat, as he used to." Willy's hot lips parted with a pleasant smile of response; his blue eyes glistened brightly. Robert Darby bent his rough, unshaven face, and took a kiss from the child's smooth one. "Yes, my boy; father *will* work."

He went out, bending his steps towards Slippery Sam's—who, by the way, had latterly tried to exact the title of "Mr. Shuck." There was a code of honour—as they regarded it—amidst these operatives of the Hunters, to do nothing underhanded. That is, not to resume work without first speaking to the Unions' man, Sam Shuck—as was mentioned in the case of Baxendale. It happened that Mr. Shuck was standing in the strip of garden before his house, carrying on a wordy war over the palings with Mrs. Quale, when Darby came up. Peter Quale had of course been locked out with the rest, but with the first hour that Mr. Hunter's yard was opened, Peter returned to his work. He did not belong to the Trades' Unions—he never had belonged to them and never would; therefore, he was a free man. Strange to say, he was left to do as he liked in peace; somehow the Union did not care to interfere with Peter Quale—for one thing, he occupied a better position in the yard than most of the men. Peter pursued his own course quietly—going to his work and returning from it, saying little to the malcontents of Daffodil's Delight. Not so Mrs. Quale; she exercised her tongue upon them whenever she got the chance. Her motive was a good one: she was at heart sorry for the privation at present existing in Daffodil's Delight, and would have liked to shame the men into going to work again.

"Now, Robert Darby! how are them children of your'n?" began she. "Starved out yet?"

"Next door to it," was Darby's answer.

"And whose is the fault?" she went on. "If I had children, and my husband wouldn't work to keep 'em out of their graves, through getting some nasty mistaken crotchet in his head, and holding out when the work was going a-begging, I'd go before a magistrate and see if I couldn't have the law of him."

"You'd do a good many things if you wore the breeches," interposed Sam Shuck, with a sneer; "but you don't, you know."

"You be wearing whole breeches now, which you get out of the blood and marrow of the poor misguided men," retorted Mrs. Quale. "They won't last out whole for ever, Slippery Sam."

"They'll last out as long as I want 'em to, I dare say," said Sam. "Have you come up for anything particular, Darby?"

"I have come to talk a bit, Shuck," answered Darby, inwardly shrinking from his task, and so deferring for a minute the announcement. "There seems no chance of this state of things coming to an end."

"No, that there doesn't. You men are preventing that."—"Us men!" exclaimed Robert Darby in surprise. "What do you mean?"

"I don't mean you; I don't mean the sturdy, honest fellows who hold out for their rights like men—I mean the other lot. If every operative in the kingdom had held out, to a man, the masters would have given in long ago—they must have done it; and you would all be back, working in triumph the nine hours per day. I spoke of those rats who sneak in, and take the work, to the detriment of the honest man."

"At any rate, the rats are getting the best of it just now," said Robert Darby.

"That they are," said Mrs. Quale, exultingly, who would not lose an opportunity of putting in her word. She stood facing the men, her arms resting on the palings that divided the gardens. "It isn't *their* children that are dropping into their winding-sheets through want of food."

"If I had my way, I'd hang every man who in this crisis is putting his hand to a stroke of work," exclaimed Sam Shuck. "Traitors! to turn and work for the masters after they had resorted to a lock-out! It was that lock-out floored us."

"Of course it was," assented Mrs. Quale, with marked complaisance. "If the Union only had money coming in from the men, they'd hold out for ever. But the general lock-out stopped that."

"Ugh!" growled Sam, with the addition of an ugly word.

"Well, Shuck, as things seem to be getting worse instead of better, and prospects look altogether so gloomy, I shall go back to work myself," resumed Darby, plucking up courage to say it.

"Chut," said Shuck.

"Will you tell me what I *am* to do? I'd rather turn a thousand miles the other way than I'd put my foot indoors at home, and see things as they are there. If a man can clam himself, he can't watch those belonging to him clam. Every farthing of allowance I had from the society last week was—"

"You had your share," interrupted Sam, who never cared to contend about the amount received. "Think of the thousands there is to divide it among. The subscriptions have come in very well as yet, but they be falling off now."

"And think of the society's expenses," interposed Mrs. Quale, with suavity. "The scores of gentlemen, like Mr. Shuck, there is to pay, and keep on the fat of the land. He'll be going into Parliament next!"

"You shut up, will you?" roared Sam. "Ryan," called out he to the Irishman, who was lounging up, "here's Darby saying he thinks he shall go to work."

"Oh, but that would be rich," said Ryan, with a laugh, as he entered the garden, and took his standing beside Sam Shuck. "Darby, man, you'd never desert the society! It couldn't spare you."

"I want to do for the best," said Darby; "and it seems to me that to hold out is for the worse. Shuck, just answer me a question or two, as from man to man. If the masters fill their yards with other operatives, what is to become of us?"

"They can't fill their yards with other operatives," returned Shuck. "Where's the use of talking nonsense?"

"But they can. They are doing it."

"They are not. They have just got a sprinkling of men for show—not many. Where are they to get them from?"

"Do you know what I heard? That Mr. Henry Hunter has been over to Belgium, and one or two of the other masters have also been, and—"

"There's no fear of the Beljim workmen," interrupted Ryan. "What English master 'ud employ them half-starved frogs?"

"I heard that Mr. Henry Hunter was quite thunderstruck at their skill," continued Darby, paying no attention to the interruption. "Their tools are bad: they are not to be called tools, compared to ours; but they turn out finished work. Their decorative work is beautiful. Mr. Henry Hunter put the question to them, whether they would like to come to England and earn five-and-sixpence per day, instead of three shillings as they do there, and they jumped at it. He told them that perhaps he might be sending for them."

"Where did you bear that fine tale?" asked Slippery Sam.

"It's going about among us. I dare say you have heard it also, Shuck. Mr. Henry was away somewhere for nine or ten days."

"Let 'em come, them Beljicks," sneered Ryan. "Maybe they'd go back with their heads off. It couldn't take much to split the skull of them French beggars."

"Not when an Irishman holds the stick," cried Mrs. Quale, looking the man steadily in the face, as she left the palings.

Ryan watched her away, and resumed. "How dare the masters think of taking on forringers? Leaving us to starve!"

"The preventing of it lies with us," said Darby. "If we go back to work, there'll be no room for them."

"Listen, Darby," rejoined Shuck, in a persuasive tone of confidence, the latter in full force, now that his enemy, Mrs. Quale, had gone. "The bone of contention is the letting us work nine hours a day instead of ten: well, why should they not accord it? Isn't there every reason why they should? Isn't there men, outsiders, willing to work a full day's work, but can't get it? This extra hour, thrown up by us, would give employment to them. Would the masters be any the worse off?"

"They say they'd be the hour's wages out of pocket."

"Flam!" exclaimed Sam. "It would come out of the public's pocket, not out of the masters'. They would add so much the more on to their contracts, and nobody would be the worse. It's just a dogged feeling of obstinacy that's upon 'em; it's nothing else. They'll come-to in the end, if you men will only let them; they can't help doing it. Hold out, hold out, Darby! If we are to give into them now, where has been the use of this struggle? Haven't you waited for it, and starved for it, and hoped for it?"

"Very true," replied Darby, feeling in a perplexing maze of indecision.

"Don't give in, man, at the eleventh hour," urged Shuck, with affectionate eloquence: and to hear him you would have thought he had nothing in the world at heart so much as the interest of Robert Darby. "A little longer, and the victory will be ours. You see, it is not the bare fact of your going back that does the mischief, it's the example it sets. But for that scoundrel Baxendale's turning tail, you would not have thought about it."

"I don't know that," said Darby.

"One bad sheep will spoil a flock," continued Sam, puffing away at a cigar which he was smoking. He would have enjoyed a pipe a great deal more; but gentlemen smoked cigars, and Sam wanted to look as much like a gentleman as he could; it had been suggested to him that it would add to his power over the operatives. "Why, Darby, we have got it all in our own hands—if you men could but be brought to see it. It's as plain as the nose before you. Us, builders, taking us in all our branches, might be the most united and prosperous body of men in the world. Only let us pull together, and have consideration for our fellows, and put away selfishness. Binding ourselves to work on an equality, nine hours a day being the limit; eight, perhaps, after a while—"

"It's a good thing you have not got much of an audience here, Sam Shuck! That doctrine of yours is false and pernicious; its in opposition to the laws of God and man." The interruption proceeded from Dr. Bevary. He had come into the garden unperceived by Sam, who was lounging on the side palings, his back to the gate. The doctor was on his way to pay a visit to Mary Baxendale. Sam started up. "What did you say, sir?"

"What did I say!" repeated Dr. Bevary. "I think it should be, what did you say? You would dare to circumscribe the means of usefulness God has given to man—to set a limit to his talents and his labour! You would say, 'So far shall you work, and no farther!' Who are you, and all such as you, that you should assume such power, and set yourselves up between your fellow-men and their responsibilities?"

"Hear, hear," interrupted Mrs. Quale, putting her head out at her window—for she had gone indoors. "Give him a bit of truth, sir."

"I have been a hard worker for years," continued Dr. Bevary, paying no attention, it must be confessed, to Mrs. Quale. "Mentally and practically I have toiled—*toiled*, Sam Shuck—to improve and make use of the talents entrusted to me. My days are spent in alleviating, so far as may be, the sufferings of my fellow-creatures; when I go to rest, I often lie awake half the night, pondering difficult questions of medical science. What man living has God endowed with power to come and say to me, 'You shall not do this; you shall only work half your hours; you shall only earn a limited amount of fees?' Answer me."

"It's not a parallel case, sir, with ours," returned Sam.

"It is a parallel case," said Dr. Bevary. "There's your friend next door, Peter Quale; take him. By diligence he has made himself into a finished artizan; by dint of industry in working over hours, he is amassing a competence that will keep him out of the workhouse in his old age. What reason or principle of justice can there be in your saying, 'He shall not do this; he shall receive no more than I do, or than Ryan, there, does? Because Ryan is an inferior workman, and I love idleness and drink and agitation better than work, Quale and others shall not work to have an advantage over us; we will share and fare alike.' Out upon you, Slippery Sam, for promulgating doctrines so false! You must be the incarnation of selfishness, or you could not do it. If ever they obtain sway in free and enlightened England, the independence of the workman will be at an end." The Doctor stepped in to Shuck's house, on his way to Mary Baxendale, leaving Sam on the gravel. Sam put his arm within Darby's, and led him down the street, out of the Doctor's way, who would be coming forth again presently. There he set himself to undo what the Doctor's words had done, and to breathe persuasive arguments into Darby's ear. Later, Darby went home. It had grown dusk then, for Sam had treated him to a glass at the Bricklayers' Arms, where sundry other friends were taking their glasses. There appeared to be a commotion in his house as he entered; his wife, Grace, and the young ones were standing round Willy.

"He has had another fainting fit," said Mrs. Darby to her husband, in explanation. "And now—I declare illness is the strangest thing!—he says he is hungry." The child put out his hot hand. "Father!" Robert Darby advanced and took it. "Be you better, dear? What ails you this evening?"

"Father," whispered the child, hopefully, "have you got the work?"

"When do you begin, Robert?" asked the wife. "To-morrow?"

Darby's eyes fell, and his face clouded. "I can't ask for it; I can't go back to work," he answered. "The society won't let me."

A great cry. A cry from the mother, from Grace, from the poor little child. Hope, sprung up once more within them, had been illumining the past few hours. "You shall soon have food; father's going to work again, darlings," the mother had said to the hungry little ones. And now the hopes were dashed! The disappointment was hard to bear. "Is he to *die* of hunger?" exclaimed Mrs. Darby, in bitterness, pointing to Willy. "You said you would work for him."

"So I would, if they'd let me. I'd work the life out of me, but what I'd get a crust for ye all; but the Trades' Union won't have it," panted Darby, his breath short with excitement. "What am I to do?"

"Work without the Trades' Union, father," interposed Grace, taking courage to speak. She had always been a favourite with her father. "Baxendale has done it."

"They are threatening Baxendale awfully," he answered. "But it is not that I'd care for; it's this. The society would put a mark upon me: I should be a banned man: and when this struggle's over, they say I should be let get work by neither masters nor men. My tools are in pledge, too," he added, as if that climax must end the contest.

Mrs. Darby threw her apron over her eyes and burst into tears; Grace was already crying silently, and the boy had his imploring little hands held up. "Robert, they are your own children!" said the wife, meekly. "I never thought you'd see them starve."

Another minute, and the man would have cried with them. He went out of doors, perhaps to sob his emotion away. Two or three steps down the street he encountered John Baxendale. The latter slipped five shillings into his hand. Darby would have put it back again.

"Tut, man; don't be squeamish. Take it for the children. You'd do as much for mine, if you had got it and I hadn't. Mary and I have been talking about you. She heard you having an argument with that snake, Shuck."

"They be starving, Baxendale, or I wouldn't take it," returned the man, the tears running down his pinched face. "I'll pay you back with the first work I get. You call Shuck a snake; do you think he is one?"

"I'm sure of it," said Baxendale. "I don't know that he means ill, but can't you see the temptation it is?—all this distress and agitation that's ruining us, is making a gentleman of him. He and the other agents are living on the fat of the land, as Quale's wife calls it, and doing nothing for their pay, except keeping up the agitation. If we all went to work again quietly, where would they be? Why, they'd have to go to work also, for their pay must cease. Darby, I think the eyes of you union men must be blinded, not to see this."

"It seems plain enough to me at times," assented Darby. "I say, Baxendale," he added, wishing to speak a word of warning to his friend ere he turned away, "have a care of yourself; they are going on again you at a fine rate."

Come what would, Darby determined to furnish a home meal with this relief, which seemed like a very help from heaven. He bought two pounds of beef, a pound of cheese, some tea, some sugar, two loaves of bread, and a lemon to make drink for Willy. Turning home with these various treasures, he became aware that a bustle had arisen in the street. Men and women were pressing down towards one particular spot. Tongues were busy; but he could not at first obtain an insight into the cause of the commotion.

"An obnoxious man had been set upon in a lonely corner, under cover of the night's darkness, and pitched into," was at length explained. "Beaten to death." Away flew Darby, a horrible suspicion at his heart. Pushing his way amidst the crowd collected round the spot, as only a resolute man can do, he stood face to face with the sight. One, trampled on and beaten, lay in the dust, his face covered with blood.

"Is it Baxendale?" shouted Darby, for he was unable to recognise him.

"It's Baxendale, as sure as a trivet. Who else should it be? He have caught it at last."

But there were pitying faces around. Humanity revolted at the sight; and quiet, inoffensive John Baxendale, had ever been liked in Daffodil's Delight. Robert Darby, his voice rising to a shriek with emotion, held out his armful of provisions.

"Look here! I wanted to work, but the Union won't let me. My wife and children be a starving at home, one of them dying: I came out, for I couldn't bear to stop indoors in the misery. There I met a friend—it seemed to me more like an angel—and he gave me money to feed my children; made me take it; he said if I had money and he had not, I'd do as much for him. See what I bought with it: I was carrying it home for my poor children when this cry arose. Friends, the one to give it me was Baxendale. And you have murdered him!" Another great cry, even as Darby concluded, arose to break the deep stillness. No stillness is so deep as that caused by emotion.

"He is not dead!" shouted the crowd. "See! he is stirring! Who could have done this!"

V

A Gloomy Chapter

The winter had come in, intensely hard. Frost and snow lay early upon the ground. Was that infliction in store—a bitter winter—to be added to the already fearful distress existing in this dense metropolis? The men held out from work, and the condition of their families was something sad to look upon. Distress of a different nature existed in the house of Mr. Hunter. It was a house of sorrow; for its mistress lay dying. The spark of life had long been flickering, and now its time to depart had come. Haggard, worn, pale, stood Mr. Hunter in his drawing-room. He was conversing with his brother Henry. Their topic was business. In spite of existing domestic woes, men of business cannot long forget their daily occupation. Mr. Henry Hunter had come in to inquire news of his sister-in-law, and the conversation insensibly turned on other matters.

"Of course I shall weather it," Mr. Henry was saying, in answer to a question. "It will be a fearful loss, with so much money out, and buildings in process standing still. Did it last very much longer, I hardly know that I could. And you, James?" Mr. Hunter evaded the question. Since the time, years back, when they had dissolved partnership, he had shunned all allusion to his own prosperity, or non-prosperity, with his brother. Possibly he feared that it might lead to that other subject—the mysterious paying away of the five thousand pounds.

"For my part, I do not feel so sure of the strike's being near its end," he remarked.

"I have positive information that the eligibility of withdrawing the strike at the Messrs. Pollocks' has been mooted by the central committee of the Union," said Mr. Henry. "If nothing else has brought the men to their senses, this weather must do it. It will end as nearly all strikes have ended—in their resuming work upon our terms."

"But what an incalculable amount of suffering they have brought upon themselves!" exclaimed Mr. Hunter. "I do not see what is to become of them, either, in future. How are they all to find work again? We shall not turn off the stranger men who have worked for us in this emergency, to make room for them."

"No, indeed," replied Mr. Henry. "And those strangers amount to nearly half my complement of hands. Do you recollect a fellow of the name of Moody?"

"Of course I do. I met him the other day, looking like a walking skeleton. I asked him whether he was not tired of the strike. He said *he* had been tired of it long ago; but the Union would not let him be."

"He hung himself yesterday."

Mr. Hunter replied only by a gesture.

And left a written paper behind him, cursing the strike and the Trades' Unions, which had brought ruin upon him and his family. "I saw the paper," continued Mr. Henry. "A decent, quiet man he was; but timorous, and easily led away."

"Is he dead?"

"He had been dead two hours when he was found. He hung himself in that shed at the back of Dunn's house, where the men held some meetings in the commencement of the strike. I wonder how many more souls this wretched state of affairs will send, or has sent, out of the world!"

"Hundreds, directly or indirectly. The children are dying off quickly, as the Registrar-General's returns show. A period of prolonged distress always tells upon the children. And upon us also, I think," Mr. Hunter added, with a sigh.

"Upon us in a degree," Mr. Henry assented, somewhat carelessly. He was a man of substance; and, upon such, the ill effects fall lightly. "When the masters act in combination, as we have done, it is not the men who can do us permanent injury. They must give in, before great harm has had time to come. James, I saw that man this morning: your *bête noire*, as I call him." Mr. Hunter changed countenance. He could not be ignorant that his brother alluded to Gwinn of Ketterford. It happened that Mr. Henry Hunter had been cognisant of one or two of the unpleasant visits forced by the man upon his brother during the last few years. But Mr. Henry had avoided questions: he had the tact to perceive that they would only go unanswered, and be deemed unpleasant into the bargain.

"I met him near your yard. Perhaps he was going in there."

The sound of the muffled knocker, announcing a visitor, was heard the moment after Mr. Henry spoke, and Mr. Hunter started as though struck by a pistol-shot. At a calmer time he might have had more command over himself; but the sudden announcement of the presence of the man in town—which fact he had not been cognisant of—had startled him to tremor. That Gwinn, and nobody else, was knocking for admittance, seemed a certainty to his shattered nerves. "I cannot see him: I cannot see him!" he exclaimed, in agitation; and he backed away from the room door, unconscious what he did in his confused fear, his lips blanching to a deadly whiteness.

Mr. Henry moved up and took his hand. "James, there has been estrangement between us on this point for years. As I asked you once before, I now ask you again: confide in me and let me help you. Whatever the dreadful secret may be, you shall find me your true brother."

"Hush!" breathed Mr. Hunter, moving from his brother in his scared alarm. "Dreadful secret! who says it? There is no dreadful secret. Oh Henry! hush! hush! The man is coming in! You must leave us." Not the dreaded Gwinn, but Austin Clay. He was the one who entered. Mr. Hunter sat down, breathing heavily, the blood coming back to his face; he nearly fainted in the revulsion of feeling brought by the relief. Broken in spirit, health and nerves alike shattered, the slightest thing was now sufficient to agitate him.

"You are ill, sir!" exclaimed Austin, advancing with concern.

"No—no—I am not ill. A momentary spasm; that's all. I am subject to it."

Mr. Henry moved to the door in vexation. There was to be no more brotherly confidence between them now than there had formerly been. He spoke as he went, without turning round. "I will come in again by-and-by, James, and see how Louisa is."

The departure seemed a positive relief to Mr. Hunter. He spoke quietly enough to Austin Clay. "Who has been at the office to-day?"

"Let me see," returned Austin, with a purposed carelessness. "Lyall came, and Thompson—"

"Not men on business, not men on business," Mr. Hunter interrupted with feverish eagerness. "Strangers."

"Gwinn of Ketterford," answered Austin, with the same assumption of carelessness. "He came twice. No other strangers have called, I think."

Whether his brother's request, that he should be enlightened as to the "dreadful secret," had rendered Mr. Hunter suspicious that others might surmise there was a secret, certain it is that he looked up sharply as Austin spoke, keenly regarding his countenance, noting the sound of his voice. "What did he want?"

"He wanted you, sir. I said you were not to be seen. I let him suppose that you were too ill to be seen. Bailey, who was in the counting-house at the time, gave him the gratuitous information that Mrs. Hunter was very ill—in danger."

Why this answer should have increased Mr. Hunter's suspicions, he best knew. He rose from his seat, grasped Austin's arm, and spoke with menace. "You have been prying into my affairs! You sought out those Gwinns when you last went to Ketterford! You—"

Austin withdrew from the grasp, and stood before his master, calm and upright. "Mr. Hunter!"

"Was it not so?"

"No, sir. I thought you had known me better. I should be the last to 'pry' into anything that you might wish to keep secret."

"Austin, I am not myself to-day, I am not myself," cried the poor gentleman, feeling how unjustifiable had been his suspicions. "This grief, induced by the state of Mrs. Hunter, unmans me."

"How is she, sir, by this time?"

"Calm and collected, but sinking fast. You must go up and see her. She said she should like to bid you farewell." Through the warm corridors, so well protected from the bitter cold reigning without, Austin was conducted to the room of Mrs. Hunter. Florence, her eyes swollen with weeping, quitted it as he entered. She lay in bed, her pale face raised upon pillows; save for that pale face and the laboured breathing, you would not have suspected the closing scene to be so near. She lifted her feeble hand and made prisoner of Austin's. The tears gathered in his eyes as he looked down upon her.

"Not for me, dear Austin," she whispered, as she noted the signs of sorrow. "Weep rather for those who are left to battle yet with this sad world." The words caused Austin to wonder whether she could have become cognisant of the nature of Mr. Hunter's long-continued trouble. He swallowed down the emotion that was rising in his throat.

"Do you feel no better?" he gently inquired.

"I feel well, save for the weakness. All pain has left me. Austin, I shall be glad to go. I have only one regret, the leaving Florence. My husband will not be long after me; I read it in his face."

"Dear Mrs. Hunter, will you allow me to say a word to you on the subject of Florence?" he breathed, seizing on the swiftly-passing opportunity. "I have wished to do it before we finally part."

"Say what you will."

"Should time and perseverance on my part be crowned with success, so that the prejudices of Mr. Hunter become subdued, and I succeed in winning Florence, will you not say that you bless our union?"

Mrs. Hunter paused. "Are we quite alone?" she asked. Austin glanced round to the closed door. "Quite," he answered.

"Then, Austin, I will say more. My hearty consent and blessing be upon you both, if you can, indeed, subdue the objection of Mr. Hunter. Not otherwise: you understand that."

"Without her father's consent, I am sure that Florence would not give me hers. Have you any idea in what that objection lies?"

"I have not. Mr. Hunter is not a man who will submit to be questioned, even by me. But, Austin, I cannot help thinking that this objection to you may fade away—for, that he likes and esteems you greatly, I know. Should that time come, then tell him that I loved you—that I wished Florence to become your wife—that I prayed God to bless the union. And then tell Florence."

"Will you not tell her yourself?"

Mrs. Hunter made a feeble gesture of denial. "It would seem like an encouragement to dispute the decision of her father. Austin, will you say farewell, and send my husband to me? I am growing faint." He clasped her attenuated hands in both his; he bent down, and kissed her forehead. Mrs. Hunter held him to her. "Cherish and love her always, should she become yours," was the feeble whisper. "And come to me, come to me, both of you, in eternity."

A moment or two in the corridor to compose himself, and Austin met Mr. Hunter on the stairs, and gave him the message. "How is Baxendale?" Mr. Hunter stayed to ask.

"A trifle better. Not yet out of danger."

"You take care to give him the allowance weekly?"

"Of course I do, sir. It is due to-night, and I am going to take it to him."

"Will he ever be fit for work again?"—"I hope so."

Another word or two on the subject of Baxendale, the attack on whom Mr. Hunter most bitterly resented, and Austin departed. Mr. Hunter entered his wife's chamber. Florence, who was also entering, Mrs. Hunter feebly waved away. "I would be a moment alone with your father, my child. James," Mrs. Hunter said to her husband, as Florence retired—but her voice was now so reduced that he had to bend his ear to catch the sounds—"there has been estrangement between us on one point for many years: and it seems—I know not why—to be haunting my death-bed. Will you not, in this my last hour, tell me its cause?"

"It would not give you peace, Louisa. It concerns myself alone."

"Whatever the secret may be, it has been wearing your life out. I ought to know it."

Mr. Hunter bent lower. "My dear wife, it would not bring you peace, I say. I contracted an obligation in my youth," he whispered, in answer to the yearning glance thrown up to him, "and I have had to pay it off—one sum after another, one after another, until it has nearly drained me. It will soon be at an end now."

"Is it nearly paid?"—"Ay. All but."

"But why not have told me this? It would have saved me many a troubled hour. Suspense, when fancy is at work, is hard to bear. And you, James: why should simple debt, if it is that, have worked so terrible a fear upon you?"

"I did not know that I could stave it off: looking back, I wonder that I did do it. I could have borne ruin for myself: I could not, for you."

"Oh, James!" she fondly said, "should I have been less brave? While you and Florence were spared to me, ruin might have done its worst." Mr. Hunter turned his face away: strangely wrung and haggard it looked just then. "What a mercy that it is over!"

"All but, I said," he interrupted. And the words seemed to burst from him in an uncontrollable impulse, in spite of himself.

"It is the only thing that has marred our life's peace, James. I shall soon be at rest. Perfect peace! perfect happiness! May all we have loved be there! I can see—"

The words had been spoken disjointedly, in the faintest whisper, and, with the last one died away. She laid her head upon her husband's arm, and seemed as if she would sleep. He did not disturb her: he remained buried in his own thoughts. A short while, and Florence was heard at the door. Dr. Bevary was there.

"You can come in," called out Mr. Hunter.

They approached the bed. Florence saw a change in her mother's face, and uttered an exclamation of alarm. The physician's practised eye detected what had happened: he made a sign to the nurse who had followed him in, and the woman went forth to carry the news to the household. Mr. Hunter alone was calm.

"Thank God!" was his strange exclamation.

"Oh, papa! papa! it is death!" sobbed Florence, in her distress. "Do you not see that it is death?"

"Thank God also, Florence," solemnly said Dr. Bevary. "She is better off."

Florence sobbed wildly. The words sounded to her ears needlessly cruel—out of place. Mr. Hunter bent his face on that of the dead, with a long, fervent kiss. "My wronged wife!" he mentally uttered. Dr. Bevary followed him as he left the room.

"James Hunter, it had been a mercy for you had she been taken years ago."

Mr. Hunter lifted his hands as if beating off the words, and his face turned white. "Be still! be still! what can *you* know?"

"I know as much as you," said Dr. Bevary, in a tone which, low though it was, seemed to penetrate to the very marrow of the unhappy man. "The knowledge has disturbed my peace by day, and my rest by night. What, then, must it have done by yours?"

James Hunter, his hands held up still to shade his face, and his head down, turned away. "It was the fault of another," he wailed, "and I have borne the punishment."

"Ay," said Dr. Bevary, "or you would have had my reproaches long ago. Hark! whose voice is that?" It was one known only too well to Mr. Hunter. He cowered for a moment, as he had hitherto had terrible cause to do: the next, he raised his head, and shook off the fear.

"I can dare him now," he bravely said, turning to the stairs with a cleared countenance, to meet Gwinn of Ketterford.

He had obtained entrance in this way. The servants were closing up the windows of the house, and one of them had gone outside to tell the gossiping servant of a neighbour that their good lady and ever kind mistress was dead, when the lawyer arrived. He saw what was being done, and drew his own conclusions. Nevertheless, he desisted not from the visit he had come to pay.

"I wish to see Mr. Hunter," he said, while the door stood open.

"I do not think you can see him now, sir," was the reply of the servant. "My master is in great affliction."

"Your mistress is dead, I suppose."—"Just dead."

"Well, I shall not detain Mr. Hunter many minutes," rejoined Gwinn, pushing his way into the hall. "I must see him."

The servant hesitated. But his master's voice was heard. "You can admit that person, Richard."

The man opened the door of the front room. It was in darkness; the shutters were closed; so he turned to the door of the other, and showed the guest in. The soft perfume from the odoriferous plants in the conservatory was wafted to the senses of Gwinn of Ketterford as he entered. "Why do you seek me here?" demanded Mr. Hunter when he appeared. "Is it a fitting time and place?"

"A court of law might perhaps be more fit," insolently returned the lawyer. "Why did you not remit the money, according to promise, and so obviate the necessity of my coming?"

"Because I shall remit no more money. Not another farthing, or the value of one, shall you ever obtain of me. If I have submitted to your ruinous and swindling demands, you know why I have done it—"

"Stop!" interrupted Mr. Gwinn. "You have had your money's worth—silence."

Mr. Hunter was deeply agitated. "As the breath went out of my wife's body, I thanked God that He had taken her—that she was removed from the wicked machinations of you and yours. But for the bitter wrong dealt out to me by your wicked sister Agatha, I should have mourned for her with regrets and tears. You have made my life into a curse: I purchased your silence that you should not render hers one. The fear and the thraldom are alike over."

Mr. Gwinn laughed significantly. "Your daughter lives."

"She does. In saying that I will make her cognisant of this, rather than supply you with another sixpence, you may judge how firm is my determination."

"It will be startling news for her."

"It will: should it come to the telling. Better that she hear it, and make the best and the worst of it, than that I should reduce her to utter poverty—and your demands, supplied, would do that. The news will not kill her—as it might have killed her mother."

Did Lawyer Gwinn feel baffled? For a minute or two he seemed to be at a loss for words. "I will have money," he exclaimed at length. "You have tried to stand out against it before now."

"Man! do you know that I am on the brink of ruin?" uttered Mr. Hunter, in deep excitement, "and that it is you who have brought me to it? But for the money supplied to you, I could have weathered successfully this contest with my workmen, as my brother and others are weathering it. If you have any further claim against me," he added in a spirit of mocking bitterness, "bring it against my bankruptcy, for that is looming near."

"I will not stir from your house without a cheque for the money."

"This house is sanctified by the presence of the dead," reverently spoke Mr. Hunter. "To have any disturbance in it would be most unseemly. Do not force me to call in a policeman."

"As a policeman was once called into you, in the years gone by," Lawyer Gwinn was beginning with a sneer: but Mr. Hunter raised his voice and his hand.

"Be still! Coward as I have been, in one sense, in yielding to your terms, I have never been coward enough to permit *you* to allude, in my presence, to the past. I never will. Go from my house quietly, sir: and do not attempt to re-enter it."

Mr. Hunter broke from the man—for Gwinn made an effort to detain him—opened the door, and called to the servant, who came forward.

"Show this person to the door, Richard."

An instant's hesitation with himself whether it should be compliance or resistance, and Gwinn of Ketterford went forth.

"Richard," said Mr. Hunter, as the servant closed the hall-door.—"Sir?"

"Should that man ever come here again, do not admit him. And if he shows himself troublesome, call a policeman to your aid." And then Mr. Hunter shut himself in the room, and burst into heavy tears, such as are rarely shed by man.

VI

The Little Boy at Rest

No clue whatever had been obtained to the assailants of John Baxendale. The chief injury lay in the ribs. Two or three of them were broken: the head was also much bruised and cut. He had been taken into his own home and there attended to: it was nearer than the hospital: though the latter would have been the better place. Time had gone on since, and he was now out of danger. Never would John Baxendale talk of the harshness of masters again—though, indeed, he never much talked of it. The moment Mr. Hunter heard of the assault, he sent round his own surgeon, directed Austin to give Baxendale a sovereign weekly, and caused strengthening delicacies to be served from his own house. And that was the same man whom you heard forbidding his wife and daughter to forward aid to Darby's starving children. Yes; but Mr. Hunter denied the aid upon principle: Darby would not work. It pleased him far more to accord it to Baxendale than to deny it to Darby: the one course gladdened his heart, the other pained it. The surgeon who attended was a particular friend of Dr. Bevary's, and the Doctor, in his quaint, easy manner, contrived to let Baxendale know that there would be no bill for him to pay.

It was late when Austin reached Baxendale's room the evening of Mrs. Hunter's death. Tidings of which had already gone abroad. "Oh, sir," uttered the invalid, straining his eyes on him from the sick-bed, before Austin had well entered, "is the news true?"

"It is," sadly replied Austin. "She died this afternoon."

"It is a good lady gone from among us. Does the master take on much?"

"I have not seen him since. Death came on, I believe, rather suddenly at the last."

"Poor Mrs. Hunter!" wailed Baxendale. "Hers is not the only spirit that is this evening on the wing," he added, after a pause. "That boy of Darby's is going, Mary"—looking on the bright sovereign put into his hands by Austin—"suppose you get this changed, and go down there and take 'em a couple of shillings? It's hard to have a cupboard quite empty when death's a visitor."

Mary came up from the far end of the room, and put on her shawl with alacrity. She looked but a shadow herself. Austin wondered how Mr. Hunter would approve of any of his shillings finding their way to Darby's; but he said nothing against it. But for the strongly expressed sentiments of Mr. Hunter, Austin would have given away right and left, to relieve the distress around him: although, put him upon principle, and he agreed fully with Mr. Hunter. Mary got change for the sovereign, and took possession of a couple of shillings. It was a bitterly cold evening; but she was well wrapped up. Though not permanently better, Mary was feeling stronger of late: in her simple faith, she believed God had mercifully spared her for a short while, that she might nurse her father. She knew, just as well as did Dr. Bevary, that it would not be for long. As she went along she met Mrs. Quale.

"The child is gone," said the latter, hearing where Mary was going.

"Poor child! Is he really dead?"

Mrs. Quale nodded. Few things upset her equanimity. "And I am keeping my eyes open to look out for Darby," she added. "His wife asked me if I would. She is afraid"—dropping her voice—"that he may do something rash."

"Why?" breathed Mary, in a tone of horror, understanding the allusion.

"Why!" vehemently repeated Mrs. Quale; "why, because he reflects upon himself—that's why. When he saw that the breath was really gone out of the poor little body—and that's not five minutes ago—he broke out like one mad. Them quiet natures in ordinary be always the worst if they get upset; though it takes a good deal to do it. He blamed himself, saying that if he had been in work, and able to get proper food for the boy, it would not have happened; and he cursed the Trades Unions for misleading him, and bringing him to what he is. There's many another cursing the Unions on this inclement night, or my name's not Nancy Quale." She turned back with Mary, and they entered the home of the Darbys. Grace, unable to get another situation, partly through the baker's wife refusing her a character, partly because her clothes were in pledge, looked worn and thin, as she stood trying to hush the youngest child, then crying fretfully. Mrs. Darby sat in front of the small bit of fire, the dead boy on her knees, pressed to her still, just as Mrs. Quale had left her.

"He won't hunger any more," she said, lifting her face to Mary, the hot tears running from it.

Mary stooped and kissed the little cold face. "Don't grieve," she murmured. "It would be well for us all if we were as happy as he."

"Go and speak to him," whispered the mother to Mrs. Quale, pointing to a back door, which led to a sort of open scullery. "He has come in, and is gone out there."

Leaning against the wall, in the cold moonlight, stood Robert Darby. Mrs. Quale was not very good at consolation: finding fault was more in her line. "Come, Darby, don't take on so: it won't do no good," was the best she could say. "Be a man." He seized hold of her, his shaking hands trembling, while he spoke bitter words against the Trades Unions. "Don't speak so, Robert Darby," was the rejoinder of Mrs. Quale. "You are not obliged to join the Trades' Unions; therefore there's no need to curse 'em. If you and others kept aloof from them, they'd soon die away."

"They have proved a curse to me and mine"—and the man's voice rose to a shriek, in his violent emotion. "But for them, I should have been at work long ago."

"Then I'd go to work at once, if it was me, and put the curse from me that way," concluded Mrs. Quale.

With the death of the child, things had come to so low an ebb in the Darby household, as to cause sundry kind gossipers to suggest, and to spread the suggestion as a fact, that the parish would have the honour of conducting the interment. Darby would have sold himself first. He was at Mr. Hunter's yard on the following morning before daylight, and the instant the gates were opened presented himself to the foreman as a candidate for work. That functionary would not treat with him. "We have had so many of you old hands just coming on for a day or two, and then withdrawing again, through orders of the society, or through getting frightened at being threatened, that Mr. Clay said I was to take back no more shilly-shallyers."

"Try me!" feverishly cried Darby. "I will not go from it again."

"No," said the foreman. "You can speak to Mr. Clay."

"Darby," said Austin, when the man appeared before him, "will you pass your word to me to remain? Here men come; they sign the document, they have work assigned them; and in a day or so, I hear that they have left again. It causes no end of confusion to us, for work to be taken up and laid down in that way."

"Take me on, and try me, sir. I'll stick to it as long as there's a stroke of work to do—unless they tread me to pieces as they did Baxendale. I never was cordial for the society, sir. I obeyed it, and yet a doubt was always upon me whether I might not be doing wrong. I am sure of it now. The society has worked harm to me and mine, and I will never belong to it again."

"Others have said as much of the society, and have returned to it the next day," remarked Mr. Clay.

"Perhaps so, sir. They hadn't seen one of their children die, that they'd have laid down their own lives to save—but that they had not *worked* to save. I have. Take me on, sir! He can't be buried till I have earned the wherewithal to pay for it. I'll stand to my work from henceforth—over hours, if I can get it."

Austin wrote a word on a card, and desired Darby to carry it to the foreman. "You can go to work at once," he said.

"I'll take work too, sir, if I can get it," exclaimed another man, who had come up in time to hear Austin's last words.

"What! is it you, Abel White?" exclaimed Austin, with a half-laugh. "I thought you made a boast that if the whole lot of hands came back to work, you never would, except upon your own terms."

"So I did, sir. But when I find I have been in the wrong, I am not above owning it," was the man's reply, who looked in a far better physical condition than the pinched, half-starved Darby. "I could hold out longer, sir, without much inconvenience; leastways, with a deal less inconvenience than some of them could, for I and father belong to one or two provident clubs, and they have helped us weekly, and my wife and daughters don't do amiss at their umbrella work. But I have come over to my old father's views at last; and I have made my mind up, as he did long ago, never to be a Union man again—unless the masters should turn round and make themselves into a body of tyrants; I don't know what I might do then. But there's not much danger of that—as father says—in these go-a-head days. You'll give me work, sir?"

"Upon certain conditions," replied Austin. And he sat down and proceeded to talk to the man.

VII

Mr. Dunn's Pigs Brought to Market

Daffodil's Delight and its environs were in a state of bustle—of public excitement, as may be said. Daffodil's Delight, however low its condition might be, never failed to seize hold upon any possible event, whether of a general public nature, or of a private local nature, as an excuse for getting up a little steam. On that cold winter's day, two funerals were appointed to take place: the one, that of Mrs. Hunter; the other, of little William Darby: and Daffodil's Delight, in spite of the black frost, turned out in crowds to see. You could not have passed into the square when the large funeral came forth so many had collected there. It was a funeral of mutes and plumes and horses and trappings and carriages and show. The nearer Mr. Hunter had grown to pecuniary embarrassment, the more jealous was he to guard all suspicion of it from the world. Hence the display: which the poor unconscious lady they were attending would have been the first to shrink from. Mr. Hunter, his brother, and Dr. Bevary were in the first mourning-coach: in the second, with two of the sons of Henry Hunter, and another relative, sat Austin Clay. And more followed. That took place in the morning. In the afternoon, the coffin of the boy, covered by something black—but it looked like old cloth instead of velvet—was brought out of Darby's house upon men's shoulders. Part of the family followed, and pretty nearly the whole of Daffodil's Delight brought up the rear. There it is, moving slowly down the street. Not over slowly either; for there had been a delay in some of the arrangements, and the clergyman must have been waiting for half an hour. It was a week since Darby resumed work; a long while to keep the child, but the season was winter. Darby had paid part of the expense, and had been trusted for the rest. It arrived at the burial place; and the little body was buried, there to remain until the resurrection at the last day. As Darby stood over the grave, the regret for his child was nearly lost sight of in that other and far more bitter regret, the remorse of which was telling upon him. He had kept the dead starving for months, when work was to be had for the asking!

"Don't take on so," whispered a neighbour, who knew his thoughts.

"If you had gone back to work as soon as the yards were open, you'd only have been set upon and half-killed, as Baxendale was."

"Then it would not, in that case, have been my fault if he had starved," returned Darby, with compressed lips. "His poor hungry face'll lie upon my mind for ever."

The shades of evening were on Daffodil's Delight when the attendants of the funeral returned, and Mr. Cox, the pawnbroker, was busily transacting the business that the dusk hour always brought him. Even the ladies and gentlemen of Daffodil's Delight, though they were common sufferers, and all, or nearly all, required to pay visits to Mr. Cox, imitated their betters in observing that peculiar reticence of manner which custom has thrown around these delicate negotiations. The character of their offerings had changed. In the first instance they had chiefly consisted of ornaments, whether of the house or person, or of superfluous articles of attire and of furniture. Then had come necessaries: bedding, and heavier things; and then trifles—irons, saucepans, frying-pans, gowns, coats, tools—anything; anything by which a shilling could be obtained. And now had arrived the climax when there was nothing more to take—nothing, at least, that Mr. Cox would speculate upon.

A woman went banging into the shop, and Mr. Cox recognised her for the most troublesome of his customers—Mrs. Dunn. Of all the miserable households in Daffodil's Delight, that of the Dunns' was about the worst: but Mrs. Dunn's manners and temper were fiercer than ever. The non-realization of her fond hope of good cheer and silk dresses was looked upon as a private injury, and resented as such. See her as she turns into the shop: her head, a mass of torn black cap and entangled hair; her gown, a black stuff once, dirty now, hanging in jags, and clinging round her with that peculiar cling which indicates that few, if any, petticoats are underneath; her feet scuffling along in shoes tied round the instep with white rag, to keep them on! As she was entering, she encountered a poor woman named Jones, the wife of a carpenter, as badly reduced as she was. Mrs. Jones held out a small blanket for her inspection, and spoke with the tears running down her cheeks. Apparently, her errand to Mr. Cox had been unsuccessful.

"We have kept it till the last. We said we could not lie on the sack of straw this awful weather, without the blanket to cover us. But to-day we haven't got a crumb in the house, or a ember in the grate; and Jones said, says he, 'There ain't no help for it, you must pledge it.'"

"And Cox won't take it in?" shrilly responded Mrs. Dunn. The woman shook her head, and the tears fell fast on her thin cotton shawl, as she walked away. "He says the moths has got into it."

"A pity but the moths had got into him! his eyes is sharper than they need be," shrieked Mrs. Dunn. "Here, Cox," dashing up to the counter, and flinging on it a pair of boots, "I want three shillings on them."

Mr. Cox took up the offered pledge—a thin pair of woman's boots, black cloth, with leather tips; new, they had probably cost five shillings, but they were now considerably the worse for wear. "What is the use of bringing these old things?" remonstrated Mr. Cox. "They are worth nothing."

"Everything's worth nothing, according to you," retorted Mrs. Dunn. "Come! I want three shillings on them."

"I wouldn't lend you eighteen-pence. They'd not fetch it at an auction."

Mrs. Dunn would have very much liked to fling the boots in his face. After some dispute, she condescended to ask what he would give. "I'll lend a shilling, as you are a customer, just to oblige you. But I don't care to take them in at all." More dispute; and she brought her demand down to eighteen-pence. "Not a penny more than a shilling," was the decisive reply. "I tell you they are not worth that, to me." The boots were at length left, and the shilling taken. Mrs. Dunn solaced herself with a pint of half-and-half in a beer-shop, and went home with the change.

Upon no home had the strike acted with worse effects than upon that of the Dunns: and we are not speaking now as to pecuniary matters. *They* were just as bad as they could be. Irregularity had prevailed in it at the best of times; quarrelling and contention often; embarrassment, the result of bad management, frequently. Upon such a home, distress, long continued bitter distress, was not likely to work for good. The father and a grown-up son were out of work; and the Misses Dunn were also without employment. Their patronesses, almost without exception, consisted of the ladies of Daffodil's Delight, and, as may be readily conjectured, they had no funds just now to expend upon gowns and their making. Not only this: there was, from one party or another, a good bit of money owing to the sisters for past work, and this they could not get. As a set-off to this—on the wrong side—*they* were owing bills in various directions for materials that had been long ago made up for their customers, some of whom had paid them and some not. Any that had not been paid before the strike came, remained unpaid still. The Miss Dunns might just as well have asked for the moon as for money, owing or not owing, from the distressed wives of Daffodil's Delight. So, there they were, father, mother, sons, daughters, all debarred from earning money; while all, with the younger children in addition, had to be kept. It was wearying work, that forced idleness and that forced famine; and it worked badly, especially on the girls. Quarrelling they were accustomed to; embarrassment they did not mind; irregularity in domestic affairs they had lived in all their lives; but they could not bear the distress that had now come upon them. Added to this, the girls were unpleasantly pressed for the settlement of the bills above alluded to. Mrs. Quale had from the first recommended the two sisters to try for situations: but when was advice well taken? They tossed their heads at the idea of going out to service, thereby giving up their liberty and their idleness. They said that it might prevent them getting together again their business, when things should look up; they urged that they were not fitted for service, knowing little of any sort of housework; and, finally, they asked—and there was a great deal in the plea—how they were to go out while the chief portion of their clothes was in pledge.

For the past few days certain mysterious movements on the part of Mary Ann Dunn had given rise to some talk (the usual expression for gossiping and scandal) in Daffodil's Delight. She had been almost continually out from home, and when asked where, had evaded an answer. Ever ready, as some people are, to put a bad construction upon things, it was not wanting in this case. Tales were carried home to the father and mother, and there had been a scene of attack and abuse, on Mary Ann's presenting herself at home at mid day. The girl had a fierce temper, inherited probably from her mother; she returned abuse for abuse, and finally rushed off in a passion, without having given any satisfactory defence of herself. Dunn cared for his children after a fashion, and the fear that the reports must be true, completely beat him down; cowed his spirit, as he might have put it. Mrs. Dunn, on the contrary, ranted and raved till she was hoarse; and then, being excessively thirsty, stole off surreptitiously with the boots to Mr. Cox's, and so obtained a pint of half-and-half.

She returned home again, the delightful taste of it still in her mouth. The room was stripped of all, save a few things, too old or too useless for Mr. Cox to take; and, except for a little fire, it presented a complete picture of poverty. The children lay on the boards crying; not a loud cry, but a distressed moan. Very little, indeed, even of bread, got those children; for James Dunn and his wife were too fond of beer, to expend in much else the trifle allowed them by the Trades Union. James Dunn had just come in. After the scene with his daughter, when he had a little recovered himself, he went out to keep an appointment. Some of the workmen, in a similarly distressed condition to himself, had been that day to one of the police courts, hoping to obtain pecuniary help from the magistrates. The result had been a complete failure, and Dunn sat, moody and cross, upon a bench, his depression of spirit having given place to a sort of savage anger; chiefly at his daughter Mary Ann, partly at things altogether. The pint of half-and-half upon an empty stomach had not tended to render Mrs. Dunn of a calmer temper. She addressed him snappishly. "What, you have come in! Have you got any money?" Mr. Dunn made no reply; unless a growl that sounded rather defiant constituted one. She returned to the charge. "Have you got any money, I ask? Or be you come home again with a empty pocket?"

"No; father hasn't got none: they didn't get any good by going there," interposed Jemima Dunn, as though it were a satisfaction to tell out the bad news, and who appeared to be looking in all sorts of corners and places, as if in search of something. "Ted Cheek told me, and he was one of 'em that went. The magistrate said to the men that there was plenty of work open for them if they liked to do it; and his opinion was, that if they did not like to do it, they wanted punishment instead of assistance."

"That's just my opinion," returned Mrs. Dunn, with intense aggravation. "There!"

James Dunn broke out intemperately, with violent words. And then he relapsed into his gloomy mood again.

"I can't think what's gone with my boots," exclaimed Jemima.

"Mother took 'em out," cried a little voice from the floor.

"What's that, Jacky?" asked Jemima.

"Mother took 'em out," responded Jacky.

The girl turned round, and stood still for a moment as if taking in the sense of the words. Then she attacked her mother, anger flashing from her eyes. "If you have been and took 'em to the pawnshop, you shall fetch 'em back. How dare you interfere with my things? Aren't they my boots? Didn't I buy 'em with my own money?"

"If you don't hold your tongue, I'll box your ears," shrieked Mrs. Dunn, with a look and gesture as menacing as her tone. "Hold your tongue! hold your tongue, I say, miss!"

"I shan't hold my tongue," responded Jemima, struggling between anger and tears. "I will have my boots! I want to go out, I do! and how can I go barefoot?"

"Want to go out, do you!" raved Mrs. Dunn. "Perhaps you want to go and follow your sister! The boots be at Cox's, and you may go there and get 'em. Now, then!"

The words altogether were calculated to increase the ire of Jemima; they did so in no measured degree. She and her mother commenced a mutual contest of ranting abuse. It might have come to blows but for the father's breaking into a storm of rage, so violent as to calm them, and frighten the children. It almost seemed as if trouble had upset his brain.

Long continued hunger—the hunger that for weeks and months never gets satisfied—will on occasion transform men and women into demons. In the house of the Dunns, not only hunger but misery of all sorts reigned, and this day seemed to have brought things to a climax. Added to the trouble and doubt regarding Mary Ann, was the fear of a prison, Dunn having just heard that he had been convicted in the Small Debts Court. Summonses had been out against him, hopeless though it seemed to sue anybody so helplessly poor. In truth, the man was overwhelmed with misery—as was many another man in Daffodil's Delight—and did not know where to turn. After this outburst, he sat down on the bench again, administering a final threat to his wife for silence. Mrs. Dunn stood against the bare wooden shelves of the dresser, her hair on end, her face scarlet, her voice loud enough, in its shrieking sobs, to alarm all the neighbours; altogether in a state of fury. Disregarding her husband's injunction for silence, she broke out into reproaches. "Was he a man, that he should bring 'em to this state of starvation, and then turn round upon 'em with threats? Wasn't she his wife? wasn't they his children? If *she* was a husband and father, she'd rather break stones till her arms rotted off, but what she'd find 'em food! A lazy, idle, drunken object! There was the masters' yards open, and why didn't he go to work? If a man cared for his own family, he'd look to his interests, and set the Trades Union at defiance. Was he a going to see 'em took off to the workhouse? When his young ones lay dead, and she was in the poorhouse, then he'd fold his hands and be content with his work. If the strike was to bring 'em all this misery, what the plague business had he to join it? Couldn't he have seen better? Let him go to work if he was a man, and bring home a few coals, and a bit of bread, and get out a blanket or two from Cox's, and her gownds and things, and Jemimar's boots—"

Dunn, really a peacefully inclined man by nature, and whose own anger had spent itself, let it go on to this point. He then stood up before her, and with a clenched fist, but calm voice of suppressed meaning, asked her what she meant. What, indeed! In the midst of Mrs. Dunn's reproaches, how was it she did not cast a recollection to the past? To her own eagerness, public and private, for the strike? how she had urged her husband on to join it, boasting of the good times it was to bring them? She could ignore all that now: perhaps really had almost forgotten it. Anyway, her opinions had changed. Misery and disappointment will subdue the fiercest obstinacy; and Mrs. Dunn, casting all the blame upon her husband, would very much have liked to chastise him with hands as well as tongue.

Reader! if you think this is an overdrawn picture, go and lay it before the wives of the workmen who suffered the miseries induced by the strike, and ask them whether or not it is true. Ay, and it is only part of the truth.

"I wish the strike had been buried five-fathom deep, I do!" uttered Dunn, with a catching up of the breath that told of the emotion he strove to hide. "It have been nothing but a curse to us all along. And where's to be the ending?"

"Who brought home all this misery but you?" recommenced Mrs. Dunn. "Have you done a day's work for weeks and months? No you haven't; you know you haven't! You have just rowed in the same boat with them nasty lazy Unionists, and let the work go a begging."

"Who edged me on to join the Unionists? who reproached me with being no man, but a sneak, if I went to work and knuckled down to the masters?" demanded Dunn, in his sore vexation. "It was you! You know it was you! You was fire-hot for the strike: worse than ever the men was."

"Can we starve?" said Mrs. Dunn, choking with passion. "Can we drop into our coffins with famine? Be our children to be drove, like Mary Ann—" An interruption—fortunately. Mrs. Cheek came into the room with a burst. She had a tongue also, on occasions.

"Whatever has been going on here this last half hour?" she inquired in a high voice. "One would think murder was being committed. There's a dozen listeners collected outside your shutters."

"She's a casting it in my teeth, now, for having joined the strike," exclaimed Dunn, indicating his wife. "She! And she was the foremost to edge us all on."

"Can one clam?" fiercely returned Mrs. Dunn, speaking at her husband, not to him. "Let him go to work."

"Don't be a fool, Hannah Dunn," said Mrs. Cheek. "I'd stand up for my rights till I dropped: and so must the men. It'll never do to bend to the will of the masters at last. There's enough men turning tail and going back, without the rest doing of it. I should like to see Cheek attempting it: I'd be on to him."

"Cheek don't want to; he have got no cause to," said Mrs. Dunn. "You get the living now, and find him in beer and bacca."

"I do; and I am proud on it," was Mrs. Cheek's answer. "I goes washing, I goes chairing, I goes ironing; nothing comes amiss to me, and I manages to keep the wolf from the door. It isn't my husband that shall bend to the masters. He shall stand up with the Unionists for his rights, or he shall stand up against me." Having satisfied her curiosity as to the cause of the disturbance, Mrs. Cheek went out as she came, with a burst and a bang, for she had been bent on some hasty errand when arrested by the noise behind the Dunn's closed shutters. What the next proceedings would have been, it is difficult to say, had not another interruption occurred. Mrs. Dunn was putting her entangled hair behind her ears, most probably preparatory to the resuming of the attack on her husband, when the offending Mary Ann entered, attended by Mrs. Quale.

At it she went, the mother, hammer and tongs, turning her resentment on the girl, her language by no means choice, though the younger children were present. Dunn was quieter; but he turned his back upon his daughter and would not look at her. And then Mrs. Quale took a turn, and exercised *her* tongue on both the parents: not with quite as much noise, but with better effect.

It appeared that the whispered suspicions against Mary Ann Dunn had been mistaken ones. The girl had been doing right, instead of wrong. Mrs. Quale had recommended her to a place at a small dressmaker's, partly of service, chiefly of needlework. Before engaging her, the dressmaker had insisted on a few days of trial, wishing to see what her skill at work was; and Mary Ann had kept it secret, intending a pleasant surprise to her father when the engagement shall be finally made. The suspicions cast on her were but a poor return for this; and the girl, in her temper, had carried the grievance to Mrs. Quale, when the day's work was over. A few words of strong good sense from that talkative friend subdued Mary Ann, and she had now come back in peace. Mrs. Quale gave the explanation, interlarding it with a sharp reprimand at their proneness to think ill of "their own flesh and blood," and James Dunn sat down meekly in glad repentance. Even Mrs. Dunn lowered her tone for once. Mary Ann held out some money to her father after a quick glance at Mrs. Quale for approval. "Take it, father. It'll stop your going to prison, perhaps. Mrs. Quale has lent it me to get my clothes out, for I am to enter for good on my place to-morrow. I can manage without my clothes for a bit."

James Dunn put the money back, speaking softly, very much as if he had tears in his voice. "No, girl: it'll do you more good than it will me. Mrs. Quale has been a good friend to you. Enter on your place, and stay in it. It is the best news I've heard this many a day."

"But if the money will keep you out of jail, father!" sobbed Mary Ann, quite subdued.

"It wouldn't do that; nor half do it; nor a quarter. Get your clothes home, child, and go into your place of service. As for me—better I was in jail than out of it," he added with a sigh. "In there, one does get food."

"Are you sure it wouldn't do you good, Jim Dunn?" asked Mrs. Quale, speaking in the emergency he seemed to be driven to. Not that she would have helped him, so improvident in conduct and mistaken in opinions, with a good heart.

"Sure and certain. If I paid this debt, others that I owe would be put on to me."

"Come along, Mary Ann," said Mrs. Quale. "I told you I'd give you a bed at my house to-night, and I will: so you'll know where she is, Hannah Dunn. You go on down to Cox's, girl; get out as much as you can for the money, and come straight back to me: I'm going home now, and we'll set to work and see the best we can do with the things." They went out together. But Mrs. Quale opened the door again and put in her head for a parting word; remembering perhaps her want of civility in not having given it. "Good night to you all. And pleasant dreams—if you can get 'em. You Unionists have brought your pigs to a pretty market."

VIII

A Descent for Mr. Shuck

Things were coming to a crisis. The Unionists had done their best to hold out against the masters; but they found the effort was untenable—that they must give in at last. The prospect of returning to work was eagerly welcomed by the greater portion of the men. Rather than continue longer in the wretched condition to which they were reduced, they would have gone back almost on any terms. Why, then, not have gone back before? as many asked. Because they preferred to resume work with the consent of the Union, rather than without it: and besides, the privations got worse and worse. A few of the men were bitterly enraged at the turn affairs seemed to be taking—of whom Sam Shuck was chief. With the return of the hands to work, Sam foresaw no field for the exercise of his own peculiar talents, unless it was in stirring up fresh discontent for the future. However, it was not yet finally arranged that work should be resumed: a little more agitation might be pleasant first, and possibly prevent it.

"It's a few white-livered hounds among yourselves that have spoilt it," growled Sam to a knot of hitherto staunch friends, a day or two subsequent to that conjugal dispute between Mr. and Mrs. Dunn, which we had the gratification of assisting at in the last chapter. "When such men as White, and Baxendale, and Darby, who have held some sway among you, turn sneaks and go over to the nobs, it's only to be expected that you'll turn sneaks and follow. One fool makes many. Did you hear how Darby got out his tools?"

"No."

"The men opposed to the Union, opposed to us, heard of his wanting them, and they clubbed together, and made up the tin, and Darby is to pay 'em back so much a-week—two shillings I think it is. Before I'd lie under obligation to the non-Unionist men, I'd shoot myself. What good has the struggle done you?"

"None," said a voice. "It have done a good deal of harm."

"Ay, it has—if it is to die out in this ignoble way," said Sam. "Better have been slaving like dray-horses all along, than break down in the effort to escape the slavery, and hug it to your arms again. If you had only half the spirit of men, you'd stop White's work for awhile, and Darby's too, as you did Baxendale's. Have you been thinking over what was said last night?" he continued, in a lower tone. The men nodded. One of them ventured to express an opinion that it was a "dangerous game."

"That depends upon how it's done," said Shuck. "Who has been the worse, pray, for the pitching into Baxendale? Can he, or anybody else, point a finger and say, 'It was you did it?' or 'It was you?' Why, of course he can't."

"One might not come off again with the like luck."

"Psha!" returned Sam, evincing a great amount of ridicule.

"But one mightn't, Shuck," persisted his adversary.

"Oh, let the traitors alone, to go their own way in triumph if you like; get up a piece of plate for them, with their names wrote on it in gold," satirically answered Sam. "Yah! it sickens one to see you true fellows going over to the oppressionists."

"How do you make out that White, and them, be oppressionists?"

"White, and them? they are worse than oppressionists a thousand times over," fiercely cried Sam. "I can't find words bad enough for *them*. It isn't of them I spoke: I spoke of the masters."

"Well, Shuck, there's oppression on all sides, I think," rejoined one of the men. "I'd be glad to rise in the world if I could, and I'd work over hours to help me on to it and to educate my children a bit better than common; but if you come down upon me and say, 'You shall not do it, you shall only work the stated hours laid down, and nobody shall work more,' I call that oppression."

"So it is," assented another voice. "The masters never oppressed us like that."

"What's fair for one is fair for all," said Sam. "We must work and share alike."

"That would be right enough if we all had talents and industry equal," was the reply. "But as we haven't, and never shall have, it can't be fair to put a limit on us."

"There's one question I'd like to have answered, Shuck," interposed a former speaker: "but I'm afeared it never will be answered, with satisfaction to us. What is to become of those men that the masters can't find employment for? If every one of us was free to go back to work to-morrow, and sought to do so, where would we get it? Our old shops be half filled with strangers, and there'd be thousands of us rejected—no room for us. Would the Society keep us?" A somewhat difficult question to answer, even for Slippery Sam. Perhaps for that reason he suddenly called out "Hush!" and bent his head and put up his finger in the attitude of listening.

"There's something unusual going on in the street," cried he. "Let's see what it is."

They hurried out to the street, Sam leading the way. Not a genial street to gaze upon, that wintry day, taking it with all its accessories. Half-clothed, half-starved emaciated men stood about in groups, their pale features and gloomy expression of despair telling a piteous tale. A different set of men entirely, to look at, from those of the well-to-do cheerful old days of work, contentment, and freedom from care.

Being marshalled down the street in as polite a manner as was consistent with the occasion, was Mr. James Dunn. He was on his road to prison; and certain choice spirits of Daffodil's Delight, headed by Mrs. Dunn, were in attendance, some bewailing and lamenting aloud, others hooting and yelling at the capturers. As if this was not enough cause of disturbance, news arose that the Dunns' landlord, finding the house temporarily abandoned by every soul—a chance he had been looking for—improved the opportunity to lock the street-door and keep them out. Nothing was before Mrs. Dunn and her children now but the parish Union.

"I don't care whether it is the masters that have been in fault or whether it's us; I know which side gets the suffering," exclaimed a mechanic, as Mr. Dunn was conveyed beyond view. "Old Abel White told us true; strikes never brought nothing but misery yet, and they never will."

Sam Shuck seized upon the circumstance to draw around him a select audience, and to hold forth to them. Treason, false and pernicious though it was, that he spoke, his oratory fell persuasively on the public ear. He excited the men against the masters; he excited them to his utmost power against the men who had gone back to work; he inflamed their passions, he perverted their reason. Altogether, ill-feeling and excitement was smouldering in an unusual degree in Daffodil's Delight, and it was kept up through the live-long day. Evening came. The bell rang for the cessation of work at Mr. Hunter's, and the men came pouring forth, a great many of whom were strangers. The gas-lamp at the gate shed a brilliant light, as the hands dispersed—some one way, some another. Those bearing towards Daffodil's Delight became aware, as they approached an obscure portion of the road which lay past a dead wall, that it bore an unusual appearance, as if dark forms were hovering there. What could it be? Not for long were they kept in ignorance. There arose a terrific din, enough to startle the unwary. Yells, groans, hootings, hisses, threats were poured forth upon the workmen; and they knew that they had fallen into an ambush of the Society's men. Of women also, as it appeared. For shrill notes and delicate words of abuse, certainly only peculiar to ladies' throats, were pretty freely mingled with the gruff tones of the men.

"You be nice nine-hour chaps! Come on, if you're not cowards, and have it out in a fair fight—"

"A fair fight!" shrieked a female voice in interruption "who'd fight with them? Traitors! cowards! Knock 'em down and trample upon 'em!"

"Harness 'em together with cords, and drag 'em along like beasts o' burden in the face and eyes o' London!" "Stick 'em up on spikes!" "Hoist 'em on to the lamp-posts!" "Hold 'em head down'ards in a horse-trough!" "Pitch into 'em with quicklime and rotten eggs!" "Strip 'em and give 'em a coat o' tar!" "Wring their necks, and have done with 'em!"

While these several complimentary suggestions were thrown from as many different quarters of the assailants, one of them had quietly laid hold of Abel White. There was little doubt—according to what came out afterwards—that he and Robert Darby were the two men chiefly aimed at in this night assault. Darby, however, was not there. As it happened, he had turned the contrary way on leaving the yard, having joined one of the men who had lent him some of the money to get his tools out of pledge, and gone towards his home with him.

"If thee carest for thy life, thee'll stop indoors, and not go a-nigh Hunter's yard again to work!"

Such were the words hissed forth in a hoarse whisper into the ear of Abel White, by the man who had seized upon him. Abel peered at him as keenly as the darkness would permit. White was no coward, and although aware that this attack most probably had him for its chief butt, he retained his composure. He could not recognise the man—a tall man, in a large loose blue frock, such as is sometimes worn by butchers, with a red woollen cravat wound roughly round his throat, hiding his chin and mouth, and a seal-skin cap, its dark "ears" brought down on the sides of the face, and tied under the chin. The man may have been so wrapped up for protection against the weather, or for the purpose of disguise.

"Let me go," said White.

"When thee hast sworn not to go on working till the Union gives leave."

"I never will swear it. Or say it."

"Then thee shall get every bone in th' body smashed. Thee'st been reported to Mr. Shuck, and to the Union."

"I'd like to know your name and who you are," exclaimed White. "If you are not disguising your voice, it's odd to me."

"D'ye remember Baxendale? *He* wouldn't take the oath, and he's lying with his ribs stove in."

"More shame for you! Look you, man, you can't intimidate me. I am made of sterner stuff than that."

"Swear!" was the menacing retort; "swear that thee won't touch another stroke o' work."

"I tell you that I never will swear it," firmly returned White. "The Union has hoodwinked me long enough; I'll have nothing to do with it."

"There be desperate men around ye—them as won't leave ye with whole bones. You shall swear."

"I'll have nothing more to do with the Union; I'll never again obey it," answered White, speaking earnestly. "There! make your most of it. If I had but a friendly gleam of light here, I'd know who you are, and let others know."

The confusion around had increased. Hot words were passing everywhere between the assailants and the assailed—no positive assault as yet, save that a woman had shaken her fist in a man's face and spit at him. Abel White strove to get away with the last words, but the man who had been threatening him struck him a sharp blow between the eyes, and another blow from the same hand caught him behind. The next instant he was down. If one blow was dealt him, ten were from as many different hands. The tall man with the cap was busy with his feet; and it really seemed, by the manner he carried on the pastime, that his whole heart went with it, and that it was a heart of revenge.

But who is this, pushing his way through the crowd with stern authority. A policeman? The men shrank back, in their fear, to give him place. No; it is only their master, Mr. Clay.

"What is this?" exclaimed Austin, when he reached the point of battery. "Is it you, White?" he added, stooping down. "I suspected as much. Now, my men," he continued in a stern tone, as he faced the excited throng, "who are you? which of you has done this?"

"The ringleader was him in the cap, sir—the tall one with the red cloth round his neck and the fur about his ears," spoke up White, who, though much maltreated, retained the use of his brains and his tongue. "It was him that threatened me; he was the first to set upon me."

"Who are you?" demanded Austin of the tall man.

The tall man responded by a quiet laugh of derision. He felt himself perfectly secure from recognition in the dark obscurity; and though Mr. Clay was of powerful frame, more than a match for him in agility and strength, let him only dare to lay a finger upon him, and there were plenty around to come to the rescue. Austin Clay heard the derisive laugh, subdued though it was, and thought he recognised it. He took his hand from within the breast of his coat, and raised it with a hasty motion—not to deal a blow, not with a pistol to startle or menace, but to turn on a dark lantern! No pistol could have startled them as did that sudden flash of bright light, thrown full upon the tall man's face. Off flew the fellow with a yell, and Austin coolly turned the lantern upon others.

"Bennet—and Strood—and Ryan—and Cassidy!" he exclaimed, recognising and telling off the men. "And *you*, Cheek! I never should have suspected you of sufficient courage to join in a thing of this nature."

Cheek, midway between shaking and tears, sobbed out that it was "the wife made him;" and Mrs. Cheek roared out from the rear, "Yes, it was, and she'd have shook the bones out of him if he hadn't come."

But that light, turning upon them everywhere, was more than they had bargained for, and the whole lot moved away in the best manner that they could, putting the stealthiest and the quickest foot foremost; each one devoutly hoping, save the few whose names had been mentioned, that his own face had not been recognised. Austin, with some of his workmen who had remained—the greater portion of them were pursuing the vanquished—raised Abel White. His head was cut, his body bruised, but no serious damage appeared to have been done. "Can you walk with assistance as far as Mr. Rice's shop?" asked Austin.

"I daresay I can, sir, in a minute: I'm a bit giddy now," was White's reply, as he leaned his back against the wall, being supported on either side. "Sir, what a mercy that you had that light with you!"

"Ay," shortly replied Austin. "Quale, there's the blood dripping upon your sleeve. I will bind my handkerchief round your head, White. Meanwhile, one of you go and call a cab; it may be better that we get him at once to the surgeon's."

A cab was brought, and White assisted into it. Austin accompanied him. Mr. Rice was at home, and proceeded to examine into the damage. A few days' rest from work, and a liberal application of sticking-plaster, would prove efficacious in effecting a cure, he believed. "What a pity but the ruffians could be stopped at this game!" the doctor exclaimed to Austin. "It will come to attacks more serious if they are not."

"I think this will do something towards stopping it," replied Austin.

"Why? do you know any of them?"

Austin nodded. "A few. It is not a second case of impossible identity, as was Baxendale's."

"I'm sure I don't know how I am to go in home in this plight," exclaimed White, catching sight of his strapped-up face and head, in a small looking-glass hanging in Mr. Rice's surgery. "I shall frighten poor old father into a fit, and the wife too."

"I will go on first and prepare them," said Austin, good-naturedly. Turning out of the shop on this errand, he found the door blocked up. The door! nay, the pavement—the street; for it seemed as if all Daffodil's Delight had collected there. He elbowed his way through them, and reached White's home. There the news had preceded him, and he found the deepest distress and excitement reigning, the family having been informed that Abel was killed. Austin reassured them, made light of the matter, and departed.

Outside their closed-up home, squatting on the narrow strip of pavement, their backs against the dirty wall, were Mrs. Dunn and her children, howling pitiably. They were surrounded with warm partizans, who spent their breath sympathizing with them, and abusing the landlord.

"How much better that they should go into the workhouse," exclaimed Austin. "They will perish with cold if they remain there."

"And much you masters 'ud care," cried a woman who overheard the remark. "I hope you are satisfied now with the effects of your fine lock-out! Look at the poor creatur, a sitting there with her helpless children."

"A sad sight," observed Austin; "but *not* the effects of the lock-out. You must look nearer home."

The day dawned. Abel White was progressing very satisfactorily. So much so that Mr. Rice did not keep him in bed. It was by no means so grave a case as Baxendale's. To the intense edification of Daffodil's Delight, which had woke up in an unusually low and subdued state, there arrived, about mid-day, certain officers within its precincts, holding warrants for the apprehension of some of the previous night's rioters. Bennet, Strood, Ryan, and Cheek were taken; Cassidy had disappeared.

"It's a shame to grab us!" exclaimed timid Cheek, shaking from head to foot. "White himself said as we was not the ringleaders."

While these were secured, a policeman entered the home of Mr. Shuck, without so much as saying, "With your leave," or "By your leave." That gentleman, who had remained in-doors all the morning, in a restless, humble sort of mood, which imparted much surprise to Mrs. Shuck, was just sitting down to dinner in the bosom of his family: a savoury dinner, to judge by the smell, consisting of rabbit and onions.

"Now, Sam Shuck, I want you," was the startling interruption.

Sam turned as white as a sheet. Mrs. Shuck stared, and the children stared.

"Want me, do you?" cried Sam, putting as easy a face as he could upon the matter. "What do you want me for? To give evidence?"

"*You* know. It's about that row last night. I wonder you hadn't better regard for your liberty than to get into it."

"Why, you never was such a fool as to put yourself into that!" exclaimed Mrs. Shuck, in her surprise. "What could have possessed you?"

"I!" retorted Sam; "I don't know anything about the row, except what I've heard. I was a good mile off from the spot when it took place."

"All very well if you can convince the magistrates of that," said the officer. "Here's the warrant against you, and I must take you upon it."

"I won't go," said Sam, showing fight. "I wasn't nigh the place, I say."

The officer was peremptory—officers generally are so in these cases—and Sam was very foolish to resist. But that he was scared out of his senses, he would probably not have resisted. It only made matters worse; and the result was that he had the handcuffs clapped on. Fancy Samuel Shuck, Esquire, in his crimson necktie with the lace ends, and the peg-tops, being thus escorted through Daffodil's Delight, himself and his hands prisoners, and a tail the length of the street streaming after him! You could not have got into the police-court. Every avenue, every inch of ground was occupied; for the men, both Unionists and non-Unionists, were greatly excited, and came flocking in crowds to hear the proceedings. The five men were placed at the bar—Shuck, Bennet, Cheek, Ryan, and Strood: and Abel White and his bandaged head appeared against them. The man gave his evidence. How he and others—but himself, he thought, more particularly—had been met by a mob the previous night, upon leaving work, a knot of the Society's men, who had first threatened and then beaten him.

"Can you tell what their motive was for doing this?" asked the magistrate.

"Yes, sir," was the answer of White. "It was because I went back to work. I held out as long as I could, in obedience to the Trades' Union; but I began to think I was in error, and that I ought to return to work; which I did, a week or two ago. Since then, they have never let me alone. They have talked to me, and threatened me, and persuaded me; but I would not listen: and last night they attacked me."

"What were the threats they used last night?"

"It was one man did most of the talking: a tall man in a cap and comforter, sir. The rest of the crowd abused me and called me names; but they did not utter any particular threat. This man said, Would I promise and swear not to do any more work in defiance of the Union; or else I should get every bone in my body smashed. He told me to remember how Baxendale had been served, and was lying with his ribs stove in. I refused; I would not swear; I said I would never belong to the Union again. And then he struck me."

"Where did he strike you?"

"Here," putting his hand up to his forehead. "The first blow staggered me, and took away my sight, and the second blow knocked me down. Half a dozen set upon me then, hitting and kicking me: the first man kicked me also."

"Can you swear to that first man?"

"No, I can't, sir. I think he was disguised."

"Was it the prisoner, Shuck?"

White shook his head. "It was just his height and figure, sir, but I can't be sure that it was him. His face was partially covered, and it was nearly dark, besides; there are no lights about, just there. The voice, too, seemed disguised: I said so at the time."

"Can you swear to the others?"

"Yes, to all four of them," said White, stoutly. "They were not disguised at all, and I saw them after the light came, and knew their voices. They helped to beat me after I was on the ground."

"Did they threaten you?"

"No, sir. Only the first one did that."

"And him you cannot swear to? Is there any other witness who can swear to him?"

It did not appear that there was. Shuck addressed the magistrate, his tone one of injured innocence. "It is not to be borne that I should be dragged up here like a felon, your worship. I was not near the place at the time; I am as innocent as your worship is. Is it likely *I* should lend myself to such a thing? My mission among the men is of a higher nature than that."

"Whether you are innocent or not, I do not know," said his worship; "but I do know that this is a state of things which cannot be tolerated. I will give my utmost protection to these workmen; and those who dare to interfere with them shall be punished to the extent of the law: the ringleaders especially. A person has just as much right to come to me and say, 'You shall not sit on that bench; you shall not transact the business of a magistrate,' as you have to prevent these industrious men working to earn a living. It is monstrous."

"Here's the witness we have waited for, please your worship," spoke one of the policemen.

It was Austin Clay who came forward. He bowed to the magistrate, who bowed to him: they occasionally met at the house of Mr. Hunter. Austin was sworn, and gave his evidence up to the point when he turned the light of the lantern upon the tall assailant of White.

"Did you recognise the man?" asked the Bench.

"I did, sir. It was Samuel Shuck."

Sam gave a howl, protesting that it was *not*—that he was a mile away from the spot.

"I recognised him as distinctly as I recognise him at this moment," said Austin. "He had a woollen scarf on his chin, and a cap covering his ears, no doubt assumed for disguise, but I knew him instantly. What is more, he saw that I knew him; I am sure he did, by the way he slunk off. I also recognised his laugh."

"Did you take the lantern with you purposely?" asked the clerk of the court.

"I did," replied Austin. "A hint was given me in the course of yesterday afternoon, that an attack upon our men was in agitation. I determined to discover the ringleaders, if possible, should it take place, and not to let the darkness baffle justice, as was the case in the attack upon Baxendale. For this purpose I put the lantern in readiness, and had the men watched when they left the yard. As soon as the assault began, my messenger returned to tell me."

"You hit upon a good plan, Mr. Clay."

Austin smiled. "I think I did," he answered.

Unfortunately for Mr. Samuel Shuck, another witness had seen his face distinctly when the light was turned on; and his identity with "the tall man disguised" was established beyond dispute. In an evil hour, Sam had originated this attack on White; but, not feeling altogether sure of the courage of his men, he had determined to disguise himself and take part in the business, saying not a word to anybody. He had not bargained for the revelation that might be brought by means of a dark lantern.

The proceedings in court were prolonged, but they terminated at length. Bennet, Strood, and Ryan were condemned to pay a fine of £5 each, or be imprisoned for two months. Cheek managed to get off. Mr. Sam Shuck, to whom the magistrate was bitterly severe in his remarks—for he knew perfectly well the part enacted by the man from the first—was sentenced to six months at the treadmill, without the option of a fine. What a descent for Slippery Sam!

IX

On the Eve of Bankruptcy

These violent interruptions to the social routine, to the organised relations between masters and men, cannot take place without leaving their effects behind them: not only in the bare cupboards, the confusion, the bitter feelings while the contest is in actual progress, but in the results when the dispute is brought to an end, and things have resumed their natural order. You have seen some of its disastrous working upon the men: you cannot see it all, for it would take a whole volume to depicture it. But there was another upon whom it was promising to work badly; and that was Mr. Hunter. At this, the eleventh hour, when the dispute was dying out, Mr. Hunter knew that he would be unable to weather the short remains of the storm. Drained, as he had been at various periods, of sums paid to Gwinn of Ketterford, he had not the means necessary to support the long-continued struggle. Capital he possessed still; and, had there been no disturbance, no strike, no lock-out—had things, in short, gone on upon their usual course uninterruptedly, his capital would have been sufficient to carry him on: not as it was. His money was locked up in arrested works, in buildings brought to a standstill. He could not fulfil his contracts or meet his debts; materials were lying idle; and the crisis, so long expected by him, had come.

It had not been expected by Austin Clay. Though aware of the shortness of capital, he believed that with care difficulties would be surmounted. The fact was, Mr. Hunter had succeeded in keeping the worst from him. It fell upon Austin one morning like a thunderbolt. Mr. Hunter had come early to the works. In this hour of embarrassment—ill as he might be, as he was—he could not be absent from his place of business. When Austin went into his master's private room he found him alone, poring over books and accounts, his head leaning on his hand. One glance at Austin's face told Mr. Hunter that the whispers as to the state of affairs, which were now becoming public scandal, had reached his ears.

"Yes, it is quite true," said Mr. Hunter, before a word had been spoken by Austin. "I cannot stave it off."

"But it will be ruin, sir!" exclaimed Austin.

"Of course it will be ruin. I know that, better than you can tell me."

"Oh, sir," continued Austin, with earnest decision, "it must not be allowed to come. Your credit must be kept up at any sacrifice."

"Can you tell me of any sacrifice that will keep it up?" returned Mr. Hunter.

Austin paused in embarrassment. "If the present difficulty can be got over, the future will soon redeem itself," he observed. "You have sufficient capital in the aggregate, though it is at present locked up."

"There it is," said Mr. Hunter. "Were the capital not locked up, but in my hands, I should be a free man. Who is to unlock it?"

"The men are returning to their shops," urged Austin. "In a few days, at the most, all will have resumed work. We shall get our contracts completed, and things will work round. It would be *needless* ruin, sir, to stop now."

"Am I stopping of my own accord? Shall I put myself into the Gazette, do you suppose? You talk like a child, Clay."

"Not altogether, sir. What I say is, that you are worth more than sufficient to meet your debts; that, if the momentary pressure can be lifted, you will surmount embarrassment and regain ease."

"Half the bankruptcies we hear of are caused by locked-up capital—not by positive non-possession of it," observed Mr. Hunter. "Were my funds available, there would be reason in what you say, and I should probably go on again to ease. Indeed, I know I should; for a certain heavy—heavy—" Mr. Hunter spoke with perplexed hesitation—"A heavy private obligation, which I have been paying off at periods, is at an end now."

Austin made no reply. He knew that Mr. Hunter alluded to Gwinn of Ketterford: and perhaps Mr. Hunter suspected that he knew it. "Yes, sir; you would go on to ease—to fortune again; there is no doubt of it. Mr. Hunter," he continued with some emotion, "it *must* be accomplished somehow. To let things come to an end for the sake of a thousand or two, is—is—"

"Stop!" said Mr. Hunter. "I see what you are driving at. You think that I might borrow this 'thousand or two,' from my brother, or from Dr. Bevary."

"No," fearlessly replied Austin, "I was not thinking of either one or the other. Mr. Henry Hunter has enough to do for himself just now—his contracts for the season were more extensive than ours: and Dr. Bevary is not a business man."

"Henry *has* enough to do," said Mr. Hunter. "And if a hundred-pound note would save me, I should not ask Dr. Bevary for its loan. I tell you, Clay, there is no help for it: ruin must come. I have thought it over and over, and can see no loophole of escape. It does not much matter: I can hide my head in obscurity for the short time I shall probably live. Mine has been an untoward fate."

"It matters for your daughter, sir," rejoined Austin, his face flushing.

"I cannot help myself, even for her sake," was the answer, and it was spoken in a tone that, to a fanciful listener, might have told of a breaking heart.

"If you would allow me to suggest a plan, sir—"

"No, I will not allow any further discussion upon the topic," peremptorily interrupted Mr. Hunter. "The blow must come; and, to talk of it will neither soothe nor avert it. Now to business. Not another word, I say.—Is it to-day or to-morrow that Grafton's bill falls due?"

"To-day," replied Austin.

"And its precise amount?—I forget it."

"Five hundred and twenty pounds."

"Five hundred and twenty! I knew it was somewhere about that. It is that bill that will floor us—at least, be the first step to it. How closely has the account been drawn at the bank?"

"You have the book by you, sir. I think there is little more than thirty pounds lying in it."

"Just so. Thirty pounds to meet a bill of five hundred and twenty. No other available funds to pay in. And you would talk of staving off the difficulty?"

"I think the bank would pay it, were all circumstances laid before them. They have accommodated us before."

"The bank will *not*, Austin. I have had a private note from them this morning. These flying rumours have reached their ears, and they will not let me overdraw even by a pound. It had struck me once or twice lately that they were becoming cautious." There was a commotion, as of sudden talking, outside at that moment, and Mr. Hunter turned pale. He supposed it might be a creditor: and his nerves were so shattered, as was before remarked, that the slightest thing shook him like a woman. "I would pay them all, if I could," he said, his tone almost a wail. "I wish to pay every one."

"Sir," said Austin, "leave me here to-day to meet these matters. You are too ill to stay."

"If I do not meet them to-day, I must to-morrow. Sooner or later, it is I who must answer."

"But indeed you are ill, sir. You look worse than you have looked at all."

"Can you wonder that I look worse? The striking of the docket against me is no pleasant matter to anticipate." The talking outside now subsided into laughter, in which the tones of a female were distinguishable. Mr. Hunter thought he recognised them, and his fear of a creditor subsided. They came from one of his women servants, who, unconscious of the proximity of her master, had been laughing and joking with some of the men, whom she had encountered upon entering the yard.

"What can Susan want?" exclaimed Mr. Hunter, signing to Austin to open the door.

"Is that you, Susan?" asked Austin, as he obeyed.

"Oh, if you please, sir, can I speak a word to my master?"

"Come in," called out Mr. Hunter. "What do you want?"

"Miss Florence has sent me, sir, to give you this, and to ask you if you'd please to come round."

She handed in a note. Mr. Hunter broke the seal, and ran his eyes over it. It was from Florence, and contained but a line or two. She informed her father that the lady who had been so troublesome at the house once before, in years back, had come again, had taken a seat in the dining-room, removed her bonnet, and expressed her intention of there remaining until she should see Mr. Hunter.

"As if I had not enough upon me without this!" muttered Mr. Hunter. "Go back," he said aloud to the servant, "and tell Miss Florence that I am coming."

A few minutes given to the papers before him, a few hasty directions to Austin, touching the business of the hour, and Mr. Hunter rose to depart.

"Do not come back, sir," Austin repeated to him. "I can manage all."

When Mr. Hunter entered his own house, letting himself in with a latch key, Florence, who had been watching for him, glided forward.

"She is in there, papa," pointing to the closed door of the dining-room, and speaking in a whisper. "What is her business here? what does she want? She told me she had as much right in the house as I."

"Ha!" exclaimed Mr. Hunter. "Insolent, has she been?"

"Not exactly insolent. She spoke civilly. I fancied you would not care to see her, so I said she could not wait. She replied that she should wait, and I must not attempt to prevent her. Is she in her senses, papa?"

"Go up stairs and put your bonnet and cloak on, Florence," was the rejoinder of Mr. Hunter. "Be quick." She obeyed, and was down again almost immediately, in her deep mourning. "Now, my dear, go round to Dr. Bevary, and tell him you have come to spend the day with him."

"But, papa—"

"Florence, go! I will either come for you this evening, or send. Do not return until I do."

The tone, though full of kindness, was one that might not be disobeyed, and Florence, feeling sick with some uncertain, shadowed-forth trouble, passed out of the hall door. Mr. Hunter entered the dining-room.

Tall, gaunt, powerful of frame as ever, rose up Miss Gwinn, turning upon him her white, corpse-like looking face. Without the ceremony of greeting, she spoke in her usual abrupt fashion, dashing at once to her subject. "*Now* will you render justice, Lewis Hunter?"

"I have the greater right to ask that justice shall be rendered to me," replied Mr. Hunter, speaking sternly, in spite of his agitation. "Who has most cause to demand it, you or I?"

"She who reigned mistress in this house is dead," cried Miss Gwinn. "You must now acknowledge *her*."

"I never will. You may do your best and worst. The worst that can come is, that it must reach the knowledge of my daughter."

"Ay, there it is! The knowledge of the wrong must not even reach her; but the wrong itself has not been too bad for that other one to bear."

"Woman!" continued Mr. Hunter, growing excited almost beyond control, "who inflicted that wrong? Myself, or you?"

The reproach told home, if the change to sad humility, passing over Miss Gwinn's countenance, might be taken as an indication.

"What I said, I said in self-defence; after you, in your deceit, had brought wrong upon me and my family," she answered in a subdued voice.

"*That* was no wrong," retorted Mr. Hunter, "It was you who wrought all the wrong afterwards, by uttering the terrible falsehood, that she was dead."

"Well, well, it is of no use going back to that," she impatiently said. "I am come here to ask that justice shall be rendered, now that it is in your power."

"You have had more than justice—you have had revenge. Not content with rendering my days a life's misery, you must also drain me of the money I had worked hard to save. Do you know how much?"

"It was not I," she passionately uttered, in a tone as if she would deprecate his anger. "*He* did that."

"It comes to the same. I had to find the money. So long as my dear wife lived, I was forced to temporize: neither he nor you can so force me again. Go home, go home, Miss Gwinn, and pray for forgiveness for the injury you have done both her and me. The time for coming to my house with your intimidations is past."

"What did you say?" cried Miss Gwinn. "Injury upon *you*?"

"Injury, ay! such as rarely has been inflicted upon mortal man. Not content with that great injury, you must also deprive me of my substance. This week the name of James Lewis Hunter will be in the Gazette, on the list of bankrupts. It is you who have brought me to it."

"You know that I have had no hand in that; that it was he: my brother—and *hers*," she said. "He never should have done it had I been able to prevent him. In an unguarded moment I told him I had discovered you, and who you were, and—and he came up to you here and sold his silence. It is that which has kept me quiet."

"This interview had better end," said Mr. Hunter. "It excites me, and my health is scarcely in a state to bear it. Your work has told upon me, Miss Gwinn, as you cannot help seeing, when you look at me. Am I like the hearty, open man whom you came up to town and discovered a few years ago?"

"Am I like the healthy unsuspicious woman whom you saw some years before that?" she retorted. "My days have been rendered more bitter than yours."

"It is your own evil passions which have rendered them so. But I say this interview must end. You—"

"It shall end when you undertake to render justice. I only ask that you should acknowledge her in words; I ask no more."

"When your brother was here last—it was on the day of my wife's death—I was forced to warn him of the consequences of remaining in my house against my will. I must now warn you."

"Lewis Hunter," she passionately resumed, "for years I have been told that she—who was here—was fading; and I was content to wait until she should be gone. Besides, was not he drawing money from you to keep silence? But it is all over, and my time is come."

The door of the room opened and some one entered. Mr. Hunter turned with marked displeasure, wondering who was daring to intrude upon him. He saw—not any servant, as he expected, but his brother-in-law, Dr. Bevary. And the doctor walked into the room and closed the door, just as if he had as much right there as its master.

When Florence Hunter reached her uncle's house, she found him absent: the servants said he had gone out early in the morning. Scarcely had she entered the drawing-room when his carriage drove up: he saw Florence at the window and hastened in. "Uncle Bevary, I have come to stay the day with you," was her greeting. "Will you have me?"

"I don't know that I will," returned the doctor, who loved Florence above every earthly thing. "How comes it about?" In the explanation, as she gave it, the doctor detected some embarrassment, quite different from her usual open manner. He questioned closely, and drew from her what had occurred. "Miss Gwinn of Ketterford in town!" he exclaimed, staring at Florence as if he could not believe her. "Are you joking?"

"She is at our house with papa, as I tell you, uncle."

"What an extraordinary chance!" muttered the doctor.

Leaving Florence, he ran out of the house and down the street, calling after his coachman, who was driving to the stables. Had it been anybody but Dr. Bevary, the passers-by might have deemed the caller mad. The coachman heard, and turned his horses again. Dr. Bevary spoke a word in haste to Florence.

"Miss Gwinn is the very person I was wanting to see; wishing some marvellous telegraph wires could convey her to London at a moment's notice. Make yourself at home, my dear; don't wait dinner for me, I cannot tell when I shall be back." He stepped into the carriage and was driven away very quickly, leaving Florence in some doubt as to whether he had not gone to Ketterford—for she had but imperfectly understood him. Not so. The carriage set him down at Mr. Hunter's. Where he broke in upon the interview, as has been described.

"I was about to telegraph to Ketterford for you," he began to Miss Gwinn, without any other sort of greeting. And the words, coupled with his abrupt manner, sent her at once into an agitation. Rising, she put her hand upon the doctor's arm.

"What has happened? Any ill?"

"You must come with me now and see her," was the brief answer.

Shaking from head to foot, gaunt, strong woman though she was, she turned docilely to follow the doctor from the room. But suddenly an idea seemed to strike her, and she stood still. "It is a *ruse* to get me out of the house. Dr. Bevary, I will not quit it until justice shall be rendered to Emma. I will have her acknowledged by him."

"Your going with me now will make no difference to that, one way or the other," drily observed Dr. Bevary.

Mr. Hunter stepped forward in agitation. "Are you out of your mind, Bevary? You could not have caught her words correctly."

"Psha!" responded the doctor, in a careless tone. "What I said was, that Miss Gwinn's going out with me could make no difference to any acknowledgment."

"Only in words," she stayed to say. "Just let him say it in words." But nobody took any notice of the suggestion.

His bearing calm and self-possessed, his manner authoritative, Dr. Bevary passed out to his carriage, motioning the lady before him. Self-willed as she was by nature and by habit, she appeared to have no thought of resistance now. "Step in," said Dr. Bevary. She obeyed, and he seated himself by her, after giving an order to the coachman. The carriage turned towards the west for a short distance, and then branched off to the north. In a comparatively short time they were clear of the bustle of London. Miss Gwinn sat in silence; the doctor sat in silence. It seemed that the former wished, yet dreaded to ask the purport of their present journey, for her white face was working with emotion, and she glanced repeatedly at the doctor, with a sharp, yearning look. When they were clear of the bustle of the streets; and the hedges, bleak and bare, bounded the road on either side, broken by a house here and there, then she could bear the silence and suspense no longer.

"Why do you not speak?" broke from her in a tone of pain.

"First of all, tell me what brought you to town now," was his reply. "It is not your time for being here."

"The recent death of your sister. I came up by the early train this morning. Dr. Bevary, you are the only living being to whom I lie under an obligation, or from whom I have experienced kindness. People may think me ungrateful; some think me mad; but I am grateful to you. But for the fact of that lady's being your sister I should have insisted upon another's rights being acknowledged long ago."

"You told me you waived them in consequence of your brother's conduct."

"Partially so. But that did not weigh with me in comparison with my feeling of gratitude to you. How impotent we are!" she exclaimed, throwing up her hands. "My efforts by day, my dreams by night, were directed to one single point through long, long years—the finding James Lewis. I had cherished the thought of revenge until it became part and parcel of my very existence; I was hoping to expose him to the world. But when the time came, and I did find him, I found that he had married your sister, and that I could not touch him without giving pain to you. I hesitated what to do. I went home to Ketterford, deliberating—"

"Well?" said the doctor. For she had stopped abruptly.

"Some spirit of evil prompted me to disclose to my good-for-nothing brother that the man, Lewis, was found. I told him more than that, unhappily."

"What else did you tell him?"

"Never mind. I was a fool: and I have had my reward. My brother came up to town and drew large sums of money out of Mr. Hunter. I could have stopped it—but I did not."

"If I understand you aright, you have come to town now to insist upon what you call your rights?" remarked the doctor.

"Upon what *I* call!" returned Miss Gwinn, and then she paused in marked hesitation. "But you must have news to tell me, Dr. Bevary. What is it?"

"I received a message early this morning from Dr. Kerr, stating that something was amiss. I lost no time in going over."

"And what was amiss?" she hastily cried. "Surely there was no repetition of the violence? Did you see her?"

"Yes, I saw her."

"But of course you would see her," resumed Miss Gwinn, speaking rather to herself. "And what do you think? Is there danger?"

"The danger is past," replied Dr. Bevary. "But here we are."

The carriage had driven in through an inclosed avenue, and was stopping before a large mansion: not a cheerful mansion, for its grounds were surrounded by dark trees, and some of its windows were barred. It was a lunatic asylum. It is necessary, even in these modern days of gentle treatment, to take some precaution of bars and bolts; but the inmates of this one were thoroughly well cared for, in the best sense of the term. Dr. Bevary was one of its visiting inspectors.

Dr. Kerr, the resident manager, came forward, and Dr. Bevary turned to Miss Gwinn. "Will you see her, or not?" he asked.

Strange fears were working within her, Dr. Bevary's manner was so different from ordinary. "I think I see it all," she gasped. "The worst has happened."

"The best has happened," responded Dr. Bevary. "Miss Gwinn, you have requested me more than once to bring you here without preparation should the time arrive—for that you could bear certainty, but not suspense. Will you see her?"

Her face had grown white and rigid as marble. Unable to speak, she pointed forward with her hand. Dr. Bevary drew it within his own to support her. In a clean, cool chamber, on a pallet bed, lay a dead woman. Dr. Kerr gently drew back the snow-white sheet, with which the face was covered. A pale, placid face, with a little band of light hair folded underneath the cap. She—Miss Gwinn—did not stir: she gave way to neither emotion nor violence; but her bloodless lips were strained back from her teeth, and her face was as white as that of the dead.

"God's ways are not as our ways," whispered Dr. Bevary. "You have been acting for revenge: He has sent peace. Whatsoever He does is for the best."

She made no reply: she remained still and rigid. Dr. Bevary stroked the left hand of the dead, lying in its utter stillness—stroked, as if unconsciously, the wedding-ring on the third finger. He had been led to believe that it was placed on that finger, years and years ago, by his brother-in-law, James Lewis Hunter. And had been led to believe a lie! And she who had invented the lie, who had wrought the delusion, who had embittered Mr. Hunter's life with the same dread belief, stood there at the doctor's side, looking at the dead.

It is a solemn thing to persist though but tacitly in the acting of a vile falsehood, in the mysterious presence of death. Even Miss Gwinn was not strong-minded enough for that. As Dr. Bevary turned to her with a remark upon the past, she burst forth into a cry, and gave utterance to words that fell upon the physician's ear like a healing balm, soothing and binding up a long-open wound.

X

The Years Gone by

Those readers will be disappointed who look for any very romantic *dénoûment* of "A Life's Secret." The story is a short and sad one. Suggesting the wretchedness and evil that may result when truth is deviated from; the lengths to which a blind, unholy desire for revenge will carry an ill-regulated spirit; and showing how, in the moral government of the world, sin casts its baleful consequences upon the innocent as well as the guilty.

When the carriage of Dr. Bevary, containing himself and Miss Gwinn, drove from Mr. Hunter's door on the unknown errand, he—Mr. Hunter—staggered to a seat, rather than walked to it. That he was very ill that day, both mentally and bodily, he was only too conscious of. Austin Clay had said to him, "Do not return: I will manage," or words to that effect. At present Mr. Hunter felt himself incapable of returning. He sank down in the easy chair, and closed his eyes, his thoughts thrown back to the past. An ill-starred past: one that had left its bane on his after life, and whose consequences had clung to him. It is impossible but that ill-doing must leave its results behind: the laws of God and man alike demand it. Mr. Hunter, in early life, had been betrayed into committing a wrong act; and Miss Gwinn, in the gratification of her passionate revenge, had visited it upon him all too heavily. Heavily, most heavily was it pressing upon him now. That unhappy visit to Wales, which had led to all the evil, was especially present to his mind this day. A handsome young man, in the first dawn of manhood, he had gone to the fashionable Welsh watering-place—partly to renew a waste of strength more imaginary than real; partly in the love of roving natural to youth; partly to enjoy a few weeks' relaxation. "If you want good and comfortable lodgings, go to Miss Gwinn's house on the South Parade," some friend, whom he encountered at his journey's end, had said to him. And to Miss Gwinn's he went. He found Miss Gwinn a cold, proud woman—it was she whom you have seen—bearing the manners of a lady. The servant who waited upon him was garrulous, and proclaimed, at the first interview, amidst other gossip, that her mistress had but a limited income—a hundred, or a hundred and fifty pounds a year, she believed; that she preferred to eke it out by letting her drawing-room and adjoining bed-room, and to live well; rather than to rusticate and pinch. Miss Gwinn and her motives were nothing to the young sojourner, and he turned a careless, if not a deaf ear, to the gossip. "She does it chiefly for the sake of Miss Emma," added the girl: and the listener so far roused himself as to ask apathetically who "Miss Emma" was. It was her mistress's young sister, the girl replied: there must be twenty good years between them. Miss Emma was but nineteen, and had just come home from boarding-school: her mistress had brought her up ever since her mother died. Miss Emma was not at home now, but was expected on the morrow, she went on. Miss Emma was not without her good looks, but her mistress took care they should not be seen by everybody. She'd hardly let her go about the house when strangers were in it, lest she should be met in the passages. Mr. Hunter laughed. Good looks had attractions for him in those days, and he determined to see for himself, in spite of Miss Gwinn, whether Miss Emma's looks were so good that they might not be looked at. Now, by the merest accident—at least, it happened by accident in the first instance, and not by intention—one chief point of complication in the future ill was unwittingly led to. In this early stage of the affair, while the servant maid was exercising her tongue in these items of domestic news, the friend who had recommended Mr. Hunter to the apartments, arrived at the house and called out to him from the foot of the stairs, his high clear voice echoing through the house.

"Lewis! Will you come out and take a stroll?"

Lewis Hunter hastened down, proclaiming his acquiescence, and the maid proceeded to the parlour of her mistress.

"The gentleman's name is Lewis, ma'am. You said you forgot to ask it of him."

Miss Gwinn, methodical in all she did, took a sheet of note-paper and inscribed the name upon it, "Mr. Lewis," as a reminder for the time when she should require to make out his bill. When Mr. Hunter found out their error—for the maid henceforth addressed him as "Mr. Lewis," or "Mr. Lewis, sir"—it rather amused him, and he did not correct the mistake. He had no motive whatever for concealing his name: he did not wish it concealed. On the other hand, he deemed it of no importance to set them right; it signified not a jot to him whether they called him "Mr. Lewis" or "Mr. Hunter." Thus they knew him as, and believed him to be, Mr. Lewis only. He never took the trouble to undeceive them, and nothing occurred to require the mistake to be corrected. The one or two letters only which arrived for him—for he had gone there for idleness, not to correspond with his friends—were addressed to the post-office, in accordance with his primary directions, not having known where he should lodge.

Miss Emma came home: a very pretty and agreeable girl. In the narrow passage of the house—one of those shallow residences built for letting apartments at the sea-side—she encountered the stranger, who happened to be going out as she entered. He lifted his hat to her.

"Who is that, Nancy?" she asked of the chattering maid.

"It's the new lodger, Miss Emma: Lewis his name is. Did you ever see such good looks? And he has asked a thousand questions about you."

Now, the fact was, Mr. Hunter—stay, we will also call him Mr. Lewis for the time being, as they had fallen into the error, and it may be convenient to us—had not asked a single question about the young lady, save the one when her name was first spoken of, "Who is Miss Emma?" Nancy had supplied information enough for a "thousand" questions, unasked; and perhaps she saw no difference.

"Have you made any acquaintance with Mr. Lewis, Agatha?" Emma inquired of her sister.

"When do I make acquaintance with the people who take my apartments?" replied Miss Gwinn, in a tone of reproof. "They naturally look down upon me as a letter of lodgings—and I am not one to bear that."

Now comes the unhappy tale. It shall be glanced at as briefly as possible in detail; but it is necessary that parts of it should be explained.

Acquaintanceship sprang up between Mr. Lewis and Emma Gwinn. At first, they met in the town, or on the beach, accidentally; later, I very much fear that the meetings were tacitly, if not openly, more intentional. Both were agreeable, both were young; and a liking for each other's society arose in each of them. Mr. Lewis found his time hang somewhat heavily on his hands, for his friend had left; and Emma Gwinn was not prevented from walking out as she pleased. Only one restriction was laid upon her by her sister: "Emma, take care that you make no acquaintance with strangers, or suffer it to be made with you. Speak to none."

An injunction which Miss Emma disobeyed. She disobeyed it in a particularly marked manner. It was not only that she did permit Mr. Lewis to make acquaintance with her, but she allowed it to ripen into intimacy. Worse still, the meetings, I say, from having been at first really accidental, grew to be sought. Sought on the one side as much as on the other. Ah! young ladies, I wish this little history could be a warning to you, never to deviate from the strict line of right—never to stray, by so much as a thoughtless step, from the straight path of duty. Once allow yourselves to do so, and you know not where it may end. Slight acts of disobedience, that appear in themselves as the merest trifles, may yet be fraught with incalculable mischief. The falling into the habit of passing a pleasant hour of intercourse with Mr. Lewis, sauntering on the beach in social and intellectual converse—and it was no worse—appeared a very venial offence to Emma Gwinn. But she did it in direct disobedience to the command and wish of her sister; and she knew that she so did it. She knew also that she owed to that sister, who had brought her up and cared for her from infancy, the allegiance that a child gives to a mother. In this stage of the affair, she was chiefly to blame. Mr. Lewis did not suppose that blame attached to him. There was no reason why he should not while away an occasional hour in pleasant chat with a young lady; there was no harm in the meetings, taking them in the abstract. The blame lay with her. It is no excuse to urge that Miss Gwinn exercised over her a too strict authority, that she kept her secluded from society with an unusually tight hand. Miss Gwinn had a motive in this: her sister knew nothing of it, and resented the restriction as a personal wrong. To elude her vigilance, and walk about with a handsome young man, seemed a return justifiable, and poor Emma Gwinn never dreamt of any ill result. At length it was found out by Miss Gwinn. She did not find out much. Indeed, there was not much to find, except that there was more friendship between Mr. Lewis and Emma than there was between Mr. Lewis and herself, and that they often met to stroll on the beach, and enjoy the agreeable benefit of the sea-breezes. But that was quite enough for Miss Gwinn. An uncontrollable storm of passionate anger ensued, which was vented upon Emma. She stood over her, and forced her to attire herself for travelling, protesting that not another hour should she pass in the house while Mr. Lewis remained. Then she started with Emma, to place her under the care of an aunt, who lived so far off as to be a day's journey.

"It's a shame!" was the comment of sympathetic Nancy, who deemed Miss Gwinn the most unreasonable woman under the sun. Nancy was herself engaged to an enterprising porter, to whom she intended to be married some fine Easter, when they had saved up sufficient to lay in a stock of goods and chattels. And she forthwith went straight to Mr. Lewis, and communicated to him what had occurred, giving him Miss Emma's new address.

"He'll follow her if he have got any spirit," was her inward thought. "It's what my Joe would do by me, if I was forced off to desert places by a old dragon."

It was precisely what Mr. Lewis did. Upon the return of Miss Gwinn, he gave notice to quit her house, where he had already stayed longer than he intended to do originally. Miss Gwinn had no suspicion but that he returned to his home—wherever that might be.

You may be inclined to ask why Miss Gwinn had fallen into anger so great. That she loved her young sister with an intense and jealous love was certain. Miss Gwinn was of a peculiar temperament, and she could not bear that one spark of Emma's affection should stray from her. Emma, on the contrary, scarcely cared for her eldest sister: entertaining for her a very cool regard indeed, not to be called a sisterly one: and the cause may have lain in the stern manners of Miss Gwinn. Deeply, ardently as she loved Emma, her manners were to her invariably cold and stern: and this does not beget love from the young. Emma also resented the jealous restrictions imposed on her, lest she should make any acquaintance that might lead to marriage. It had been better possibly that Miss Gwinn had disclosed to her the reasons that existed against it. There was madness in the Gwinn family. One of the parents had died in an asylum, and the medical men suspected (as Miss Gwinn knew) that the children might be subject to it. She did not fear it for herself, but she did fear it for Emma: in point of fact, the young girl had already, some years back, given indications of it. It was therefore Miss Gwinn's intention and earnest wish—a very right and proper wish—that Emma should never marry. There was one other sister, Elizabeth, a year older than Emma. She had gone on a visit to Jersey some little time before; and, to Miss Gwinn's dismay and consternation, had married a farmer there, without asking leave. There was nothing for Miss Gwinn but to bury the dismay within her, and to resolve that Emma should be guarded more closely than before. But Emma Gwinn, knowing nothing of the prompting motives, naturally resented the surveillance.

Mr. Lewis followed Emma to her place of retirement. He had really grown to like her: but the pursuit may have had its rise as much in the boyish desire to thwart Miss Gwinn—or, as he expressed it, "to pay her off"—as in love. However that might have been, Emma Gwinn welcomed him all too gladly, and the walks were renewed.

It was an old tale, that, which ensued. Thanks to improved manners and morals, we can say an "old" tale, in contradistinction to a modern one. A secret marriage in these days would be looked upon askance by most people. Under the purest, the most domestic, the wisest court in the world, manners and customs have taken a turn with us, and society calls underhand doings by their right name, and turns its back upon them. Nevertheless, private marriages and run-a-way marriages were not done away with in the days when James Lewis Hunter contracted his.

I wonder whether one ever took place—where it was contracted in disobedience and defiance—that did not bring, in some way or other, its own punishment? To few, perhaps, was it brought home as it was to Mr. Hunter. No apology can be offered for the step he took: not even his youth, or his want of experience, or the attachment which had grown up in his heart for Emma. He knew that his family would have objected to the marriage. In fact, he dared not tell his purpose. Her position was not equal to his—at least, old Mr. Hunter, a proud man, would not have deemed it to be so—and he would have objected on the score of his son's youth. The worst bar of all would have been the tendency to insanity of the Gwinns—but of this James Hunter knew nothing. So he took that one false, blind, irrevocable step of contracting a private marriage; and the consequences came bitterly home to him. The marriage was a strictly legal one. James Hunter was honourable enough to take care of that: and both of them guarded the secret jealously. Emma remained at her aunt's, and wore her ring inside her dress, attached to a neck ribbon. Her husband only saw her sometimes; to avoid suspicion he lived chiefly at his father's home in London. Six months afterwards, Emma Gwinn—nay, Emma Hunter—lay upon her death-bed. A fever broke out in the neighbourhood, which she caught; and a different illness also supervened. Miss Gwinn, apprised of her danger, hastened to her. She stood over her in a shock of horror—whence had those symptoms arisen, and what meant that circle of gold that Emma in her delirium kept hold of on her neck? Medical skill could not save her, and just before her death, in a lucid interval, she confessed her marriage—the bare fact only—none of its details; she loved her husband too truly to expose him to the dire wrath of her sister. And she died without giving the slightest clue to his real name—Hunter. It was the fever that killed her.

Dire wrath, indeed! That was scarcely the word for it. Insane wrath would be better. In Miss Gwinn's injustice (violent people always are unjust) she persisted in attributing Emma's death to Mr. Lewis. In her bitter grief, she jumped to the belief that the secret must have preyed upon Emma's brain in the delirium of fever, and that that prevented her recovery. It is very probable that the secret did prey upon it, though, it is to be hoped, not to the extent assumed by Miss Gwinn.

Mr. Lewis knew nothing of the illness. He was in France with his father at the time it happened, and had not seen his wife for three weeks. Perhaps the knowledge of his absence abroad, caused Emma not to attempt to apprise him when first seized; afterwards she was too ill to do so. But by a strange coincidence he arrived from London the day after the funeral.

Nobody need envy him the interview with Miss Gwinn. On her part it was not a seemly one. Glad to get out of the house and be away from her reproaches, the stormy interview was concluded almost as soon as it had begun. He returned straight to London, her last words ringing their refrain on his ears—that his wife was dead and he had killed her: Miss Gwinn being still in ignorance that his proper name was anything but Lewis. Following immediately upon this—it was curious that it should be so—Miss Gwinn received news that her sister Elizabeth, Mrs. Gardener, was ill in Jersey. She hastened to her: for Elizabeth was nearly, if not quite, as dear to her as Emma had been. Mrs. Gardener's was a peculiar and unusual illness, and it ended in a confirmed and hopeless affection of the brain.

Once more Miss Gwinn's injustice came into play. Just as she had persisted in attributing Emma's death to Mr. Lewis, so did she now attribute to him Elizabeth's insanity: that is, she regarded him as its remote cause. That the two young sisters had been much attached to each other was undoubted: but to think that Elizabeth's madness came on through sorrow for Emma's death, or at the tidings of what had preceded it, was absurdly foolish. The poor young lady was placed in an asylum in London, of which Dr. Bevary was one of the visiting physicians; he was led to take an unusual interest in the case, and this brought him acquainted with Miss Gwinn. Within a year of her being placed there, the husband, Mr. Gardener, died in Jersey. His affairs turned out to be involved, and from that time the cost of keeping her there devolved on Miss Gwinn.

Private asylums are expensive, and Miss Gwinn could only maintain her sister in one at the cost of giving up her own home. Ill-conditioned though she was, we must confess she had her troubles. She gave it up without a murmur: she would have given up her life to benefit either of those, her young sisters. Retaining but a mere pittance, she devoted all her means to the comfort of Elizabeth, and found a home with her brother, in Ketterford. Where she spent her days bemoaning the lost and cherishing a really insane hatred against Mr. Lewis—a desire for revenge. She had never come across him, until that Easter Monday, at Ketterford. And that, you will say, is scarcely correct, since it was not himself she met then, but his brother. Deceived by the resemblance, she attacked Mr. Henry Hunter in the manner you remember; and Austin Clay saved him from the gravel-pit. But the time soon came when she stood face to face with *him*. It was the hour she had so longed for: the hour of revenge. What revenge? But for the wicked lie she subsequently forged, there could have been no revenge. The worst she could have proclaimed was, that James Lewis Hunter, when he was a young man, had so far forgotten his duty to himself, and to the world's decencies, as to contract a secret marriage. He might have got over that. He had mourned his young wife sincerely at the time, but later grew to think that all things were for the best—that it was a serious source of embarrassment removed from his path. Nothing more or less had he to acknowledge.

What revenge would Miss Gwinn have reaped from this? None. Certainly none to satisfy one so vindictive as she. It never was clear to herself what revenge she had desired: all her efforts had been directed to the discovering of him. She found him a man of social ties. He had married Louisa Bevary; he had a fair daughter; he was respected by the world: all of which excited the anger of Miss Gwinn.

Remembering her violent nature, it was only to be expected that Mr. Hunter should shrink from meeting Miss Gwinn when he first knew she had tracked him and was in London. He had never told his wife the episode in his early life, and would very much have disliked its tardy disclosure to her through the agency of Miss Gwinn. Fifty pounds would he have willingly given to avoid a meeting with her. But she came to his very home; so to say, into the presence of his wife and child; and he had to see her, and make the best of it. You must remember the interview. Mr. Hunter's agitation *previous* to it, was caused by the dread of the woman's near presence, of the disturbance she might make in his household, of the discovery his wife was in close danger of making—that he was a widower when she married him, and not a bachelor. Any husband of the present day might show the same agitation I think under similar circumstances. But Mr. Hunter did not allow this agitation to sway him when before Miss Gwinn; once shut up with her, he was cool and calm as a cucumber; rather defied her than not, civilly; and asked what she meant by intruding upon him, and what she had to complain of: which of course was but adding fuel to the woman's flame. It was quite true, all he said, and there was nothing left to hang a peg of revenge upon. And so she invented one. The demon of mischief put it into her mind to impose upon him with the lie that his first wife, Emma, was not dead, but living. She told him that she (she, herself) had imposed upon him with a false story in that long-past day, in saying that Emma was dead and buried. It was another sister who had died, she added—not Emma: Emma had been ill with the fever, but was recovering; and she had said this to separate her from him. Emma, she continued, was alive still, a patient in the lunatic asylum.

It never occurred to Mr. Hunter to doubt the tale. Her passionate manner, her impressive words, but added to her earnestness, and he came out from the interview believing that his first wife had not died. His state of mind cannot be forgotten. Austin Clay saw him pacing the waste ground in the dark night. His agony and remorse were fearful; the sun of his life's peace had set: and there could be no retaliation upon her who had caused it all—Miss Gwinn.

Miss Gwinn, however, did not follow up her revenge. Not because further steps might have brought the truth to light, but because after a night's rest she rather repented of it. Her real nature was honourable, and she despised herself for what she had done. Once it crossed her to undo it; but she hated Mr. Hunter with an undying hatred, and so let it alone and went down to Ketterford. One evening, when she had been at home some days, a spirit of confidence came over her which was very unusual, and she told her brother of the revenge she had taken. That was quite enough for Lawyer Gwinn: a glorious opportunity of enriching himself, not to be missed. He went up to London, and terrified Mr. Hunter out of five thousand pounds. "Or I go and tell your wife, Miss Bevary, that she is not your wife," he threatened, in his coarse way. Miss Gwinn suspected that the worthy lawyer had gone to make the most of the opportunity, and she wrote him a sharp letter, telling him that if he did so—if he interfered at all—she would at once confess to Lewis Hunter that Emma was really dead. Not knowing where he would put up in London, she enclosed this note to Austin Clay, asking him to give it to Lawyer Gwinn. She took the opportunity, at the same time, of writing a reproachful letter to Mr. Hunter, in which his past ill-doings and Emma's present existence were fully enlarged upon. As the reader may remember, she misdirected the letters: Austin became acquainted with the (as he could but suppose) dangerous secret; and the note to Lawyer Gwinn was set alight, sealed. If Austin or his master had but borrowed a momentary portion of the principles of Gwinn of Ketterford, and peeped into the letter! What years of misery it would have saved Mr. Hunter! But when Miss Gwinn discovered that her brother had used the lie to obtain money, she did not declare the truth. The sense of justice within her yielded to revenge. She hated Mr. Hunter as she had ever done, and would not relieve him. A fine life, between them, did they lead Mr. Hunter. Miss Gwinn protested against every fresh aggression made by the lawyer; but protested only. In Mr. Hunter's anguish of mind at the disgrace cast on his wife and child; in his terror lest the truth (as he assumed it to be) should reach them—and it seemed to be ever looming—he had lived, as may be said, a perpetual death. And the disgrace was of a nature that never could be removed; and the terror had never left him through all these long years.

Dr. Bevary had believed the worst. When he first became acquainted with Miss Gwinn, she (never a communicative woman) had not disclosed the previous history of the patient in the asylum. She had given hints of a sad tale, she even said she was living in hope of being revenged on one who had done herself and family an injury, but she said no more. Later circumstances connected with Mr. Hunter and his brother, dating from the account he heard of Miss Gwinn's attack upon Mr. Henry, had impressed Dr. Bevary with the belief that James Hunter had really married the poor woman in the asylum. When he questioned Miss Gwinn, that estimable woman had replied in obscure hints: and they had so frightened Dr. Bevary that he dared ask no further. For his sister's sake he tacitly ignored the subject in future, living in daily thankfulness that Mrs. Hunter was without suspicion.

But with the dead body of Elizabeth Gardener lying before her, the enacted lie came to an end. Miss Gwinn freely acknowledged what she had done, and took little, if any, blame to herself. "Lewis Hunter spoilt the happiness of my life," she said; "in return I have spoilt his."

"And suppose my sister, his lawful wife, had been led to believe this fine tale?" questioned Dr. Bevary, looking keenly at her.

"In that case I should have declared the truth," said Miss Gwinn. "I had no animosity to her. She was innocent, she was also your sister, and she should never have suffered."

"How could you know that she remained ignorant?"

"By my brother being able, whenever he would, to frighten Mr. Hunter," was the laconic answer.

XI

Relief

We left Mr. Hunter in the easy chair of his dining-room, buried in these reminiscences of the unhappy past, and quite unconscious that relief of any sort could be in store for him. And yet it was very near: relief from two evils, quite opposite in their source. How long he sat there he scarcely knew; it seemed for hours. In the afternoon he aroused himself to his financial difficulties, and went out. He remembered that he had purposed calling that day upon his bankers, though he had no hope—but rather the certainty of the contrary—that they would help him out of his financial embarrassments. There was just time to get there before the bank closed, and Mr. Hunter had a cab called and went down to Lombard Street. He was shown into the room of the principal partner. The banker thought how ill he looked. Mr. Hunter's first question was about the heavy bill that was due that day. He supposed it had been presented and dishonoured.

"No," said the banker. "It was presented and paid."

A ray of hope lighted up the sadness of Mr. Hunter's face. "Did you indeed pay it? It was very kind. You shall be no eventual losers."

"We did not pay it from our own funds, Mr. Hunter. It was paid from yours."

Mr. Hunter did not understand. "I thought my account had been nearly drawn out," he said; "and by the note I received this morning from you, I understood you would decline to help me."

"Your account was drawn very close indeed; but this afternoon, in time to meet the bill upon its second presentation, there was a large sum paid in to your credit—two thousand six hundred pounds."

A pause of blank astonishment on the part of Mr. Hunter. "Who paid it in?" he presently asked.

"Mr. Clay. He came himself. You will weather the storm now, Mr. Hunter."

There was no answering reply. The banker bent forward in the dusk of the growing evening, and saw that Mr. Hunter was incapable of making one. He was sinking back in his chair in a fainting fit. Whether it was the revulsion of feeling caused by the conviction that he *should* now weather the storm, or simply the effect of his physical state, Mr. Hunter had fainted, as quietly as any girl might do. One of the partners lived at the bank, and Mr. Hunter was conveyed into the dwelling-house. It was quite evening before he was well enough to leave it. He drove to the yard. It was just closed for the night, and Mr. Clay was gone. Mr. Hunter ordered the cab home. He found Austin waiting for him, and he also found Dr. Bevary. Seeing the latter, he expected next to see Miss Gwinn, and glanced nervously round.

"She is gone back to Ketterford," spoke out Dr. Bevary, divining the fear. "The woman will never trouble you again. I thought you must be lost, Hunter. I have been here twice; been home to dinner with Florence; been round at the yard worrying Clay; and could not come upon you anywhere."

"I went to the bank, and was taken ill there," said Mr. Hunter, who still seemed anything but himself, and looked round in a bewildered manner. "The woman, Bevary—are you sure she's gone quite away? She—she wanted to beg, I think," he added, as if in apology for pressing the question.

"She is *gone*: gone never to return; and you may be at rest," repeated the doctor, impressively. "And so you have been ill at the bankers", James! Things are going wrong, I suppose."

"No, they are going right. Austin"—laying his hand upon the young man's shoulder—"what am I to say? This money can only have come from you."

"Sir!" said Austin, half laughing.

Mr. Hunter drew Dr. Bevary's attention, pointing to Austin. "Look at him, Bevary. He has saved me. But for him, I should have borne a dishonoured name this day. I went down to Lombard Street, a man without hope, believing that the blow had been already struck in bills dishonoured—that my name was on its way to the *Gazette*. I found that he, Austin Clay, had paid in between two and three thousand pounds to my credit."

"I could not put my money to a better use, sir. The two thousand pounds were left to me, you know: the rest I saved. I was wishing for something to turn up that I could invest it in."

"Invest!" exclaimed Mr. Hunter, deep feeling in his tone. "How do you know you will not lose it?"

"I have no fear, sir. The strike is at an end, and business will go on well now."

"If I did not believe that it would, I would never consent to use it," said Mr. Hunter.

It was true. Austin Clay, a provident man, had been advancing his money to save the credit of his master. Suspecting some such a crisis as this was looming, he had contrived to hold his funds in available readiness. It had come, though, sooner than he anticipated.

"How am I to repay you?" asked Mr. Hunter. "I don't mean the money: but the obligation."

A red flush mounted to Austin's brow. He answered hastily, as if to cover it.

"I do not require payment, sir. I do not look for any."

Mr. Hunter stood in deep thought, looking at him, but vacantly. Dr. Bevary was near the mantelpiece, apparently paying no attention to either of them. "Will you link your name to mine?" said Mr. Hunter, moving towards Austin.

"In what manner, sir?"

"By letting the firm be from henceforth Hunter and Clay. I have long wished this; you are of too great use to me to remain anything less than a partner, and by this last act of yours, you have earned the right to be so. Will you object to join your name to one which was so near being dishonoured?"

He held out his hand as he spoke, and Austin clasped it. "Oh, Mr. Hunter!" he exclaimed, in the strong impulse of the moment, "I wish you would give me hopes of a dearer reward."

"You mean Florence," said Mr. Hunter.

"Yes," returned Austin, in agitation. "I care not how long I wait, or what price you may call upon me to pay for her. As Jacob served Laban seven years for Rachel, so would I serve for Florence, and think it but a day, for the love I bear her. Sir, Mrs. Hunter would have given her to me."

"My objection is not to you, Austin. Were I to disclose to you certain particulars connected with Florence—as I should be obliged to do before she married—you might yourself decline her."

"Try me, sir," said Austin, a bright smile parting his lips.

"Ay, try him," said Dr. Bevary, in his quaint manner. "I have an idea that he may know as much of the matter as you do, Hunter. You neither of you know too much," he significantly added.

Austin's cheek turned red; and there was that in his tone, his look, which told Mr. Hunter that he had known the fact, known it for years. "Oh, sir," he pleaded, "give me Florence."

"I tell you that you neither of you know too much," said Dr. Bevary. "But, look here, Austin. The best thing you can do is, to go to my house and ask Florence whether she will have you. Then—if you don't find it too much trouble—escort her home." Austin laughed as he caught up his hat. A certain prevision, that he should win Florence, had ever been within him.

Dr. Bevary watched the room-door close, and then drew a chair in front of his brother-in-law. "Did it ever strike you that Austin Clay knew your secret, James?" he began.

"How should it?" returned Mr. Hunter, feeling himself compelled to answer.

"I do not know how," said the doctor, "any more than I know how the impression, that he did, fixed itself upon me. I have felt sure, this many a year past, that he was no stranger to the fact, though he probably knew nothing of the details."

To the fact! Dr. Bevary spoke with strange coolness.

"When did *you* become acquainted with it?" asked Mr. Hunter, in a tone of sharp pain.

"I became acquainted with your share in it at the time Miss Gwinn discovered that Mr. Lewis was Mr. Hunter. At least, with as much of the share as I ever was acquainted with until to-day."

Mr. Hunter compressed his lips. It was no use beating about the bush any longer.

"James," resumed the doctor, "why did you not confide the secret to me? It would have been much better."

"To you! Louisa's brother!"

"It would have been better, I say. It might not have lifted the sword that was always hanging over Louisa's head, or have eased it by one jot; but it might have eased *you*. A sorrow kept within a man's own bosom, doing its work in silence, will burn his life away: get him to talk of it, and half the pain is removed. It is also possible that I might have made better terms than you, with the rapacity of Gwinn."

"If you knew it, why did you not speak openly to me?"

Dr. Bevary suppressed a shudder. "It was one of those terrible secrets that a third party cannot interfere in uninvited. No: silence was my only course, so long as you observed silence to me. Had I interfered, I might have said 'Louisa shall leave you!'"

"It is over, so far as she is concerned," said Mr. Hunter, wiping his damp brow. "Let her name rest. It is the thought of her that has well nigh killed me."

"Ay, it's over," responded Dr. Bevary; "over, in more senses than one. Do you not wonder that Miss Gwinn should have gone back to Ketterford without molesting you again?"

"How can I wonder at anything she does? She comes and she goes, with as little reason as warning."

Dr. Bevary lowered his voice. "Have you ever been to see that poor patient in Kerr's asylum?"

The question excited the anger of Mr. Hunter. "What do you mean by asking it?" he cried. "When I was led to believe her dead, I shaped my future course according to that belief. I have never acted, nor would I act, upon any other—save in the giving money to Gwinn, for my wife's sake. If Louisa was not my wife legally, she was nothing less in the sight of God."

"Louisa was your wife," said Dr. Bevary, quietly. And Mr. Hunter responded by a sharp gesture of pain. He wished the subject at an end. The doctor continued—

"James, had you gone, though it had been but for an instant, to see that unhappy patient of Kerr's, your trammels would have been broken. It was not Emma, your young wife of years ago."

"It was not!—What do you say?" gasped Mr. Hunter.

"When Agatha Gwinn found you out, here, in this house, she startled you nearly to death by telling you that Emma was alive—was a patient in Kerr's asylum. She told you that, when you had been informed in those past days of Emma's death, you were imposed upon by a lie—a lie invented by herself. James, the lie was uttered *then*, when she spoke to you here. Emma, your wife, did die; and the young woman in the asylum was her sister." Mr. Hunter rose. His hands were raised imploringly, his face was stretched forward in its sad yearning. What!—which was true? which was he to believe?—"In the gratification of her revenge, Miss Gwinn concocted the tale that Emma was alive," resumed Dr. Bevary, "knowing, as she spoke it, that Emma had been dead years and years. She contrived to foster the same impression upon me; and the same impression, I cannot tell how, has, I am sure, clung to Austin Clay. Louisa was your lawful wife, James." Mr. Hunter, in the plenitude of his thankfulness, sank upon his chair, a sobbing burst of emotion breaking from him, and the drops of perspiration gathering again on his brow. "That other one, the sister, the poor patient, is dead," pursued the doctor.

"As we stood together over her, an hour ago, Miss Gwinn confessed the imposition. It appeared to slip from her involuntarily, in spite of herself. I inquired her motive, and she answered, 'To be revenged on you, Lewis Hunter, for the wrong you had done.' As you had marred the comfort of her life, so she in return had marred that of yours. As she stood in her impotence, looking on the dead, I asked her which, in her opinion, had inflicted the most wrong, she or you?"

Mr. Hunter lifted his eager face. "It was a foolish deceit. What did she hope to gain by it? A word at any time might have exposed it."

"It seems she did gain pretty well by it," significantly replied Dr. Bevary. "There's little doubt that it was first spoken in the angry rage of the moment, as being the most effectual mode of tormenting you: and the terrible dread with which you received it—as I conclude you so did receive it—must have encouraged her to persist in the lie. James, you should have confided in me; I might have brought light to bear on it in some way or other. Your timorous silence has kept me quiet."

"God be thanked that it is over!" fervently exclaimed Mr. Hunter. "The loss of my money, the loss of my peace, they seem to be little in comparison with the joy of this welcome revelation."

He sat down as he spoke and bent his head upon his hand. Presently he looked at his brother-in-law. "And you think that Clay has suspected this? And that—suspecting it, he has wished for Florence?"

"I am sure of one thing—that Florence has been his object, his dearest hope. What he says has no exaggeration in it—that he would serve for her seven years, and seven to that, for the love he bears her."

"I have been afraid to glance at such a thing as marriage for Florence, and that is the reason I would not listen to Austin Clay. With this slur hanging over her—"

"There is no slur—as it turns out," interrupted Dr. Bevary. "Florence loves him, James; and your wife knew it."

"What a relief is all this!" murmured Mr. Hunter. "The woman gone back to Ketterford! I think I shall sleep to-night."

"She is gone back, never more to trouble you. We must see how her worthy brother can be brought to account for obtaining money under false pretences."

"I'll make him render back every shilling he has defrauded me of: I'll bring him to answer for it before the laws of his country," was the wronged man's passionate and somewhat confused answer.

But that is more easy to say than to do, Mr. Hunter!

For, a few days subsequent to this, Lawyer Gwinn, possibly scenting that unpleasant consequences might be in store for him, was quietly steaming to America in a fine ship; taking all his available substance with him; and leaving Ketterford and his sister behind.

XII

Conclusion

With outward patience and inward wonder, Florence Hunter was remaining at Dr. Bevary's. That something must be wrong at home, she felt sure: else why was she kept away from it so long? And where was her uncle? Invalids were shut up in the waiting-room, like Patience on a monument, hoping minute by minute to see him appear. And now here was another, she supposed! No. He had passed the patients' room and was opening the door of this. Austin Clay!

"What have you come for?" she exclaimed, in the glad confusion of the moment.

"To take you home, for one thing," he answered, as he approached her. "Do you dislike the escort, Florence?" He bent forward as he asked the question. A strange light of happiness shone in his eyes; a sweet smile parted his lips. Florence Hunter's heart stood still, and then began to beat as if it would have burst its bounds.

"What has happened?" she faltered.

"This," he said, taking both her hands and drawing her gently before him. "The right to hold your hands in mine; the right—soon—to take you to my heart and keep you there for ever. Your father and uncle have sent me to tell you this."

The words, in their fervent earnestness carried instant truth to her heart, lighting it as with the brightness of sunshine. "Oh, what a recompense!" she impulsively murmured from the depths of her great love. "And everything lately has seemed so dark with doubt, so full of trouble!"

"No more doubt, no more trouble," he fondly whispered. "It shall be my life's care to guard my wife from all such, Florence—heaven permitting me." Anything more that was said may as well be left to the reader's lively imagination. They arrived at home after awhile; and found Dr. Bevary there, talking still.

"How you must have hurried yourselves!" quoth he, turning to them. "Clay, you ought to be ill from walking fast. What has kept him, Florence?"

"Not your patients, Doctor," retorted Austin, laughing; "though you are keeping them. One of them says you made an appointment with him. By the way he spoke, I think he was inwardly vowing vengeance against you for not keeping it."

"Ah," said the Doctor, "we medical men do get detained sometimes. One patient has had the most of my time this day, poor lady!"

"Is she better?" quickly asked Florence, who always had ready sympathy for sickness and suffering: perhaps from having seen so much of it in her mother.

"No, my dear, she is dead," was the answer, gravely spoken. "And, therefore," added the doctor in a different tone, "I have no further excuse for absenting myself from those other patients who are alive and grumbling at me. Will you walk a few steps with me, Mr. Clay?"

Dr. Bevary linked his arm within Austin's as they crossed the hall, and they went out together. "How did you become acquainted with that dark secret" he breathed.

"Through a misdirected letter of Miss Gwinn's," replied Austin. "After I had read it, I discovered that it must have been meant for Mr. Hunter, though addressed to me. It told me all. Dr. Bevary, I have had to carry the secret all these years, bearing myself as one innocent of the knowledge; before Mrs. Hunter, before Florence, before him. I would have given half my savings not to have known it."

"You believed that—that—one was living who might have replaced Mrs. Hunter?"

"Yes; and that she was in confinement. The letter, a reproachful one, was too explanatory."

"She died this morning. It is with her—at least with her and her affairs—that my day has been taken up."

"What a mercy!" exclaimed Austin.

"Ay; mercies are showered down every day: a vast many more than we, self-complaisant mortals, acknowledge or return thanks for," responded Dr. Bevary, in the quaint tone he was fond of using. And then, in a few brief words, he enlightened Austin as to the actual truth.

"What a fiend she must be!" cried Austin, alluding to Miss Gwinn of Ketterford. "Oh, but this is a mercy indeed! And I have been planning how to guard the secret always from Florence." Dr. Bevary made no reply. Austin turned to him, the ingenuous look upon his face that it often wore. "You approve of me for Florence? Do you not, sir?"

"Be you very sure, young gentleman, that you should never have got her, had I not approved," oracularly nodded Dr. Bevary. "I look upon

Florence as part of my belongings; and, if you mind what you are about, perhaps I may look upon you as the same."

Austin laughed. "How am I to avoid offence?" he asked.—"By loving your wife with an earnest, lasting love; by making her a better husband than James Hunter has been enabled to make her poor mother."

The tears rose to Austin's eyes with the intensity of his emotion. "Do you think there is cause to ask me to do this, Dr. Bevary?"

"No, my boy, I do not. God bless you both! There! leave me to get home to those patients of mine. You can be off back to her."

But Austin Clay had work on his hands, as well as pleasure, and he turned towards Daffodil's Delight. It was the evening for taking Baxendale his week's money, and Austin was not one to neglect it. He picked his way down amidst the poor people, standing about hungry and half-naked. All the works were open again, but numbers and numbers of men could not obtain employment, however good their will was: the masters had taken on strangers, and there was no room for the old workmen. John Baxendale was sitting by his bedside dressed. His injuries were yielding to skill and time: and in a short while he looked to be at work again.

"Well, Baxendale?" cried Austin, in his cheery voice. "Still getting better?"

"Oh yes, sir, I'm thankful to say it. The surgeon was here to-day, and told me there would be no further relapse. I am a bit tired this evening; I stood a good while at the window, watching the row opposite. She was giving him such a basting."

"What! do you mean the Cheeks? I thought the street seemed in a commotion."

Baxendale laughed. "It is but just over, sir. She set on and shook him soundly, and then she scratched him, and then she cuffed him—all outside the door. I do wonder that Cheek took it from her; but he's just like a puppy in her hands, and nothing better. Two good hours they were disputing there."

"What was the warfare about?" inquired Austin.

"About his not getting work, sir. Cheek's wife was just like many of the other wives in Daffodil's Delight—urging their husbands not to go to work, and vowing *they'd* strike if they didn't stand out. I don't know but Mother Cheek was about the most obstinate of all. The very day that I was struck down I heard her blowing him up for not 'standing firm upon his rights;' and telling him she'd rather go to his hanging than see him go back to work. And now she beats him because he can't get any to do."

"Is Cheek one that cannot get any?"

"Cheek's one, sir. Mr. Henry took on more strangers than did you and Mr. Hunter; so, of course, there's less room for his old men. Cheek has walked about London these two days, till he's foot-sore, trying different shops, but he can't get taken on: there are too many men out, for him to have a chance."

"I think some of the wives in Daffodil's Delight are the most unreasonable women that ever were created," exclaimed Austin.

"*She* is—that wife of Cheek's," rejoined Baxendale. "I don't know how they'll end it. She has shut the door in his face, vowing he shall not put a foot inside it until he can bring some wages with him. Forbidding him to take work when it was to be had, and now that it can't be had turning upon him for not getting it! If Cheek wasn't a donkey, he'd turn upon her again. There's other women just as contradictory. I think the bad living has soured their tempers."

"Where's Mary this evening?" inquired Austin, quitting the unsatisfactory topic. Since her father's illness, Mary's place had been by his side: it was something unusual to find her absent. Baxendale lowered his voice to reply.

"She is getting ill again, sir. All her old symptoms have come back, and I am sure now that she is going fast. She is on her bed, lying down."

As he spoke the last word, he stopped, for Mary entered. She seemed scarcely able to walk; a hectic flush shone on her cheeks, and her breath was painfully short. "Mary," Austin said, with much concern, "I am sorry to see you thus."

"It is only the old illness come back again, sir," she answered, as she sunk back in the pillowed chair. "I knew it had not gone for good—that the improvement was but temporary. But now, sir, look how good and merciful is the hand that guides us—and yet we sometimes doubt it! What should I have been spared for, and had this returning glimpse of strength, but that I might nurse my father in his illness, and be a comfort to him? He is nearly well—will soon be at work again and wants me no more. Thanks ever be to God!"

Austin went out, marvelling at the girl's simple and beautiful trust. It appeared that she would be happy in her removal whenever it should come. As he was passing up the street he met Dr. Bevary. Austin wondered what had become of his patients.

"All had gone away but two; tired of waiting," said the Doctor, divining his thoughts. "I am going to take a look at Mary Baxendale. I hear she is worse."

"Very much worse," replied Austin. "I have just left her father." At that moment there was a sound of contention and scolding, a woman's sharp tongue being uppermost. It proceeded from Mrs. Cheek, who was renewing the contest with her husband. Austin gave Dr. Bevary an outline of what Baxendale had said.

"And if, after a short season of prosperity, another strike should come, these women would be the first again to urge the men on to it—to 'stand up for their rights!'" exclaimed the Doctor.

"Not all of them."

"They have not all done it now. Mark you, Austin! I shall settle a certain sum upon Florence when she marries, just to keep you in bread and cheese, should these strikes become the order of the day, and you get engulfed in them."

Austin smiled. "I think I can take better care than that, Doctor."

"Take all the care you please. But you are talking self-sufficient nonsense, my young friend. I shall put Florence on the safe side, in spite of your care. I have no fancy to see her reduced to one maid and a cotton gown. You can tell her so," added the Doctor, as he continued on his way.

Austin turned on his, when a man stole up to him from some side entry—a cadaverous-looking man, pinched and careworn. It was James Dunn; he had been discharged out of prison by the charity of some fund at the disposal of the governor. He humbly begged for work—"just to keep him from starving."

"You ask what I have not to give, Dunn," was the reply of Austin. "Our yard is full; and consider the season! Perhaps when spring comes on—"

"How am I to exist till spring, sir?" he burst forth in a voice that was but just kept from tears. "And the wife and the children?"

"I wish I could help you, Dunn. Your case is but that of many others."

"There have been so many strangers took on, sir!"

"Of course there have been. To do the work that you and others refused."

"I have not a place to lay my head in this night, sir. I have not so much as a slice of bread. I'd do the meanest work that could be offered to me."

Austin felt in his pocket for a piece of money, and gave it him. "What misery they have brought upon themselves!" he thought.

When the announcement reached Mrs. Henry Hunter of Florence's engagement, she did not approve of it. Not that she had any objection to Austin Clay; he had from the first been a favourite with her, though she had sometimes marked her preference by a somewhat patronizing manner; but for Florence to marry her father's clerk, though that clerk had now become partner, was more than she could at the first moment quietly yield to.

"It is quite a descent for her," she said to her husband privately. "What can James be thinking of? The very idea of her marrying Austin Clay!"

"But if she likes him?"

"That ought not to go for anything. Suppose it had been Mary? I would not have let her have him."

"I would," decisively returned Mr. Henry Hunter. "Clay's worth his weight in gold."

Some short while given to preliminaries, and to the re-establishment (in a degree) of Mr. Hunter's shattered health, and the new firm "Hunter and Clay" was duly announced to the business world. Upon an appointed day, Mr. Hunter stood before his workmen, his arm within Austin's. He was introducing him to them in his new capacity of partner. The strike was quite at an end, and the men—so many as could be made room for—had returned; but Mr. Hunter would not consent to discharge the hands that had come forward to take work during the emergency.

"What has the strike brought you?" inquired Mr. Hunter, seizing upon the occasion to offer a word of advice. "Any good?" Strictly speaking, the men could not reply that it had. In the silence that ensued after the question, one man's voice was at length raised. "We look back upon it as a subject of congratulation, sir."

"Congratulation!" exclaimed Mr. Hunter. "Upon what point?"

"That we have had the pluck to hold out so long in the teeth of difficulties," replied the voice.

"Pluck is a good quality when rightly applied," observed Mr. Hunter. "But what good has the 'pluck,' or the strike, brought to you in this case?—for that was the question we were upon."

"It was a lock-out, sir; not a strike."

"In the first instance it was a strike," said Mr. Hunter. "Pollocks' men struck, and you had it in contemplation to follow their example. Oh, yes! you had, my men; you know as well as I do, that the measure was under discussion. Upon that state of affairs becoming known, the masters determined upon a general lock-out. They did it in self-defence; and if you will put yourselves in thought into their places, judging fairly, you will not wonder that it was considered the only course open to them. The lock-out lasted but a short period, and then the yards were again opened—open to all who would resume work upon the old terms, and sign a declaration not to be under the dominion of the Trades' Unions. How very few availed themselves of this you do not need to be reminded."

"We acted for what we thought the best," said another.

"I know you did," replied Mr. Hunter. "You are—speaking of you collectively—steady, hard-working, well-meaning men, who wish to do the best for yourselves, your wives, and families. But, looking back now, do you consider that it was for the best? You have returned to work upon the same terms that you were offered then. Here we are, in the depth of winter, and what sort of homes do you possess to fortify yourselves against its severities!" What sort indeed! Mr. Hunter's delicacy shrank from depicting them. "I am not speaking to you now as your master," he continued, conscious that men do not like this style of converse from their employers. "Consider me for the moment as your friend only; let us talk together as man and man. I wish I could bring you to see the evil of these convulsions; I do not wish it from motives of self-interest, but for your sole good. You may be thinking, 'Ah, the master is afraid of another contest; this one has done him so much damage, and that's why he is going on at us against them.' You are mistaken; that is not why I speak. My men, were any further contests to take place between us, in which you held yourselves aloof from work, as you have done in this, we should at once place ourselves beyond dependence upon you, by bringing over foreign workmen. In the consultations which have been held between myself and Mr. Clay, relative to the terms of our partnership, this point has been fully discussed, and our determination taken. Should we have a repetition of the past, Hunter and Clay would then import their own workmen."

"And other firms as well?" interrupted a voice.

"We know nothing of what other firms might do: to attend to our own interests is enough for us. I hope we shall never have to do this; but it is only fair to inform you that such would be our course of action. If you, our native workmen, brothers of the soil, abandon your work from any crotchets—"

"Crotchets, sir!"

"Ay, crotchets—according to my opinion," repeated Mr. Hunter. "Could you show me a real grievance, it might be a different matter. But let us leave motives alone, and go to effects. When I say that I wish you could see the evil of these convulsions, I speak solely with reference to your good, to the well-being of your families. It cannot have escaped your notice that my health has become greatly shattered—that, in all probability, my life will not be much prolonged. My friends"—his voice sunk to a deep, solemn tone—"believing, as I do, that I shall soon stand before my Maker, to give an account of my doings here, could I, from any paltry motive of self-interest, deceive you? Could I say one thing and mean another? No; when I seek to warn you against future troubles, I do it for your own sakes. Whatever may be the urging motive of a strike, whether good or bad, it can only bring ill in the working. I would say, were I not a master, 'Put up with a grievance, rather than enter upon a strike;' but being a master, you might misconstrue the advice. I am not going into the merits of the measures—to say this past strike was right, or that was wrong; I speak only of the terrible amount of suffering they wrought. A man said to me the other day—he was from the factory districts—'I have a horror of strikes, they have worked so much evil in our trade.' You can get books which tell of them, and read for yourselves. How many orphans, and widows, and men in prisons are there, who have cause to rue this strike that has only now just passed? It has broken up homes that, before it came, were homes of plenty and content, leaving in them despair and death. Let us try to go on better for the future. I, for my part, will always be ready to receive and consider any reasonable proposal from my men; my partner will do the same. If there is no attempt at intimidation, and no interference on the part of others, there ought to be little difficulty in discussing and settling matters, with the help of 'the golden rule.' Only—it is my last and earnest word of caution to you—abide by your own good sense, and do not yield it to those agitators who would lead you away."

Every syllable spoken by Mr. Hunter, as to the social state of the people, Daffodil's Delight, and all other parts of London where the strike had prevailed, could echo. Whether the men had invoked the contest needlessly, or whether they were justified, according to the laws of right and reason, it matters not here to discuss; the effects were the same, and they stood out broad, and bare, and hideous. Men had died of want; had been cast into prison, where they still lay; had committed social crimes, in their great need, against their fellow-men. Women had been reduced to the lowest extremes of misery and suffering, had been transformed into viragos, where they once had been pleasant and peaceful; children had died off by scores. Homes were dismantled; Mr. Cox had cart-loads of things that stood no chance of being recalled. Families, united before, were scattered now; young men were driven upon idleness and evil courses; young women upon worse, for they were irredeemable. Would wisdom for the future be learnt by all this? It was uncertain.

When Austin Clay returned home that evening, he gave Mrs. Quale notice to quit. She received it in a spirit of resignation, intimating that she had been expecting it—that lodgings such as hers were not fit for Mr. Clay, now that he was Mr. Hunter's partner.

Austin laughed. "I suppose you think I ought to set up a house of my own."

"I daresay you'll be doing that one of these days, sir," she responded.

"I daresay I shall," said Austin.

"I wonder whether what Mr. Hunter said to-day will do any of 'em any service?" interposed Peter Quale. "What do you think, sir?"

"I think it ought," replied Austin. "Whether it will, is another question."

"It mostly lies in this—in the men's being let alone," nodded Peter. "Leave 'em to theirselves, and they'll go on steady enough; but if them Trade Union folks, Sam Shuck and his lot, get over them again, there'll be more outbreaks."

"Sam Shuck is safe for some months to come."

"But there's others of his persuasion that are not, sir. And Sam, he'll be out some time."

"Quale, I give the hands credit for better sense than to suffer themselves to fall under his yoke again, now that he has shown himself in his true colours."

"I don't give 'em credit for any sense at all, when they get unsettled notions into their heads," phlegmatically returned Peter Quale. "I'd like to know if it's the Union that's helping Shuck's wife and children."

"Do they help her?"

"There must be some that help her, sir. The woman lives and feeds her family. But there was a Trades' Union secretary here this morning, inquiring about all this disturbance there has been, and saying that the men were wrong to be led to violence by such a fellow as Sam Shuck: over eager to say it, he seemed to me. I gave him my opinion back again," concluded Peter, pushing the pipe, which he had laid aside at his young master's entrance, further under the grate. "That Sam Shuck, and such as he, that live by agitation, were uncommon cute for their own interests, and those that listen to them were fools. That took him off, sir."

"To think of the fools this Daffodil's Delight has turned out this last six months!" Mrs. Quale emphatically added. "To have lived upon their clothes and furniture, their saucepans and kettles, their bedding and their children's shoes; when they might, most of 'em, have earned thirty-three shillings a week at their ordinary work! When folks can be so blind as that, it is of no use talking to them: black looks white, and white black." Mr. Clay smiled at the remark, though it had some rough reason in it, and went out. Taking his way to Mr. Hunter's.

"Austin! You must live with me."

The words came from Mr. Hunter. Seated in his easy chair, apparently asleep, he had overheard what Austin was saying in an undertone to Florence—that he had just been giving Mrs. Quale notice, and should begin house-hunting on the morrow. They turned to him at the remark. He had half risen from his chair in his eager earnestness.

"Do you think I could spare Florence? Where my home is, yours and hers must be. Is not this house large enough for us? Why should you seek another?"

"Quite large enough, sir. But—but I had not thought of it. It shall be as you and Florence wish."

They both looked at her; she was standing underneath the light of the chandelier, the rich damask colour mantling in her cheeks.

"I could not give you to him, Florence, if it involved your leaving me."

The tears glistened on her eyelashes. In the impulse of the moment she stretched out a hand to each. "There is room here for us all, papa," she softly whispered.

Mr. Hunter took both their hands in one of his; he raised the other in the act of benediction; the tears, which only glistened in the eyes of Florence, were falling fast from his own.

"Yes, it shall be the home of all; and—Florence!—the sooner he comes to it the better. Bless, oh, bless my children!" he murmured. "And grant that this may prove a happier, a more peaceful home for them, than it has for me!"

"Amen!" answered Austin, in his inmost heart.

The End

A Note About the Author

Mrs. Henry Wood (1814–1887) was an English novelist. Born in Worcester, she married Henry Wood—a banker and merchant—in 1836, moving with him to the South of France. After twenty years abroad, they returned with their children to England, where Wood supported the family with her writing. Throughout her career, she published over thirty novels, including *East Lynne* (1861) and *The Channings* (1862). In 1867, she purchased *Argosy*, an English magazine she would edit and publish for the next twenty years. Wood maintained a dedicated readership worldwide, especially in Australia, and counted among her many fans the legendary Russian writer Leo Tolstoy.

A Note from the Publisher

Printed in the USA
CPSIA information can be obtained
at www.ICGtesting.com
JSHW022221140824
68134JS00018B/1195

9 781513 281094